THE SECRETS WE HIDE

ALSO BY PATRICIA SANDS

The Bridge Club

The Promise of Provence (Love in Provence Book 1)

Promises to Keep (Love in Provence Book 2)

I Promise You This (Love in Provence Book 3)

Drawing Lessons

The First Noël at the Villa des Violettes (Villa des Violettes Book 1)

A Season of Surprises at the Villa des Violettes (Villa des Violettes Book 2)

Lavender, Loss & Love at the Villa des Violettes (Villa des Violettes Book 3)

THE SECRETS WE HIDE

PATRICIA SANDS

Cover Design by Sharon Clare

www.claritybookcoverdesigns.com

"In the end, only three things matter: how much you loved, how gently you lived, and how gracefully you let go of things not meant for you." ~ Buddha

PROLOGUE

SEPTEMBER 2012

*K*aito Tanaka locked the door to his house before he walked out to a waiting taxi. And quite possibly to a change of everything in his life.

He smiled as doves in the garden sent him on his way with gentle cooing, a sign all was right with his world.

The golden glow of a quintessential Hawaiian sunrise washed over the peak of Diamond Head. Soft waves of light bathed the silhouettes of stately palm trees that lined the street like sentries.

As he climbed into the car, he could feel the dawn bringing warmth to his Manoa-Makiki neighborhood in the Punchbowl.

"Aloha! It's going to be another hot one. Nice to see you, Kaito," the driver greeted him in a hoarse, early-morning voice.

Kaito was pleasantly surprised to see Ben Okalani, a friend from his martial arts studio.

"Aloha *oe*," Kaito responded, "Good to see you too! You're right about the weather!"

The men carried on a polite conversation for a few minutes before Kaito rested the back of his head against the beige leather seat. He rubbed his hand across his closely cropped steel-gray hair, a subconscious habit. Closing his eyes, he drew deeply within himself.

For twenty years he had used this taxi ride to decompress. It seemed easier this year, unencumbered by a shadow of guilt.

Kaito acknowledged a twinge of sadness in his heart as his fingers brushed the white gold wedding band he had worn for forty-three years. He also accepted the complete absence of regret in this departure. It was his time.

Stealing away in September, as he was now, had been his secret for twenty years. It had also been his salvation.

For a moment, conflicting thoughts filled his mind, as the taxi glided silently along still-deserted streets. Anticipation was mixed with lingering remembrance. He felt tears build and blinked them back.

Then he closed his eyes for a moment and let himself be drawn to the light within himself, referring to the Buddhist philosophy that was the core of his strength.

"I am enough," he murmured under his breath as he turned his gaze outward to the familiar streets.

A sense of new possibilities cut through the jumble of thoughts. As dawn grew lighter, shapes and blooms of lush vegetation began to emerge from the shadows. Gardens were a riot of color with well-established plumeria, hibiscus, and bougainvillea in full blossom. A shudder of pleasure and anticipation ran through him.

Like the rebirth of each day at sunrise or the blooming of new buds, Kaito felt his heart opening to opportunities. But he also was aware of indecision and doubt simmering below his calm exterior. At the age of sixty-three, was there still time to begin a new chapter in his life? Did it make sense? And was his heart really in it?

The taxi ride from the quiet Punchbowl streets to the Honolulu International Airport took twenty minutes, with little traffic at this hour. Even the *wikiwikis*—the local shuttle buses—had few people to pick up between terminals.

"*Mahalo nui loa*," Kaito said as he paid Ben, who wished him a safe trip.

As Kaito walked into the international terminal, he sighed as he noted the long line waiting to go through the security checkpoint and was glad he had left in plenty of time.

He checked in at the ticket counter and continued on with his carry-on bag and small backpack. No extra luggage for him. He had his packing down to a fine art.

Without feeling rushed, he finally made it through to the departure lounge for his nonstop flight to Tokyo. At just under nine hours, he would have plenty of time to snooze, meditate, and prepare for the next part of his journey.

After takeoff and the usual attentions from the airline staff, Kaito set his seat at a comfortable angle and relaxed, thankful there was no passenger sitting next to him.

Closing his eyes, Kaito's thoughts returned to those he had been contemplating in the taxi. There was so much to consider.

Before long he was lost in the past.

CHAPTER 1

1958

*W*hen he was not at school or helping with chores in their small fishing village, eight-year-old Kaito's favorite thing was to play games of fantasy with friends. This included his best friend, Hana Suzuki. The same age and without siblings, they were like brother and sister. Their families spent a great deal of time together helping each other make ends meet as the entire country struggled to recover from WWII.

Even more than a decade later, there was rebuilding underway and most families struggled to stay above the poverty line. Fishing was the main source of income and involved everyone in the village. There were tasks for all ages. Little hands helped with harvesting seaweed, untangling nets and stacking baskets.

But there were times when the kids could let their imaginations soar.

Bombed-out buildings, rubble remaining from the war, provided plenty of possibilities for their games about samurai warriors and other adventurers. They took turns being the *shogun,* the chief, or the *samurai,* the warriors under him, or the *daimyo,* the feudal lord the warriors protected throughout history. There was no problem finding scraps of wood and metal to use in making the swords, shields, or whatever their game called for. Kaito loved to be the *shogun* and, even in those early years, he liked to think of himself as a protector for shy and delicate Hana.

Life was not easy in postwar Japan. In villages like Kaito's, every day was a struggle. The fishermen of the village set out to sea in the early predawn hours, often for long stretches of days or weeks.

At home, community nets were set each day along the vast beaches and hauled back in by everyone, including children, to harvest sardines, a main staple of the economy. The abundance of seafood made coping with the severe food shortage marginally easier.

Unloaded from these nets or from the returning fishing boats, the fish would be heaped in wicker baskets and taken to market. Larger fish would be cleaned and filleted by the women and made ready for sale. When not in school, Hana joined other girls helping their mothers, while the boys learned at early ages to gather natural materials like hemp and bamboo to help in the never-ending repair of the nets.

In the surrounding hills that tumbled down to the sea, the children would often hike up with their mothers to collect greens and vegetables for pickling. Flat stretches of land were filled with rice paddies. Everything was done by hand, as it had been for centuries, and the work was exhausting. But somehow the resilient children could always find moments for play.

To Kaito, a happy child with smiling eyes and an easy laugh, life was good.

One evening, as he was finishing his favorite meal of ramen noodles, with a ubiquitous book close at hand, his parents included him in a conversation that changed his young life.

"We are going to move and live on a beautiful island far away, to work hard and have a better life," his father told him. "I know we are all going to like it there."

Kaito looked at his mother in desperation, hoping she would say it was not happening. He gulped as she confirmed his father's words, adding, "Many others from our village have gone to a place called Hawaii to work at the pineapple farms and are writing letters back that we should join them."

Wide-eyed, Kaito listened quietly, looking from one parent to the other as they continued to speak of all the good things they foresaw with the move.

He was accustomed to never questioning what they said. But inside he was feeling a frenzy of emotions. His head was dizzy with confusion and fear. He tapped his chopsticks nervously on the rim of his bowl as he wondered how his parents could take him away from everything he had ever known … his friends, his books, his beloved teacher.

As his parents spoke, inwardly Kaito dissolved into a mess of alarm and dread. Nothing else registered. He slept little that night.

The next morning on his way to school, he panicked and hid in a ramshackle wooden shed on one of the fishing wharfs. He had to think of a plan to change his parents' minds. Surely they would not really move away if they saw how badly he wanted to stay.

He knew the schoolmaster would notify his parents first thing in the morning of his absence, so he had chosen his hiding place well. The abandoned shed was more ruin than anything and one he knew through play.

He could hear the number of voices growing, calling his name, throughout the day. He was sure the whole community was looking for him and felt badly he was causing such distress to others. He had only meant to convince his parents to change their minds about moving.

When rain began to fall, he moved into a more sheltered spot under the roof. It was typhoon season and he began to worry that he had chosen a bad day to make his stand.

Nightfall approached, and with it the intensifying storm. Rain hammered on the metal roof and waves pounded the boards of the dock below him. Swirling winds began to shriek through the cracks in the wooden structure. He shivered from the damp and his stomach rumbled. The thought of his ramen noodles became more important than the thought of moving away. He was certain his parents would have changed their minds about leaving Japan by now.

Hearing his father's loud voice mixed with others nearby, Kaito stumbled onto the dock and waved his arms, frantically drawing attention. Then he climbed down the wooden ladder to the dirt road and ran into his mother's outstretched arms. His father was right behind her. It was the only time he saw both of his parents weep. Their tears did not subside as they expressed how they feared all day that he had drowned.

Kaito was filled with reactions he had not experienced before. His shoulders sagged and his chin dipped to his chest as he kept his eyes on the ground. Sobbing, he felt terrible as he bowed and whispered apologies.

His parents immediately walked with him a few streets away to offer prayers of gratitude in the primitive Shinto that had protected his village for a century. This simple act of forgiveness was etched into his memory.

Kaito bowed with his parents as they passed through the simple gate at the entrance and then stopped at the *temizuya* to slowly perform the cleansing ritual in the stone water basin.

He bowed again with them before the dimly lit shrine as tradition demanded. They rang a bell and bowed twice and clapped twice before tossing some money in an offering box. As they stood quietly with heads respectfully lowered, Kaito knew they were lost in prayer. He copied them again as they turned to leave after one last long bow.

He told Hana many days later, "I don't know why they feel so good after going to the temple and clapping. Some day I want to find out. It's like magic."

When they were back home, his parents sat with him before he prepared for bed. "But why, Kaito? Why did you do this?"

"I-I don't want to go a-away," he stammered, as he shuffled his feet and stared at the floor. He had always been such an obedient child.

His voice was barely audible. "I'm afraid to leave our home ... our friends. I'm scared."

Gently, his parents acknowledged and soothed his fears. They stressed that listening to them and trusting them was always the ultimate act of love. "We would never, dear son, make decisions that were not good for you."

The lasting impact was that obedience and loyalty became the cornerstones of his personality.

His parents had gently instilled in him the meaning of *gaman*, the fundamental core of the Japanese psyche, since he was a toddler. Now he understood.

"It means we must always try our best in difficult circumstances ... like now when you were so frightened ... and always have self-control and discipline," his father explained. "Do the right thing. It is our duty, son."

These values were everything to him from that moment on.

It wasn't until many years later that he recognized the feelings that night had been of shame. All he knew right then was that he never wanted to experience that feeling again.

Kaito was quiet after he said goodnight. His heart leapt when his mother said, "We should have told you that the Suzuki family is going to make this move to Hawaii too. Your friend Hana will be there with you."

He lay on his tatami mat and pulled the thin cover up to his chin. His fears began to subside as exhaustion overtook him. He heard his father's words as he drifted off to sleep. *"Shikata ga nai. It is what it is."*

CHAPTER 2

*L*iving in Honolulu two years later felt like a fantasy come true to ten-year-old Kaito after life in war-torn Japan. His fears had evaporated before the plane landed as he and Hana peered out the windows. He felt the glistening sea and waving palm trees were welcoming him to his new home.

Kaito was fascinated by the big flashy cars he saw everywhere on Oahu. He hung on the promise from his father that one day they would have their own Chevrolet.

Hana couldn't get enough of all the pop music played on the radio every day. Her mother played 78 rpm records of Alfred Apaka's Hawaiian songs all the time and Kaito would join them trying to mimic the words.

The beach in their village in Japan was strictly for fishing boats, so the freedom and fun of Waikiki Beach with its board riders and outrigger canoes was an astonishing surprise to the new immigrants.

Kaito was happy to have his best friend experiencing so many new firsts with him. He had always felt a sense of freedom and safety in Japan and to discover it here as well was comforting. There were thrilling new experiences as the families hiked the rain forests together and went on a boat trip to see the powerful breechings of majestic humpback whales.

Living with natural wonders all around was a discovery that had a powerful impact on the little boy who had been filled with dread about moving. He felt drawn into the unique environment, and the ancient legends fired his young imagination. The tales expressed sacred, deep connections to nature and were filled with gods, ghosts, and goblins. These beloved myths provided explanations for everything, beginning with the creation of the Earth.

Kaito memorized each legend his father told him on their hikes. It seemed each natural wonder or blooming flower had a mystical story. Maui, the God of the Sun, and Pele, the Goddess of Fire and Volcanoes, were two of his favorites.

In his spookiest voice Kaito shared the often-scary tales with a wide-eyed Hana. "Remember," he warned her, "if you see the Night Marchers with their torches, you must crouch low to the ground and play dead. Don't look at them. Ever! They are the ghosts of chiefs and gods and we must respect them. But don't worry. If I'm there I will protect you."

"I believe you, Kaito," Hana would say when he made promises such as that, childish innocence pledging her trust in him.

From the beginning they had each other to laugh with and talk about what was happening in their new lives. It eased their embarrassment as they learned the language of their adopted country.

Going barefoot, especially to school, was a novelty both kids thought was cool.

Young Kaito dutifully attended prayers at the Shinto shrine with his parents long before he understood what it was all about. He liked the continuity of this from his life in Japan. All he knew was that whatever stress his parents displayed seemed to evaporate into calm serenity after a visit.

In his teens, Kaito became more aware of Buddhist philosophy through conversations with friends and began to visit temples with them. He was mesmerized by the hushed chanting of the monks and found the peaceful prayers to his liking.

In high school, Hana and Kaito took several of the same classes and often studied together. They rolled their eyes at each other as their parents clung to their ancestral ways, but did not disrespect the traditions, which they could see were highly valued by their elders. Education was a strong focus as both youngsters were guided by constant reminders that learning was the pathway to success.

During their high school years, Kaito, a natural athlete, played on school baseball and basketball teams. He was popular, with a quick sense of humor, and oblivious to his good looks. He often hung out with his teammates for a while after practice. But he did not get involved in their parties and was often teased good-naturedly for being a bookworm. He laughed at this and agreed with them. He loved to study and learn in general and almost made it seem cool.

Hana was also studious and not inclined to gossip or party with the girls her age.

Soon after their arrival in Honolulu, her mother had resumed an earlier love of embroidery. After years of sheer survival in postwar Japan, there had been no time for that. The war had brought an abrupt halt to this craft in Japan as materials vanished and every spare moment was spent simply trying to find enough food to survive.

The family's reputation for exquisite silk obi, the long belt worn with kimono, passed through generations of women in her family. It was widespread in Japan and Hana's mother brought that history with her to Honolulu.

Hana knew of this through stories her mother and grandmother told, and through one treasured kimono and obi carefully wrapped in special *washi* papers and protected in a small basket. Now that thread and silk were available once again, her mother had the time to return to working her magic.

While Hana watched her mother, she begged to learn the craft and showed an immediate talent. She became fascinated about the family history of creating this unique stitching for more than a century. As she learned more, Hana became deeply connected to the art and spent much of her spare time stitching and learning new techniques.

She had an innate shyness about her, but also had Elvis Presley posters in her bedroom and knew the words to all of his songs. For the most part she only socialized with her best friend, Lailani Mahelona, a fourth-generation Hawaiian girl who was one year older, and her cousin, Sara, on her mother's side.

Lailani was the polar opposite to Hana in many ways. She exuded confidence and optimism and liked to believe the world was as she saw it, in spite of the realities. The two girls became friends almost immediately as they discovered their shared love of books and music. Lailani made everything about high school so much easier for Hana.

Sara's mother was Hana's father's sister and they had immigrated to Honolulu a few years before the Suzukis. Though Sara's family moved from Honolulu to the mainland before high school graduation, the cousins' friendship continued as pen pals.

Family social engagements generally only involved Japanese families who also had immigrated and were happy to share their experiences to help the newcomers settle in. Although often there were several other young people their ages, Hana and Kaito always seemed to end up together in a corner chatting and laughing or outside exploring nature.

Their friendship was rooted in familiarity before there was ever a hint of romance.

For as long as they could remember, they had said they were going to marry each other. At first it was more of a childish game, as kids sometimes play. In their teens, their parents talked to them about this reality and spoke about the tradition of arranged marriage that was not uncommon in the Japanese culture. Hana and Kaito had grown up with the idea and were comfortable with it. To not accept it would be to disrespect their parents.

In time, the childhood friendship evolved into a boyfriend-girlfriend connection. Kaito saw sweetness in Hana's shy nature and beauty in her dark eyes.

Their first kiss happened at the movies when they were fourteen. An Elvis movie festival was playing for the weekend and they had gone to see *Blue Hawaii*, one of Hana's favorites.

Sitting in the back row with Lailani and her date, who were cuddled together from the start of the film, Kaito slipped his arm around Hana's shoulder while Elvis sang the theme song. The dulcet tones and sensuous scenery of their very own surroundings stirred feelings for Hana that Kaito's teenage heart could not resist. Hana turned her face to him and their lips met in a kiss that surprised them both. The page turned on a new chapter in how they saw each other. As they held hands on the walk home, Kaito, having learned from his American friends, asked her if she would like to go steady. Without hesitation, Hana said yes.

They teased each other about checking out options but the truth was, they admitted, that neither felt attracted to the American dating scene.

As much as they made fun of their parents' conservative lifestyle, Kaito also appreciated the loving home in which they had been raised. And he knew Hana did too. It was one of the things he admired about her.

Like Kaito, even as a young child she hadn't been spoiled and was encouraged to be independent but always well behaved. In his home, virtues like honesty, honor, humility, and trust were emphasized through conversation and the calm manner in which the family interacted with one another. When he spent time with Hana's family Kaito felt equally comfortable because of their similar dynamics.

There was much discussion during meals and often debate, but never vitriol or angry dissention. Conflict served no one, his parents had taught him. He knew he and Hana would be a good match.

Peace and harmony within the family was of the utmost importance, even if it meant not showing anger or worry.

Hana and Kaito often expressed to each other how they had always felt loved by their parents. But like many of their high school friends, they were eager to leave the nest and explore the world on their terms without having to answer to anyone else.

They talked about going to university. Kaito wanted to be an engineer and work with environmental projects to build a better world. Hana wanted to study psychology, as she had become immersed in the writings of Freud and Jung. She was increasingly puzzled about moodiness and anxiety creeping into her days, although she was adept at hiding it from others, including Kaito and her parents.

On long hikes or sitting on the beach or just hanging out, Kaito and Hana would occasionally plan how the future might look. Sometimes they dissolved into laughter and other times they seriously examined their differences. They both agreed on a house with a big yard. Kaito was all about developing the gardens and Hana was more interested in interior decorating. The topic of children went unresolved. Kaito believed he wanted to be a father, but Hana was uncertain about becoming a mother.

Kaito felt perplexed when Hana repeatedly said she wanted

to understand herself before she tried to guide another life. His efforts to get her to open up more about these feelings did not produce much in the way of results. He hoped once they were settled into their married life, Hana would feel differently.

Kaito became more involved with aikido in his teens and took a part-time job in the *dojo*, where they practiced, to learn even more. He liked that the sport was more about protection than causing damage. Hana dove deeply into the existentialist writings of Kierkegaard and Nietzsche. These were very different sides of their lives that did not impact their feelings about each other. Kaito was attracted to Hana's deepening sensitivity about life and felt the hours they spent talking strengthened their relationship.

It wasn't all serious and they teased each other about their differences. Stolen make out sessions when their parents were out for the evening or during weekend hikes were part of their growing connection, adding sparkle and innuendo to many of their passing glances.

But when it came down to it, they agreed that what they valued most was the comfort and safety they felt with each other as they saw other couples breaking up. They knew they were in love, or what they thought was love.

CHAPTER 3

*B*efore Christmas 1968, in his last year of high school, Kaito made plans to speak to Hana's father. He chose a night when he knew she was going shopping with her best friend, Lailani, who was already engaged to his good mate, Brett.

He carefully prepared his words to ask Mr. Suzuki officially for his daughter's hand in marriage. Even though their union was a foregone conclusion, Kaito felt strongly about following this proper tradition. He vowed he would never forget the promise he made that evening.

"I love Hana with all my heart and vow to you I will cherish and protect her. I hope I may have your blessing."

They bowed to each other as Mr. Suzuki's eyes glistened. "I have been waiting for the day to call you 'son.' We are all blessed to know this union in which we have believed forever will soon happen. We would like to have a *yuino* a few months before the wedding."

Kaito expected this, as it was a tradition for the families to gather after the engagement and exchange symbolic gifts as they wished for prosperity and old age for the couple.

ON NEW YEAR'S EVE, milling about on Waikiki Beach with throngs of people, Kaito felt a rush of emotion as he looked at Hana awash in moonlight. He suddenly was consumed by how much he loved her. Taking her hand, he knelt in the sand and proposed. Fireworks began to boom and light the sky in a dazzling display. He laughed as Hana kept nodding and murmuring her reply over and over. The timing of him popping the question was a surprise and so was the ring. Hana could not control her excitement when she recognized it as one she had admired at least a year before.

"I asked the jeweler to put it away for me and went in each month to make a payment," Kaito explained. He had saved part of the pay each week from his part-time job at the local martial arts studio. In his typical fashion, he knew what he wanted and made a plan to make it happen.

After several attempts to get her words out, Hana threw her arms around Kaito, tossed her head back, and shouted a loud "Yes, yes, yes!" to the colorful fireworks-infused skies.

Kaito lifted Hana off her feet as they shared a passionate kiss. When it finally ended, Hana breathlessly sighed as Kaito pressed himself to her. His thoughts were reminding him to slow down and control his urges. He had made a promise to Hana to respect her wish to remain a virgin until their wedding, but it wasn't always easy to stop wanting to go all the way.

"Soon, Kaito, soon. Let's set our wedding date right away," Hana said. "I want you, too, but I'm glad we are waiting."

THEIR WEDDING WAS PLANNED for summer, after graduation.

It was 1969 and not uncommon for couples to marry right out of high school. Hana and Kaito had attended the weddings of several of their friends. Each time they had been more convinced of their love for each other and their plans to move into this new chapter together grew in intensity.

Influenced by their parents, but totally in agreement, they planned a traditional Japanese wedding, a *"shinzen shiki,"* with immediate family, followed by a small reception with friends. As their venue, they chose the Izumo Taisha Shinto Shrine.

Taking the first step to making things legitimate, Kaito and Hana shared nervous excitement when they visited the city hall in May, thirty days before the marriage, to arrange for a wedding certificate. They were both nineteen.

"This really is happening!" Hana said, joyfully tucking the paper into her purse as they walked out to the parking lot. Then she slipped her arm through Kaito's as he held her close, thinking he had never seen her so exuberant.

Before he opened the car door for her, Kaito took Hana's hand and drew her to him for an ardent kiss. Hana responded with equal intensity. "We can do this in public whenever we want now. It's official!"

They grinned at each other and agreed some Japanese barbecue on Waikiki would be the perfect way to celebrate.

THERE WERE few details to be considered for the small reception. The couple's suggestions about food, flowers, and the Hawaiian wedding chant were respected as the parents made the arrangements for fifty guests. Hana's and Kaito's mothers sewed white tablecloths, adding some red and gold stitching to match the color theme of the party.

Both sets of parents had shipped their carefully stored wedding clothes to Hawaii when they originally immigrated in 1960. Kaito and Hana felt honored to wear them. They both knew how meaningful it was for their parents and they felt happy to honor them as well as their heritage.

For the ceremony, Hana was dressed in her mother's pure white wedding kimono, *shiromuku*, which was finished with a short train. Tradition stated that this signified pureness, cleanliness, and virginity, and the bride as a blank canvas was open to accepting her husband and his ideas and values. Her mother whispered these values to Hana as she helped her into the outfit. Although a teenager of the sexually liberated 1960s, Hana still trusted her mother's words and felt proud she was still a virgin.

A wide white obi wrapped around the kimono and over all that was a white overcoat, *uchikaki*. The weather had definitely played a role in choosing the wedding date, as a scorching summer day would not have worked with her outfit.

As the final touch, Hana wore a white headdress, *wataboshi*, considered the equivalent of the western bridal veil. More of a tall hood, it hid her face from all but Kaito until the end of the ceremony. Hana had declined to wear a traditional wig that many brides wore under this headpiece. Instead she had her hair pinned up and decorated with the same gold hair ornaments worn by Kaito's mother on her wedding day.

An abundance of clothing for Hana's diminutive frame, everything had been tailored to fit her perfectly. Looking in a mirror, she felt proud and hoped Kaito would be pleased.

Rather than flowers, Hana carried a folding fan and a small colorful clutch purse, *hakoseko*, which contained a few traditional good luck charms. Now it was also a convenient cosmetics case.

Kaito and his parents arrived in a limousine to collect his bride and her parents. He had wondered if he might feel some trepidation as this day arrived, after anticipating it for so long. But his reaction was just the opposite. He felt a warmth in his chest, an almost calm elation that this new chapter in his life was about to begin.

As Hana stepped out of the house in her stunning outfit, for a brief moment Kaito pictured the young Japanese girl he had known for so long. Then his heart surged as he saw a gracious bride who appeared to have stepped from a painting centuries back. It was a dramatic moment that spoke to him in a most romantic way and filled his heart.

Kaito took her hand to help her into the limo and they paused together for a moment. His fingers caressed the silkiness of her cheek. He leaned in to softly kiss her and felt a sense of bliss mixed with protection for her. He knew she was all he wanted in his life.

When Hana shyly lifted her eyes to meet his, he detected a new look of hope combined with emotion that promised more than friendship. The warmth he had felt in his chest flooded through him. The love he felt for Hana had never been stronger.

Kaito wore his father's traditional *hakama,* black-and-white pleated voluminous skirt-like trousers, gray kimono with the family crest, and black overcoat, *haori.* Tall and slim as he was with a sturdy build, the clothing sat well on his frame and made him look distinguished.

He smiled inwardly with pride when his father placed his hands on his shoulders and said, "My son, the high-ranking samurai."

The drive to the shrine was short and filled with light conversation. The parents reminisced about their own wedding day.

Upon their arrival, the group bowed at the *torii* gate. Next they stopped to symbolically purify their hands and mouths with wooden ladles at the springs near the entrance.

Before entering the shrine, Kaito pulled on large colorful woven cords hanging down to ring a loud bell. This was meant to invite God's appearance and repel evil, bringing confidence and power to the ringer.

A donation was made to the collection box and a priest

invited them inside, where he offered prayers. Then the couple shared three nuptial cups of sake, called *san-san-kudo*. They each took three sips from a small, then a medium, and finally a large cup. These small sips represented deliverance from human flaws and bound the couple together to overcome life's challenges: the symbolic beginning of their life as husband and wife.

As they gazed into each other's eyes, Kaito leaned in and whispered, "You look so beautiful, Hana. The perfect bride." He was filled with wonder at how they had grown up together and already shared so much up to this magical moment.

She whispered back, "And you look funny in your outfit ... funny but handsome. I am so lucky to be marrying you, my best friend."

To complete their marriage, they returned to the limousine and drove forty-five minutes to the stunning Byodo-In Buddhist Temple.

The elaborate temple had recently been constructed to commemorate the 100-year anniversary of the first Japanese immigrants to Hawaii. In a beautiful setting on expansive grounds, this was a smaller-scale replica of the over 950-year-old Byodo-In Temple, a United Nations World Heritage Site in Uji, Japan, and a popular venue for wedding photos.

The limo turned onto the paved road through the lush gardens of the Valley of Temples Memorial Park. The backdrop of jagged green cliffs of the Ko'olau Mountain Range created a striking setting. The first stop was at the entrance to a long picturesque bridge leading to the stunning temple with its cluster of red buildings and sweeping, curved tile roofs.

The photographer they had hired was waiting to greet them. Hana slipped her hand into Kaito's and a flicker of uncertainty showed in her eyes. Even when Kaito was the photographer, she never enjoyed having a camera trained on her. He gently squeezed her hand and leaned his head to her ear.

"Just a few photos and this part will be over. You will be so glad to have these later and so will I."

As they paused to pose on the bridge over the two-acre koi pond, other visitors to the temple discreetly took photos of them.

On the lawns, wandering peacocks and black swans stopped to look with curiosity.

Kaito was relieved that brief moment of anxiety on the bridge had passed. Now he watched as Hana's face glowed and she could not stop the sweet smile he knew so well. Kaito beamed with pride, eager to begin this new step as a couple.

A Buddhist monk was waiting for them in the temple to offer a simple blessing. Fragrant incense filled the air as Kaito and Hana stood holding hands with heads bowed. Then the formalities were complete.

Kaito was elated. His sweetheart was now his wife.

As they held hands during the drive to the reception hall, there was excited conversation about the future. Both sets of parents shared their joy and wishes for their children.

Kaito let his thoughts wander as he pictured how they would build a life together in their own space. There was so much to discover with careers and possibly a family. He knew Hana would need some time to get her head around that. Even when he joked about having children, her ambivalence was clear. But today was not the time for such thoughts. He just wanted to celebrate.

And the celebration was about to commence.

In twenty minutes they were at a trendy reception hall perched on a ridge with a panoramic view down to the sea.

After the photos at the Temple, they both were thankful to change into cooler clothing. The June weather with its heat and humidity was taking its toll.

Hana removed the headdress and changed into a festive red and gold kimono, *iro-uchikaki*, with a bright, colorful design she and her mother had worked on together. The embroidered details included cherry blossoms and cranes plus other Japanese symbols of good luck and fortune. Months of dedicated work had gone into preparing this outfit. Hana told Kaito she felt it represented her commitment to the marriage and the change it would bring to her life.

In a touching surprise, Kaito's mother gifted Hana her original obi, the decorative kimono sash that had been handed down in her family through four generations.

Kaito changed into a tuxedo for the party, like his father and now father-in-law, and more photos were taken in the gardens before the party began.

There was more of a Hawaiian touch included in the atmosphere and decorations for the reception. Kaito and Hana greeted each guest with a lei and a kiss on the cheek as they entered the spacious room.

The red, white, and gold color theme was bright and festive. A tall vase with white calla lilies gave a dramatic touch to each table and a colorful origami crane was found at each place setting.

When everyone had found their table, trays of champagne were served through the room.

Then Lailani and her fiancé, Brett, stood to get everyone's attention. Brett blew on the *pu*, a conch shell horn that symbolized the ancient Hawaiian tradition of announcing a community gathering or blessing a home or a wedding. Everyone clapped and called out to the newlyweds to kiss. Kaito grinned as Hana blushed profusely when he took her in his arms to respond.

Next, Lailani recited an Oli Aloha wedding chant as a welcome and to bless the newlyweds. Champagne glasses were raised in a boisterous toast and the party began.

Hana and Lailani held each other in a long hug and then touched noses in *honi ihu*, as they had since they first became friends. Their eyes locked as Hana said, "You are my best friend forever. We will always be family."

"*Ohana* today, tomorrow, and always," Lailani replied.

Brett and Kaito shook hands and patted each other on the back, smiling and laughing.

"We can't thank you enough for helping to make today so special," Kaito said, as Hana smiled warmly at them both and echoed his words, adding, "You brought the spirit of Laka to the room."

Brett gave them a thumbs-up. "The goddess of love is one of my favorites."

"*He alo a he alo*," Lailani replied. "May you always share aloha —love, peace, and compassion—in your marriage. You two were meant to be together and we are so happy to be part of the celebration."

A trio of musicians in white pants and brightly patterned shirts began to play the traditional Hawaiian wedding song. They were joined by three hula dancers, along with Lailani, who performed the slow and hypnotic wedding dance, their graceful hand movements expressing the beauty and emotion of the day.

A long buffet table was adorned with profusions of fuchsia and white orchids. Platters of sushi and teriyaki dishes mixed with traditional Hawaiian cuisine including many types of fish, poi, *laulau*, and vegetarian dishes. Hand-carved monkeypod wood bowls overflowed with salads. Artistic sculptures of luscious fresh fruit decorated an enticing sweet table with a chocolate waterfall as its centerpiece.

The four-tiered wedding cake, another nod to Western weddings, with its buttercream icing decorated in a cherry blossom motif, held the place of honor on a separate table. An antique Japanese saber lay next to it for the official cutting.

Lush, colorful flowerbeds bordered the expansive glass walls of the room. Majestic palms dotted the luxuriant lawns that seemed to stretch to the horizon. The walls were open on three sides, framing the spectacular view. Gentle breezes wafted through the open space with soft Hawaiian music filling the gaps between short speeches.

Kaito and Hana circulated amongst the tables. The room buzzed with lively conversation and laughter as the guests enjoyed the food and camaraderie. Typical at this type of Japanese wedding, there was no dancing.

Time passed quickly. To end the party, Kaito wielded the antique saber dramatically to cut the wedding cake. Hana passed servings to her parents and Kaito's, who delivered them to the tables.

Kaito had not given a lot of thought to the wedding preparations, feeling it really was Hana's show. But as he looked around the room now at their family and friends, he was warmed by the sentiment. The day was filled with emotion and joy—a true blend of the Japanese and Hawaiian traditions of hospitality that filled him with pride for his ancestry and adopted homeland.

CHAPTER 4

*a*fter the cake was cut and shared with thanks, *mahalo*, to everyone, Kaito led Hana to a waiting limousine.

With a look of puzzlement, Hana asked, "Is this how we are going home?"

"Going home is for two days from now," Kaito replied, his eyes twinkling. "Step inside. There is a bag packed with everything we need."

They waved goodbye to their guests and parents gathered outside. Hana giggled with excitement and Kaito drew her into his arms. "I am so in love with you, my sweet Hana. Our adventure together begins right now!" The limousine took them on a short drive to an exclusive resort they had frequently read about.

As they turned through ornate gates onto a long driveway that wound through manicured lawns and sculptured gardens, Hana gasped with delight. "What? How?"

Kaito could not stop smiling.

"This is my surprise for you. I've been saving all year. Yesterday while you were out with your mother, Lailani went over and packed for you ... under my guidance, of course. But I figured she might think of some things I would not. I'm sure you will see she didn't forget anything. And if she did, there are shops here."

With a sly grin, Hana murmured, "She even knew of my surprise for you."

Kaito smiled. He was usually the one springing surprises and wondered what she had planned.

Hana looked as excited as Kaito had ever seen her. "This is an amazing gift! The location is breathtaking! Even more spectacular than photos I've seen."

He took her in his arms, with all of his senses on high alert. Passion mixed with piety. He wanted to make this Hana's perfect day. "I hope today was everything you wanted it to be ... my *tsuma*, my *wahine*, my wife! We are together forever now and about to begin an entirely new adventure."

Kaito felt his body respond to the thought of making love to Hana. He had waited so long for this day and fantasized about it endlessly. He had been patient ... and frustrated when their intimacy had never involved him entering her. He had respected her wish to remain a virgin until this night. He craved the moment.

Hana's eyes reflected her happiness. "Today was everything, yes ... and more ... my *shujin*, my *kane*, my husband. And now let's go to the beach!"

"Absolutely! I'm boiling in this suit and you must be too," Kaito said.

Hana agreed. "I can't tell you how many times today I said a silent thank you to air conditioning!"

As much as Kaito wanted to take his wife in his arms and satisfy her in every way, he could see she was not on that wavelength. It would all happen tonight.

They quickly changed and were soon comfortably settled on padded chaise lounges placed sporadically for privacy on the horseshoe-shaped beach dotted with clusters of coconut palm trees. Shaded by a large palapa of dried palm leaves, the newly-weds sipped mai tais in frosted glasses with bright paper umbrellas. The soft white sand felt like sugar between their toes and the turquoise waves of the crystal clear lagoon lapped gently a few steps away, beckoning them.

After a refreshing swim, interrupted by many embraces and long kisses, they both fell asleep on the lounges. In time, they were gently awakened by a server who asked if they were dining on the lawn to watch the sunset.

Kaito confirmed they had reservations for a prime table. As they hurried back to their room to change, they laughed at their carefree feelings.

Hana hiccuped. "I think that last mai tai went straight to my head! But it was soooo delicious, I might have some more tonight."

Kaito laughed at this side of her he had not seen before. Hana had generally been a teetotaler, but today at the reception she had begun by drinking a glass of champagne after she tipped it to him, saying, "Here's to our freedom!"

THE SETTING for dinner in the warm air of dusk was magical. Tables were scattered on a broad terrace that overlooked the sea and the setting sun.

A group of musicians wearing brightly colored tropical-patterned shirts and white slacks played traditional Hawaiian music. Six hula dancers entertained with graceful, sensuous movements that told stories of history, nature, and love.

"Tonight I feel like a tourist!" Hana exclaimed. "Thank you for planning this wonderful secret!"

Kaito's heart swelled to see Hana so happy. Her eyes sparkled and her skin glowed with a radiance he had not seen before.

Dinner commenced as the sun was beginning to set. A crystal flute of champagne was set before each of them as they perused the menu.

"*Ho'o maika!* Congratulations on your marriage," the server said, as a woman in a vibrant full-length sarong muumuu placed a fragrant white-flower lei on Hana and one of green maile leaves on Kaito.

They toasted each other, "*Kampai!* To us!"

Hana giggled. "I am making up for years of not drinking alcohol today!"

Kaito nodded and chuckled. "And why not? As long as we are enjoying our special day, let's make the most of it."

Both were still full from their reception and ate sparingly, although they could not resist having some of the classic Kalua pua'a. This dish of pork rubbed with sea salt, covered with ti leaves and cooked in an underground oven, was one of the restaurants specialties and a favorite of Hana's wherever it was served.

"Today has been more than I hoped for, in every way," Hana said as she took Kaito's hand in hers. "Isn't it amazing that we have already shared so much of our lives with each other."

Kaito kissed the palm of her hand and smiled. "You are so right. Including hiding from our parents when they tried to get us to go to bed on camping trips when we were ten, to sharing my math homework all through high school."

Hana laughed and gave his hand a playful swat. "We've grown up together."

"And now we will have untold adventures and grow old together," Kaito said, touching his champagne glass to hers as her face shone with happiness. "Fasten your seatbelt!"

They reminisced through dinner, sharing laughs and recollections, as the champagne flowed with the memories. Kaito thought he had never seen Hana so relaxed and full of life. It seemed as though she had suddenly blossomed into a young woman, ready to take on the world.

Nature's show began with the first sounding of a pu—conch shell horn—when the bottom of the sun touched the sea. A card on the table described the details of this ceremony. The pu was blown three more times as the sun sank below the horizon, and then a final note of goodbye and thanks was sounded.

The moment the sun disappeared, the edge of sky along the sea became ablaze with a slow blending of vivid reds, oranges, and pinks that began to fill the sky. Above that, softer shades of purples, blues, and gold slowly swirled like a kaleidoscope into the sudden darkness of nightfall. The gentle breeze from the ocean still held the heat of the day.

There were exclamations of "What a stunning spectacle!" along with enthusiastic applause and cheers.

Hana sighed. "Even though we are fortunate to live with Hawaiian sunsets every night, there's something special about watching it here ... in this setting ... with you ... on our wedding night."

Kaito took her hand in his and kissed each finger slowly. "It truly is our new beginning."

HANA AND KAITO strolled to the elevator with their arms around each other. Hana had enjoyed another mai tai before their scrumptious meal and several glasses of champagne had been included with the dinner.

She stumbled slightly as they got on the elevator. "Ooops! I think I'm tipsy!"

"I'd say we both might be," Kaito replied with a laugh.

Hana had been more nervous than curious about making love for the first time whenever she and Kaito talked about it in their courtship. Sex had never been a big part of their relationship until they became engaged, and then only moderately.

There had been lustful kissing sessions, with their hands exploring each other's bodies. But he had never entered her, although she would help him climax.

Hana had shyly broached the subject early on when she asked Kaito if he would understand that she wanted to remain a virgin until her marriage. Kaito's teenage hormones had not been pleased with the idea, but he respected Hana. They would be married one day and he would wait.

Many girls she knew had been sleeping with their boyfriends in these years of increasing sexual liberation. Candid conversations about "how far" everyone was going seemed to be commonplace and discussed with pride. Hana sometimes felt like a loser for not wanting to go that route. Not that she spoke about it, but she would question herself when she heard other girls talking freely.

Hana shared secret thoughts with Lailani on overnight stays and she was surprised that her friend, by comparison, was so sexually liberated.

"You did that?" Hana would gasp, as Lailani rolled her eyes and giggled.

But Lailani also encouraged Hana to stick to her beliefs. "What is important to you is what counts. Then you have to be sure that your boyfriend agrees or nothing will last long. You and Kaito are such good friends, hopefully he will understand."

And Kaito did respect her wishes. Hana had been the only girl he had a relationship with. Even when it was simple friendship in the early years, he did not date anyone else. He became good-looking in his teens and girls were attracted to him. But even then he felt a loyalty to Hana that seemed predestined. Not that he found it easy, but he devoted his time to studies and sports and remained that guy all the girls wanted to date but was not available. His sex education came from locker room bragging by his friends and the dog-eared *Playboy* magazines he kept hidden in a box under his bed.

As they began to date more seriously and Hana explained her wishes, he felt it was only right to agree. They set some boundaries, and there were many serious make out sessions where Kaito had to quickly remove himself.

Tonight would be the night.

Once in their hotel room, as Kaito took Hana in his arms, she returned his kisses and caresses but then said she wanted to change. Removing an item from her suitcase, she disappeared into the bathroom.

Kaito's pulse quickened in anticipation as he stood on the balcony waiting for her, and he felt himself responding to his thoughts. He had imagined this night so many times.

It was a few minutes before Hana returned wearing a pale pink long, sheer negligee that complemented her in every way.

"All the girls...s-s-s-said every bride should have one on her wedding night," she said, her words slurring slightly. "Good thing I showed it to Lailani or it might not have been packed."

With her eyes cast down shyly, she went to Kaito.

"I hope this pleases you," she whispered, and then hiccupped, as they folded into each other's arms.

The silk against her body felt sensuous, and Kaito covered her with kisses as he felt himself reacting to his growing passion. Tonight he could fulfill a hunger he had kept in control for too long. As his tongue parted Hana's lips he felt her respond with an unfamiliar intensity as she helped him undress.

Hana's soft curves melting into his hard body ignited an explosion of fireworks that surged through him. Her hands were all over him and she wrapped her legs around him, almost too eager. Kaito reminded himself to take his time and not let excitement take over. He wanted this more than anything right now, but it had to be right for them both.

They whispered erotic words to each other as he guided her

THE SECRETS WE HIDE

to touch, taste, and enjoy, slowly savoring each other in the most sensuous ways. Their lovemaking was everything he had imagined it might be.

As passion took over and Kaito gently pressed into Hana, she suddenly recoiled in pain and confusion, pushing him away, gasping, "You are hurting me!"

Kaito pulled back, confused. Hana leapt out of bed and dashed into the bathroom where he could hear her throwing up.

Kaito went to her side to make certain she was okay. Then he dampened a washcloth with cold water and held it to her forehead, murmuring comforting words.

In between bouts of loud vomiting, Hana apologized over and over again.

When she appeared to be finished, Kaito gently wiped her face and led her back to bed. The moment her head hit the pillow, he realized she had passed out.

He lay beside her for a moment. The desire and excitement he had felt about finally making love to his bride had dissipated. Now he felt frustrated—and empty. He walked out to sit on the balcony. The sky was filled with stars and the moon cast a gentle reflection across the sea.

Kaito was stunned by how this perfect night had suddenly fallen apart. He worried he had done something terribly wrong, but soon decided that alcohol was probably the cause of everything. He had never seen Hana drink so much and decided it must suddenly have hit her.

So this wedding night would not be memorable in the way Kaito had dreamt. He was shaken and disappointed. But he also was calm enough to realize this would be smoothed over. He would be patient with his new bride.

CHAPTER 5

*T*he last thing Lailani Mahelona expected after Hana's beautiful wedding was for her best friend to phone her two days later, barely able to speak through her sobs. What Lailani did understand was that Hana ... now Mrs. Kaito Tanaka ... was on her way over and needed her help.

And help is what Lailani was all about when it came to Hana. Their long friendship was rooted in help to begin with and had flowered into a true sense of family. Since their teens they had been as close as any sisters, with a connection built on trust and laughter.

They had first met in elementary school when Hana Suzuki arrived as a shy ten-year-old from Japan. Her knowledge of English was remarkably good from the excellent schooling in her small village. Suddenly shifting to life in Hawaii was not so easy.

Lailani was a year older and assigned to be Hana's reading buddy. And from that point on, a friendship flourished between the two young girls who were different in every way but loyalty. Avid readers, their early friendship was based on sharing and exchanging books. This passion carried through the years, as did the way they greeted each other by touching noses, the *honi*. Lailani had explained this Hawaiian tradition when they first met, and Hana said it was like a secret handshake that she would do with no one else.

As timid as Hana was, Lailani was outgoing and boisterous in the most delightful way. Everyone loved her. A proud native Hawaiian, her family history had been traced back to Polynesian roots. More recently her family had been part of four generations of luthiers—makers of stringed instruments—and she had been raised with a ukulele in her hands. It helped that she had the voice of an angel.

She was known throughout the island for the way she sang traditional Hawaiian songs while her father accompanied her on the slack-key guitar. Her favorite songs were the old ones that were simple and rhythmic, involving chanting and often using just a double gourd and drums to accompany hula dancers.

The one song Lailani refused to sing was "Tiny Bubbles," which had become popular in 1966. "Leave that to Don Ho!" she would say.

That gift of music broke barriers when the girls first met.

Although Hana was quite a good reader, she was extremely self-conscious of her accent and did not want to read aloud. Lailani found the key to helping Hana overcome this through songs and ditties she made up.

At first Hana's reaction was to hide behind her hand, close her eyes, and swallow anything resembling a laugh. In time, she could be found with her arms wrapped around her sides attempting to gain control over loud laughter that eventually dissolved into giggles.

Lailani would look at her with a grin, brush her hands together, and say, "I believe my work is done!"

Another of Lailani's gifts was her sense of humor, usually accompanied with a sound as pure as light musical ringing bells that often ended in peals of laughter. Her laughter was contagious.

While Hana was delicate and willowy with straight, silky black hair, Lailani was full-figured with an abundance of dark, wild curls. Both girls were the same height. They soon discovered they shared a love of music and art. Their athletic pursuits were limited to hiking and spending time at the beach. Doing homework was a pleasure and they often worked together at one home or the other.

Lailani always had her sights set on being a nurse like her widowed mother. Hana was uncertain where life would take her after high school. She was dedicated to continuing the art of sewing that was an ongoing talent of the women in her family through many generations. But by graduation she had also developed a keen interest in psychology.

As they approached their twenties, both had grown into responsible young women.

Almost twenty, Lailani was finishing her first year of nursing school. She was engaged to her high-school sweetheart, Brett Moana, star football player, and state surfing champion who was just finishing his first year of premed at Honolulu University.

The two couples were great friends, sharing many good times through the high school years. Protesting the Vietnam War brought them together even more, as they expressed shared values while they were drawn into the politics of the times that were shattering their youthful ideals.

Hana and Lailani continued to spend a great deal of time together in between studies and other commitments. They bared their hearts to each other, sharing their hopes for the future.

But obviously they hadn't shared enough about everything.

~

STANDING in the doorway of Lailani's home, weeping with mascara running down her cheeks, Hana blurted, "I feel like I ruined our marriage before it began! How could I have been so stupid?"

Shocked, Lailani took her friend's hand and pulled her into her arms. "For heaven's sake, what happened?"

It took several attempts before Hana was calm enough to explain. Lailani led her to the sofa and held her hand as they sat together. She felt perplexed at what could possibly have happened to cause distress.

Between gulps, Hana said, "My sweet Kaito planned a special surprise for us to spend two days at the Sunset Dreams Luxury Resort. We had such a magical time. First on the stunning beach and then at dinner on the terrace watching a magnificent sunset."

"Maik`i... wonderful!" Lailani said. "So what went wrong?"

Hana dissolved into sobs again.

Lailani put her arms around her friend and patted her back softly.

After a few minutes, Hana pulled herself together and began to explain, "I feel like such an idiot ... and this is so personal ... but I have to talk to you about it ..."

"There's nothing best friends can't talk about," Lailani murmured. "We already know that."

Looking around, Hana asked, "Is your mother home?"

Lailani shook her head. "No, she is working a double shift in Emergency and won't be home for hours."

Hana sat back, wiped her eyes with the backs of her hands, and sniffed loudly as she reached for a tissue from a box on the coffee table. "Well, this is something I should have talked to you about before the wedding. So I'm just going to say it and get it out there. Have you and Brett ever had sex? I mean like the whole thing?"

Lailani looked at her, wide-eyed. "Um, in a word ... yes. Did you and Kaito never do it? You swore to me you were going to be a virgin when you married, and then we never talked about it again."

"I don't remember you telling me that you and Brett had gone all the way," Hana said, as a flush crept up her face. She twisted a tissue in her hands. "But I might just have shelved that information because I was so embarrassed about wanting to stay a virgin. Seriously, I avoided the topic of sex with you—and now I know that was so stupid!"

"No, no! I never told you we did do it ... it was just a few weeks ago ... we both got all emotional about the war and the possibility of him shipping out, and the next thing you know ... well, that was that. You were busy and excited with your wedding arrangements. I always got the impression you didn't want to talk about sex and I respected that. Actually, because you told me you were going to stay a virgin, I started thinking you might think I was a slut for going all the way."

Hana sniffled. "I would never have thought that—never. But it doesn't matter. This isn't your fault. It's all mine! I always felt too shy talking about it. I just never thought it would be like it was."

Lailani held Hana by the shoulders and looked into her eyes. "But it should have been ... umm ... well, great ... I mean wow! I have to tell you, I love having sex."

Hana looked at her in surprise. Then she stood up and burst into loud, ugly bawling. "Well, great ... now I really feel like I messed up in the worst way!"

"What the heck happened?" Lailani asked, pulling her back to the sofa. "Did you wear that beautiful negligee you bought when we were shopping?"

"Yes, I wore it and Kaito loved it. Everything started off perfectly. He was strong and sexy and made me feel like he knew what he was doing. He made me feel beautiful and loved and—" She buried her face in her hands and rocked back and forth.

"It can't be that bad," Lailani said.

"Oh, it is! I spoiled everything when we got to the serious part. It hurt … and I panicked. I thought I was doing something wrong and started to cry … and pushed him away."

"Oh Hana!" was all Lailani could murmur.

"It hurt so much and I didn't know what to do … and when I pushed him away, he didn't know what to do. He told me he didn't want to upset me or hurt me and that it was okay, that we didn't have to do anything more."

"Oh Hana," Lailani murmured again.

"And then, to make matters worse, did I mention I had way too much to drink? The room started spinning and I ran into the bathroom and threw up. Big time!"

"Oh man," Lailani muttered. Her heart went out to her dearest friend who was always the epitome of grace and good manners. She understood how mortifying this would be for her. She searched for the right words. "It happens …"

Hana got to her feet and began pacing. "But you know I never drink very much! I feel like such a loser. I know I should have let passion sweep me away and get the pain over with. But I think the drink kicked in and I was out of control …"

She explained how Kaito had truly been sweet and loving.

Lailani murmured, "I'm sure he was. Kaito adores you and is so thoughtful. I'm sure he was understanding."

"He was. Imagine! After I behaved like that! He stayed with me and put a cold cloth on my forehead in the bathroom. When I felt better, he took me back to bed and held me in his arms, whispering everything was all right."

Hana looked at Lailani with a pained expression. Her voice was filled with sorrow. "I'm devastated. I feel such disgrace. How could I let him down like that?"

"I hear you," Lailani said in her most comforting voice. She stood and hugged Hana to stop her pacing. Then she held her by the arms and gave her a little shake. "But you need to know you are not the first person this has happened to. There are many brides who overindulge at the wedding—and who knows how their wedding nights end up. It's history and you need to forgive yourself. Kaito obviously did."

Hana blew her nose. She shrugged her shoulders as she shook her head. "Easier said than done."

Hana let herself be drawn back onto the sofa and they sat side by side for a moment. Then Lailani turned her head and looked directly into her eyes.

"So now, three days later," she asked, "what's happened with everything? Any more koochie moochie?"

"That's just it. Nothing. We've just gone to bed and kissed and cuddled. Kaito said he would wait until I feel comfortable about trying again. And I do want to try again but I'm afraid I'm going to mess it up again. So I keep putting it off."

The two friends talked for quite a while. In the back of her mind, Lailani wondered if perhaps Hana had a medical problem and should see her doctor, but she decided that should be the backup plan. With her urging, she and Hana came up with an idea as to how to begin to smooth things over.

CHAPTER 6

$\mathcal{K}$aito was right about being patient and understanding with his new bride. As frustrating as it had been for him to continue to suppress his desire to make love to her, he was giving her time to come to him about it. He understood how embarrassed she was about overdrinking and he had needed to reassure her a few times that he was not angry.

A few days after they had settled into their apartment, Hana prepared his favorite meal, ahi poke, for dinner. She cubed the tuna, purchased fresh at the market that morning, and added the Hawaiian salt, seaweed, and kukui nuts in the traditional way of preparing the dish. Sometimes Kaito liked to have crunchy chopped green onions added—an American touch—but she decided to leave that out for tonight. Everything she planned was for "tonight."

She had not been able to stop thinking of the fiasco of their wedding night. She blamed herself entirely and was anxious to banish the guilt she carried. After all the years of sticking to her vow to save herself for her wedding night, she could not forgive herself for messing up. And Kaito! She loved him all the more for being understanding.

Their favorite Elvis album was playing on the stereo.

After dinner, Hana moved the needle to replay "Love Me Tender," and she brought Kaito out to the balcony to dance in the moonlight.

They held each other close and as the song was ending, she whispered in his ear. "Let us try again, Kaito. I want you to make love to me so much I can't think of anything else. I hope you still feel the same."

Kaito had been waiting since their wedding night for Hana to say these words. He felt his mouth go dry and his stomach tighten as he hoped this time everything would be fine. Within a moment, he felt a surge of desire and kissed her gently before answering, "Of course I do. I've never stopped wanting you."

She asked him to wait until she called him to the bedroom.

There Kaito found her in the silky negligee she had worn on their wedding night. Candles lit the room.

Kaito reminded himself to let Hana's responses guide him and not to rush her. Their lovemaking was tender and erotic as they finally discovered what pleased each other. They took their time until they climaxed in unrestrained passion.

Hana cried softly as she lay in Kaito's arms. "That was everything I hoped it would be, my darling," she said. "It is how I wanted our first time to be." Her voice caught as she added, "I'm so sorry that I ruined our wedding night."

"Our wedding night was wonderful in many other ways, my love," Kaito whispered to her as he stroked her hair and covered her face and neck with kisses. "Put those thoughts out of your head … this was worth waiting for. It was beautiful."

Hana sighed and murmured, "Yes, it was." She hugged him tightly as they drifted off to sleep.

I have to remember to thank Lailani for that tube of lubricating gel … was Hana's last thought as her eyes closed.

THAT AUTUMN, Kaito enrolled in university to become a biological engineer, as he had dreamed after this new degree program was announced. His love for the environment had grown into a desire to have a job that enabled him to help the planet. He had been awarded an ROTC scholarship for his outstanding marks and would attend military training along with his studies.

The scholarship would help defray tuition costs along with income from Kaito's part-time job at the martial arts studio and Hana's growing sewing business. Kaito's parents had set aside money in an education account since they first arrived in Honolulu; and although the newlyweds did not have a lot of money to spare, they had enough to be comfortable. For that they were immensely grateful.

Kaito supported Hana's wishes to pursue a university degree in psychology. However, this was something her father would not consider. He was a kind and loving father but was still stuck in an old-fashioned mentality about girls not going to college. No matter how Kaito encouraged Hana to try and persuade him to change his mind, he had to accept her decision to acquiesce to her father's feelings. She had adamantly refused to allow Kaito to raise the subject with him.

Hana's skill in the sewing and stitchery that had been passed along from generations of women in their family continued to be her favorite pastime. She was blessed with nimble fingers, an artful eye, and a love for the feel of the silk threads and fabrics. Her talent was honed under her mother's watchful eye and direction, and there was no denying she worked magic as she stitched. She had a knack for combining unusual colors that created spectacular visuals, some soft and muted and others absolutely eye-popping.

"I do love it," Hana often told Kaito. "I wish Papa had

changed his mind about me going to university, but this is what I will do. I'll do my best and stitch wishes into my work so these obi will bring happiness to others."

Kaito worried as Hana struggled for a while with the disappointment of being denied her own wish. He was concerned that it might affect the intermittent periods of deep sadness she sank into from time to time.

He watched her closely and did his best to cajole her when she became withdrawn. However, he had also learned that there were times when she needed to be left alone until she felt better. Her despondency was irregular and unpredictable.

As time went by, Hana became increasingly inspired by the referrals she was receiving from clients as far away as Japan, where it had become popular to hang the obi or use it as a table decoration. She treasured the positive notes they wrote to her about her beautiful embroidering.

"You've achieved a PhD in sewing," Kaito told her. "A piece of paper from the university is not worth any more than all of the letters you receive for your awesome creations. People don't write this kind of praise unless they truly mean it."

He could see that his words inspired her confidence and was happy to watch her begin to enjoy the sewing orders that were flowing in. She was skillful and talented and gradually acquired a high-paying clientele for her sought-after designs that featured nature-inspired motifs. Birds, blossoms, and butterflies were her trademarks. Each one she chose had special significance, which made every one of her obi special to the owner. The blend of colors and textures she created, down to the smallest details, were unique, and she explained to Kaito that was because of the sense of magic she felt as she stitched.

"I'm bringing happiness to others. I feel it as I sew."

However, Kaito wished he could feel she was also bringing happiness to herself. When Hana was not sewing, she often retreated to a dark place within herself. He would sometimes find her weeping softly to herself, unable or unwilling to give him an explanation. She would simply say she could not control the urge. And this caused him ongoing consternation.

LAILANI, Brett, Hana, and Kaito's friendship flourished. Saturday morning often became a date to visit Young's Fish Market and choose the freshest pieces for lunch together. Kaito and Brett called themselves "Men with Knives" and entertained with an exaggerated display as they prepared sushi and sashimi. Lailani and Hana put together traditional maki rolls, sometimes competing with each other to create new taste sensations with different ingredients.

Sundays were reserved for hikes in the winter and beach days in the summer. Many of those beach days involved cheering on Brett in thrilling surfing competitions at the north beaches. The excitement of standing on the golden sand at the Banzai Pipeline and holding their breath as they watched their friend disappear into the pull of a wild twenty-foot wave with the gusting wind and roar was indescribable. And the cheer as he suddenly shot through the other end was exhilarating.

These times brought out the best side of Hana's behavior and he was always aware of how thankful he was for her friendship with Lailani.

CHAPTER 7

*A*part from the good times, Hana and Kaito were settling into the serious side of life that adulthood brought. Kaito's studies were demanding but he thrived on the challenge. At times, Hana felt the burden of deadlines in her sewing projects and did not deal so well with that. The pressure weighed on her; but once she was in her studio, needle in hand, she lost herself in her work.

The four friends were involved in the anti-war movement, delivering pamphlets and attending rallies as the Vietnam issue continued to be divisive, often splitting families apart. Along with many school friends, they joined in demonstrations and marches in the city.

Kaito knew Hana had felt as proud as he had when they received their American citizenship at age twelve. The families had attended citizenship classes together, quizzing each other on the required facts they had to learn. Kaito and Hana had stood side by side, flanked by their parents, with hands over hearts as they proudly recited the Oath of Allegiance on that special day.

Now they felt strongly about their abhorrence to this war that was enflaming households.

Military service was very much a topic of conversation. The conflict in Vietnam had dominated newspaper headlines for years. So it was a major surprise when Lailani and Brett arrived for dinner one evening and shared the news that Brett had enlisted in the Navy. He would be leaving soon for training and then deployment to the war zone.

The news was a shock after two years of demonstrating together.

"I decided I didn't want to take a chance being drafted," Brett explained. "This way I could choose which arm of the services I wanted. It's going to be a conflict—no pun intended—because I sure as hell don't believe in this war, but at the same time I want to serve my country. And I will be able to continue my medical degree when I return."

Lailani's eyes betrayed her calm demeanor as she whispered to Hana while they were alone in the kitchen. "I'm terrified, Hana. But I want to support his decision. He suggested we get married before he leaves but I want to wait until he is safely home again."

"We will be here for you, like always, and trust the war ends before too long."

Deep in her heart, Hana said a prayer that Kaito would not suffer the same fate.

The first two years of marriage were relatively happy, filled with studies and work. As they began to explore their relationship in their own home, away from protective parents and opinionated comments, their love blossomed.

Kaito grew accustomed to Hana's need for solitude from time to time and did not try to talk her out of one of her dark moods if he saw it would be impossible. He had learned that Hana reacted badly to any persuasion to "snap out of it" on those days, so he would go to the aikido studio, take a walk on the beach with his camera, or work in the garden.

As time went by, they became comfortable with the intimacy that developed but nights of passion were not exactly how their love life could be described. Hana, without Kaito's knowing, consulted Lailani on a regular basis for advice on lovemaking, which simply did not come naturally to her. Lailani was an endless source of good advice, as well as articles and books on the subject. To her disappointment, as much as Hana wanted to please Kaito sexually and also be pleased herself, she could not truly enjoy it.

Lailani also experienced Hana's dark moods through the years. There were occasions when she might not answer the phone, and if Lailani dropped by when Kaito was at work or out, she would ignore the doorbell. Her explanation a day or two later would be that she had a headache or she had been asleep. She never admitted to not feeling well in those instances, and Lailaini did not press her.

Lailani and Kaito confided in each other as they worried about Hana getting help if the episodes got any worse. At this point, Kaito felt she really was just moody like many other people and did not see the serious aspect that Lailani raised based on her medical studies.

Kaito appreciated Hana's quiet demeanor as she established an organized schedule keeping their small apartment tidy, in spite of demanding sewing projects. It was in his nature to help out with chores and, after initial protestations from Hana, it was not long before she accepted his pitching in. A contented rhythm filled their days.

They adhered to traditional weekly tea visits to and from their parents' homes, but they also made time to pursue their mutual passions, particularly hiking and exploring. Since their teenage years, they had become familiar with the lush tropical jungle rainforests and conservation areas with well-marked trails, many near their home and others along breathtaking seaside and rugged mountainous drives.

In no time at all they could be at the Diamond Head Trail, which took them to the top of the crater with its panoramic view that often included a rainbow, since sudden rain showers were common. Only a three-hour hike, leaving early to avoid tourists and intense tropical sun and heat, they would get their exercise and still have the rest of the day for other things.

Other times they would pack a lunch and fill the day with visits to trails known mainly to locals. They hiked in every season but avoided some days during the winter rainy periods when the trails became slippery and humidity, sometimes 100%, could be a problem. Spring and summer were the favorite times when speckled light filtered through dense jungle greenery and gave welcome shade as temperatures soared. Fragrances of wild ginger and guava scented the air. These hikes often led to waterfalls that offered invigorating freshwater pools. On days like these, Kaito and Hana talked for hours and chuckled with smugness that their locations were not overrun by tourists.

On the good days, they would amuse each other by repeating local folklore, of which there was a wealth. Hana would sketch flora, birds, and butterflies in her journal, developing ideas for sewing projects. Kaito's contribution was taking photos that Hanna could refer to later.

Kaito teased her with a nickname of *pulele*, a shortened version of the Hawaiian word for butterfly, *pulelehua*. He told her she was as delicate and beautiful as those she drew. A shy smile was always his reward.

Lailani often was included in their plans, and the frequent Saturday sushi meals continued. Brett's presence was sorely missed.

These were their best times together—as long as Hana did not have a sudden mood swing where she would retreat into herself. And that was something that simply could not be predicted. When it did happen, they drove home in silence and Hana would go straight to her sewing.

Usually a few hours later she would reappear. Sometimes she would apologize to Kaito, often tearfully. But she would also say she did not want to talk about how she felt and that it was best if they simply moved on. Other times she would simply act as though there hadn't been any incident, and Kaito would be left to seek his own peace deep within himself.

~

ONE SATURDAY LAILANI arrived in tears and handed them a telegram.

"Brett is missing in action," she blurted, before she dissolved into sobs.

With a horrified expression, Hana threw her arms around her best friend and led her to the sofa. She held her, with her own face wet with tears, until Lailani's sobs eventually subsided.

Kaito brought a glass of water for each of them. He read the telegram over several times and tried to find something positive to say. Shock had rendered him speechless.

Lailani stood and paced the room as she explained that two senior military officers had delivered the message that morning. "Missing in action. I guess that is better than deceased," she mumbled. "But I feel shattered."

Kaito hugged her. "We have to keep believing in the best outcome."

Lailani nodded, hugging him back. "I absolutely will do that until I am given proof that it won't happen." She sniffed and took the tissue Hana offered.

Hana felt more shaken by the announcement than anyone. She admired how Lailani could regain her composure and maintain such a brave face.

LATER THAT WEEK, Lailani was at Kaito and Hana's for dinner.

"I'm glad to see you are eating," Hana said.

Lailani smiled ruefully. "You know me! Even in my worst moments, food is always a comfort."

"And your mother is about the best cook in town. After all the years we have been welcomed at her table, we can vouch for that," Kaito said.

Hana nodded her enthusiastic agreement.

"Bless my mother! You know all about that! Thank goodness she was home when the telegram was delivered. I spent a good part of the morning crying on her shoulder, so I thought I would be fine when I came to share it with you. But the minute I walked to your front door, I lost it again."

"Your mother is always an enormous help and support ... and not just in the food department," Kaito said, hoping to offer some comfort.

"For sure," Lailani agreed. "Having her with me that morning made a difference. I don't know what I would have done if I had been alone. She is helping me realize that I can find the strength to deal with this. I have to."

Hana could not get her head around that. "I'm so devastated by Brett's situation that my heart hurts. I only think negative thoughts whenever I let it get into my mind. I can't seem to help myself."

Lailani explained, "You know I have been involved in a group at the hospital looking into happiness studies and how to reduce stress in our patients and workplace. Trust me, I've learned a lot."

"Well, you might have to try a few techniques on me," Hana said. "Seriously ..."

"I'm serious too, my friend. Let's plan a time," Lailani replied. She continued talking about how many more people were seeking help for depression and anxiety because of the war and other pressures in society in general.

"It's bizarre how these studies came into my life this year and how learning about it has helped me. What a coincidence. And then there is my mom, bless her ..."

Kaito and Hana nodded together and chuckled.

"She is happiness personified," Kaito said. "I've never known anyone who sings and laughs as much as she does."

Hana added, "And her stories that tell the myths and legends of the islands are always so full of positivity. We never walk away from her without a smile."

"Well," Lailani said, her smile crinkling the sides of her eyes, "Imagine how it is living with that your entire life. I guess it's genetic—and I'm thankful for that!"

Kaito impulsively gave Lailani a hug. "And we are thankful for that too! You bring sunshine with you wherever you go and we're glad so much of it lands on us! Right, Hana?"

It was Hana's turn to hug her friend. "Kaito is so right. We love you, Lailani, and I hope you always know that."

Kaito grinned at them both and silently gave thanks for the close friendship the women shared. He knew Lailani's influence often helped Hana through difficult days when anxiety or depression was dragging her down.

He hoped that somehow they were able to help Lailani in return with her concern about Brett.

CHAPTER 8

*K*aito continued with his hobby of photography that had begun in high school. Lailani also expressed an interest back then, and Hana was always happy to see them take courses and workshops together. Hana told Kaito she enjoyed having those times to herself.

Since the news about Brett, Kaito tried to encourage Lailani to join him on some photo excursions. Hana had pointed out to him that Lailani was spending all her time devoted to her nursing studies and did not seem to be enjoying other aspects of her life.

Kaito became more involved in aikido, a form of martial arts that his father introduced to him as a boy of six in Japan. He was intrigued by the use of tactics and moves that bring an opponent under control with minimal effort and little harm. Hana had tried to become interested in the sport but did not enjoy the physical contact, saying it exhausted her mentally.

"It's not for everyone," Kaito reassured her when she thought badly of herself for not sharing his love of the sport. "You have your hobbies and I have mine. No problem."

The two of them loved to swim and surf in the sparkling

waters of the endless beaches, but Hana was becoming paranoid about the dangers of too much sun. Before long she became increasingly cautious about the amount of time they spent there.

Kaito was disappointed in Hana's growing aversion to being out in the sun and attempted to persuade her with different sun-blocking lotions. But to no avail.

As time went by, it became more apparent that Hana needed her own time and space more often. Her sewing was her refuge. She would withdraw into herself and become silent for hours, letting the silken threads slip through her fingers as she considered the shades and strand counts of the floss to choose next.

Afterward, she sometimes would thank Kaito for his understanding and he felt a sense of relief hearing her light tinkling laughter again. He knew by now that every time she immersed herself in the embroidery, she was searching for the *ki*—the life force, the energy that guided her with every stitch. She explained how it sustained her as she worked.

Kaito hoped one day she could bring that life force into the rest of their life.

There were a few aspects of their Japanese heritage that remained a part of their lives. Most important was the tea ceremony. The *chado* was a tradition both sets of parents continued, although somewhat modified as the years passed.

Kaito and Hana both remembered how, as youngsters in Japan, their grandparents served the family tea once a week in a small *tatami*-floored hut, a *chashitsu*, standing separately in a corner of their garden.

As children, they heard reminiscences of ceremonies that were preceded by long meals and would last for hours, but those had vanished with modern times. Now a sweet would be served, before her mother prepared the green tea leaves for matcha.

The tools for the ceremony were kept in an ornate wooden

chest that had on its lid a detailed etching of a pagoda with mountains in the backdrop. A small brass gong was struck softly to begin. Fine linen cloths were used to wipe the bowls. Shallow bowls were used in summer so the tea would cool more quickly. Kaito's mother had earthenware bowls that had been passed through the family for more than a century. Sadly those of Hana's family had been lost in the war. A small tea caddy contained the leaves to be used that day, and a bamboo tea scoop transferred the powdered leaves to each bowl. Water was heated in a small kettle placed on a brazier. A bamboo whisk mixed the powder and water in each bowl. Each bowl of tea was accompanied with a bow, by both the presenter and recipient, as it was served.

At times, Kaito and Hana would have their own private tea ceremony in their tiny apartment as a way of relaxing and sharing quiet thoughts.

IN MAY, weeks before their second anniversary, Kaito was called up to ship off to Vietnam courtesy of the American military draft program. He had three years left on his engineering degree when he opened the notice to report to the local military base for more intensive training than he had received in his ROTC courses. In spite of being shocked and not supportive of the war, they always knew this was a possibility.

This news did not sit well with Hana. She could not stop crying and questioning if he would meet the same fate as Brett, about whom no further word had been received. Kaito felt distraught at the thought of going to Vietnam and worried how Hana would cope. However, he knew that Lailani would be a rock for Hana just like Hana had made every effort to be there for her best friend as they still waited for word about Brett.

Both sets of parents assured Kaito they would go out of their way to offer Hana support.

Three weeks later, as he prepared to board the military transport, the families were at the base to see him off. Both sets of parents stoically bowed and wished him well. Hana sobbed as she threw her arms around him in an uncharacteristic public display of emotion as the parents all looked away. Kaito stroked her long black hair, soft as silk.

"I love you and will miss you, *pulele*," he whispered, his lips brushing her cheek as he breathed in the scent of her, a refreshing blend of citrus and floral he knew he would carry with him.

Their love had blossomed slowly and now the prospect of being apart was difficult to accept. They clung to each other in one final embrace and then bowed as they backed away from each other, too overcome for more words.

CHAPTER 9

*S*ix weeks later, Hana discovered she was pregnant. She wrote to Kaito that she was nervous about motherhood. "I'm worried I am not ready for this. I wish you were not so far away."

Kaito wrote back expressing his surprise and pleasure about the baby and encouraging Hana to find joy in the situation.

"My love for you cannot be expressed deeply enough in letters. I think of you and our child you are carrying all the time. It's truly a miracle and I have smiled every single day since you shared the news with me. I want to put my arms around you and have you feel that love. One day that will happen, and the moment we hold our child in our arms I know we both will feel the powerful love of being in this new chapter together. It will be such a gift."

Each week Hana sent Kaito details of how she was feeling and later began to send photographs of her growing baby bump. Lailani had taken the pictures one afternoon at the beach as a lark. Kaito requested they continue so he could feel part of what was happening. He was thankful their friendship with Lailani had never dimmed and that the women continued to spend a lot of time together.

It was difficult for letters to be mailed and received in Vietnam, but Hana and Kaito tried their best to keep in close touch as the months passed. There was a constant nagging concern in the back of Kaito's mind as to how Hana would adjust to being a mother. She had always been reluctant to have a serious conversation about having children and certainly this pregnancy was not planned.

Kaito did his best to be positive and encouraging in all of his communication with her. He kept hoping and looking for some eagerness in Hana's letters, but his heart sank each time he felt there was none.

With his environmental engineering education, he was assigned to a maintenance unit working with civilian contractors that took care of resupply of drinking water for the troops. The extreme subtropical humidity caused severe sweating, which made rehydration a constant challenge. Combat duty was not part of this assignment and there were times this filled him with guilt. Especially since a medical unit also stationed with them meant there was contact with injured combat soldiers coming through that gave a very clear picture of the horrors they faced. There were unpredictable bombing incidents on their encampment and the threat of danger hung heavily.

Being situated deep in the jungle, it was a day after the birth on April 5, 1972, that Kaito learned the happy news by wire from his central command.

It was several days before he could gain access to a satellite phone. The conversation was brief due to a tenuous connection, and at the sound of Hana's gentle voice, with no sign of anxiety, Kaito's normally stoic composure crumbled. Silent tears slid down his cheeks. He felt relief to know the birth had not been difficult and suddenly he was awash with joy as he heard the sounds the baby was making. It all became real.

"Everything went well. I even managed the pain without an epidural," Hana proudly told him. She sounded more positive than he had ever imagined. "And our daughter is perfect. All fingers and toes."

"And will we call her Kiana?" Kaito asked, speaking loudly over the static on the line.

This was the name they had chosen earlier through letters. It felt exactly right, as it was a combination of Kaito and Hana. The Hawaiian meaning was "divine."

"It is absolutely the perfect name for her. She is beautiful, my husband, truly divine ... with a mass of dark hair and your ebony eyes." Hana promised to mail photos right away.

Her words and tone of voice made Kaito's heart leap. A brief but deep thought crossed his mind. He wondered if the birth of their daughter was the answer to past anxieties and dark moments that had plagued Hana for years.

"Lailani took lots of photos and so did our parents when they were here to see us. And they are all coming to take us home tomorrow ... so funny! I have never seen them so animated—truly so very happy. I feel grateful to have a healthy baby. I will wait four more days to honor the *oshichiya* and tell them our daughter's name on the seventh night after her birth. They are already planning the *omiyamairi*."

Kaito laughed as Hana described the grandparents' reactions to the baby's arrival and the fact they were already planning the traditional first shrine visit and photo shoot at cherry blossom time.

He felt heavy-hearted that he would not be home to be part of these Japanese traditions.

Hana was sad as they spoke of this, but she seemed heartened by the support of Lailani and their parents. She also expressed she felt the weight of the deeply engrained culture of Japanese wifehood, which dictated she maintain the household when the husband is absent.

"Be sure to ask Lailani to take lots of photos," he reminded her.

"I will," she replied. "I think this will be one spoiled little girl by the *baa-chan* and *jii-chan*," Hana said, referring to their parents.

WAITING to see photos was torment to Kaito, on top of coping with the depressing atmosphere within his unit. Morale was low as the US was well into its withdrawal of troops, and there was an ominous sense within Kaito's unit that the North Vietnamese were preparing another offensive.

It was weeks before a thick packet arrived.

His hands trembled as he tore open the envelope to see the promised pictures of the baby.

As he gazed at the first photograph, he caught his breath at the tiny face, her perfect eyes, nose, and lips.

His daughter. His child.

His entire body flushed with something he could not explain. War brought fresh ugliness every day, not just the blood and the filth, the screams, but the way it revealed the worst of men's souls—the casual cruelty, the numb resignation to atrocities that would break you if you didn't make yourself stop caring.

But this...this perfect little girl in the photo in his hand who was his and Hana's, something they'd made together...that was the beauty of the world. A reason to hope. A reason to get through this hateful war.

In the days and weeks after receiving the photos and remembering his phone call with Hana over and over, Kaito was aware of a strength and determination he had struggled to find in the midst of this abhorrent war.

This renewed sense became more visceral and Kaito felt a

different commitment to his service in Vietnam: an additional urgency that would get him back home to care for his daughter and wife. The word "family" took on another meaning for him. So many soldiers were fathers who wanted to return to their families and now he was one too.

As infrequent letters from Hana, and the odd one from Lailani, attested, both mother and mother-in-law provided assistance in the first weeks Hana and Kiana were back home from the hospital.

Kaito's mother had dutifully written short letters to her son every week since he left for Vietnam. She always told him how proud they were of him, how much they missed him and how the weather had been recently. After Kiana was born she also added gushing descriptions of their sweet granddaughter.

The letters from Hawaii arrived bundled in a packet, and Kaito took pains to make certain he read them in order. Each one was a treasure and, although they made him homesick, they also kept him grounded through the hellish living conditions in the jungle and the fear and vulnerability of surprise attacks.

It wasn't until two months after Kiana was born that Hana's letters became infrequent. Lailani wrote of her concerns to Kaito.

"Hana alternates between being short-tempered or sad, with infrequent periods of seeming happy. She treats Kiana well but often is quietly crying as she feeds or holds her. Breastfeeding has been a struggle from the beginning. I'm sure Hana's doctor will arrange some help with that, if only I could get her to go ..."

Thanks to her training as a nurse, Lailani expressed herself clearly and Kaito felt confidence in her observations, but unspeakable anxiety seeped into his mind as he read on. She mentioned that his mother and Hana's mother behaved as though nothing was amiss, but their expressions told a different story.

"Honestly, Kaito," she wrote. "I can see they are concerned.

But when I try to address some of Hana's behavior, they simply shake their heads and refuse to say anything, except to promise they are coming every day and everything will be fine. But they know everything won't be fine. I can see it. In fact, I have discovered they are taking turns staying overnight too. Hana needs medical attention. Do I have your permission to call her doctor?"

As he read Lailani's letter, Kaito's heart dropped and he was hit with an overwhelming sadness. He felt the muscles strain in his neck and his entire body tensed. To suddenly be aware of Hana in trouble, but also confirm an insipid fear and anxiety he had harbored in years past, and to be so far away in the last place he ever wanted to be, he felt helpless … and angry.

He stuffed the letter in his pocket and went behind the shed where he was helping stack empty munitions crates for pickup. Walking over to a crude exercise area the men had patched together, he spent several minutes pounding a punching bag … not his normal reaction to stress. But this was all that would help for the moment.

After just a few minutes he was dripping with sweat and swatting flies. He pulled his thoughts together, stripped off his clothes, and stood under the outdoor shower where the water was perpetually warm with no heating. He needed to find time to meditate—later.

Now he carefully folded the crumpled and damp letter and tucked it with others in his backpack. He immediately walked to the office area to reply by telegram, asking Lailani to do whatever she felt necessary as quickly as possible.

Stressing the importance of his need to call his wife, the next day he was able to organize a satellite phone call. Working to control his concern, he tried to gently prompt Hana to express how she was feeling. She insisted she was fine. But Kaito heard despondency in the tone of her voice, in spite of her words. He felt even more unsettled and worried afterward.

Lailani made the call. The doctor was hesitant at first since Lailani was not a family member. But she listened as Lailani explained all of the family complications with an absent husband at war and parents who were not acknowledging any problem.

"It is good of you to call and you are right to be concerned," the doctor said to Lailani. "Hana is due for a routine visit with the baby. I will have my office call and say we want her to come this week due to some scheduling issues. We will make it seem like our office problem."

As Lailani explained in her next letter to Kaito, at the appointment the doctor was thorough and sensitive in her conversation with Hana. Medication was prescribed and a woman from the Lamaze group was scheduled to help with breastfeeding techniques. The doctor also recommended counseling, which could not begin for a month due to a backlog.

Kaito felt helpless and frustrated at being so far away. He spoke to his senior officers about the possibility of getting home for a few weeks but was given little hope of anything they could do to help.

CHAPTER 10

*T*hree months after his daughter's birth, Kaito was suddenly removed from his unit. A medical request from Hana's obstetrician had outlined the need for his involvement in his wife's developing health issues. There was a concern that her postpartum depression was in fact the more serious postpartum psychosis due to periods of anxiety and disorganization Hana was presenting.

Less than a week later, he was debriefed with orders to take up a military desk position in Honolulu, where he would put his engineering skills to use as he completed his degree at night school. He knew it was highly unusual for someone of his lowly position in the military to be sent stateside. His Commanding Officer had obviously sensed an urgency in the situation.

Kaito could not stop worrying about Hana and how she must be feeling and how his daughter's care was being managed; his stomach was in a knot until the day he landed in Honolulu. He could not rid his mind of the traditional Japanese expectation of the duties of a wife and mother, and he wrestled with his conflicting feelings.

He was flown to Seoul by military transport and then after a lengthy wait, a commercial carrier took him the rest of the way home. The change happened so quickly Kaito felt he was in an alternate reality. Attempting to adjust to the extreme contrasts of what he had left behind was an unsettling challenge.

On the uncomfortable and seemingly endless flight home, Kaito worried whether his inability to be home for the birth was the cause of Hana's difficulties. He could not rid himself of guilt and concern.

As they began the approach to the landing, the stunning view of turquoise waters and lushly forested craggy volcanic slopes brought a welcome familiarity and a rush of memories for his love of the paradise he called home. Stepping from the plane into the nostalgic warm embrace of the early Hawaiian morning, he breathed in the familiar scent of the frangipani lei that was placed over each passenger's head. It was the smell of home.

The worrisome feelings that plagued him on the flight melted momentarily when Hana greeted him at the door of their apartment with the baby in her arms. He could not help noticing how wan and thin Hana appeared. He hugged his wife and daughter gently together and kissed them before she handed the tiny bundle to him.

"I love you, my *pulele*, and missed you more than I can express. Thank you for this exquisite gift of our Kiana."

Hana's eyes glistened, but there was something in her expression that caused Kaito concern. "I love you too and am so relieved you are home." Her words were loving but he was appalled by her voice, which was flat and emotionless.

Holding his three-month-old daughter for the first time, overpowering feelings swept through him. As her eyes locked onto his, he became aware of a completely different dimension of love: something pure, strong and deeper than he had ever known. He understood he would do anything to protect and guide this little being that now owned his heart.

Tenderly his finger caressed her plump cheeks. When her tiny hand grasped his finger, he gently examined each of hers, kissing the tips before he enfolded her hand in his palm. Then he unwrapped the light cotton swaddling blanket and examined each toe in the same manner.

"You are right, *pulele* … ten perfect fingers and toes," he whispered to Hana. She smiled but without the glow he hoped to see.

Kiana cooed and gurgled as he wrapped her snugly, holding her to his chest and feeling the warmth of this new love press into his being. He kissed the mass of jet-black hair framing her face and marveled at how angelic she appeared.

"You are my *keiki*," he whispered, "my child."

That first night Kaito fell asleep in a chair with his daughter in his arms. He was exhausted from the flight and the emotion of his return and had no memory of how he had gotten to bed.

In the following days, conversation often was awkward, particularly when Hana asked about his time in Vietnam. He begged her to understand his inability to elaborate on the experience. They agreed it was a topic to be left until he wanted it raised. And that never happened.

By most comparisons, he had missed the worst of that war.

Even so, there were nightmares. The sounds of bombs and gunfire. The screams and moans of human suffering. The extreme heat and humidity that created unbearable living conditions. All of this was just part of what would trigger terrible lasting emotions he would learn to live with.

Added to all this was the ongoing pain and worry about Lailani's fiancé, Brett. No further news had been received. He was like family to them and from the beginning his situation had haunted Hana more than anyone. His status remained "missing and presumed dead."

Kaito's reliance on Buddhist teachings, meditation, and his

aikido were all sources of strength to him. He tried to share his understanding of this strength with Lailani.

He had explained this more than once, hoping Lailani would find the same strength. "Buddhism teaches me to find the self-reliance to deal with chaos in my life. I seek the power to endure by my own strength. Buddha cannot save me, but his way of living guides me to find my 'I.'" He would share books with her and often they would discuss Buddha's words. Hana, on the other hand, found these conversations exhausting.

In spite of her perpetual sunny outlook, as time passed Lailani found it difficult to accept the idea of always living in the present and not worrying or mourning the past.

One evening when Hana had gone to bed early before Lailani left, Kaito asked how she was doing while he gave Kiana a bottle.

"Once the truth of the situation is known, I can begin to move on," Lailani said. "Until then, I will have moments of struggle. I continue to work on it and try to encourage Hana to do the same. It's the best I can do right now, but she truly cannot let it go. She was convinced the same would happen to you when you were in 'Nam ... or worse. She worried about it constantly."

Kaito did his best to keep Lailani's spirits up, knowing how much effort she put in to doing the same for Hana in her down periods. She loved bringing little gifts for Kiana and would often soothe her—and Hana—with gentle songs and melodies as she strummed her ukulele. She encouraged Hana to get more involved in "Mom and Baby" groups. But Hana would only go if Lailani went with her, which she did.

There was no debate when Hana suggested to Kaito that they ask Lailani to be the *kari-oya* for Kiana. An old tradition in Japan, this esteemed title was the equivalent of godmother in Western culture, one who would protect and foster a child in addition to the parents.

Lailani beamed as she joyfully accepted. "She will always be like a daughter to me. Thank you for this honor."

∽

KAITO WAS ASTONISHED by his desire to be involved with the baby. He felt good giving Hana a break from all the demands when he arrived home from work. Changing diapers and helping mix formula became part of his regimen. Hana had struggled with breastfeeding and given up even before Kaito returned from Vietnam.

After just a few days back at home, he noticed Hana's extreme mood swings and insomnia. Anytime he tried to talk to her about it, she became irritable and brushed off his concerns.

When he found the right moment to broach the subject, he asked about doctor appointments and Hana showed him a calendar.

"Lailani marked these appointments, and you and I are to go together," she said. "I don't think it is necessary. And if you agree, I will cancel them."

Kaito insisted that it was important he know what problems had occurred. He wanted to speak with the doctor and try to gain an understanding of what Hana was dealing with.

Hana had not been forthcoming, but Lailani shared troubling details with him. She described instances of arriving at Hana's to discover Kiana had not been changed or bathed when it was obvious both were needed and other times when she was there that Hana would fall asleep, leaving the care and feeding to Lailani.

Lailani explained to Kaito that depressed people often find the simplest request an act of regression: driving a car, meeting new people, even opening a door. "Everything can take so much energy out of them."

Hana cried when Kaito pressed her about this. He could hear

her remorse and confusion as to why she was having those types of behavior from time to time. He knew that above all Hana was an organized and responsible person; he could understand her growing fear about these instances where pieces of her life seemed to fall apart.

His heart went out to her and he gently offered comfort.

"We will go together, and together we will work through whatever is needed. Don't worry, my sweet. I'm here and will fix this."

At their first appointment together with Hana's doctor, her serious demeanor worried Kaito. And Kaito realized Hana's problems were not necessarily something he could fix. All he could do was be supportive and positive, encouraging Hana in every way and listening to her when she needed him.

After explaining his concerns in detail, the doctor said, "Hana, I feel you may be struggling with postpartum depression and I am going to send you to a specialist." Kaito was grateful to the doctor, who patiently answered all of his questions and assured him they would have ongoing medical support.

Barely into their twenties, Kaito and Hana, along with their parents, had no idea about postpartum depression. In Japan, such personal struggles were not discussed. For his parents' generation, emotional issues were common, but they were to be kept strictly private. The scars of WWII were raw and deep. Feelings were buried. Loyalty and respect were expected, but love was not something to outwardly demonstrate.

Both families went together to generously purchase a new home for them. With great excitement Kaito, Hana, and Kiana moved from the small apartment to a three-bedroom house with a screened-in lanai and, best of all, a spacious garden.

The lanai was set up as a studio with a roomy walk-in cupboard at one end so Hana could keep her art and sewing materials ready to use. The hope was she would be inspired to take more of an interest in working with her mother again. She had not picked up a needle since Kiana was born. There was a growing demand for the obi, Hana's mother explained to Kaito. She said many young people were using them as table runners or wall hangings rather than the traditional belt, and Hana's talent would be appreciated.

On weekends Kaito would take the baby in a backpack so he and Hana could hike the trails she had previously enjoyed. He encouraged her to continue sketching and felt hopeful to see it still gave her pleasure.

Kaito often asked Hana to describe to him how she would transfer the vision she had sketched into a unique design on silk. He was heartened as her eyes lit up when she envisioned the beauty of the finished product. He could feel her passion and wanted so badly for it to burn more brightly within her. He wanted her to feel the "ki" of it again. The life force. He hoped she was ready to get back to it.

The hiking exercise usually guaranteed a period of good days and Kaito would be heartened. But by the end of the following week, a curtain of darkness and excruciating sadness would drop over Hana again.

One particularly beautiful day stayed in Kaito's mind as a turning point to trouble. It began with them walking along a sidewalk bordering Waikiki Beach.

Kiana babbled happily in her stroller as Kaito held hands with Hana and was filled with contentment. The sea glistened, a palette of blues, greens, and turquoise reflected in the sky. Scattered cotton-puff cumulus clouds danced along with the trade winds.

Surfers of all ages rode the waves, children snorkeled and rode boogie boards, while the sparkling white sand beach was dotted with families sharing picnics. Hana agreed, with a chuckle, when Kaito observed it was only tourists who baked on the beach without shade.

They chatted and Hana giggled often as they stopped for a

plastic cup of shave ice, the popular refreshing treat covered with fruit syrup or assorted other toppings. Kaito never varied from his strawberry syrup choice, but Hana was often adventurous in her topping and this day it was pineapple ice with *li hing mui* powder, a sweetened concoction of ground plum skin. They laughed as Hana tried to convince him her choice was so much more delicious and she teased him for being so unwavering in his order.

Kaito thought the mood of the day was unbeatable when it began.

It ended with him leading Hana home as he pushed the stroller with one hand and wrapped his other arm around her heaving shoulder. She had dissolved into uncontrollable weeping. For no reason. That was the troubling part. He was thankful Kiana was sleeping peacefully at that point. After that day, nothing was ever the same.

Days of relative calm would alternate with increasing irritability and anxiety.

There were constant counseling sessions for them together and Hana on her own. The doctors tried many changes in medication. It troubled Kaito as he gained more of an understanding that there was not a great deal of health care available for the symptoms Hana was displaying. He spent hours poring over research papers and contacting specialists, often to no avail. Slowly it became clear to Kaito that Hana's battle with postpartum depression was the beginning of what appeared to be a descent into more serious mental health problems.

The only thing that seemed to calm the demons that were distressing her was when she closed herself in her sewing studio and worked for hours. She had begun to stitch again.

There were days when Kaito despaired and felt discouraged, but he never stopped being positive and optimistic with Hana. In spite of this, Kiana was a bright light, always happy and full of energy. Her smile lifted his heart and made the day better. He would take charge of her as soon as he walked in from work and made certain bedtime was special. Above all, he wanted her to know she was loved.

Kaito tried to make life as easy as possible for Hana by helping with chores and joining her in the kitchen preparing meals. With their love of ramen, meals were often quick and easy. The kitchen was one place where he could usually make her laugh with his antics.

And Lailani continued to work her magic with Hana. She would call from work to see how things were going and drop by on her way home, often staying until Hana fell asleep. Her calm manner, soothing voice, and gentle humor would most often bring Hana to a better frame of mind. There might be tears and, although rarely, apologies from Hana ... until the next time.

CHAPTER 11

*A*fter three more years in the military, Kaito graduated with a commitment to continue in the Army Reserve. He joined a small engineering company dedicated to the burgeoning focus on environmental projects. The workload was such that he was able to continue to have extra time to parent Kiana as he tried to make up for what she was not getting from her mother.

During those three years, all four grandparents and Lailani worked out a schedule to ease the pressure on Hana and ensure Kiana received love and stimulation. She was a curious and bright little girl who loved to laugh and sing and went off to nursery school with great enthusiasm.

Bookshelves in the house were full, and Kaito praised Hana for sharing her love of reading with Kiana. Reading books together before Kiana's bedtime was part of their daily schedule, although Hana needed to have Kaito involved. Sometimes she would insist that he do the reading and he gladly obliged.

If Hana felt unwell during the week, one of the grandparents or Kari-oya Lailani would step in depending on her nursing shift.

Music was something to which Hana responded in a positive way. The house was usually filled with tunes on the radio or recordings, from the popular hit parade songs like those of the Beach Boys of the 1970s to classical and jazz. Concerts at the Waikiki Bowl were the main entertainment indulgence. On good evenings Hana would go along, but more often than not as time went by she became anxious in crowds and chose to remain home.

Lailani's impromptu ukulele concerts always guaranteed a positive response from all of them. Kiana would dance around the room while the others clapped along. Hana might join her with a *hula noho*, her arms and hands gracefully moving to the music while she remained seated.

Those were special times that brought what Kaito felt was calm and happiness into the home.

Requests for custom orders continued to grow from the local shop that sold the Suzukis' stunning obi. With Kiana in school full time, Hana became more involved. Her work focused on the larger particulars of the design ... flowers, trees, birds, and butterflies ... all stitched with intricate detail.

Hana became so involved with her designs that there now was an application with each order asking a few personal questions. She wanted to know who the recipient of the belt would be so that she could stitch something meaningful for that person into the details of her design.

"This is my life, Kaito," she began to tell him. "This is what I was meant to do. I feel the spirits of my ancestors speaking to me as I work. They guide the needles so smoothly no matter how difficult the stitch. I hear their voices."

Hana's mother cut and sewed the long bands of silk and filled in backgrounds if needed. Kaito was happy to see mother and daughter collaborate so effectively. There were few outbursts in the studio and little conversation. Hana chose to work silently or hum to soft koto music that played soothingly in the background.

The studio was a picture of organization and harmony with skeins of silk threads in all shades and bolts of lustrous silk arranged in the most efficient manner. Hana had taken to keeping the door locked most of the time and no one was to touch anything in the room.

Since Hana did not take the initiative, Kaito kept up with all the local entertainment advertisements and was pleased when he could convince her to go with him. He had long learned to swallow his disappointment when Hana changed her mind at the last minute and would often invite Lailani to go since she continued to be on her own. Hana was happy to see them go off together. Most often Kaito bought tickets for concerts where it was appropriate to take Kiana along.

THE LARGE GARDEN behind the house allowed father and daughter to indulge in many projects without being away from home. Like most other things, Hana's interest in helping in the garden was unpredictable. Kaito built a tree house and play area and taught Kiana about growing flowers from seed.

Kaito had encouraged Hana to take on the care of a bonsai tree. After a two-hour tour of the Dragon Garden Nursery, they both fell in love with the beautiful mature species offered for sale. Hana chose a Torch of Thai Bougainvillea and Kaito a Golden Gate Banyan.

The gardener who guided them on the tour was passionate about raising bonsai. He expressed to them with such conviction that "the power of bonsai is to portray the utmost beauty of nature" and that a bonsai owner must commit to being responsible for carrying on an ancient tradition.

77

PATRICIA SANDS

"I can't believe that tiny plant will actually have blossoms," Hana exclaimed.

She was assured that it would bloom with the proper care and good sunlight each day and she promised this was important to her. Initially, Hana was committed to caring for her bonsai with great dedication.

And bloom it did. In the spring for a month or so it was covered in bright pink blossoms that caused Hana great delight, and the family celebrated with her.

Kaito found caring for his tree a satisfying hobby and continued to take courses to understand every aspect of nurturing it more fully. There was much of the philosophy of raising bonsai that connected to Buddhism, connecting man, the soul, and the natural world.

In time Kiana came to enjoy caring for the garden plants. She spent hours helping Kaito, and Hana when she was interested, prune the flowering shrubs and trim the bonsai, as well as weeding and keeping the fast-growing beds under control. There were many orchid plants in pots in the garden and these became her favorites. She would help tend them and later hang the pots in shaded places from tree branches to watch them continue to flower each year.

When he knew he would be home, Kaito encouraged Kiana to bring her friends to spend time in the garden. It gave him great pleasure to see it used as a playground. He was aware Hana often observed Kiana flourishing with her friends. He sometimes watched her peering through the windows in her sewing studio, her safe place.

Even in these seemingly happy moments, Kaito would observe Hana carefully for mood swings. There had been some unfortunate incidents of Hana suddenly flying off the handle and verbally tearing a strip off Kiana in front of her friends.

As time passed, Kiana stopped taking a chance on inviting friends unless she knew her father would be home.

Through the years, the garden remained a well-used part of their lives thanks to the tropical weather. Even the daily rainstorms were welcomed there. The tranquil environment provided fun and entertainment as well as being a peaceful place to meditate and find healing.

A family of bright green parrots visited the garden frequently. Their noisy squawking and colorful show delighted Kiana but sent Hana scurrying indoors in a fury. It was another simple situation where Kaito felt torn over whose reactions he should accommodate. Should he keep encouraging birds in the garden for his daughter, or chase them away for his wife?

It seemed there was always an issue, either major or insignificant, that required attention. Although the garden had so far been spared many of Hana's violent occurrences.

In the ongoing attempts by Hana's doctors to find the best combination of medications for her, Hana's difficult episodes varied in intensity and were impossible to predict.

Breakfast was generally peaceful as Hana enjoyed preparing eggs in a variety of ways and Kiana loved to make pancakes with fruit. They made a colorful schedule of alternate days and hung it on the wall where artwork done by all of them was displayed. On days Hana chose to stay working in her studio, Kaito filled in.

The schedule also had room for Kiana to note any plans she had with friends or her dad. They were always adding decorations to the poster and it presented the image of a happy home blessed with activity. Unless Hana ripped it down, which happened more than once.

After the shock of the first time this occurred, Kaito wiped Kiana's tears and they talked about Hana not intending to be mean.

"Mommy acts like this when she is tired. Her illness does this to her," Kaito explained, avoiding words critical of his wife. He and Kiana would make a project of it and create a new, happy calendar. On rare occasions Hana would join them in this, possibly with a muted apology but more often not.

"It's all about forgiveness." Kaito often repeated to Kiana from early childhood on. "It's part of how we help Mama. We forgive and move on and we never stop loving her. We can always replace paper." Or whatever else she had destroyed.

As the years progressed, Kaito's role at home became savior and mediator. Although worry and fear found their way into Kaito's thoughts on a regular basis, meditation would bring him some relief. He lived with hope that things would improve for all of them, although in his heart he had long known this was unlikely. He could see that his focus had become as much about keeping Kiana happy as maintaining Hana's world on an even keel. It was about raising a happy child who would grow up strong enough not to be crushed by her mother's erratic mood swings.

Deep inside he believed that as long as he could sustain the balance, his family would be okay.

The uncontrolled treatment Hana dealt their daughter was often physical—slapping, pinching, pushing. There were periods when Hana took her medication as prescribed and a sense of normalcy prevailed. Until she stopped her pills, which led to the next blowup.

Paranoia and delusional thoughts would cause Hana to lash out in anger. As the years had progressed, her withdrawing into herself had morphed to include some extreme reactions. Slamming doors, banshee-like screaming, or guttural wailing would fill the house with a sense of evil and dread ... and sadness as silence eventually followed.

Virtually no sufficient mental health support was available for Hana's erratic problems. After reaching the end of recommended specialists, the diagnosis was possibly ... never definitively ... major depressive disorder or MDD. The doctors were quick to prescribe more pills and additional counseling, none of which were very effective and lasted only a short period of time. Hana often refused to attend her counseling sessions. Tranquilizers simply turned her into a zombie—but a zombie still capable of frightening behavior.

Through these years, Hana was able to continue her sewing business on a reasonably regular basis. Phone calls from clients went to her mother, who looked after a schedule and eliminated the need for Hana to communicate with strangers.

When she was feeling calm, Kaito could see Hana still took pleasure and pride in her skills. She taught Kiana some simple needlework stitches and there were times they worked side by side. But Kaito also learned to take Kiana's little sewing projects away and hide them so in her darker days Hana would not destroy them.

"Why does Mama do this?" Kiana blubbered, her cheeks tearstained, after the first incident.

"I'm so sorry, my *keiki*," Kaito said as he folded his arms around her and kissed the top of her head. "Mama is ill and cannot help it when she loses control. I know it is hard for you to understand, but she loves you. Always remember that."

"I don't know, Papa. I just don't know."

His heart wrenched as he hugged his daughter and tried to offer words of comfort.

He fought feelings of despair for Kiana's pain and disappointment often mixed in with his anger and frustration at Hana's loss of control.

Those were times when he worked out with his aikido exercises to the point of exhaustion. Kaito often feared his own loss of temper might break through and he could not risk that for Kiana's sake.

Kaito struggled within himself constantly to battle those conflicting feelings. No matter how upset he felt about Hana's behavior, he always reminded himself how it was the illness causing her to lash out. Deep sadness often engulfed him.

But always he tried to find ways to show Kiana that her mother loved her. He praised Hana in front of Kiana on a regular basis and made a fuss over all of her beautiful sewing projects. It was important to Kaito that Kiana appreciate Hana's talents. He made certain Hana did the most reading during the bedtime ritual, which they never missed, knowing how this intimate time together strengthened the family bond.

CHAPTER 12

*A*s a child in Japan, Kaito's first introduction to the teachings of Zen Buddhism came through the tea ceremony with his grandparents. Much of the philosophy of calm and ritual was infused into daily life as he grew up. It became something taken for granted, but also appreciated and diligently practiced.

Faced with the ugly brutality of his time in Vietnam, it was his Buddhist grounding that helped him through his worst days. The memories were clear of how he would pray for the souls of innocent victims rather than be consumed by fear, as bombing and gunfire filled the air not far from where he went about his tasks. The Buddhist saying "Avoid killing, or harming, any living thing" resonated at all times. While some turned to narcotics, meditation became Kaito's drug of choice.

He delved more seriously into Buddhism as Hana continued to lose her grasp on reality. Simple readings calmed him as he searched for a way to bring peace into his soul ... and his home. He had to stay strong for their daughter.

The teachings began to sustain him in a quiet and private

way. Patience was a key part of his learning. He knew he had to "quiet the waters of his mind" and wait for as long as necessary to deal with a problem. Monkey mind, as Buddhism described being unsettled or confused, was something that happened and was not to be judged as one tried to achieve the calm.

Going to temple was sometimes his best recourse, but the socializing aspect did not appeal to him. He felt he had no time to cultivate new friendships and did not want to have to explain Hana's erratic behaviors to anyone. He tried not to feel the shame his culture traditionally associated with mental illness.

So he did not join groups. Instead, he withdrew more into his garden, his photography, and his world with Hana and Kiana, where his family secret was safe and protected.

When Kiana was eight, Kaito had the opportunity to purchase the local martial arts club to which he had belonged going back to his school days. It was an uncharacteristically impulsive move but the timing felt right. He was spending a great deal of time there after work and on weekends. Kiana had been in a children's program since she was four. He saw the studio as a peaceful escape for them both. With good management, he could run the business and still keep his day job.

As much as Kiana was learning the techniques of the sport, he knew she also was learning skills that would help her at home. Aikido was as much about what happened off the mat as it was about the physical contest. From an early age, the philosophy of harmony in life was learned through games and drills all based on having fun and being thoughtful. The main tenet was to be kind and gentle—yet powerful. And on time! The Vince Lombardi philosophy of being on time or ahead of time for everything was taught from the beginning. And kids got it.

Younger students mainly had fun jumping and rolling on mats, much like gymnastics. But for older children when it came to contests on the mat, using their physical skills, they employed these *ukemi* skills with confidence. Learning to fall softly and rebound ready to go again was the goal of the match. And the goal of life. Rebounding from Hana's dark times was something Kiana had been doing all of her young life. This tormented Kaito. His constant goal was to make amends. His focus always was to help Hana in every way possible. He never lost sight of himself as her protector. This was his family and he was determined to not have it disintegrate.

With a good support staff, the newly named K&K Studio ran smoothly. Kiana was thrilled that she was part of the studio name. Kaito and Kiana were able to use it as a place to work out frustrations. Kiana built a network of friends and it took the place of her not being able to play as often with friends at her own home. Hana had no interest in going to the studio, as the physical interactions of the activities there upset her dramatically and made her feel exhausted.

Kaito expended his physical energy with aikido. His conjugal intimacy with Hana was diminishing and there would often be long periods of time without any sexual or physical interaction. Pushing himself physically helped work through some frustrations.

He became a respected sensei, a teacher in his own dojo where classes were regularly fully attended. As he put most of his physical energy into this, he struggled to release the many emotions he knew he was smothering inside. For that he turned to meditation.

Both sets of grandparents expressed concern about Hana in their own ways. But they never spoke of the specific problems, choosing to ignore the obvious tensions and shameful family secret by bringing food and offering to spend days with her. They continued to help with their involvement with Kiana, who loved them dearly.

· · ·

KAITO CONTINUED to stay connected to her work by supplying endless photos of images she would find inspiring. This was the one area of communication that remained open between them and he nurtured those conversations and interactions.

On good days, Hana asked Kiana to model an obi she was working on, which she did with great excitement. Kaito always held his breath until the moments passed without incident.

There weren't many options for father and daughter to escape the rage-filled atmosphere of Hana's bad days, but Kaito took advantage of every opportunity. Anything to have a break from the often toxic atmosphere that frightened and confused their daughter. His gratitude to Lailani knew no bounds.

After work, she would stay with Hana on bad days or spend time with Kiana, whichever helped them all the most. Her magic ukulele was always close at hand.

From time to time Kaito and Kiana would attend parent-child workshops at the Hawaii Nature Center. If Hana was having a good day, she would join them. This always filled Kiana with hope. And caused a searing pain in Kaito's heart.

Other times father and daughter would go to Waikiki Beach, just minutes away, and surf the smaller waves. With Hana's growing paranoia about getting too much sun, she now chose not to go to the beach at all.

As a newly arrived ten-year-old, Kaito had been drawn to surfing at the local beaches with his father. In high school, all of his friends hung out there and most were far more adept at the sport than he was. Lailani's boyfriend, Brett, was a champion surfer and they spent many exciting days at the North Shore watching breathtaking competitions. It was part of the DNA in Hawaii and Kaito quickly grew to love it. But he remained a casual Waikiki surfer and never was tempted to ride the big waves. Hana had no interest in the sport, but liked to be at the beach in their early years. Kaito was happy when Kiana showed an interest in surfing and it became another activity they enjoyed together.

The sad thing about days that were relatively calm was that everyone felt they were walking on eggshells, never knowing what would set off another storm. It was almost impossible to relax and let a sense of peace prevail, which was something Kaito never stopped hoping for.

Lailani regularly provided Kaito with conversation, friendship, and laughter in the long hours he spent at home with Kiana. Her knowledge and compassion as a nurse were important factors in her dedication to Hana, which never faltered, even as she realized her efforts were, in the end, never going to achieve what the family hoped to see.

She had not become involved in a serious relationship since Brett had been killed in Vietnam. It had taken years for his remains to be found and identified, and that time took a toll on Lailani. She devoted herself even more to her nursing career, taking additional accreditations and working long hours.

She continued to live with her mother. Often when she stopped by on her way home from the hospital she would find Kaito, and usually Kiana as well, in the back garden tending the various beds of annuals and perennials and fussing over the growing section of bonsai.

There were many days when Hana would be there with them and they would chat about events going on in the islands. Hana had a habit of watching, or listening to, the television in the evening but in time had to avoid the news, as any tragedy affected her deeply and would set her on a cycle of anxious worry.

She continued to keep music on constantly, especially her beloved *koto*, as she worked in her studio. Her preference was for the traditional compositions of centuries before. Kaito agreed that the gentle plucking of the strings was soothing and almost dreamlike.

As a fourth-generation Hawaiian, Lailani had an island calmness about her. She was able to distract Hana with conversation and coax her to go for walks occasionally. On good days they would go to the local hula dance club and practice new steps and laugh. Hana never stopped loving other music, outside of her favorite *koto* or Lailani's Hawaiian songs, but the times she participated in anything became fewer.

Their shared love of reading was a constant, and a week seldom passed without the two of them engaged in passionate exchanges about their current book. Their book discussions sometimes took place in Hana's sewing studio where Hana continued to chat as she stitched. Lailani praised her skill and bemoaned her own inability to even sew on a button.

Hana was always happy to have her friend stay at the house while Kaito and Kiana went off hiking or camping.

When Lailani was alone with Kaito, they would talk in the peace of the garden about the part of his life that was tearing him apart. He despaired of losing Hana completely.

"Since we were kids, I have felt protective of her. I keep thinking of her as an injured butterfly, so delicate and needing to be treated gently. No matter how bad things get and how frustrated or angry I feel at times, my love is there. It never will leave because I know she cannot help herself when she loses control. I know how regretful she feels. It is so heartbreaking all around—for all of us."

Lailani was a good listener and Kaito appreciated that she did not attempt to give him directions about how to handle Hana unless he asked specifically. Her nursing experience was a bonus and Kaito respected her opinions and careful observations. She often reminded him that no one could predict Hana's behavior.

When Kaito spoke to Lailani of how he did not want to be both father and mother to Kiana, she understood. "I want to be the best father I can be and I know I have to do many things

Hana should be doing. But I still want Kiana to feel that she has a mother. A mother who loves her but whose illness does not always allow her to show it. Does that make sense?"

In many ways her support and compassion meant more than the professionals working with him and Hana because he knew she loved Hana and wanted the best for them all.

CHAPTER 13

*A*s both sets of grandparents aged, their involvement with Hana became less helpful, although they all tried as best they could. Kiana would sometimes stay at their places for overnights, but was always eager to return to her father.

Kaito's father passed away when Kiana was thirteen and his mother was best cared for in a nursing home. The passing of Hana's parents followed very close to one another just a year later. Those were difficult times for Kaito, Hana, and Kiana. But the grandparents had left behind strong memories of happy times with Kiana even as Hana slipped more and more away from them into the darkness of her illness.

Determined to keep the sewing business flourishing, as Hana's mother's health began to fail, Mrs. Suzuki arranged with Hana and Kaito to hire a Japanese seamstress to take over the organization and the machine sewing that had been her responsibility.

Hana found the transition difficult and Kaito took on the role of go-between to ensure continuity. Productivity diminished somewhat, but Hana's desire to continue stitching wishes of happiness into all of her work remained her focus.

Kaito was astonished and troubled that after each of their parents passed, Hana made no mention of them again. It was as if those parts of her life were erased.

Around the same time, Hana lost her interest in hiking. Her medications caused weight gain, and this decrease in physical activity did not help, adding another source of irritation to Hana on a regular basis.

Hiking the lush mountain trails continued to be a favorite weekend activity for Kaito, however, who would share the legends and mysteries of the islands with his wide-eyed daughter. Kiana giggled and laughed as they both made up stories of imaginary creatures and gods living in the jungles around them. Kaito loved her vivid imagination.

If Lailani was not available to stay with her, she supplied Kaito with a list of personal support workers she knew from the hospital who could provide homecare. Hana still took care of bathing and dressing herself and accepted their presence as housekeepers and cooks.

Kaito planned short hikes so they would be home by dinnertime, but increasingly over the years, Kiana thrived on the challenge of longer explorations. They spent treasured time exploring the breathtaking natural beauty of the nearby dense rainforests. Arriving at heart-stopping panoramic views or thrilled by waterfalls, there was always something special to anticipate. As a teenager, she began talking about studying to become a botanist when she grew up.

Hana was never alone overnight, but if Lailani was available for a "girls" night, father and daughter sometimes camped by tranquil blue waters in the summer or drove up between November and February to see the fiercely towering winter swells along the legendary Seven Mile Miracle on the North Shore. At that mecca for world-class surfers, they gasped in awe at the waves that sometimes reached thirty feet. Kaito told his daughter stories of the days he, Hana, and Lailani went to watch Brett.

THE DRIVE to the north shore guaranteed a stop in the charming surf town of Haleiwa at Matsumoto Shave Ice for their rainbow-flavored specialty. It was the only time Kaito changed from his standard selection.

Kiana loved to explore this historic colorful old town with some original frame buildings still in use. Lailani told them many tales through the years about early life there, passed on to her by her mother, who had grown up in this town, when a long-gone railway brought visitors up from Honolulu. Now a big bypass was under construction and Lailani and her mother lamented how it would impact the shop owners.

"We will still come here, Lanilani," Kiana would say each time, calling her by the name she had used forever. "And we will take the old road into town. I promise!"

Occasionally, they could convince Hana to join them on the drives but then there was inevitably tension in the air. The unknown was whether the day would progress without an unpleasant outburst. Since the passing of the grandparents, there were fewer instances when Hana did leave the house. And never without Kaito.

In her teens, Kiana was curious about her father's photography. Taking photos and making notes, they would identify native and exotic plants as well as indigenous birds. He was thrilled she shared his love of the art, whether it was capturing fleeting beauty or simply composing an image for her own pleasure. She had an excellent eye for the craft.

Father and daughter volunteered repairing the floating lanterns used for the emotional Memorial Day Lantern Festival in Waikiki in memory of loved ones. Hana helped decorate them but never attended the ceremony.

Thousands of lanterns were floated out to sea in the ceremony with four rice paper sides surrounding the candle, each decorated with personal remembrances and affirmations for the future. They were collected the next day and returned to be repaired, stored, and used again the next year.

Kiana was artistic in this way, too, and was good at working with her hands. She took a calligraphy course at school with friends so she could inscribe her own words of remembrance on her lantern.

It pleased Kaito to remind her she had inherited these talents from Hana. He desperately wanted her to have loving thoughts about her mother, despite Hana making that difficult. Working on and decorating lanterns was something that also gave Hana peace, and it was one of the few activities they shared for some years—as long as Hana's head was in the right space.

She still took some pleasure in working on drawings with Kiana and together they created some lovely patterns for stitching. But there was usually something that set Hana off at some point that would leave mother and daughter in tears or exchanging angry words. Each time it happened, Kaito's heart would break a little more.

Kaito maintained a regular counseling schedule and found it helpful. Kiana was included in family counseling sessions for years but there were seldom any suggestions that made a difference. Hana sometimes agreed to go but then never communicated at the meeting.

Kaito often shared with Kiana the history and traditions of the Hawaiian culture that he had taken for his own. In high school, few of his friends spoke the Hawaiian language outside of home and he was in shock to learn that in 1893 a law was passed that made English the official language of the islands. It was severely frowned upon to speak Hawaiian in public at the time. His friends used many of the words as a sign of rebellion, and Kaito tried to slowly learn it, particularly when Lailani was around to correct him.

Hana never expressed an interest in learning the language. She had always been self-conscious about the Japanese accent she insisted she still had in speaking English, even though no one else seemed to notice it.

Lailani had shared with Kaito and Hana that her parents and grandparents continued to speak Hawaiian in their home. She described how they did not want the language to die. "They explained to me that they agreed with the government it was best if everyone in the islands learned to speak English. But they were determined that our family and friends were to speak Hawaiian at home."

Then she would tease Kaito. "Come on. This language has the smallest alphabet in the world with just five vowels and eight consonants. How difficult can it be?"

The trick was to speak each syllable slowly, and eventually the word would tumble out. A great deal of hilarity was involved, since the easiest way for him to learn the words was from songs.

Hana would play records and Lailani would help Kaito pronounce as they sang. Lailani had a wonderful voice. Kaito did not. Often the attempts were drowned out by the laughter.

Not so many of Kiana's friends used the native language, although there were quite a few words that had become seamlessly woven into everyday life. They would often laugh at each other's attempts to pronounce many of the challenging words and help each other until they got it. In 1978 laws were passed making the native language official again. So by the time Kiana reached high school, there actually were immersion courses beginning to help bring the language back to life.

Increasing tourism and artists' appreciation of the authentic aspects of Hawaiian culture and traditions became popular again, which helped immensely with the revival of the language.

Kaito was thankful for the close relationship Lailani had with Kiana in her gentle, understated way. And Lailani was the best language teacher there was.

Kiana told him one day, "Lanilani is like a fairy godmother to me. Whenever there is something wrong, she arrives and waves her magic wand. She is *ohana* and I love her like I wish I loved my mother."

Kaito's heart twisted in conflict. He was thankful that Kiana had someone with whom to feel that kind of love. "Yes, Lailani is family. And she loves you like a daughter. I think she would love to know she is your fairy godmother. You should share that with her one day."

How he wished those feelings were about Hana.

Lailani's close connections to the family became even more intimate as Kiana began dating and Hana proved reticent to have some of the necessary mother/daughter conversations.

But she had managed to guide Kiana into puberty and prepared her for when her period first arrived.

When boyfriends began to appear, Hana asked Lailani to join her for a conversation about how to behave with them. They talked about values and expectations before things became a bit awkward getting into the nitty-gritty of touch. Kiana told them she was having sex education at school, which was teaching her everything she needed to know. She really did not want to have a discussion with them.

Hana was happy to accept that. Lailani remembered how uncomfortable Hana had been about those discussions when they were teenagers and hoped she would not instill the same attitude in Kiana. However, Lailani was also quite certain from Kiana's flippant responses that she was already much farther ahead in knowing things than they had been at her age.

Kaito was relieved to see that those discussions were not in his domain. Although he did try to have short chats with Kiana about her being in charge of her decisions when she was with a boy, most of the time he felt he was bumbling. Thoughts would sometimes come in the middle of a hike or while they were working in the garden. Somehow his messages were relayed.

And there were other seriously important issues to talk about.

There was growing crime in Honolulu then, unlike the carefree days of Kaito and Hana's youth. The newspapers were full of reports of a suspected serial killer at large. Kaito hoped he was not being too alarming as he kept reminding Kiana to be vigilant.

CHAPTER 14

1988

*A*s her sixteenth birthday approached, Kaito was delighted to see Kiana feel excited about it. She was even hoping to invite friends to the house, which was something that never happened. She had asked for one condition.

"Please may we have Lanilani at the house? She can keep Mama in the bedroom or perhaps even take her out for a drive."

Kaito understood and agreed it was a good idea.

Kiana spent weeks planning her party, listing everything on pieces of paper covered with colorful doodles and whimsical sketches of balloons, candles, palm trees, and smiling faces. She had begun to use some of her drawings to create invitations and was keeping everything in a file.

Kaito smiled as she showed it to him over breakfast a few weeks earlier and they talked about the details. He was pleased she wanted a party, and knowing Lailani would be there relieved her of the fear of her mother's irrational behavior. It made him happy to hear excitement in her voice.

"And what gift would you like, my sweet *keiki?*"

Kaito's love for her filled his voice. He so wanted her to be happy.

Kiana loved her father with the same intensity. He had been the best father to her all along. Even though he wanted Kiana to recognize and respect her mother, that was hard for her to do. Her father was her everything and never, ever hurt her.

"Papa, this party will be my gift. That's all I want."

Nodding, Kaito said, "You have planned every detail. It will be easy and fun to make this happen. We can decorate the garden together."

As Kiana beamed, Kaito added, "Perhaps driving lessons would also be a good gift."

Kaito was engulfed in her excitement as Kiana threw her arms around him. "Really? That would be the best thing ever! Thank you!"

"Hurry and get ready to catch the bus. We can talk more about it later today."

Leaving the file on the table, Kiana went to her room. Kaito smiled at the lightness of her steps. It wasn't often he could see such obvious joy in his only child, his treasure.

She was delicate in stature, thanks to her Japanese heritage, with large, dark almond-shaped eyes and porcelain skin. Her face radiated the same classic beauty he had once seen in her mother's face.

Too often Kiana's innocent face was tearstained, her expressions frustrated, pained, and sad. It was difficult enough for Kaito to deal with the challenges of Hana's erratic, often hurtful behavior. It was simply too much to ask of a child.

On a bad day, Hana would criticize everything Kiana was wearing, how her hair was styled, the way she walked or spoke. Nothing was beyond her negative assessment.

After too many dreadful confrontations between Hana and Kiana, Kaito did not allow his daughter to arrive home at the end of the day without him anymore. Nor did Kiana want to. They had established a ritual of meeting after school either at the martial arts studio or at a friend's house.

When father and daughter did return home, Hana typically would be sequestered in her room or her studio. Kaito would make a simple dinner or serve one left by the caregiver, while Kiana began her homework. They never knew for certain if Hana would join them but always made a point of asking her.

If Kiana's homework was light, she would help in prepping. They both liked to cook uncomplicated stir-fries and traditional Hawaiian meals like the cubed fish of poke and variations of *laulau*.

Kiana had been the family's poi expert since she was old enough to pound the steamed taro root and add the water to create the delicious pudding-like consistency. She loved to eat this beloved Hawaiian staple as much as make it. Kaito swore no one made it better.

In the car on the way home that day, they debated whether to add salmon or tuna to the dinner menu. Kaito planned to work on a repair to one of their garden lanterns at his potting bench and Kiana said she might join him.

As soon as they entered the house, however, it was clear there was a problem. The entire living room and kitchen were in disarray. Cushions were strewn about and art hung at crooked angles on the wall. The kitchen counter and floor were covered in pots, bowls, and food. Hana stood in the middle of the room, wild-haired and trembling, clutching a paper in her hand.

"You stupid girl!" she screamed at Kiana, following by a string of scathing words. She waved pieces of paper from the birthday file in her daughter's face. Then she tore everything into pieces and threw them at Kiana and Kaito, who stood in stunned silence.

"A birthday party? With what friends? No one likes you!" Hana shrieked in a voice that pierced the air and clearly cut like a dagger into Kiana's heart. And Kaito's.

Kaito seldom lost his temper, understanding Hana's illness,

but this time was too much. His face red with anger, he reached for Hana's arm. His eyes blazed and his seething voice stopped Hana abruptly. "Stop this, Hana. Immediately. Calm down!"

Hana dodged Kaito's reach and stormed off to her room muttering, while Kiana stumbled, weeping, to hers. Two doors slammed.

Kaito walked to the wall of windows that ran along the back of their modest bungalow and overlooked his peaceful garden. He always had such a physical reaction to these outbursts of Hana's. It was as if she kicked him in the stomach. It was one thing for her to screech at and insult him, but when it involved Kiana, he ached with a fierceness only his Buddhist teachings could help assuage. And this time he wondered if even that would work.

He knew he had to control the rancor seething within him. He had learned that anger is one of the three poisons, along with greed and ignorance. To begin to rid himself of the poison, he needed to be mindful. To acknowledge his feelings.

He needed to cultivate *metta,* a loving-kindness toward the one who had caused the anger. How often had this practice saved him from the opposite reaction that raged within him? Hana was ill. This he understood. But today had pushed him to the limit of understanding.

He stood looking out at the neatly trimmed shrubs and hedges. The blooming season was reaching its peak and the garden was a riot of color, from the dusty pink blossoms of the rainbow shower tree to the mix of white, yellow, pink, and red plumeria Kaito had carefully cultivated. In one corner the fiery bloom of a royal poinciana tree created an outrageously flamboyant contrast to the calm of the rest of the yard.

As he sought to bring his thoughts to a better place than the scene in the kitchen, Kaito focused on the minutiae of his yard. The grass needed trimming where it bordered the stone path down to the koi pond, overlooked by a wise Buddha. A cluster

THE SECRETS WE HIDE

of weeds seemed to have suddenly sprung up in a far corner. This garden was a refuge for him. It brought him peace to plan and plant and maintain.

He lost himself in the calm of it and murmured to himself the now-familiar.

mantra: "*Conquer anger by non-anger. Conquer evil by good. Conquer miserliness by liberality. Conquer a liar by truthfulness.*"

He waited, eyes closed, in a meditative state. *Patience* ... his heart told him.

After a while, he tapped on Kiana's door.

Kaito sat beside where she had thrown herself on her bed and burrowed under the covers. He waited quietly for several minutes with his head in his hands. He knew he would be saying words Kiana had heard from him before. He struggled to answer how he could comfort her and take the sting out of her mother's words this time.

"*Keiki*, I promise I will make the party happen just as you planned. We must forget this happened."

But the damage was done and Kiana refused to even consider the party or any alternatives.

Kaito's heart ached as she said, "I don't even want to acknowledge my birthday. She makes me wish I had never been born. I hate her."

"My sweet *keiki*, you are so precious to me, *ko aloha makamae e ipo*," he murmured softly to her. She accepted the shelter of his arms, which he wrapped around her as she lay on the bed. "You know Mama cannot help herself. She is truly possessed by demons at times. She was so happy to be carrying you and eager to begin a family. She did love you. She does love you. She just doesn't know how to show that anymore. She has no concept of the hurt she causes us. Really, she is not with us in so many ways."

Kiana said nothing.

Kaito's voice was stilled momentarily as he tormented

himself with the thought he had not been at her birth. His tour to Vietnam had shipped a month before Hana knew she was pregnant. He often wondered if things might have been different if he had been with Hana from the moment Kiana took her first breath. Maybe Hana's postpartum depression might have been avoided.

The doctors had told him it would not have made a difference, but even after all this time there was a shadow of guilt that haunted Kaito.

"Well, I wish she was gone." Kiana spat out the words, interrupting his thoughts. "Nothing helps her. She is like a nightmare that never ends."

"There, there," Kaito whispered, his heart breaking yet again, thinking that no child should ever feel like that. "We've been through this so many times. I'm sorry. I'm sorry."

Kiana sat up and slipped her arms around her father. They rocked gently together as they had so often through so many years. "I'm going to see if Lailani can come over to soothe your mother."

"Lanilani is always the best one to help," Kiana murmured.

He left to make the phone call and returned within minutes. "She is on her way."

Kiana nodded wordlessly as she sat slumped on her bed.

"Then we will sit and have tea," Kaito continued. "I will do the ceremony and we will be calm."

"The tea ceremony has been calming me as far back as I can remember," Kiana told her dad as she reached out and squeezed his hand. "I like when you do it."

Kaito appreciated her efforts to appease the situation and admired the maturity she was showing in this instance. He felt reassured about her and thought perhaps he had overreacted to her behavior recently. For several weeks she had not been checking in as usual and instead came home later than agreed. It had caused him concerns but Lailani had assured him it was typical of teenagers.

Now he shook off his anxieties and kissed the top of her head lightly. "I understand your frustration with your mother. I'm proud of the way you help us get by, in spite of the difficult days. We're a team, you and I, and always have been. Let's go and sit in the garden while we wait."

As they walked through the mess in the kitchen and living room, Kiana's eyes filled with tears again. Kaito put his arm around his daughter and quickly guided her outside.

LAILANI KNOCKED on the front door before letting herself in. She rushed through the house, into the garden, where she hugged the still-shaken girl and looked past her to Kaito. "It appears a hurricane came through the house!"

Kaito nodded and began to speak but Lailani gently hushed him. "I don't need an explanation. You two leave and let me deal with this. *Hele aku ...* scoot!"

Ashen-faced, Kiana sounded relieved. "Let's not have tea now, Father. Let's go to the noodle house at the beach and take a walk."

CHAPTER 15

hey sat at wooden tables on the sugary sand outside their favorite noodle shop for ramen. The popular restaurant had a '60s vibe to it. Beach Boys music floated out from the speakers and down to the turquoise waters gently brushing the shore. The calm of the setting helped lessen the tension Kaito and Kiana were seeking to shed.

Quietly sipping the delectable noodles floating in the broth, they ate the tofu, chicken, and vegetable pieces with chopsticks.

"This is my comfort food," Kiana said, color beginning to return to her pale complexion. "I got that from you, of course! I love your stories about eating ramen all the time as a kid in Japan."

Kaito nodded in agreement. "I couldn't get enough of it. Your dearly departed grandmothers both made delicious *saimin* meals. All the day's leftovers went into them."

When they finished eating, they walked down to the water's edge and watched surfers working the last waves of the afternoon. Surfing was like walking to Hawaiian children. Tourists were always easy to spot and could be counted on to provide a few chuckles.

They stepped out of their *slippahs* and left them under a shrub. After a long barefoot saunter on the warm sand, they decided to sit beneath some palm trees and watch a stunning sunset.

Kaito's eyes shone with love as he looked at the beautiful young woman who would always be a little girl to him. He was trying not to admit to himself that he was worried about the irrational behavior he was seeing from her recently. Secretive at times and headstrong at others, she was trying to figure her life out. *Who could blame her?* he asked himself.

Kaito also realized she was more than a little attractive and young men were paying attention to her. This was obvious even now as the heads of young men swiveled while she strolled beside him. He worried when she was out at night on the weekends and thought that some of her friends were allowed much more freedom than he approved. He was only too aware of how times had changed since his teens.

Now he repeated some unsettling concerns Lailani had shared lately, remembering her cautions that he should remind Kiana to be aware for her personal safety.

"Kiana, I'm going to sound like an overly protective father here—"

She interrupted and gave him a playful pat on his arm. "But that is what you are, Papa."

He continued. "Lailani has passed along to me some information about the streets not being as safe as they once were. In fact, there is some frightening talk about a possible serial killer in Honolulu. Please promise me you will pay attention to your surroundings and your choice of friends. I want to know where you are going and what you are doing ..."

"Thank goodness for Lanilani, letting us know," Kiana said, interrupting again. "I wish you had married her instead of Mother."

Kaito's jaw tightened with regret that Kiana harbored such a thought. It was not the first time she had shared those words with him, and the pain they caused him never dulled.

When she was younger, he had talked to her about how fortunate they were that Lailani and her mother were such close friends of the family's.

He encouraged her to love Lailani in a way that grew from gratitude for how the friendship helped her mother and, in turn, all the family. She had been a constant presence in Kiana's life since the day she was born and this was never lost on Kiana.

Now he could address the situation more realistically and remind Kiana that it was Hana he loved as his wife and her mother. "Lailani is like a sister to me. She really is part of our family. Our chosen family."

BACK AT THE HOUSE, Lailani's red Mustang convertible was still in the driveway. She was in the kitchen sweeping the floor as Kaito and Kiana walked in. Pulling Kiana into her warm embrace, she whispered, "I'm sorry about what happened, *mea aloha*. We all know your mom can't help herself. We must forgive her."

Kiana nodded wordlessly.

Kaito and Lailani bowed to each other in their usual way. Then he took her hands in his, clasping them tightly. For a moment their eyes met with a connection of gratitude and caring before Kaito shivered slightly, overcome with emotion, and stepped back. "As always, thank you for coming to rescue us. I don't know what we would do without your help and the big part of our lives it has been for a very long time."

Lailani lowered her eyes modestly. "It's what friends are for. I'm glad I can be of support in some way to all of you."

Kaito motioned to the living room. "Let's sit and talk."

Kiana suggested they do the tea ceremony they had planned earlier. "I will get everything set up and prepare it."

Lailani smiled and said, "Kiana, this will be very special for me ... the first time I've seen you do it."

Kiana beamed at her words and grinned even more broadly when her father praised how well she knew the entire ceremony.

As each one of them was presented with their tea, in turn they reflected on the warmth of the ceramic bowl and the color of the bright green *matcha* before sipping, all a standard part of the tradition to focus entirely on the ceremony and leave other thoughts behind.

As the soothing fragrance steamed into the air, Kaito thought to himself how, yet again, the tea ceremony had the power to ease tension and bring peace to the participants. How he wished Hana had been part of this one.

CHAPTER 16

$\mathcal{H}$ana spent the next few days in her studio or her bedroom. Kaito prepared meal trays for her and she received them silently, avoiding eye contact and ignoring any words he shared with her. Often the food was barely touched.

Kaito would tell her what a beautiful day it was and suggest some time in the garden and then exit when she chose not to respond. He never left her without saying, "We love you and would be happy if you were with us."

He knew from past experience not to address the elephant in the room. He learned years earlier that just as she never appeared to grieve the passing of loved ones, neither was there often remorse for her hurtful behavior. She simply seemed to block it from memory.

Kaito's counselor had explained that Hana often realized her actions had been hurtful but chose to blame everyone but herself. He advised Kaito that the best way to move forward was to try to put the episode behind him and agreed with Kaito this was not easy and made forgiveness elusive.

From the time Kiana was young, she would always kiss her

mother's cheek when she was going out or to bed, even though there were many times she was roughly pushed away. The hurt in his daughter's eyes caused his pain as well. But to Kiana's credit she had never given up. Until now. She wanted no contact with her mother if at all possible, leaving early for school and coming home late.

If Kaito was alone, he would say, "My *pulele*, you are loved. I am waiting for you to join me." Her response to his kiss on her cheek would be the same. Sometimes accepted. Other times not. But always emotionless.

When Hana finally did appear in their presence after an incident, it usually would have taken a visit from Lailani. Unlike the early years, there were never words of remorse anymore but rather a complete avoidance of any mention of upset.

Even after the birthday debacle.

~

THERE WAS no Sweet Sixteen party.

No luau buffet spilling over with *lomilomi* salmon, chicken long rice, *kalua* pork and all the poi you can eat. No mounds of juicy fresh fruit and an overflowing sweets table. No giggling girlfriends wearing grass skirts and fresh flower leis. No awkward boys in loud Hawaiian-print shirts vying for the Big Kahuna prize. No laughter-filled games of pineapple bowling with coconuts or noisy Hula-Hoop and limbo contests. No vivid June sunset followed by an hour or two of loud music and wild dancing that teenagers do so well.

Kaito had gifts waiting in Kiana's room when she awoke, as was their tradition. She opened them with glee and was thrilled when one contained a photo of the car key with a note that her first driving lesson was scheduled for that afternoon after school.

To their surprise, Hana had risen early to bake Kiana's

favorite chocolate cake. She had decorated the icing with delicate flowers that formed the number sixteen.

Kaito attempted to turn his anger into some sort of positive response for Kiana's sake. To try to smooth over something so broken was a challenge. It required all of his perseverance to be calm.

No mention was made of the destruction of her birthday plans.

As sad as Kaito felt for Kiana's hurt and disappointment of Hana's earlier actions, he admired the mature way she handled these extreme fluctuations of Hana's behavior.

Some of Kiana's friends convinced her to go out to dinner with them. Kaito was happy for her to do something special. But he was shocked when a good-looking young man appeared at the door to pick her up. An expensive car sat in the driveway.

"Papa, this is Jake Akana," Kiana said as she introduced him to a tall, handsome young man who looked a little too old for his daughter.

Jake seemed to have good manners and chatted in a relaxed way with Kaito for a few minutes before they left. But there was something that did not sit right. For one thing, after just those few minutes of conversation, Kaito was certain of his suspicions about Jake's age. The familiarity between him and Kiana caused Kaito to suspect they had already gotten to know each other quite well.

Kiana kissed her father lightly on his cheek and promised not to be late.

Kaito hugged her and wished her happy birthday again. He brushed off his concerns, admonishing himself for being so judgmental.

The thought occurred to him that she might be safer with this fellow looking out for her while they are out with her flighty girlfriends.

But he would definitely have a conversation with Kiana soon about this new person in her life.

CHAPTER 17

*L*ife at home settled into a period of relative calm after the birthday fiasco. Hana's violent reaction and the hurt she had inflicted on Kiana were the worst Kaito had ever seen of her actions. He felt at his wits' end and wondered how they were going to continue as a family if this was to be the new reality with Hana. He would never stop loving his wife and caring about her, but worried that her destructive behavior was tearing their little family apart.

Kaito went with Hana to a series of counseling sessions where he seemed to do most of the talking. Her medications were changed. As days went by, she became more quiet and docile but still sat with Kaito for some meals. She had no interest in any sewing projects at the moment and turned down all requests.

Kiana had dug in her heels and refused to accompany them, but she had gone to see the counselor in private sessions so that the entire domestic picture was understood. She also spent more time at the K&K Studio or with friends after school and had dinner later when Hana was in her room.

Lailani made a point of coming over several times a week to

keep Hana occupied. She asked Hana to help her with a needle-point project that she had been working on for ages, and to her surprise, Hana took an interest in it. Lailani had worked her magic once again.

It wasn't long before Kaito noticed that Lailani was preoccupied. Her normal sunny demeanor seemed forced and she looked disturbingly gaunt. When he first asked if she was fine, she brushed it off, blaming a demanding schedule at the hospital.

Even Kiana noticed something amiss. "Lanilani is my rock and now I feel there is something wrong between us. She's just not the same at the moment. Papa, please talk to her."

One evening as Lailani prepared to leave when Hana had settled for the night and Kiana was at the library, Kaito confronted her.

"Lailani, I know something is not right with you. What has happened? Is your mother ill?"

She motioned to him to be quiet and beckoned him to the garden.

Speaking in hushed tones she said, "You can't believe what is going on in my life right now."

She paused as Kaito gasped at the frightened expression on her face.

Her hands shook as she whispered, "This started a few weeks ago. Right after Kiana's birthday, so I didn't want to say anything to you. You had enough on your plate. I had to go to the police station and identify a man in a lineup."

She stopped as Kaito stared wide-eyed at her. Then her words tumbled out in an almost hysterical flow. "It appears this is the man suspected of being responsible for the murders in this area in the last few months, and he has been arrested and of course has to go to trial. I almost bumped into him as he was coming out of the woods by the parking garage at the hospital, and I stared at him and he stared at me and I felt the most evil and threatening vibes from him … Then I ran to the hospital entrance and he ran in the opposite direction … it was so bizarre … I didn't think anything of it until I saw a sketch on the news and I knew right away it was the same guy."

She stopped to catch her breath.

Kaito reached for her shaking hands, taking them in his. "This is shocking! How frightening for you. So you went to the police and reported this, viewed a lineup—and? End of story?"

Lailani shook her head as the color drained from her face and her eyes filled with tears. "It's been a nightmare. It turns out the guy I identified is a member of the Wong family!"

Kaito blanched, filled with concern. "The Company! Everyone who lives here knows about that crime syndicate. They've been solidly entrenched for years."

Lailani nodded. "And I'm paying the price."

She gulped before she continued. "A week ago my sweet Sugar was killed and left on our front doorstep." She burst into sobs.

Kaito went over and put his arms around her, knowing how she loved that little dog. Bile rose in his throat. "I'm so sorry. This is terrible!"

Stammering through her sobs, she said, "And that's not all. There—there've been phone calls and m-m-messages … threats … left in the mailbox…"

She took the handkerchief Kaito offered and buried her face in it.

"This is unbelievable! What do the police say about all of this?" Kaito asked, his voice resonating with alarm.

Lailani took a deep breath and composed herself. "They are distressed and fearful for my safety. They have put me up in the Holiday Inn near the hospital and are keeping an eye on my house and doing who knows what else. I've sent my mom to stay with her sister on Maui until I'm assured there's nothing to worry about."

"My dear! You should have told me sooner. I'm not sure what I could have done, but I hate to think you were going through this without any other support."

"The police said not to say a word, but I know you won't say anything. I'm so glad you know."

Kaito nodded. Worry creased his face. "Of course! In fact, I think you should keep a low profile and not worry about coming to us for now. I wonder if you should even be out in public right now."

"The police are watching me every minute and feel they may catch the guy if I am going to the hospital every day. I feel like a bit of a target though."

She gestured to Kaito to come to the window. "See that van down the street? That's them. I don't want to stop coming here but may have to cut back a bit as long as Hana doesn't have a bad episode."

"This new medication seems to be helping her, don't you agree?' Kaito asked.

Lailani shrugged her shoulders. "I know it is keeping her very quiet but I'm not sure what sort of a help that is. At least it makes life easier for you and Kiana, and for now that's a help. Unfortunately the health services here still have a rather negative view of psychological treatments. We could be doing a lot more work on mental health than we are, I'm sorry to say."

Kaito grunted. "How many times have we had that conversation? We are just so thankful for all you do to help keep us sane here. But now you'd better go ... and be careful. Please keep me posted on whatever is going on. Promise you will check in with me every evening, please!"

Lailani promised. "I give you permission to explain to Kiana what happened, but please leave out the details. Don't mention any names. Just say I was feeling anxious about having to view a lineup."

They embraced warmly before she went on her way.

Kaito had been stunned to hear what Lailani was experiencing. After Kiana returned home, he was somber as he went to her room and explained what had happened. Her teenaged eyes widened as her jaw dropped. "It sounds like some crazy cop movie, not like my safe and friendly hometown. It's hard to believe that sort of stuff happens here. And especially to sweet Lailani!"

"Well, now we know. Life is very strange and unpredictable at times. So please choose your friends carefully," he said, giving her a long hug. His love for her was the fuel that kept him getting up every morning to try and make their day the best it could be. He had to admit that she was his priority. His love for Hana was a given but one fraught with challenges. His love for Kiana was pure and strong.

"Papa, you know I will," she assured him. But there was something about her expression that made Kaito feel nervous. He thought to himself how the world seemed to be changing so quickly in the 1980s. Divorce rates were climbing and the concept of the family unit as he knew it was on the decline. He could see for himself that the younger generation of girls was bold and defiant with a different approach to values. It was hard to lose so much control over his teenaged daughter's choices.

Lailani called each night for another few days and then let him know she was coming to spend an evening with Hana. She accepted his invitation for dinner and was pleased that Hana joined them as well. Hana did not contribute much to the conversation unless it centered around their needlework project, the only subject to which she responded these days.

After dinner, while it was still light out, Hana and Lailani went for a brief walk in the neighborhood. Shortly after that, Hana said she was ready to go to bed and left them.

As Kaito and Lailani sat in the garden, the setting sun painted the sky and a peaceful calm filled the air. Lailani sighed a long, deep breath as she admired the sunset. "We should have our cameras out for this one," she said.

Kaito nodded. "You are so right. Tonight's display is quite remarkable. I have to say I haven't been using mine these past few weeks. I've been so focused on Kiana and trying to understand the ways of a teenager today."

Lailani smiled. "You should be proud of the way you are handling things, and how you have done, all these years. It hasn't been easy."

"No it hasn't. And your friendship and help has been immeasurable. But I don't need to tell you that."

They sat without speaking for a few moments.

Then Lailani announced she was going to take a week's vacation.

"I'm so stressed about this crazy situation and can't deal with living in the hotel and going to work as if nothing is amiss. I need to get away. I'm going to stay with Mama and Auntie on Maui and hope the police can put an end to everything before we return."

"Good plan." Kaito said, but his voice betrayed his misgivings. "I worry about you every day and wake up some nights with shivers! I hope with all my heart you are truly being well protected. Please keep in touch when you can."

They stood and hugged for a long time, then bowed as they backed from each other. "You, Hana, and Kiana are my family along with my mother. I just want this to be over so we can get back to normal life, whatever that is these days! I will definitely call you when I can."

A WEEK LATER, Lailani and her mother were back at their home.

Personal care workers from the hospital had taken several shifts during the week to be with Hana, who had otherwise remained sequestered in her room. It was unsettling for Kaito and Kiana to have strangers in the house, but they accepted this was necessary and the women were kind and helpful. Hana appeared passively resentful, communicating with nonverbal nods and remaining unwilling to leave her room.

"We are feeling rested, thanks," Lailani said when she stopped by Kaito's the day after her return.

After Kaito first replied to her inquiry about how Hana's week had gone, he asked about Lailani's trip.

"Mom and Auntie loved their time together, and I'm wondering why I had to wait for something like my current crisis to happen to get them together. Life is crazy sometimes, isn't it?"

Kaito was relieved to see a glimmer of Lailani's good humor again.

"And everything is under control as far as the police are concerned?" he asked.

"The police kept a watch on our house, and even had a man posted by my auntie's—imagine! Everything was fine. They did say they will remain vigilant, so that's somewhat comforting. The trial is not for a few months and that is when I will have to testify. I'm sure I'll be full of stress then. Now I have to move forward with life."

"Kiana will be delighted to hear that! Thanks for sending her the postcards from Maui. She loved them and we both felt reassured you were okay."

Lailani smiled. "I'm sorry she isn't here now but I will make a date with her."

Kaito nodded and chuckled, accompanied by a wry smile. "I practically have to make an appointment to see her these days. She's turned into quite the social being and can't wait until she's ready to try for her driver's license. You can imagine how I feel about that!"

"Kids grow up a lot faster these days than we did, that's for sure. Is she still dating Jake?"

Kaito's expression was not particularly happy. "As far as I know, yes. I feel I'm not privy to a lot of information these days."

.

CHAPTER 18

*E*arly in the afternoon two days later, Kaito's doorbell was rung impatiently several times. He peered through the long window beside the door and was surprised as he recognized his friend from the police department.

"Aloha, Mitch Alika—or should I say, Detective Alika," Kaito greeted his old friend. *"Ho'omaika'i 'ana!* Congratulations! I read about your promotion. To what do I owe this pleasure?"

Knowing his daughter was at school and Hana was in the house, there was no concern in his voice.

"Always Mitch to you, Kaito-san," his friend replied. "It's been a very long time since we saw each other. Too long."

Kaito bowed slightly and gestured for him to enter. "Is everything okay?"

"I'm afraid not," was the response.

Kaito was shocked. "What's up? How am I involved?"

"It's about Lailani Mahelona and her mother, Ulani. You do know them?"

Kaito's gut tightened. He thought of the previous threats.

"Yes, of course. They're close friends ... *ohana*—family.

Lailani's fiancée was tragically killed in 'Nam when I was there. We see her often. In fact, two nights ago she was here for dinner …"

Detective Alika indicated to Kaito that they should sit down. He took a deep breath and rubbed the palms of his hands along his thighs. His voice was low and throaty as he said, "I have terrible news. I'm afraid they both were killed in an auto accident at Morgan's Corner last night."

Kaito's head jerked back. His hand flew to his throat as if he was about to choke. "No!"

The detective lowered his eyes and spoke softly. "I'm so sorry. We've identified their remains, such as they were. The Mustang was a fireball, totally obliterated … but the license was readable. Now we're contacting people we know were friends of theirs to see if they were having any problems."

"But why … wasn't it an accident?" Kaito asked, having an out-of-body experience as he heard his words but felt he was not there.

"In all likelihood, yes. However, we have to check out all possibilities."

Kaito hung his head and then rested it in the palms of his hands. His voice shook. "This is terrible. They are such good people. Lailani is Hana's closest—no, make that only—friend. As I said, we are *ohana* … What a catastrophe."

They spoke for a few minutes. Kaito was completely shrouded in disbelief.

"Lailani mentioned some recent trouble and that the police were handling it," Kaito said. His voice trembled and he felt nauseous. He labored to get words out. "Surely this was not related!"

Mitch held up his hand and took out a notebook. "We are investigating all possibilities. So she did say something to you. Please tell me what you can recall."

∽

AFTER THE DETECTIVE LEFT, Kaito stumbled to the garden. He threw himself into a chair feeling he might pass out. Then he wept.

His shoulders heaved as sobs wracked his body. Uncontrollable cries escaped his lips from time to time as he sagged into a chair. He made no effort to stop it. He knew he couldn't do anything until the fierce pain and anguish he felt worked its way out and left him exhausted.

He cried for Lailani's loss of life. And her mother's. They had so much more living to do. He cried for the loss of their friendship … of family. For all that Lailani meant to him and Kiana and Hana.

He had never allowed this kind of emotion to break through his solid wall of control before.

He had shed some tears, briefly, in the past. In 'Nam, for the birth of Kiana, and at times late at night for Hana and his sorrow and frustration at the illness that was consuming her.

But nothing like this.

At one point, he saw Hana watching him through her bedroom window. He was thankful she did not come out.

His mind replayed the detective's story many times over. Questions swirled through his head. Did it have anything to do with The Company? Was it really an accident?

Everyone on Oahu knew that supposedly haunted hairpin curve, the object of several spooky legends. The canopy-covered road that runs through lush vegetation was also one of the most beautiful drives on the island. But it was also known to be pitch black there at night. He wondered why Lailani and her mother would even be out there then. They would have known better.

He needed to know more before he could process this unthinkable disaster.

The absence of her friendship would leave a gaping hole in their lives. It was a loss that was heartbreaking and he knew it would be an unbearable shock to Kiana. He could already feel the weight of the pain Kiana's despair would bring to him. He could deal with how badly his heart hurt, but to try to take away a child's heartache is another thing altogether. Grief dragged him down.

When Kiana returned from school, she found Kaito tending plants in the garden. He had worried all afternoon how he would share this terrible news.

They sat side by side on a lounge in the gazebo and he held her hand. His words came slowly and gently. His voice broke as sentences he would never have wished to utter explained the accident.

Indescribable pain stabbed through him as he watched her face shatter in agony.

"No! It's not possible! How can we live without Lanilani?"

Tears poured silently down her cheeks as her entire body shook. She folded into his comforting embrace as he searched for words that might somehow help. At this moment there were none.

All he could do was try to absorb some of the pain as sobs racked her body. In time they rocked together gently, drained.

There would be no work or school for either of them for days as they comforted each other in mourning, at times together and other times apart.

THE NEXT DAY, Kaito composed himself as best he could and explained the loss of Lailani to Hana in the gentlest way possible. Confused and blaming herself for losing her one friend, Hana withdrew into silent darkness.

Taking Hana to the memorial service seemed the right thing to do. Something that perhaps would help her understand the finality of what had happened. Kiana agreed to support him in this decision.

The service was packed but seats had been set aside for them in the family section. Kaito and Kiana held Hana between them as they slowly walked down the aisle, heads bowed. She kept her hands clamped on theirs the entire time they were there and they hurried back to the car as quickly as possible afterward.

To Kaito's surprise, she had reacted calmly at the time and said not a word. Nor did she shed a tear. Once home, she went straight to her studio and began stitching.

To his even greater surprise, she stopped mentioning Lailani after this, as if she had never existed.

The loss of Lailani's vital friendship created an agonizing void in the house for the three of them, even if Hana never acknowledged it. Kaito was certain that within the confused recesses of her mind, Hana understood Lailani was gone.

Grief is never easy, Kaito explained to a heartbroken Kiana as they sat in the garden a few days later. Uncontrollable bursts of tears had been part of their days and nights.

"It's a long and difficult process and we must all find our way through as best we can. We need to help each other but also understand that each of us will have different responses. I'm so sorry you have to experience this at your age, my *keiki*. I would give anything to take away this hurt to your heart."

Kiana wept quietly, as she tucked her hand into his.

Kaito fought an urge to completely break down. He could not stop the feeling of anguish that no child should hear these words. Taking a few deep breaths, he forced himself to continue. "This heartache will always be with us, but we will slowly find a way to manage it. That is the reality of grief."

Kaito felt everything he was saying settle into the depths of his heart. The pain was palpable. The vital source of calm and friendship Lailani brought to his life had vanished. He felt truly bereft.

He began to visit the Buddhist temple on his way to work, after Kiana left for school. Meditating at home was proving elusive but the soothing chants piped into the temple began to help Kaito calm his feelings of being overwhelmed. Eventually he could feel a center of peace return that carried him through the day.

～

SOON AFTER THE ACCIDENT, a full-time caregiver named Roselani Kamealoha was hired.

Kaito had become aware of just how much Lailani had helped them in so many ways. Kiana's schoolwork was becoming more demanding and he did not want her stressing about doing housework too. Kaito had always been quick with the vacuum and duster but had lost his will for it now. And Hana became increasingly morose and disinterested in doing anything for herself or anyone else. She began to stay in her room and seldom go to the studio. Her business languished.

A neighbor recommended Roselani.

A robust, full-bodied woman with a smile that lit the world around her, her greeting to Kaito and Kiana on her first morning was, "*Aloha kakahiaka!* My name is Roselani, but I would be honored if you choose to call me Auntie! It's up to you. I hope we will become family."

Her eyes sparkled with such intensity and sincerity, her immediate expression of affection and familiarity was hard to resist.

She was hired as a companion for Hana and to make lunch and do housekeeping while Kaito was at work. She hummed and sang as she worked and from what Kaito could see, she seldom sat doing nothing. The house gleamed within days.

"May I please offer to make your dinner?" she asked at the end of the first week. "It is so much nicer to arrive home to a meal and I can simply make it as I prepare lunch. You will see I love to cook … and to eat! And I love others to love my cooking!"

She patted her round middle and laughed warmly, "Never trust a skinny cook!"

Kaito explained to Hana that this woman was a housekeeper and cook to help all of them. Her response was a shrug and a dull stare back to the television.

But Auntie was much more than that. Kaito soon realized he had struck gold finding her. She was a special type of woman who exuded warmth and good cheer. Her capacity to show caring as well as humor to Hana appeared to know no bounds. Her very presence in the house brought a lightness that had been missing since Lailani's passing.

She was gentle with Kiana. Shortly after she took on her position with the family, she discreetly spoke with Kaito about her observations. It was obvious to her a problem existed and she was subtle enough when she asked Kaito about it. He appreciated the degree to which she showed commitment to the family.

She understood the dark hole of grief she could feel Kiana was in. Gradually Kiana responded to her kind, thoughtful ways and began to laugh and be a teenager again.

She was extensively trained as a caregiver and could coax Hana into the shower and fresh clothing on a daily basis. Even if Hana's temperament was not improved, her appearance was.

And then it was as if a prayer had been answered. As Auntie became aware of Hana's talent in her sewing studio, she gradually enticed her back to stitching. She also connected with the woman who had taken over from Mrs. Suzuki.

Kaito was beyond thankful as he watched business grow again and Hana return to her long days in her studio. Auntie was the perfect support for her. He hoped that the optimism and positivity once again alive in their home would be of some help to his ongoing issues not just with Hana but also with Kiana.

CHAPTER 19

1989

*W*ithin six months of Lailani's death, Kiana fell in even more with the wrong crowd, of which Jake seemed to be a leader. Kaito had been unnerved hearing gossip at the studio that linked Jake's name to local drug dealing. When he confronted Kiana with this, she denied it and became belligerent, unwilling to listen to reason from her father.

Suddenly there was no interest in old pastimes they had enjoyed together. She was still loving towards him but seldom home on the weekend until the early hours of the morning. Her responses to his questions about where she was going and what she was doing were short and vague. He struggled with this increasingly difficult behavior of secrecy and lies that were exacerbated by the absence of Lailani's stabilizing influence.

Even Auntie's gentle humor began to have little effect on Kiana, although she was never disrespectful to her.

When her behavior became erratic, with irregular mood swings, Kaito worried that Hana's demons had passed to their daughter. The helplessness he felt tortured him.

Kiana agreed to go to grief counseling with him as they had years before, but these sessions did nothing to alter her attitude.

During the meetings, she expressed her sorrow at Lailani's death and her love for her father. But there was never a crack in the anger and hurt she felt regarding Hana.

The counselor met privately with both of them and reported to Kaito that Kiana would require intensive private counseling in that regard. He stressed that Kiana herself was very healthy and that her psychological problems revolved around Hana's behavior and the emotional abuse Kiana suffered from her. She also reassured Kaito that it was obvious he was instrumental in Kiana coping as well as she did.

Kiana steadfastly refused to attend more counseling.

"Papa, there is too much water under the bridge when it comes to Mama. I can't begin to go there. You have saved me and loved me and my love for you is what has brought me this far. But now I also have found a safe haven where I laugh and think about the future with happiness. I need these friends."

It was almost no surprise, although a wound to Kaito's heart forever, when wanton and uncontrollable seventeen-year-old Kiana ran off with Jake. He heard more rumors of the long-haired artist's drug habits and wild lifestyle, widely circulated at the K&K Studio and was terror-stricken at Kiana's involvement with him.

Kiana packed a small overnight bag to stay at a girlfriend's, something she had done several times before. Kissing her father goodbye on Saturday afternoon, she assured him she would be home Sunday evening.

When she was not home by ten o'clock, Kaito began pacing. He did not want to be the nagging father, but Lailani's car crash was still fresh in his mind. He knew most of Kiana's friends drove now and Jake, in particular, had a fast model. It was difficult to keep his mind from going to dark places. At eleven he phoned the friend's home, apologizing for calling so late, and was told Kiana had not been there at all.

His heart sank. He felt nauseous and began to sweat as his head filled with horrific scenarios.

Feeling helpless, he called Mitch Alika and asked what to do. The detective said he would alert all the divisions after taking down Kiana's description.

Just before sunrise, the phone rang. Kaito's pulse raced as he reached for the receiver.

"Papa, I am not going to talk to you but I want you to know I am fine. I am not coming home but I will be in touch. Try not to worry. I love you." Kiana's voice was sad but firm.

Stunned, Kaito attempted to interrupt, to no avail, before the line went dead. He felt numb, unable to move, as if he might be dead too.

He advised Mitch of the call but asked him to keep looking for Kiana. For the next forty-eight hours, Mitch kept him updated to the fact there was absolutely no information about Kiana's whereabouts. Someone else seemed to be living in Jake's apartment and any of his friends they questioned said they knew nothing.

"To no one's great surprise," the detective muttered in disgust.

And to Kaito's utter despair.

ON THE THIRD day after her disappearance, a letter arrived for Kaito, who had barely slept or eaten during that time. He had spent hours driving aimlessly, hoping to find her somewhere in town. He arranged for posters to be printed that would be ready in a day to put up throughout town. Friends of Kiana's from school and the studio offered to help.

There was no postmark on the envelope and it had obviously been placed in his mailbox during the night. He took it out to the garden to read.

. . .

Dear Papa,

I am sorry for the anguish I know I have caused you. I did not plan to do this when I left on Saturday. I was just going to spend the weekend with Jake and come home. But when it was time to leave, I did not want to go and Jake asked me to stay. We are going to get married. He is going into hiding and I will go with him.

I know you will say I am too young. But I feel safe with Jake ... and loved. In spite of how he earns his living, he treats me with love and respect.

I felt loved with you too, Papa, and always have. You have never let me down. But you have so much pain to deal with from Mama's behavior. I know if I am not there things will be better. She cannot stand me. And I don't want either of us to have to live with that anymore.

I hope you can find it in your heart to forgive me. Your love will always live inside me. You have made me who I am.

I feel it is not fair to ask but, if you agree, would you have Auntie pack my clothes and books in a few storage cartons? I would also like the treasures you have given me and that you and I have made together, they are all on the top bookshelf.

If you leave all that one night next week by the mailbox, someone will collect them.

Whoever does will not know where I am, so please do not try to detain them or tell the police. Trust me on this. That would only complicate things for me and would not bring me back.

I promise to be in touch—that's the most important thing, Papa.

I want to write to you but if anyone else knows, then I will have to stop. Please tell no one.

I will always love you.

Your keiki

. . .

A LIGHT DRIZZLE fell on Kaito. He sat stunned for some time, mulling over everything that had transpired in the past year. His memory took him back to the day he learned Lailani had died. The explosion of emotions that had occurred that day had left an indelible mark on him. Emotions he had kept solidly in place throughout his life had risen to the surface and left cracks in the unshakeable exterior behind which he lived.

He felt himself losing control again. This time his tears were a mixture of despair and relief. At least he knew his daughter was not hurt or being forced to stay where she was. The fact that she chose to leave him was a stab to his heart, but she was safe and he believed he would see her again.

As the warm rain soaked through his clothes, endless thoughts tortured him as he wept with no sign of stopping. Surrounded by the beauty he and Kiana had spent so many years creating together, he searched for the answer to how things had come to this. How was it possible? How had he failed?

He felt there was nothing more he could do. If the police could not find Kiana, how would he? And why were they going into "hiding"? For the first time he had a sense that the rumors he heard about Jake's involvement in drugs might be true. His heart sank.

And if Kiana was right ... if she was to remain safe ... he had to make up a story to tell them that he knew this and they should stop looking. He promised himself he would never give up hope.

In time he felt drained, numb, despondent. He could not stop the one thought that would always haunt him: he had failed at the most important task in his life, being a father.

Auntie watched him, filled with sorrow herself. She stayed later than usual and finally coaxed him inside with a warm pot of tea.

After a long shower that helped to clear his head, he wrote a response for Kiana and hoped it might reach her. It sat in the mailbox until her next note arrived. Then, just as mysteriously, his note disappeared.

A few days later, he put out three plastic storage boxes that Auntie packed up. He stayed up very late watching to see if they were collected before he fell asleep in the chair. In the morning they were gone.

Kiana thanked him after his first note, so he was relieved to know she had received it. She thanked him again after the boxes were collected. This connection lifted his spirits in a small way. It was something.

A week after Kiana left, on an evening when Hana had joined him for dinner, Kaito suggested they sit in the garden. He led her over to where an abundance of orchids were in full bloom and pointed out some that had been birthday or Christmas gifts.

Hana nodded, making comments about some that bore a profusion of blossoms and were growing in trees. "Kiana likes to put those plants there. I never do but she does it all the time. They seem to like to grow there."

Kaito was pleased that she had brought up Kiana's name and connection to the orchids.

He took Hana's hand and had her sit beside him on the garden swing. As it gently rocked, he told her that Kiana had moved out to live with some friends. Hana barely gave any notice to his words. She looked straight ahead and said, "That's good. I'm glad she is gone."

And that was the end of it. There was no questioning why or where. Nothing. Not that Kaito was overly surprised, but somewhere deep inside he had hoped for some expression of remorse or regret—or love. But there was none. Kaito added that to the collection of hurts he stored deep inside. When he meditated that night he would put this in the grief compartment, which is how he viewed his psyche. Lots of compartments.

Buddhist teachings stressed how grief was an expression of love. It was how people felt when love was lost or torn away from them. Without grief there would be no love and vice versa. They went together. People needed to be mindful and then recognize grief was impermanent and let it pass. He walked with Hana to the bedroom and wondered how long it would take him to let this grief pass. If ever.

His hope vanished for some expression of warmth for their daughter to be spoken by her. He kissed Hana goodnight on the cheek and went to light a candle at his small shrine.

From time to time, Kaito raised the question with Hana about having Kiana return home if possible. He could not stop his dream of one day tracking her down or her arriving on their doorstep. Hana's response never changed. She insisted Kiana remain cut off from their family, with no looking back.

Kaito knew in his heart that he would never stop looking for Kiana. If there was ever a chance to have her back in their home, he would see that it happened and deal with Hana then. He suspected she would simply accept it in spite of what she said now.

CHAPTER 20

*A*t this point, Hana still had days when she would join Kaito for a meal. He tried to cajole and reason with her that Kiana needed her parents in her life. Hana would have none of it and made disturbing threats if Kaito went against her wishes. He felt trapped by his commitment to Hana and after a time did not mention it.

And he struggled to suppress the anger he felt towards her at times like this.

He had always tried to maintain a level of conversation with Hana, even when her responses were limited. Now his focus was on keeping the edge of acrimony from his voice.

Many months later, Detective Alika called Kaito and arranged a meeting for the next evening at his office.

"This will not be easy for you to hear, *pilialoha*," Mitch said, using the term for dear friend. "I am here as a father and friend, not an official. But what I have to tell you I would only know through my work. Kiana and her deadbeat husband … forgive me but I must be blunt … he is *karaima*."

Kaito held up his hand in a gesture of understanding. "Sadly,

I am well aware of this. You are right. He is nothing but a criminal. Please continue."

"They are running with a very tough crowd and Jake's 'posse' has been under surveillance for some time. He is a master at evading us and without a doubt a big player in the drug world, not just on Oahu but throughout the islands. I fear for Kiana. They appear to have moved from their apartment and gone into hiding."

Kaito's heart constricted with a terrible ache. His hands trembled. The emotions he felt were visceral. Even though he and Kiana were communicating, this news made his heart sink even more. Now he knew he had to do the best acting of his life and not give an inkling that they were in touch.

"I feel so helpless ... and stupid ... there must be something I can do," Kaito said, digging deep to not let on the contact he had with her. "I can't believe she would leave me like this. She has always been a good girl and—"

His voice caught and he covered his face with his hands. His shoulders sagged. All of his reactions came straight from his heart.

The detective put his hand on Kaito's shoulder. His eyes were filled with sympathy.

"You are not the first parent to deal with this, my friend. It is a terrible shock and nothing can remove the pain. If there is any consolation at all, you know she is with someone and not a victim of trafficking, which is becoming more of a problem these days."

Kaito nodded. "You are right, but somehow that doesn't help. Losing Lailani from our lives was the worst thing that could have happened. She was a link to keeping our family connected. Suddenly we were adrift ..." His voice faded as he dropped his head into his hands.

"I'm heartbroken for you and wish I could do something more to help," Mitch continued. "I hoped that by letting you know the situation, there might be some way of rescuing Kiana from the grips of this beast of a man."

Mitch promised he would do all he could to keep him informed.

After Kaito thanked him and saw him to the door, he leaned against the wall and breathed an enormous sigh. He felt terrible for deceiving Mitch, who was doing his best to help. And his deception about the notes was a minor part of the bigger picture. His daughter was lost to him in every way but a few non-descriptive lines of words every once in a while. It really was small compensation for his heart.

The apparent truth was that Jake Akana had drawn his young wife under his spell. Before long Mitch reported they had discovered evidence that Jake and his crew were becoming more and more involved in the island's drug world. Crime was a growing factor in the once idyllic life on Oahu and all of the other islands.

"But I can assure you, if it is any consolation," Mitch told him, "I never hear your daughter's name mentioned apart from the fact she is Jake's wife."

In spite of the occasional missives from Kiana, Kaito feared for her safety. Her notes to him were always superficial and unrevealing, but he was relieved to have whatever she wanted to send him. It was so much better than nothing. Worry and regret became his constant companions.

CHAPTER 21

*S*ix months later, Kaito had reason for a glimmer of hope that there might be a change in his life.

The day a black-and-white photo arrived in the mail of the sweetest looking baby girl, with a halo of dark curls and cherubic face, Kaito's heart soared. Although Kiana had continued to surreptitiously have letters left for him, there was never any indication as to how he could reach her. Again, the letter was left in his mailbox at night.

Her note to him was brief.

Dear Papa,

I hope you are well. I want you to know I am fine and now the mother of this blessed bundle of love. I wish you could see her.

I have named her Kailani to remind me of you, my dearest father, and Lanilani, who was like a mother to me. I carry you both in my heart.

Please believe we live a good, simple life by the sea. Even though Jake is involved in a world which I, in all honesty, regret, he loves me and looks after me. We want for nothing.

I am filled with sorrow at the pain I have caused you. It is my pain too but the way it must be.

When you are by the sea, please think of me as I do you and of this new star in my universe.

I love you.

Your keiki

HE FERVENTLY HOPED that somehow this might be the opportunity to bring Kiana back to him. He wondered if she could be persuaded. As unlikely as that seemed, the hope never left him.

Perhaps, he pondered, the birth of their granddaughter might signal a shift in Hana's attitude. But any mention of reconciliation threw her into a fierce rage and now he was quite certain Hana had no idea why. Her doctors had explained that these manic outbursts were beyond Hana's control and she was a patient who had shown no process for remorse, nor sometimes even remembrance.

All along, in spite of Kaito's efforts, there had been no point in arguing with her completely irrational thinking. He had tried reasoning so vehemently in the early years and always hit a wall. A wall that usually exploded.

It would always be a puzzle to him how the birth of an innocent child could be the undoing of a mother. But he had come to understand from Hana's health care professionals that in her case it was simply the key that unlocked her more serious condition of manic-depressive disease, which her meds seldom helped.

Doctors and counselors repeatedly told him no one could have predicted it. Kaito had been advised through discussions with specialists through the years that Hana did not simply have a clear case of being bipolar or manic. There were many complicating factors in her diagnosis, making it a challenge to effectively medicate.

~

TIME PASSED SLOWLY without Kiana in his daily life. Kaito focused on keeping himself busy during the day with work and the K&K Studio. But evenings were often a challenge. There were fewer occasions when Hana stayed awake long enough to have more interactions. Kaito was acutely aware that although they were a couple, he was living his life alone.

There were times, when Hana was not in the depths of depression, they would occasionally have a pleasant evening and go for a walk or a drive. It had been years since they had shared any intimacy. Knowing how hesitant Hana had become about having sex after Kiana was born, Kaito resisted any desire to approach it. These moments troubled Kaito tremendously. He felt conflicted about feeling no desire for her now.

These occasions sent him back to counseling. Many difficult emotional days of guilt and anguish would follow. Kaito would beat himself up for the way he had handled everything. Perhaps if he had made different decisions Kiana would still be at home. But really, he asked himself how could he have done things differently? He loved Hana in spite of her illness. He would always be there for her. Loyal. He believed she did not want to be the way she was … she did not realize how she was. If he had not cared for and supported her through the years, what would have happened to her?

The sessions gave him the release of expressing his feelings out loud but that still did not ease the pain he carried until time allowed it to fade.

He felt himself protecting what was left of his heart by consciously shutting down his emotions. Hana was his wife and he felt compelled to honor his vows to care for her in sickness and in health. At home he became a prisoner of her bitterness, anger, and emotional distance. He knew in many ways this was the choice he was making. It was not in his nature to go off looking for fun and enjoyment on his own. Kiana had been the impetus for that from the day she was born. She had been the catalyst, his motivation to make life good and happy.

Since she was gone, he accepted how his life was at this time and would be for as long as it lasted.

Fortunately, through whatever force of nature, there was this angel in their lives now named Roselani Kamealoha. She removed a tremendous weight from Kaito's shoulders as he saw how Hana accepted the cheerful assistance of Auntie, who helped her maintain a balance of nutrition and hygiene.

Kaito would never forget his feeling of gratitude over how Auntie had brought Hana back into her sewing studio. Her ability to create magnificent embroidery again improved as the weeks went by. Auntie was a benevolent taskmaster and Hana stitched many hours away each day.

Outside the home, Kaito managed to maintain his own balance, mentally and physically. Committed to projects at the engineering firm, he was respected as an intelligent, quiet man with an unknown home situation. He never felt inclined to accept social invitations. He had no desire for small talk or the usual niceties required in the company of others at parties of any sort. He did not want to disclose to others his situation at home. Whether it was shame or embarrassment he felt, it did not matter. This was his choice.

After a while the invitations stopped.

He was devoted to his martial arts studio. The discipline of the art kept his body strong and his mind alert and he enjoyed his interaction with others there. This did not require any chat about his home life. The time there delayed his arrival to what-ever awaited him with Hana.

Some evenings on her good days, Kaito and Hana would read together. They shared books and chatted about them. Hana sometimes asked Kaito to read to her and this was a time when he felt close to her and warmed to memories of earlier years together.

But frequently, he arrived home to nothing more than Hana's darkened room and no response. He had become accustomed to the emptiness this caused him to feel.

Those times Kaito would read, watch some television, and end his day with meditation that helped keep him centered. As he knew from the words of Buddha, this was a path to shedding anger, depression, and frustration—and would lead to nirvana. That was his focus and he knew there was still a long way to go.

At one point, Detective Alika let him know that the police department discovered Kiana and Jake had moved to the island of Kauai.

"We've been running undercover surveillance and found Jake is overseeing things from there. He's crafty and sly and keeps himself just beyond the reach of the law," Alika told him. "He seems to live a double life and on the other side of things appears to be a devoted family man."

Kaito was stunned as Mitch said, prefacing it with the hope it would put things in perspective, "As long as you have not been contacted to say she is dead, you know she is alive."

THE PAIN of accepting the news Mitch had shared was mildly relieved by the notes Kaito continued to receive from Kiana. They were always brief but filled with affection for him and assurances that she and his granddaughter were happy. She talked about hikes they went on and plants she was nurturing in her garden, as she had done with Kaito. She described all of the milestones little Kailani was reaching and promised they would see each other one day. Kaito held on to that promise.

He still did not reveal their correspondence to the detective or anyone else.

CHAPTER 22

$\mathcal{A}$ s years went by, Kaito spent even more time at K&K Studio, increasing his skills and participating in local competitions. Now that he had time on his hands on weekends, he slowly began to develop more interactions with other people there. Most important to him were the opportunities he had to work with students of aikido who were around Kiana's age—in their early twenties. His sense of failure at losing her was partially eased when he watched a commitment to the art grow in a student.

Over time he developed a friendship with Bob Johnston, an acquaintance from high school and a regular at the studio. Rehashing memories from those carefree days evolved into deeper conversations about Buddhism after they bumped into each other at a photographic exhibit at the Byodo-In Temple, where their conversation led them to discover more shared interests.

After many invitations, Bob finally convinced Kaito to have dinner with him and Gail, his wife. They included Hana in the invitation, although Bob had gathered from Kaito that she was ill and did not go out. But they were thoughtful people and

Kaito appreciated that. They also understood when he confirmed Hana would not be with him.

The couple was close to his age and they all knew many of the same people from school days. There was much laughter as they dredged up old memories. Gail still kept in touch with some of the women and had some current gossip.

Kaito accepted an increasing awareness of how much he had cut himself off from a social life. He had never been bothered about it as his devotion to and time spent with Kiana and his other interests kept him busy. His dedication to Hana was unwavering, even when unrequited. He loved her in spite of the difficulties, perhaps even more so, as he saw how broken she was. How alone within herself. His sense of loyalty went back to his childhood and was a powerful part of who he was.

But now, as more time passed without Kiana in his life, he sensed a shift within himself that welcomed this new interaction.

After that first dinner, Kaito enjoyed getting together occasionally. Hana was always included in the invitation and Kaito asked her every time, knowing full well she would always refuse. He never stopped hoping that would change.

The Johnstons lived on the east side of town with breathtaking views out to sea and a constant breeze from the trade winds. Gail was an avid gardener and a member of The Garden Club of Honolulu. Her table flower arrangements caused Kaito to exclaim out loud and he was at ease immediately as they shared tips on some of the same plants they grew.

A few months later on, as they became familiar with each other, Gail asked Kaito more specifically about Hana. She wondered if there was any way she could be of assistance.

Kaito was touched by her genuine concern and desire to help.

"That's kind of you and much appreciated. But Hana is very much a recluse and has no ability or desire to interact with others, apart from myself and our indispensable Auntie. Rosie is our housekeeper, caregiver, cook, and general guardian of good spirits in our home. We would be lost without her."

This was the first time that he had opened up to anyone other than people in health care about his situation at home. He was surprised at how it freed him in some ways. He found himself able to rise above the shame that had engulfed him for years. Gail's empathy encouraged straightforward conversation about the difficulties of mental health problems and the challenges borne.

He felt pride as he described Hana's beautiful embroidery work on the belts and how this special talent was her lifeline. After listening, Gail brought out that day's copy of *The Honolulu Advertiser* and Kaito showed her the standing ad for Hana's work.

"Kaito, these are stunning! I would love to meet Hana one day. I hope we can make it happen. And I'm ordering one of these belts immediately!"

It was a new sensation to speak glowingly of something Hana was doing and to have someone respond in such a way. Kaito experienced a wave of shame when he thought about it later. He realized that in some ways he had marginalized Hana and kept her hidden away from the rest of his life. Even though this was what Hana wanted, he felt it had not been fair of him to never speak of her in public to any extent. He wrestled with guilt about this now. She was more than just her illness, he told himself.

But he also knew he had to continue to be the gatekeeper in their world. Her protector.

Gail was a social worker who had some experience with clients dealing with illnesses similar to Hana's. Kaito always knew he was not alone in what he faced, but to hear a friend talk about it with him rather than a counselor was a new experience. He felt he had crossed an invisible hurdle he had placed before himself many years ago.

The more they talked, the more Kaito relaxed in their company.

One day, Gail said, "Kaito, I want to tell you how much I respect your attitude about Hana's health issues. It takes a great deal of inner strength to continue to live with those demands year after year. I can see you do that with compassion and love."

"Thank you for that," Kaito replied. "Since I have spoken about Hana to you, I've been battling guilt over not recognizing her as more than her illness. That has caused me many sleepless nights."

Gail looked at him with great sympathy. "Kaito, that's not an unusual situation with mental illness, particularly when the afflicted person shies away from social interaction with others. Your response is to protect Hana's privacy as well as your own. Do not feel guilty. Your devotion to her is exemplary."

Kaito nodded and looked down, unsure of how to respond.

Gail's voice caught for a moment before she continued. "And to have your daughter leave home as well ... my heart goes out to you. You carry a heavy load. Plaudits to you, my friend."

Kaito flushed with embarrassment. "It's just how our lives are. We deal with what we are handed in the best possible way. To quote Buddha, 'Do not dwell in the past, do not dream of the future, concentrate the mind on the present moment.'"

"And that, as we know, is easier said than done," Gail said.

"And have the good fortune to discover a gem like Auntie," Kaito said, which made them laugh in agreement. "But in all seriousness, she truly is our saving grace."

It was from Bob that Kaito first learned about Buddhist retreats and courses in Koyasan. He had seen posters at the temple but never paid any attention to them.

Now he was intrigued by the possibilities.

"Seriously, Kaito, you might want to consider a visit there. I try to go every two years and it has made a tremendous difference in my attitude towards life. You can get information at most of the temples in Honolulu, and some have an organized trip every year. That's how I went the first time. Now I prefer to go when the timing is right for me."

Kaito plied Bob with questions. The thought of being immersed in the Buddhist atmosphere for two weeks intrigued him and he thought perhaps it was time to get in touch with his Japanese roots.

He was surprised to learn that Gail did not accompany Bob on those trips and he asked about it at dinner one evening.

"She went with me once," Bob said, and Gail nodded as he continued. "The spartan lifestyle and uncomfortable sleeping mats were not for her. She appreciated the solitude of the experience at the time and the immersion into more of the Buddhist way. Right, my dear? But not enough to go back."

Gail interjected. "Exactly. When I go away I am looking for comfort. Not necessarily luxury but definitely a good bed and pillows. So now I plan a holiday with a girlfriend or two and that way we are both happy."

"Sometimes we meet at the end of our time away … so far in Thailand and Bali," Bob continued.

"That's worked out really well," Gail grinned, "and I'm looking forward to doing it again."

The following week, Bob handed Kaito some brochures and photocopied pages with information about Buddhist retreats in Koyasan. He was familiar with information about Kyoto, but this sacred site, 120 miles southwest, was less well-known to him.

"As advertised, my friend. I'm going to go in September and you are welcome to join me. No rush. It's still a few months away and never busy there."

After Kaito visited the library and searched through a number of books he checked out, his interest was piqued.

The next issue he had to face was his guilt at the thought of leaving Hana for two weeks.

It had never occurred to Kaito to actually go away and leave her for an extended time. Overnight camping was one thing, but to be out of the country for a couple of weeks was another. It went against his sense of duty and loyalty to Hana.

The odd time that he was away overnight, Auntie stayed with Hana so there was never any worry about her safety.

He seriously doubted she would even be aware of the time he was gone and realized he was struggling with self-inflicted guilt. In the three years since Kiana had left, Kaito had spent time reflecting on choices he had made with his life. He was finally taking a look at himself and realizing it was time to do something just for him.

CHAPTER 23

KOYASAN 1992

*I*n time, Kaito convinced himself that taking a trip to a Buddhist retreat was not the equivalent of dashing off to Club Med. He felt justified in giving himself the gift of a change of scene and the opportunity to become more involved in his spiritual beliefs.

It was at this point that Kaito made arrangements for a two-week trip to Koyasan. He was forty-two years old, and for a good part of twenty years he had lived in the grips of Hana's illness.

"I deserve this," he kept telling himself. Setting aside his innate sense of duty, he acknowledged that he needed to find space to breathe again, to gather himself and mentally stand upright.

He discussed with Auntie how the news should be shared with Hana. It was decided he would simply say he was going to be away on business for a little while and see whether her reaction warranted more details.

At breakfast one morning a week before his departure, he said to Hana, "My *pulele,* I am going to be going away for a short while on a business trip."

Hana looked up from her bowl of fruit for a moment and nodded.

Kaito continued. "Auntie will be here with you the entire time I am gone. You will never be alone and you know she will take very good care of you."

Hana nodded again with no particular indication of concern.

"Do you have any questions about where I am going or what I am doing?" he asked.

This time her expression did not change. She shook her head and continued eating.

Kaito sat with her until Auntie came to clear the dishes and suggest to Hana they go out to the garden. Without looking at Kaito, Hana followed Auntie to the patio doors. Then she turned and waved as she sometimes did on a normal morning.

Kaito felt a surge of sadness mixed with relief. He nodded to himself, having expected nothing more … really. He was free to go.

A FEW MONTHS LATER, in September, he accompanied Bob to Japan and was glad to have his friend's experience guide him with decisions on that first trip.

During the nine-hour flight, Kaito felt a new sense of freedom as he physically moved further and further away from his daily regimen of worry about Hana. There was a lingering disbelief as he enjoyed a meal and a beer, chatted with Bob, and settled into a relatively undisturbed sleep.

The arrival at Haneda International Airport in Tokyo was a reminder to Kaito of how insular his life had been. He questioned how he could have spent all of his adult life without ever leaving the islands of Hawaii apart from his stint in Vietnam.

As they waited in line to present their passports he admitted as much to Bob.

"You've got to be kidding, man!" Bob exclaimed, taken aback. "So you are taking your first trip away from Hawaii with me? Whoa! I'm blown away!"

"So am I," Kaito admitted, feeling his face redden. "It's just never been an issue because of Hana's illness. I honestly never considered leaving her for more than a day or two camping. It was talking to you that started me thinking about it."

Bob's voice was filled with sympathy. "I'm so sorry—for both of you. And I know from what you have told us that there is no hope your wife could travel. But once you get a taste of this, you may decide to go other places. This year my Gail is going to Bali with a friend for two weeks and then we're going to Cambodia and Vietnam for two weeks before we go home."

Kaito nodded. "Just going to Koyasan is a big step for me and who knows if I will ever do it again. This is the test run."

"Trust me, my friend. You will not be disappointed."

After the uncrowded, quiet life in Hawaii, even with the increase of tourists coming to the islands, he was shocked by the throngs of people in the Tokyo air terminal. He was so intent on keeping close to Bob that he failed to take in all of the surrounding scene.

"For God's sake, don't lose me! I feel completely like a fish out of water!" Kaito muttered.

He explained it was his first flight to his former homeland since traveling there with his parents as a child. They had returned several times to visit his grandparents before they passed, but the last trip was during high school days.

"I remember going with them to Tokyo," he said as he declined when Bob asked if he wanted to go there on this trip.

He had visions seared in his young mind making it a city of ghosts and charred, bombed-out ruins.

He was surprised how his recollections transported him back to childhood memories as he set foot in the country of his birth.

"Perhaps I will visit Tokyo on another trip, if I come back here," he said to Bob.

Bob's reply was full of confidence. "Trust me, you are going to want to come back."

~

GETTING to Koyasan felt complicated with various buses and trains and he was grateful not to be doing the trip on his own. Bob proved to be an excellent travel guide and had recommended some advance reading for Kaito. But in spite of all his reading, the initial experience of this destination was something he could not have imagined.

His first adjustment was to being so far away from Hana. He had worked through that part long before he made the decision to go on the trip. Knowing she would be well looked after 24/7, he had left with only a small sense of guilt or worry about her welfare. All details were in place and he had gone over them endless times to be certain nothing was forgotten, as was his nature.

Accustomed to the diverse culture in Hawaii, Kaito was aware he was in the majority back in the land of his birth. The observation surprised him, as he never felt marginalized in Hawaii.

What immediately impacted him the most was the complete change of scenery and surroundings. It was one thing to read about it, but he felt electrified to be in the midst of it. There was something comforting about the dense forests and the intense shades of greens so different from those on Oahu, some of which were already showing hints of blazing color to come.

He knew Mount Koya was one of the highest mountains in Japan after Mount Fuji, but was surprised as the funicular climbed at dizzying angles on the trip up from the base town of Gokurakubashi.

"The town name translates to 'The Bridge of Heaven,'" Bob said, his voice solemn. "I always feel that sets the tone for this experience."

The ten-minute ride was exhilarating and steep through a dense forest, with occasional glimpses of the countryside far below. Bob explained there was also the option of hiking up to Koyasan on the original pilgrimage trail. "It only takes about an hour, so is not overwhelming. But I admit I have not done it."

"I imagine one would have to pack more lightly than I did to hike up," Kaito replied.

Bob nodded, cleared his throat, and added, "I should tell you about the huge spiderwebs you have to watch for along the way too. The *jorogumo* are the most common spiders in Japan. They have long spindly legs and yellow and black stripes and apparently can catch small birds. I haven't actually seen one but I've been told it's really best to hike when you can take a big stick with you to clear the way."

"Duly noted," Kaito said, with a chuckle. "I'll save that experience for another time ... or maybe not ..."

At the Koyasan stop, Kaito was immediately struck by the silence around them. Then he became aware of the freshness of the air and breathed in deeply the strong scent of cedar. He noted leaves were beginning to turn and the temperature was cooler, so he took his jacket out of his backpack.

One of the holiest places in Japan, Koyasan was established in 819 by the Buddhist monk Kobo Daishi. Now headquarters of the Shingon school of Buddhism, there were more than one hundred temples, recognized by their soaring cypress bark roofs. The town was also filled with accompanying monasteries, pagodas, halls, and statuary.

Bob indicated a bus waiting outside the station, and in just a few minutes it dropped them a short walk from the thousand-year-old setting in which was their *shukubo*, a temple with pilgrim lodging. Kaito felt exhilarated as he glimpsed soaring rooftops of some of the eighty temples in the town.

"There is so much beauty here, it will take your breath away," Bob said. "Once you go through the doors of these buildings, you enter an entirely different world. We have missed the evening meal, so let's stop at this noodle shop before we check in to our temple. As long as we are there by eight o'clock, the doors will be open."

~

AFTER A BOWL of deliciously full-flavored udon noodles, they walked down a dimly lit street and through the carved wooden gates to find their accommodation.

Kaito could not contain his pleasure and exclaimed often as they walked up the stone path. Surrounded by ornamental gardens, the path took them to wide steps leading to a broad porch of what appeared to be the main building. He was surprised at the cluster of structures on the property and the density of the cedar forest surrounding them. The elegant lines of the curved tile rooftops and the stone walls with lanterns lining the path gave him a thrilling sense of history and a satisfaction that he was really there. He had done it. The sense of accomplishment caught him off guard for a moment. He wondered if he had denied himself this kind of experience longer than he should have.

Bob had stayed here before and recommended it for atmosphere and location.

"You will see what I mean tomorrow when we take a walk. I can't wait to hear what you have to say then," Bob said, enjoying Kaito's obvious enthusiasm.

Inside, they were warmly welcomed now by a young monk with a shaved head who was dressed in a simple orange robe. He came around from behind a counter and bowed as he handed each of them a small board with a room number and some Japanese slippers of straw and cloth.

Kaito murmured to Bob, "No keys?" and Bob shook his head in response.

"Simply not necessary. And no telephones, television, or newspapers," he reminded him.

They removed their shoes and put on the slippers. Kaito followed Bob down the dark wooden corridor the monk had indicated.

"The shared bathrooms are just a little further along. The hot spring bath is outstanding. Not private but you are welcome to use it whenever," Bob said. "I'm ready for a good sleep though. How about you?"

"No kidding," Kaito replied. "I can barely keep my eyes open."

He bowed to Bob. "Thank you, my friend, for getting me started on this adventure."

Bob returned the bow. "My room is next door. See you in the morning. As Buddha says, 'A good laugh and a long sleep are the two best cures for anything.'"

Kaito chuckled. "*Oyasumi.* Good night."

Sliding open a rice paper door, screened with drawings of animals, mountains, and people, Kaito entered his simple room. Sparsely decorated in typical Japanese fashion, there was a low table and tatami mats for sitting. His eyes went to a small altar decorated with a scroll, not unlike the one in his home.

With a deep bow, he picked up three incense sticks at the altar. Lighting the incense, he knelt three times and placed the incense in front of the altar. The sweet fragrance filled the air as he prayed in a soft, low voice.

"May I be free from fear.

May I be free from suffering.

May I be happy.

May I be filled with loving-kindness.

May you be free from fear.

May you be free from suffering.

May you be happy.

May you be filled with loving-kindness.

May all people everywhere be happy and filled with loving-kindness."

He prayed for the souls of his dead ancestors and that they would protect Hana in his absence.

At home he liked to begin and end each day with the loving-kindness blessing, after praying to his ancestors. But there were days he struggled to get through it. Now, here in Koyasan, saying the blessing felt like so much more. He thought of Hana and prayed for her, as he would every day he was gone. He gave thanks for the good care he knew she had every day, whether he was there or not.

A light rap interrupted his thoughts. A different young monk bowed and gestured he would come in. Kaito watched as he took down the thin *shikibuton* that was folded on a shelf. After rolling this sleeping mattress on top of a tatami mat on the floor, he placed a folded, equally thin, blanket on top. Then he set an odd-looking sack on the mattress as well that Kaito recognized as the pillow: a thin rectangular cushion he knew was filled with buckwheat chaff and seriously uncomfortable until one got used to it.

The monk pointed to a heavier duvet on a shelf, which Kaito was certain would come in handy.

He placed on the mattress a folded thin cotton robe, *yukata*, and a cotton coat, *tanzen*, thickly padded, he explained, to help keep out the cold. Kaito had read he was expected to wear these to the baths and to dinner, but not breakfast.

When the monk finished preparing the room, he bowed and left. Kaito held his bow longer than usual, reminding himself that Buddha had considered comfort of secondary importance. And now so would he.

He slid open the rice paper door leading outside and took a deep breath. Candles were lit all along the wooden walkway outside and throughout what he could see of an ornamental garden and pond. In the dim light it was still possible to appreciate the mystical juxtaposition of rocks and vegetation. He was filled with a sense of being in an ancient and holy place.

Kneeling on the walkway outside his room, he practiced his *ki* breathing. A daily part of his aikido training, he had long ago discovered it harmonized with his meditation and was an effective way to prepare for sleep.

Childhood memories flooded his mind as he settled on the hard mattress and pulled the threadbare blanket over him. This was how he had slept until he had his first bed when his family immigrated to Hawaii. He drifted off recalling how happy those early years had been despite poverty and discomfort.

He knew he was stronger in many ways as an adult because of those childhood hard times.

CHAPTER 24

*T*he deep rich gong of the monks' prayer bell rang at six a.m. promptly. Kaito's surprisingly deep sleep had been welcome, but cold. He woke with excitement and eager anticipation. And then felt as if he hit a wall.

Something was missing. After so many years of waking to responsibility. Of wondering how the state of affairs would be in his home that morning. Now, with no one to take care of but himself at this time, the sensation was strange and almost frightening—as if something major was missing from his psyche.

Slowly he sat up, his joints stiff from the cold, hard floor. He moved his legs into the lotus position and let his hands rest softly on his knees with his palms up. He focused all of his attention on his breathing. Willing each breath to sink deeply into his core and then just as slowly releasing it, he knew he was also letting go of worry and fear.

As his shoulders relaxed, he felt free of tension. He could face the day. He would not worry. He was where he was supposed to be. His responsibilities at home were being looked after.

THE SECRETS WE HIDE

He continued with his usual routine of aikido stretches and a few basic strengthening exercises. Although his focus was to be humble and banish pride, his level of fitness was important to him.

Bob came into the darkened hall at the same time as Kaito and they exchanged bows and shivers as they quietly followed others to the monks' main hall of prayer.

The wooden floor was shiny and slippery, having been well polished by novices for centuries, according to Bob. Silence echoed through the frigid air of the corridor.

Leaving their slippers outside the hall, they followed a vivid crimson carpet laid across beige tatami mats through the candlelit temple, indicating the way for prayer-goers.

As Kaito's eyes became accustomed to the light of the flickering candles, he took in the scene. Stacks of black and gold boxes stood neatly on a shimmering altar. Mounds of pink grapefruit and bright flowers interspersed with red candles were all carefully arranged.

Four monks with shaven heads knelt in silent contemplation. The beating of a single drum signaled the beginning of the prayer session. Symphonic chanting in unison was accompanied by the occasional clash of cymbals. A fire ritual followed.

Kaito felt as if he were held in a suspended hypnotic state, until it was his turn to make his way down the crimson carpet on his knees. Once again he was thankful to have Bob showing him the ropes. When he reached the altar, he pushed sweet-smelling incense sticks into the ash of a burner and offered a private prayer as the smoky "breath of gods," with its supposed curative powers, wafted over him.

Then he joined the monks in meditation for the remainder of the hour and a half, surrounded by repetitive chanting, incense, and a slight warmth from the fire. The scene mesmerized Kaito. The steady flow of low guttural chants was hypnotizing. Swirling trails of incense smoke curled through the space and the occasional muted tone of a gong punctuated the air.

A light vegetarian breakfast was waiting in his room after this. Kaito smiled as the tray with small porcelain and ceramic bowls and plates of modest amounts of different dishes again rekindled childhood memories. He recognized a round tofu-and-vegetable cake like his mother used to make, which tasted much like an omelet. Then he took seaweed and put it in a bowl of miso soup that was so deliciously simple and light he wished there had been more. He knew the Buddhist kitchen used no animal products of any kind and the richness of the broth attested to that. He finished two small pieces of okra and then the light, tart, and crunchy bamboo and carrot salad, saving the pickled seaweed and pickled plum—his favorite—for last.

The meal was not filling, but hearty in spite of the small amounts. Since Buddhists traditionally eat two meals a day, he was certain this would sustain him without a problem.

Bob was at Kaito's door after half an hour, full of praise about the breakfast.

They had agreed that on this first day he would help Kaito discover how to tap into many of the options open to him, and then they would go their separate ways.

BOB HAD BEEN RIGHT about the location.

They were situated precisely at the entrance to Okunoin, the ancient cemetery set amidst towering cedar trees.

Kaito immediately reached for his camera.

Bob chuckled. "No surprise there, my friend. Your shutter will be clicking furiously every day you are here. I guarantee that!"

"There's no doubt about that," Kaito agreed.

"But as cool and beautiful as you will find it here now, wait until evening and come back through when all the lanterns are lit. That is a spectacle unto itself … haunting in every respect," Bob said, letting out a sigh. "And the Torodo Hall! Man, it's the coolest!"

The two-kilometer cobblestone path through the sacred cemetery led to the mausoleum of Kobo Daishi, the founder of Shingon Buddhism and one of the most revered religious people in Japanese history.

At the Ichinohashi Bridge, monks and pilgrims traditionally washed their hands and faces before entering what they believe to be the "pure land," or paradise. Kaito and Bob joined other pilgrims in the ritual and bowed before they walked over the bridge.

Across that bridge was a dense wood filled with giant cedar trees, some thousands of years old, along with cypresses and conifers. Ferns, grasses, and low-spreading greens carpeted the forest floor. Kaito knew there were more than 200,000 graves marked by all manner of moss-covered stone sculptures, tomb-stones, pagodas, and statues as well as family and corporate mausoleums. He noticed offerings of flowers and other small gifts left at some.

He was surprised to learn from Bob, who was acting as a well-informed guide, that anyone could still be buried in this cemetery.

"I was amazed to learn that too," Bob said. "For centuries, many prominent citizens, monks, and feudal lords had their tombstones erected there. I thought it was exclusive, but that is not so. It seems for everyone the hope is that salvation will be received simply by being buried close to Kobo Daishi."

Kaito was moved by the solemn beauty of the setting. Ornate grave markers, as well as simple ones, were offset by the varied monuments. Historic figures, war heroes, royalty, busi-ness leaders, children, and pets were all memorialized here.

In what seemed bizarre at first glance, some of the little

Buddha-like statues wore what appeared to be handcrafted red bibs or tiny hats of all sorts or both. Bob explained these small statues held the spirits of children and babies.

"No one is considered dead here but rather waiting for spirits."

They walked along for twenty minutes and then turned back to the entrance.

"Thanks, Bob. I know you've spent a lot of time in here, so I'll come back by myself ... no doubt more than once ... and take my time with my camera. And I will come at night too. Thanks for that tip."

"Oh, I should tell you too that further up when you get to the bridge leading to the mausoleum where Kobo Daishi is believed to rest, there's no photography allowed past that. But there are signs to remind you."

Kaito well knew that Kobo Daishi was the most revered Buddhist saint ... a poet, scholar, and monk ... the founder of Shingon Buddhism in the 8th century. He had read that the monks in Koya visited his shrine, the most sacred place, every day to bring food and other offerings as a symbolic gesture. They believe he lives on in eternal meditation, awaiting the Buddha of the future.

The rest of the day was spent visiting some of the many temples, the spectacular Daimon Gate, the Daito Bell, and admiring the artistic gardens that abounded as Kaito became familiar with the map containing the stops in town.

By mid-afternoon, they were back at their shukubo and had time to sink into the relaxing hot spring baths before catching a meditation class. There was so much to take in during the day that Kaito truly only fleetingly thought about Hana or what was happening at home. He acknowledged the strange feeling and also his acceptance of it.

He knew she was safe and had her own agenda. That gave him the peace to focus on his goals for this trip.

As he sat submerged to his neck in the thermal water, he pictured Hana going through her daily routine.

Thankful for Auntie, he wondered if his absence would be remarked upon as the days went by. Auntie had promised to send a telegram to the Western Union office in Koyasan if there was anything to report. He had agreed he would stop by each day to check.

Dinner was served at 5:30 in an attractively but simply decorated room. Each person had their own small table and tatami mat, all set up in rows.

A monk explained the Buddhist cuisine to the newcomers.

Shojin ryori adheres to a strict belief of nonviolence towards living things. It spread across Japan in the 13th century with the rise of Zen Buddhism and refers to its basic tenets.

Certain patterns of five apply.

For cooking: stewing, boiling, steaming, roasting, and leaving the food raw.

Five primary colors: red, green, white, black, and yellow. The food pyramid of Japanese antiquity, it is believed to provide a healthy balance of nutrients.

Flavor is the final rule of five: balanced across the palate on the sweet, salty, sour, bitter, and savory spots of the tongue.

The meal was a vision in itself, once again served in colorful small bowls and plates.

Sitting side by side, Kaito and Bob savored and analyzed each dish. They began with a miso-style soup, as delicious as the broth at breakfast. This was followed by steamed rice, pickled radish, vegetable tempura, hijiki seaweed, tofu with shoyu and a dab of wasabi, seaweed with cucumber, snow peas, pumpkin, daikon, a bowl of soba noodles and broth. As a refreshing finish, a juicy orange was cut into sections.

Water and the ubiquitous hot tea were on every table.

That night before he went to sleep, Kaito studied a schedule of the classes and meditation groups and prepared to begin his new regimen in the morning.

As he drifted off, he felt as though he had just fallen head over heels in love. This time in Koyasan was to be his ongoing muse and he would be back. But for longer. This he already knew.

He thought of Buddha's words. *There is no path to happiness, happiness is the path.* For the first time in a long time, he felt excited and at the same time content. It seemed he was rediscovering the meaning of being happy.

CHAPTER 25

*J*ust one week into Kaito's newfound happiness, his
bliss was shattered as information filtered through
from new arrivals that a fierce hurricane was due
to strike Hawaii.

There had been some talk of an impending storm before
they left on their trip, but Kaito had been so busy with preparations to leave that he had not paid a lot of attention. Serious
hurricanes had not hit Hawaii for decades and he assumed this
one would miss the islands too.

He and Bob shared their fear at hearing about events
unfolding from so far away. The monks told them of a tearoom
in town that had a television set up in the window for the
general public. The two men interrupted their daily schedules
to walk over and see the latest news.

"Just my luck!" Kaito exclaimed. "The first time I leave Hana
… and not just go around the corner … all hell breaks loose! Do
you think the gods are trying to tell me something?"

"I'm thankful we can at least get an update at this place," Bob
said as they hurried up the street. "All of a sudden, there's a real-
ization of how cut off we can be when something like this

happens. Never really thought much about it. I'm glad Gail is away too and our kids are at university on the mainland."

Lost in thought, Kaito mumbled, "Mmmhmm." He was thinking of Hana's safety and hoped Auntie and her husband had battened down the house sufficiently. He felt certain they had. He had to assume that Kiana's family had prepared for the storm in Kauai.

As he gathered his thoughts, he apologized for being distracted. "Sorry. I'm trying to sort through this logically. The bottom line is that we are here and basically helpless. It's a disturbing sensation, but I'm glad my phone call went through."

The night before, Kaito had joined a long line of people at the Visitor Center where emergency telephone calls could be placed. Once his call went through, Auntie assured him her husband had prepared the house with hurricane shutters. She reported that thousands of people on Oahu were being evacuated to public shelters, but Kaito's house was on a high enough elevation and in a well-protected setting. She and her husband would stay at the house with Hana.

"We are praying to Paka'a, our God of Wind, to keep everyone safe," she said.

There was nothing more anyone could do but hope and pray.

THE NEXT DAY, on September 11, Category-4 Hurricane Iniki struck the Hawaiian Islands. The name meant "strong and piercing wind," which well described the worst hurricane to ever hit the islands. The damage left behind was profound.

Oahu managed to escape the worst of it, with moderate storm surge and wind damage. Kauai was a disaster.

With power and communication lines destroyed, there was great frustration and fear, with no way of contacting loved ones.

Kaito awoke after a restless night, desperate for news. He and Bob rushed to a café to see what news was available. Television reports were few, as all power was down in Hawaii. Newspaper headlines in town offered no more details and the photos simply increased his concern. In his heart and head he felt Hana would be safe. But what of Kiana and Kailani on Kauai? Reports of the destruction there were dismal.

The men's first reactions were to return home immediately, but there was simply no flight for a number of days.

"And really, what can we do right now?" Bob said. "But we need to know your wife and our homes have survived unscathed."

Kaito focused all meditation and prayer on the gods to speed the recovery.

To everyone's surprise that day, it was announced that one of the monks was a ham radio operator and he was able to bring some news to the guests. He also was working on connecting with the Red Cross. The organization had established lists for missing people and some comfort was gained as the day went on when no names requested by Kaito and Bob were on them.

Still unable to contact anyone directly, it was not easy to clear his mind of the guilt he was feeling at having left Hana at this time.

Finally a telegram was delivered to him at his shukubo. His chest tightened as he opened it, filled with concern. Then he breathed a long sigh of relief as he read Auntie's words that they were all safe, had food, and the house was fine. She had also checked about Bob's house. There was no need to come back now.

Kaito was filled with gratitude as he lit some incense and gave thanks for this Hawaiian angel in his life.

His remaining days were busy with classes, meditation, and long, challenging hikes. At the end of the two weeks, he left to fly back home. He had been told he would have to be prepared for cancellations and might be stuck in a hotel near the Tokyo airport for a day or two. The cleanup on Honolulu was moving slowly.

Bob left at the same time to meet up with his wife in Bali for a few days. They had canceled their tour of Cambodia and Vietnam and were going back to Honolulu to volunteer to help in whatever way they could.

The news reported it would take months to clear up the debris of trees and damage to gardens and parks. Food distribution was requiring ongoing organization, as power still had not been reestablished. Everything was hampered by the lack of electricity.

AS THE PLANE flew low over the islands, Kaito was shocked to see that miles into the ocean from the shoreline the water looked reddish brown. The pilot advised they were seeing the results of volcanic sediment washed down from the hills.

The amount of debris and destruction Kaito saw from the taxi on his way to his house stunned him. The storm surge had littered the usually pristine Waikiki Beach with all manner of flotsam and jetsam, palm fronds and pieces of surfboards that had blown in from along the coast, which crews were busy raking and collecting.

As the car pulled into his driveway, he could see piles of branches from shrubs and trees that had already been collected and were waiting for pickup. Someone had been hard at work to tidy things for his arrival.

Auntie was at the door to greet him.

"Welcome back! You missed all the excitement ... and I must say it was something else! I have to admit there were long hours of frightening conditions—moaning winds and torrents of rain you can't imagine! But as you know we were fortunate. The gods were with us. Kauai got the worst of it, sadly."

Kaito half expected Hana to come to the door, but she was nowhere to be seen. He looked around expectantly.

"Hana is asleep now," Auntie said, noting his concern. "And she pretty much slept through the storm. I don't know how because that wind was a-howling! The studio windows were covered with hurricane shutters so it was off limits. But she did come outside to rake the yard with us afterward, much to our surprise."

"Did she even notice I was gone?" he asked, almost tentatively.

Auntie gave him a very direct look before she answered. "I made a decision not to tell you this while you were gone. I did not want anything to ruin your time away. Hana was fine ... but she did notice you were not here. Twice she became anxious and asked where you were. I told her you were on a business trip and would be home in a few days. This seemed to satisfy her and everything was as it usually is. She has been immersed in her sewing, as usual."

Kaito nodded, as much to himself as to Auntie. "You did the right thing. Thank you for taking such excellent care of everything."

Kaito was surprised by the small satisfaction he felt in knowing that Hana might have missed him. He realized that somehow, somewhere deep inside him, he had been hoping for some indication of this. If there had been no awareness of whether he was there or not, he wondered if he might have questioned how he was living his life. That thought had most definitely been on his mind during the flight home.

If his caring presence was somehow important to Hana's well-being, that justified the sacrifices he made the rest of the year.

~

FROM THAT FIRST trip to Koyasan, Kaito vowed September would be blocked off for Japan. It took him no time at all to realize that he wanted to stay for a month. The days had flown by and when it was suddenly time to return to Hawaii, he had felt he was just getting settled. He knew there was so much more to see and do and to be accomplished within himself. For as much spiritual peace as he was able to achieve with his meditation at home and at the temple, there was no comparison to the internal strength he felt he gained from his time away. Added to that was the pleasure of being in this completely different environment to explore and expand his mind.

From this one experience he realized it would not be his last, and the effect his absence had on Hana cemented this in his mind. If she was only mildly aware of his being away, his guilt was definitely relieved.

Kaito paced and worried for a week about Kiana and Kailani as communications were still down between the islands. The Red Cross had set up a center in Honolulu where people could go to obtain information about all the islands. He checked there constantly but did not find their names on any lists. His mind was not at rest until a note arrived in his mailbox from Kiana assuring him they were safe. Their west end of Kauai had been spared the worst of the storm, but she was heartbroken at the massive destruction she had seen everywhere else.

The more he contemplated his time in Koyasan, the more he came to the conclusion that he had six weeks' vacation from work, the total of which he never took each year, so going for that month would not be a problem.

He knew Bob might be there for part of future visits but not always. Kaito was not bothered by that in the least. It actually suited him to think he would be on his own.

CHAPTER 26

1998

ate works in mysterious ways that are often difficult to understand or accept. Through six years after the hurricane, the mailbox correspondence with Kiana continued. Each time Kaito opened the flap and discovered a new note, his entire being felt flushed with relief and with love. He would put the paper to his face and try to breathe in something of Kiana's being. She had held the paper in her hands and he willed that sense of her to come through his fingers.

Around the time of Kailani's birthday, a photo would be included and Kaito felt bittersweet emotions as Kiana described her as a happy, spirited little girl. The hole in his heart grew with each passing year with his desire to be reunited with Kiana … and now a granddaughter too. He had gone to Kauai several times and driven around, hoping a stroke of luck would bring him a glimpse of them. Difficult as it was, he respected her admonitions to not contact her in any way but their mailbox exchange.

As he began to prepare for his sixth visit to Koyasan, Kaito received gut-wrenching news, once again delivered by his friend, now Chief of Police, Mitch Alika.

Kaito knew Mitch had long been removed from direct involvement in Kiana's case. He was now in charge of the entire police force for Oahu, but never stopped checking for new developments.

Mitch bowed low to Kaito after he was invited into the house. His eyes were filled with sorrow as he said, "Aloha, Kaito. I'm so sorry that I am the bearer of bad news once again … all these years later."

Kaito took in a sharp breath. What now? What could be worse than had already happened?

Mitch continued, his voice somber. "There was a crash of a seaplane yesterday in which Kiana and her husband were the only passengers. I regret to say that Kiana was killed."

Once again Kaito's tattered heart broke into pieces. He steeled himself to keep control now. But his mind immediately carried him back to the first time Kiana came into his life and the light and love she brought to him.

How could this happen? Why?

His *keiki*. His little child. The startling impact of the moment he first held her in his arms had never left him. The unconditional love he had felt looking into her eyes, knowing she had brought an entirely new understanding of the word "love" to him.

He treasured a wealth of happy memories from Kiana's childhood in spite of the rupture Hana's illness had caused in their family, driving Kiana away. That part had left him with inconsolable heartache and regret.

He had never recovered from the pain of losing her physical presence when she ran off with Jake, but at least they still had a connection. Now even that was gone. He gripped his chest to stop his heart from being ripped out and reached to the wall to steady himself.

Mitch looked at him with alarm and put his hand on Kaito's

shoulder as he continued, "Are you going to be okay? Should I call an ambulance?"

Kaito shook his head. "No, no. I will be okay."

"I wish it were otherwise," Mitch continued. "I am so, so very sorry. The pilot was also killed. Jake survived. He was arrested in the hospital and will be placed on trial for a long list of charges."

They spoke briefly before Mitch left, nothing of which Kaito would recall later. In a state of shock, he struggled to find words that made any sense.

As he did whenever he was attempting to process bad news, Kaito went into the garden. He crumpled onto the bench near the play area he and Kiana had created so many years before. Memories rolled gently over him, as he wiped tears away with the backs of his hands.

She had been twenty-six on her last birthday, but in his mind she remained a little girl full of sweetness and energy.

They had spent so many happy times in that spot and some of those times had even included Hana. He closed his eyes and could picture Kiana swinging and going down the slide, climbing up into the playhouse and waving merrily out one of the windows. He could hear her sweet laughter and her little footsteps running toward him to leap up and throw her arms around his neck. Even as a teenager, she would swing on the bigger swing he had made. He recalled how she refused to let him take down the parts she had long outgrown.

"No, papa," she had implored. "We need to save those for the grandchildren."

Kaito groaned out loud at that thought. His tears fell more freely until there was an uncontrollable flood of them along with a guttural roar. Then he wept as he had never before.

His daughter was dead. Gone. Forever.

Through the painful times where he had sought solace in this garden, never had he felt pain this intense.

There was no reason to stop his weeping, even if he could.

So much of those happy dreams had never and now would never come true.

Auntie hurried into the garden, asking how she could help. But all he could do was shake his head and wave her away.

KAITO'S NINE-YEAR-OLD GRANDDAUGHTER, Kailani, was left homeless. Social services contacted him to advise of the situation. The little girl had been placed in temporary care until all options were explored.

Jake was sent to prison for his role as the head of a widespread narcotics ring. He would be incarcerated for years.

Kaito was torn. He would have loved nothing more than to have Kailani come to live with them. However, with Hana's condition, he knew there was no way this would even be considered. And although it hurt to admit, he understood. As much as he loved the idea of family, it seemed that was something fate did not have in store for him.

He was impassive as the woman from social services advised that Kailani had gone to live with Hana's cousin, Sara, in Oregon. This request had come directly from legal documents Kiana and Jake had drawn up after Kailani was born.

Kaito had always been in contact with Sara, although fleetingly. When he made the offer now, she declined to have him pay for his granddaughter's expenses. She advised him that Jake had a trust fund set up for his daughter and she felt it best if Kaito had little involvement in Kailani's life with her. She did not hold anything against Kaito. She understood his pain. But she did not want Kailani to suffer any of the poison Hana might spew. Hana also had inflicted deep wounds in her relationship with her cousin.

CHIEF OF POLICE Mitch Alika kept Kaito abreast of news about Jake, including the date he had been sentenced and entered prison.

A few days after that, Kaito received a jarring phone call from the lawyer who had handled Jake's case. In a solemn voice he explained that Jake had requested Kaito be called to see if he would take care of Kiana's ashes.

"I am sorry to call you about this and realize it is a highly sensitive topic," the lawyer began. "Mr. Akana asked if you would consider taking ownership of your late daughter's ashes. He knows you do not wish to have any contact with him. Since he will be in prison, he wanted to be certain his late wife's ashes would be respected."

Kaito found himself speechless at first. His throat constricted with emotion. He managed to agree and the lawyer said that he personally would deliver the urn to Kaito's home that evening at whatever time was convenient.

At 9 p.m., a somber middle-aged man in a gray business suit was at Kaito's door with a simple white box. Kaito had requested that time, knowing Hana would be asleep by then.

"Thank you, Mr. Tanaka. May I express my sincere condolences," the man said as Kaito opened the door.

Kaito murmured a response and bowed to the man.

"PLEASE COME IN," Kaito said, his voice quiet and soft.

The man respectfully waited for Kaito to reach for the box.

"I am Thomas Armstrong, and if there is anything I can do to help, please let me know."

Unable to find his voice, Kaito nodded wordlessly and reached for the box with trembling hands.

The lawyer lowered his hands, whispered "I am so sorry," and backed out the door.

Kaito quickly shut the door and felt as though he might faint. He could not have imagined the impact of holding the remains of his beloved Kiana.

Putting the box on the hall table, he lifted out a light green polished marble urn. The beauty of it brought a lump to his throat. It was just right for Kiana. She would have approved, he thought. He carried it out to the garden and set it amidst the orchids she had so carefully cultivated.

There was a heaviness in his chest as he pulled a chair over and sat looking at this last physical connection to his daughter. After the ten years she had been away from him, all that he could envision of her … her long legs, her beautiful face and bright smile, her shiny black hair … all of it was in that vessel. He felt tears building and knew he did not have the strength to fight them. Nor should he. Memory after memory flooded his mind and he closed his eyes allowing them to play out as hot tears covered his cheeks.

This was part of his life … sorrow, pain, loss, sadness … and he would deal with it as he did with everything else. He had to. He could.

And tomorrow he would get up and see what the new day brought.

CHAPTER 27

onths of isolated torment within himself followed. In reflection, much later, he would recognize that it was the steadfast friendship of Bob and Gail and the blessing of Auntie in his home every day that kept him sane. And the teachings of Buddha.

And his ability to *gaman*, taught since he was a toddler. Persevere. Be patient, accept the situation and see it through. *Shikata ga nai*—it can't be helped. Built into the Japanese psyche.

Kaito lived a quiet, resigned life inside his home. His role continued to become more of a caregiver, but his love was steadfast. He would always be her protector. Buddha taught that love is kindness. Unselfish love is freeing and leads to nirvana. Kaito believed this was part of what kept him going.

Certainly this was a love with little reciprocity. There was not the conventional relationship of husband and wife. But they were married to each other and he had vowed to love her in sickness and in health. As much as he could he tried to help Hana have the best life she could manage.

His meditation strengthened his soul. His work, martial arts studio, photography, and garden remained his sanctuaries. Auntie made certain, after a respectful time, that she filled each day with laughter and song, as she successfully encouraged Hana's sewing business. Although Hana remained out of contact with customers, her artistic embroidery increasingly became prized and there was an endless stream of requests for her work.

The shop in Honolulu had advised Auntie that they were receiving even more requests from Japan for Hana's obi belts.

Gail made a gentle suggestion to Kaito to go through his photos and create a collage of family images he had taken since he and Hana were teenagers. He included photos of their parents and also Lailani and Brett. Then he focused on the life he and Hana and Kiana had built together.

In her wisdom, Gail knew very well that few sad memories are recorded in photos.

There were moments of melancholy … and sorrow. Kaito searched for fragments of the happiness he knew had been there. He desperately wanted to reclaim those memories. Surely his life should not be all about pain and loss.

He could not turn back time but he could move forward. He would.

Kaito worked his way through the years and had photos mounted or framed. The project became a source of healing. He tried to involve Hana as much as possible. At times together they planned how some of the images would be displayed on the long hallway wall.

He was perplexed that she did not react negatively to images of Kiana. There were few words said about those but Hana seemed content to include them. Kaito had to rein in his anger at Hana in some of those instances, filled with frustration at how life might have been different for all of them. *How could she show no feeling?*

In those moments he would put a stop to the project for a time.

He discovered his patience had a limit. And so did his heart.

AS THE YEARS PASSED, one slim but strong thread to the memory of his Kiana was the long-distance relationship that Kaito maintained with his granddaughter, Kailani. He was thankful that Hana's cousin, Sara, kept in touch with him from the day Kailani had gone to live with her family.

Through occasional letters and phone calls she let him know that Kailani was happy and doing well.

He never stopped sending his granddaughter a birthday card each year, which included a short letter and fifty dollars. He knew that Sara had a hand in young Kailani sending him brief thank-you notes. When Kailani became a teenager, she began to reply with polite, well-written letters giving him small windows into her life.

For her sixteenth birthday she received a phone and they began having occasional video conversations. Hana wanted no involvement with any of that, which saddened but did not surprise Kaito. With her continuing to grow less communicative, these moments connecting with Kailani took on great importance in filling some holes in Kaito's heart.

When Kailani was ready to begin university, with Sara's encouragement, she had agreed to accept Kaito's offer to pay her tuition. Even though she explained that the trust fund, set up by her parents when she was born, more than covered the costs.

"My sweet Kailani, this is one small way I might begin to make up for my absence in your life and that of your mother. I hope you will forgive me in time."

It warmed Kaito's heart to feel this connection with Kailani. From everything he could see, she was a fine young woman who was studying to be a nurse. He knew Kiana would be proud of her daughter.

CHAPTER 28

2010

*S*ince that first trip to Japan with Bob, Kaito's now annual trip to Koyasan was his saving grace.

The month of September each year became a major focus, second only to Hana's well-being. His immersion in the study of Buddhism and meditation offered by the monks was what he needed to recharge. Sometimes Bob was there for part of his visit but not always. Kaito was so accustomed to solitude and not socializing widely that it suited him to be on his own.

After eighteen years of making the trip, he was now a seasoned traveler within the limited boundaries of Hawaii to Japan and back. He had acquired a level of confidence that made the voyage easy and enjoyable.

On a previous trip when Bob had also been there, they rented a car at the airport a day before their departure home and drove to the fishing village where Kaito's family had lived before they left for Hawaii.

On this drive, the two friends got into a philosophical conversation about childhood memories. Feeling the connection to his past, Kaito was compelled to explain to Bob how *gaman* was an integral part of being Japanese.

Listening thoughtfully, Bob eventually said, "I've always admired your positive approach to life in spite of so many challenges you've faced. Now I understand." He paused before blowing out a long, frustrated sigh. "My culture could benefit from a similar approach."

Kaito assured Bob he had no expectations. "I'm not even certain why I decided to return to this village. No family lives here now from my side or from Hana's. I've never really harbored any desire to connect with these roots since my last visit with my parents when I was twelve. But for some reason, this time I felt like doing it."

They drove through dense oak and cedar forests and suddenly passed a golf course carved into the picturesque countryside. Kaito laughed. "Ah yes! Even here!"

The surroundings changed as they neared the coast. Groves of bamboo lined the roadway, with towering green stalks swaying gracefully in the breeze. Soon the vista opened up beyond terraced rice paddies to an endless expanse of glistening sea, studded with unusual rock formations. Kaito felt a melancholic wash of memories come over him as he inhaled the briny sea air.

But those memories faded quickly, mainly because they were those of a ten-year-old.

Now the harbors were filled not only with fishing boats as Kaito remembered, but also with pleasure craft. In postwar Japan, as recovery progressed through more than six decades, an entirely new beach culture laid claim to the sparkling clear waters of his childhood. Simple villages had been transformed by the addition of apartment buildings, warehouses, hotels, restaurants, and shops.

He turned off the highway and searched along a coastal road for his village. Bob took over driving so Kaito could watch for familiar places. But it was to no avail; the streets he recalled appeared to have been swallowed by progress and the beach was now a popular surfing destination.

Disappointed but not surprised, Kaito suggested they stop for lunch at a cluster of old wooden fishermen's stilted houses that were now cafés and shops.

"At the very least, we will have the freshest seafood possible," Bob said with a chuckle.

Kaito nodded. "That, for certain, is something that has not changed through the years. I'm going to order sardines and see if they make them as delicious as my mother did."

The sardines were good, but not like his mom's.

On the drive back to the airport hotel, Kaito and Bob's conversation reflected on their pasts.

"I guess Thomas Wolfe was right when he wrote, 'You can't go home again,'" Kaito said.

"I wouldn't know where to call home from my early days," Bob said. He spoke of how his military family moved constantly and how he never felt he belonged anywhere.

He described how once he met Gail at university on the mainland and fell in love, his life finally had consistency. She had grown up in Honolulu. They moved there a few years after they married and never left except to travel. Every year they took a trip, even if it was just to the mainland.

Kaito's story was the opposite. Apart from leaving Japan, Honolulu had been his home. Period. As his life with Hana became complicated by her illness, he had never desired to go anywhere until his trips began to Koyasan.

"Interesting how our circumstances direct us to make such opposite decisions about our lives," Kaito said. "Now I'm beginning to wonder about what I've missed. And Hana too. I wonder if travel might have helped her. She never wanted to even discuss it and I simply acquiesced."

~

THIS TIME KAITO made the decision to visit Tokyo. Communicating solely in Japanese came easily again and despite the population being around twelve million, he did not panic at the crowd sizes this time. However, the sheer numbers and frenetic pace of the city didn't appeal to him.

He stayed in a modern, well-located hotel and walked to many of the places he wanted to visit in the three days he planned to be there. He had studied tourist guides and had an organized plan to follow. The subway system was impressive and took him wherever he needed that was too far to walk. But exploring on foot was his first choice, despite the endless crowds and bustle that surrounded him.

Bob's advice had been invaluable.

"Here's what I recommend for a quickie trip. The first thing you absolutely have to experience is the Shibuya Crossing."

Kaito had laughed. "I've seen videos of that. Do I really need to actually go there? It's just a big shopping district with the biggest mob of people I've ever seen all crossing the street in different directions at the same time!"

"True that!" Bob replied. "And yes, you need to do it." He explained that it's the intersection of seven roads and on a signal, everyone crosses at once. "There may be hundreds or even thousands of people and it's unbelievable that it works. But it does."

Kaito shook his head. "If you say so."

"Everyone goes to see it," Bob said. "And you will want to take photos. There are two coffee shops that have elevated views where you can go and grab some incredible visuals. It's hypnotic and crazy, man!"

And Bob had been absolutely right. Kaito thought the experience was a buzz and enjoyed the opportunity to take photos there. He spent the rest of his time in the city visiting shrines and museums and eating at the endless selection of excellent restaurants. From snacks to sushi to more involved meals at

Michelin-star restaurants, the trip had been a gustatory delight.

But Kaito also felt Tokyo had morphed into a jungle of concrete and wires, with masses of neon and blaring loud-speakers that he found offensive. Even so, Tokyo had seemed surprisingly safe as he wandered and every person with whom he came in contact was unfailingly polite and helpful.

After being almost completely bombed out by the end of WWII, there were few historic sections of the city left, and he found most of the newly built areas modern and flashy. What did appeal to him were the many beautiful gardens, parks, and open spaces throughout. He noted there were no trash containers visible and the city was extremely clean. In the subway he was impressed with blackboards where people could leave messages for others if their train was late or plans changed or just whatever. People communicated.

Tokyo was a city that gave him the sense people cared about each other in spite of the size. The courtesy and kindness of every person he interacted with made him feel proud of his heritage.

He was glad to have visited.

ON SOME OTHER TRIPS, Kaito had visited Kyoto for a few days to experience the opposite side of Japan from Tokyo, in a bigger way than Koyasan. Often referred to as the "storehouse of Japan's traditional culture," the population was under one million and one could wander the town in a very relaxed way by foot or bicycle.

There were so many spectacular shrines, temples, and gardens that Kaito realized on his first visit there that he would be back. The three-hour bus ride made it an easy day trip.

But in his heart, it was still Koyasan that called him back.

The small town and ease of access to hiking trails as well as the basic familiarity that he experienced each year upon his return were incomparable. His sense of well-being, spiritual and physical, was renewed with each visit.

Kaito returned home from each trip feeling more enlightened and with the determination he knew he needed to face the months ahead. Every year he seemed to reach a new level of understanding with his meditation. In some ways he felt he was redefining the man he wanted to be and becoming that.

There was no question in his mind that this was his greatest tool in achieving patience with Hana and reminding him of the duty and commitment he felt for her, as broken as she was. He had long ago recognized this did not encompass all the same feelings of love as when they married. But it still was love. "In sickness and in health," he often reminded himself. His wife needed him and he would not forsake her.

Certainly his physical desire for her had long ago ceased. But the tenderness and devotion to his promise to love and protect her remained in place.

It amazed him how quickly a year could pass with the promise of a return to Koyasan dangling in front of him.

CHAPTER 29

SEPTEMBER 2010

*I*t all began with a walk on which Kaito planned to take some particular photos. In the two weeks he had already been at the temple, he had been waiting for just the right weather, light, and time of day to capture specific images.

That morning felt right.

At the beginning of the two-kilometer cobblestone path through the sacred Okunoin cemetery he stopped at the Ichino-hashi Bridge. As usual, he joined monks and pilgrims who were washing their hands and mouths before entering the "pure land," or paradise. After that ritual, he bowed before he walked over the bridge along the path leading into the towering forest of ancient cedar trees.

From time to time, the plaintive cry of a turtledove resonated from deep within. Its doleful sound seemed to leave a lament hanging in the air.

After all his years coming here, Kaito still was deeply touched by the solemn beauty of the setting and the haunting atmosphere of the timeworn, mossy tombstones.

Kaito knew he could only take photos on the first half of the walk. After that, it was forbidden, out of respect. In his efficient way, he had notes from previous trips of the particular tomb-stones he wanted to focus on today using the specific light now available.

As he walked along, Kaito stopped to admire a state-of-the-art tripod and camera set up by the path. A new lightweight zoom lens that had recently come on the market grabbed his attention. The petite woman preparing to take photos smiled and nodded as she acknowledged his compliments about her equipment.

"Please excuse me for interrupting you, but how do you like the results you're getting with that lens?" he asked. "I've been considering getting one."

When the woman began to answer, Kaito moved closer. He peered intently at her, jolted by what he perceived.

Those eyes.

For a moment he felt faint and began to perspire. A knot formed in his gut.

How can this possibly be? I am seeing a ghost.

He thought about turning and leaving immediately but his feet were rooted to the spot.

The woman was staring back at him with a look of annoy-ance at his seeming rudeness.

Before he could stop himself, he blurted, "I beg your pardon. You remind me of someone I knew many years ago."

He noticed the woman's eyes flicker with shock before she looked away. She began to pick up her tripod and equipment quickly, preparing to leave.

His words tumbled out. "Did you ever live in Hawaii? I am Kaito Tanaka from Honolulu." His eyes were wide and his mouth agape. He felt out of control, and stupid for his outburst.

The woman looked nervously away and abruptly turned her back to him. She continued packing up her equipment.

Without turning to him, she replied in a voice that was tight and definitely not encouraging. "You are mistaken. I do not know anyone in Honolulu."

Her stiff body language left no doubt that she considered the conversation over.

Kaito bowed politely and backed away, feeling foolish and embarrassed. "Of course, please pardon my poor manners."

As he continued along the path, Kaito tried to collect himself. It was unlike him to be so forthright, but that meeting had been uncanny. The woman resembled his close friend Lailani, who, along with her mother, had died in Honolulu decades earlier in a terrible car accident.

He, Hana, and Kiana had attended her funeral.

For a moment he thought he might be ill.

What sort of tricks is my mind playing on me? How could I have thought such a thing?

Sadness filled his heart as he recalled Lailani now.

Twenty-two years. A lifetime. That's how long ago it was. My mind must be slipping to think I saw her just now!

He sat on the first bench he came to and tried to settle himself. He couldn't stop thinking about Lialani as memories came rushing back.

He hadn't realized how important she was to him until she was gone. As Hana had sunk more and more into the depths of her mental illness, Lailani had offered so much to them. She had filled an enormous void in Kiana's life, as a mentor and friend. And at times a disciplinarian, knowing just the right words to say.

She had been the sweetness in Kaito's life next to Kiana, that offset the sadness—and sometimes bitterness—of Hana. She reminded him to laugh and to take care of himself. She had been a true friend in every way.

When the car accident happened, it had been horrifying and shocking to think something like that could happen to not just one but two people he knew, Lailani and her mother.

He shuddered. Too many horrible flashbacks now had been triggered. The ground felt unsteady under his feet.

Those few years had been the worst of his life, since they also included the time Kiana ran off and Hana insisted they consider their daughter dead too.

He remembered now how he had worked to put his life back into some sort of balance. Deep inside he knew then it would never be the life he wanted. But he also knew it was the life he had been handed and it was up to him to come to terms with it. So he had done his best. *Shikata ga nai.*

He got up and walked a little further, thinking perhaps he would forget the photography for today. But then he reminded himself that the light was just what he had been waiting for. He had learned long before that, as Henri Cartier-Bresson said, "Photography is an immediate reaction." He knew he did not want to miss this light.

Stopping, he leaned against the trunk of one of the enormous ancient trees. He closed his eyes as he rubbed his hand across his hair. He knew there was no way to fight the memories pushing their way into his thoughts. He would just give himself permission to let them happen until he felt a semblance of calm again.

CHAPTER 30

*T*he roughness of the bark was unpleasant as Kaito let the ancient cedar hold him up. It even jabbed through the vest he wore over his shirt. It pricked his skin and made him itch. Discomfort poked him back to the present. The flashbacks evaporated.

The resemblance of that woman to Lailani continued to haunt him. She had the same dark curly hair, although now streaked with silver. She was the same height, although slimmer. But it was her eyes ... that face ...

He berated his mind for playing ghoulish tricks on him.

Walking further along the path, he passed familiar yellow signs warning about the presence of bears. Never having seen one in the ten years he'd been visiting Koyasan, he was more curious than concerned.

Several viewpoints along the way offered opportunities for taking pictures. He'd stopped at them all in the preceding years. This time he had a particular area in mind and reached it after walking another ten minutes.

He began to feel he had pulled himself together, thanks partly to breathing in the intoxicating fragrance of the cedar forest, which energized his senses. He pushed the incident with the woman from his thoughts and set up his equipment.

His hands, slightly disfigured by arthritis, made it difficult at times to steady his camera. Kaito carefully set up his new Nikon on the lightweight travel tripod he unfolded.

Never a man to fixate on possessions, he did love this camera. He still had his trusty old Canon that had served him well for a very long time, but it had become heavy as his hands became less nimble. Finally he had succumbed and was thrilled with his decision. He had treated himself. Possibly for the first time ever.

He focused on a series of three ancient grave markers that he had captured many times before. After reviewing his photo files, Kaito knew he was trying for a specific shot. It had to be timed for precisely when shadows were beginning to fall across these distinctly ornate markers in a particular way as the light filtered through the trees. Such attention to detail pleased his artistic sense.

Now he studied the subtle values and textures of the handsomely carved markers, considering how to also capture the intricate, weathered inscriptions. Visualizing the image he sought, he considered the stones, the light, the shadows, and the background details that he would fade into a soft blur by adjusting the depth of field with his lens setting.

The creative process of capturing an image filled him with satisfaction. He took care positioning the camera, knowing that an inch here or there could dramatically affect the result he sought. He allowed his eye to rove and experiment and he gave thanks to the ancient souls that surrounded him here. Surely those spirits were guiding him.

From studying the work of Ansel Adams, he had come to believe in the term "intuitive rightness", signifying the moment to release the shutter. It had become visceral to him. He often thought he should apply that to how he lived his life in general.

But he knew he didn't. As he grew older he struggled with accepting that through all his years he often had not listened to his intuition. Instead he had shut out the rightness of his decisions and let the scientific part of his brain make the analytic choice. He wondered if he would have been happier in life if he had listened to his gut for everything and not just in his photography.

And wasn't that his intuition, his gut, that had caused him to speak to that woman? What was that all about?

He pushed the thought aside again and pressed the shutter.

A frisson of excitement shot through him, as it always did when he knew he had captured the desired image he was tracking. The sound of his shutter echoed in the mist-shrouded forest.

Kaito stood aside after taking a number of shots. Straightening his back, he stretched and blew out a long breath. He was pleased with how he had timed the setup of this shoot. He knew he had been right about the light and congratulated himself for going ahead with it even when he had felt like quitting just a while ago.

"Hmm!" he murmured. Intuitive rightness, he thought to himself.

"Kaito?" A quiet voice spoke behind him.

Startled, he turned to see the woman he had addressed earlier along the path.

"Yes," he replied, but feeling his mind was playing tricks on him.

She paused before speaking again.

Kaito was confused by what he thought he had heard. He peered at her.

Her expression seemed sorrowful. Almost apologetic.

The woman bowed slightly to him. Kaito returned the bow politely, but baffled.

Her voice was soft and hesitant, wavering in an almost

fearful fashion. "You are right. We do know each other. I am Lailani," she said, looking deep into his eyes. "I am stunned to see you."

Kaito remained motionless. His heart palpitated and a vein in his neck throbbed. He thought he might pass out.

This cannot be.

His breath caught as he stared at her. She held his gaze.

The intensity of the moment hung in the air.

His mind worked to process what his eyes and ears were seeing and hearing.

"Lailani," he repeated. "Lailani." His voice no more than a whisper. "*Hoaloha* ... dear friend ... this is unbelievable."

Nodding, the woman stared back at him. Then they bowed to each other once more, a long, slow bow. When they straightened up, tears poured from Lailani's dark shining eyes, running down her cheeks.

Kaito's eyes glistened. His entire body trembled with shock.

And then they were locked in an embrace, sobbing.

Shock, fear, disbelief rushed through Kaito. He stepped back, holding the woman by her shoulders to peer at her face and then enveloping her in his arms once again.

She clung to him with the same intensity. Their arms wrapped around each other in an embrace that was loving and tender. An embrace between two people who knew each other well.

Slowly, they gained control.

Kaito took the woman's hand and guided her to a nearby bench. Sitting beside each other, he pulled a handkerchief from his pocket and handed it to her while he wiped his face with his hands.

He sighed a very deep sigh, looking straight ahead, while she dabbed at her eyes.

After a moment, he stammered. "You ... you and Ulani ... you died ... how can this be you?"

"But we didn't …," Lailani murmured through her tears. "It was all a lie."

Kaito shook his head, dazed. "Unbelievable. Somehow the spirits have made this happen. I thought … everyone thinks … " He felt confused, nauseous, as his questions spilled out. "But how can this be? We went to your funeral! Why …? What …?"

"I know. Everyone thinks Mama and I died in that car accident."

"There was a touching memorial service for you both. It was a terrible shock to the community … especially to Hana … and Kiana … to me … everyone who knew you and your mother."

Lailani's eyes searched his face before she spoke again. She clasped her hands together nervously. "I can only imagine. It was a shock to us to have to steal away as we did."

"But how did you? And why?"

Lailani gulped and took a moment to compose herself.

"The police planned it all. It happened in the blink of an eye and we were gone. That was the worst for me, really … not being able to talk to anyone from the past. To Kiana, to you. We felt terrible leaving Honolulu without a word. We were frightened, Mama and me. Terrified. We were ordered to say nothing. To accept we could not contact anyone … ever."

"Where did you go? Why did you go? What happened? The accident?"

"That's just it. There was no accident. I need to tell you everything and I will. Let's go somewhere to talk."

Kaito packed up his equipment. His heart was pounding and his mind racing. Everything felt surreal.

Lailani waited on the bench. Her shoulders were hunched and a pained expression was etched on her face.

"But first, please tell me. How is Hana?"

Kaito sat beside her again. "Not good. She has never gotten better. Only worse. And now her medications keep her in a docile state."

195

Lailani's face crumpled as silent tears covered her cheeks. When she finally spoke, her voice was tinged with sorrow. "I never stopped praying that she would get better. That someone would find the key to her illness. I loved her so dearly."

Kaito nodded solemnly. "And she loved you. You were sisters. You were *ohana*. But she continued in a gradual slide to be less communicative and now is showing signs of dementia."

"Oh Kaito, what a load you have carried all these years. My heart goes out to you."

"My heart has been broken for her for many years," he murmured.

Lailani nodded. "You always were a man of honor and compassion. And Kiana? That delightful girl. The apple of your eye."

Before Kaito could answer, she said, almost as an apology, "I've never forgotten that sixteenth-birthday fiasco. It's one of those horrible memories you want to erase and cannot."

Kaito swallowed hard and looked down. "That was a fiasco, all right. Sweet Kiana's story is such a tragedy." His words came tersely as he shared the details.

Lailani's voice was choked. "I'm so sorry. Oh Kaito ..."

They sat in silence for a moment.

The woman's voice was soft and low. "Life can be so cruel. I can't imagine the grief of losing a child."

Kaito's words came haltingly, his pain evident. "Accepting her absence in my life when she ran off was painful enough." He cleared his throat. "It was almost as if she had died then, but always, there was still a flicker of hope in me ..."

Lailani put her hand on his arm. "Please, you don't have to relive that if it is too difficult."

Kaito looked at her, knowing the truth of who she was and how she had loved Kiana.

He continued. "I want to tell you. I have not spoken about it like this to anyone. But you knew her ... you loved her ... and how she loved you."

"She was a daughter to me," the woman whispered, her eyes filled with tears. "I loved how she never stopped calling me Lanilani, from the time she was a toddler. So sweet."

Kaito continued Kiana's story to its end. "When she died in the airplane accident, I experienced the true cut of grief."

He uttered a low groan.

"Grief is a double-edged sword. It makes you vividly aware of your loss while your reality confronts you day after day," Lailani said softly, indicating she spoke from experience.

The memories made him feel weak. Color drained from his face. "You are supposed to want to go on," he said. "To care for those you love who are left behind. But I honestly didn't want to care for Hana or anyone else at that point. My commitment to her insisted I do so. But I had so much resentment and anger, I struggled relentlessly for some time. And then she refused to even acknowledge our granddaughter. That is when I truly turned to Buddhism to survive. I had to find something in which to deeply believe. And I became more immersed in aikido."

No more than a whisper now, Lailani's words came hesitantly and apologetically, "That causes me great sadness. I remember you as quiet and strong, but quick to smile and be pleased by life. I recall you owning the K&K Studio and spending happy hours there with Kiana."

Kaito closed his eyes briefly. Lailani's voice was as he remembered: sweet and caring. His heart raced now as feelings buried under years of rubble attempted to stir. This desire to communicate was so unfamiliar and yet so strong. He felt a sense of trust that he recognized from long ago. He had missed this kind of friendship.

"Pleasure and peace come to me through the teachings of Buddha, and the simple interests that have filled my life: my photography, my aikido, my bonsai and nature. As much of a recluse as Hana has become, so have I within my own world."

They spoke for a while about the progression of Hana's condition and how it had taken years for a diagnosis.

"And even now, there is doubt. As time goes by and more research and studies are available, specialists keep going between borderline personality disorder and bipolar illness. The doctors have never been exactly certain."

Kaito grew silent and stared ahead.

Lailani looked downcast. "I often wondered what happened after we were whisked away. But what of her amazing embroidery? She was so talented."

Kaito smiled. "That is the one positive in her sad story. She creates the most beautiful obi that sell amazingly well."

"Obi!" Lailani exclaimed. "What an excellent way to use her skills. I remember how effortlessly she could stitch the most intricate details."

He told her about Auntie and how she was the glue that held their home together.

"Not only is she a caregiver and housekeeper, she also organizes Hana's sewing projects with another woman, which has resulted in Hana obsessively creating for years. She spends long hours in her sewing studio, which overlooks the garden, and that is where her heart lies. I don't know what she would do without it. Or what I would do, for that matter."

"I feel in shock hearing all this," Lailani said, her voice breaking as her eyes glistened. "But I am happy to know that Hana continued with the gift handed down to her through so many generations."

She pulled her woolen jacket tightly around her and did up the zipper. It was becoming cool so deep in the dense forest with the sun's rays barely breaking through.

"Let's go to a teahouse, if you have time. There is much to talk about."

The stern lines of Kaito's face softened with affection and he smiled. "Of course, I will make time—are you kidding? I would like to know what has happened to you—to this ghost I have stumbled upon—during the past." He paused suddenly, struck by the reality of what was happening.

"Twenty-two years, Kaito. Twenty-two years."

They stood staring at each other for a moment. Then suddenly they were in each other's strong embrace again, sobbing and incredulous.

CHAPTER 31

*F*inally they stepped apart.

Kaito's handkerchief was of absolutely no use now. Tissues wiped away tears as the long-lost friends both fought for control of the eruption of emotion they had just shared.

Kaito packed up his camera equipment and noted that Lailani carried hers in a similar type of backpack. They chuckled as he pointed it out.

"You know, you were the reason I became interested in this hobby," she said. "You helped me choose all my equipment back in the day. Is it any wonder I would still be psychically guided by your choices all these years later?"

They walked to a nearby *kissaten* on the main street that served coffee as well as black or green tea. These were recent contemporary additions to the town, Kaito explained, offering an alternative to the traditional tearoom with its ancient tea ceremony rituals.

Lailani pointed to a table in a quiet corner, although the place was almost empty. "It looks like we might have some privacy here. I have a feeling I'll be shedding more tears."

"I would like green tea, please," Kaito said, placing his order. "Lailani, what would you like? His voice remained shaky and his face was still filled with wonder.

"In truth," Lailani sighed, "I would give anything for a double espresso. But I know I'm not going to find that here."

Kaito raised his eyebrows questioningly. "You sound like a committed coffee person."

"Once I tell you that I've spent the past eighteen years living in France, that should not surprise you," she said.

Kaito could not help staring at this woman, this ghost from the past, and shaking his head in wonder. "I'm ... I'm ... remembering you always did love the Kona coffee from the Big Island."

Lailani smiled. "Your memory has not failed you. It was a thrill to recently discover I could order that coffee on the internet. How the world has become a different place since we last saw each other."

"I'm waiting," Kaito implored. "Tell me this mystery you have been living, the story of your world."

Lailani began to relate what had transpired in her life since the last time they'd seen each other in Honolulu, all those decades ago. He listened in disbelief.

She lowered her voice and in hushed tones reminded him of the shocking case of a serial killer strangling three women over a period of two years. The police had arrested a man, and Lailani correctly identified him out of a lineup.

She paused to sip her coffee.

Kaito said, "I recall all of that and can picture us sitting in the garden as you told me you had to identify the man and the terrible things that followed. It was distressing and frightening. You stayed at a hotel and then went to Maui, to your aunt. You had sent Ulani there."

Lailani nodded, "An enormous task force was set up. The FBI were involved. It was all over the national news."

"Right," Kaito said, as Lailani's words triggered the return of buried memories. "Kiana was still at home." He paused, caught in the past. "We were driving back from the grocery story early one evening. The police had set up a roadblock. They stopped us and I had to show ID I had to prove I was her father. Now I remember!"

"I began to receive weird, frightening phone calls and I felt like I was being stalked. One morning I found our sweet poodle, Sugar, dead on our doorstep."

"So long ago ... but I remember you told me that and nothing afterward," Kaito said.

"I was terrified and the police warned me not to speak of what was happening. They gave me protection and tried to set traps—like that roadblock you were in—to catch him, but nothing worked. Or so they said."

Kaito's eyes widened. "You think they weren't on the level?"

"Here's what I know now," Lailani said, raising her eyebrows. She looked at him matter-of-factly. "He was connected to the Wong family, who ran the biggest crime syndicate in the Islands, which also had connections on the mainland with the Mafia. The cops were never going to arrest him."

Kaito's eyes widened.

Barely taking a breath, Lailani continued. "Then my mother's car was set on fire in our driveway. That was the last straw. The only option I was offered was a chance to leave Hawaii with a new identity. They whisked us off the next morning."

Lailani paused again as her entire face twisted with regret and sadness. "You can't imagine how terrified we were, how agonizing it was to completely walk away from everything and everyone in our lives, especially you, Hana, and Kiana—my extended family. Years have softened the experience but telling you about it now is bringing back the trepidation we felt. We were in shock for some time."

Kaito reached out and put his hand over hers, without giving it a second thought. It was something he would have done in the past. Almost a reflex action.

Lailani gripped it tightly.

As she continued speaking, Kaito registered one horrified expression after another while Lailani disclosed the reality of what they had experienced.

"And you couldn't tell me! I feel terrible about all this! And your mother? How was she coping?"

"Of course they sent both of us off. All we had was each other. We were both scared stiff every day. It was no way to live. So we left on a private FBI plane, just like in the movies. Before dawn, with new names, new passports, a driver's license for me, private health insurance for us both, and enough money to allow us to live—frugally, I might add. They didn't want me to work as a nurse. It was too identifying."

Kaito exhaled a long breath. "Are you talking about the Witness Protection Plan?"

"Exactly. What choice did we have?"

Kaito shook his head. His voice was sympathetic as he struggled to process what he was hearing. "So where did you go?"

"For the first few years we lived in Tokyo. Mama requested that at first; she thought it would be a good fit culturally. But she was not happy there and the pollution made her asthma very bad. I went back to school and studied languages for something to do. I thought I might be a good translator, as languages always came easily to me."

She blew out a long sigh, before her voice tightened with tension. "But my biggest problem—and it was enormous—was that every time I turned around I thought I saw the guy coming for me. I couldn't get past it. I was constantly looking over my shoulder."

"That must have been very hard to live with, along with leaving everything from your past behind. More than your past, actually. You had to abandon your heritage."

Her face became ashen. Ghosts of buried traumas seemed to return. "My poor mama was even more involved with her ancestry. I was so lucky to have her with me or I might have gone crazy. But you know how I was, Kaito. Never actually such a candidate in that regard."

Kaito shook his head. "Never. You brought sunshine into our home every time you entered. You were such an optimist, so happy with your life."

"I was." As she spoke, color returned to her cheeks with each good memory. "I loved nursing. I loved our beautiful flower-filled islands with their velvet-covered hills and endless beaches. I loved my friends and most of all you three. Even after Brett died in Vietnam, my life was full, thanks to you. And once grief and I learned how to coexist."

Kaito bowed his head, lowering his eyes. "Yes, Brett. That was horrible—"

"Yes, it was. I was heartbroken. But, as we know, life goes on. Your family became my family. You and Kiana were a big part of that happiness. And Hana, on her good days. I have memories of such good times with her, my chosen sister. Even as she deteriorated there was satisfaction in knowing I was able to help her in small ways."

Kaito looked off into space, remembering. "We were all so close. You saved us many times, Lailani. You truly did."

They sat quietly for a few moments. A slideshow of memories played in Kaito's head. Happy and sad memories etched forever that he, Hana, Kiana, and Lailani had made together.

Lailani was the first to speak again. "When the murders started happening in Honolulu—that bastard. He killed those women, and for a while I felt like he murdered me, too."

Lailani finished her coffee and ordered another. Kaito still had some tea in his pot and encouraged her to continue.

She looked down at the table for a moment, tapping her

fingers nervously. "I hope you take what I'm going to say the right way."

"Try me."

"I knew I couldn't live in an Asian country. I had to get away from men who looked like that guy. That killer."

Kaito squinted as he pursed his lips and nodded, looking deeply into her eyes. "I understand. I hope I'm not scaring you."

Lailani's expression softened. A smile returned and her demeanor became more relaxed.

"No, dear Kaito. You would never scare me."

"That's a relief," he said, and they both chuckled. Kaito felt some of the tension of the past few moments of conversation dissipate. "I just realized how hard it must have been just now for you to relive that terrifying time and the challenges that followed. Do you want to stop talking about it now?"

Lailani shook her head. "No! Not at all. It actually is a relief to be able to speak to someone ... to you ... about it."

"It's so hard to digest all of this and to understand how you coped. I feel sadness and anger all mixed in together. Yet I have to admit I'm fascinated by it all."

"It's pretty confusing, isn't it? And a shock to you to hear all this for the first time. It's really just part of my life now, and a distant part in many ways because, as you will see, I've had the chance to live again in the most unexpected way."

"So where did you go? And how?"

"As I mentioned, I'd been taking language courses in Tokyo and fell in love with French. My mother was resigned to our life on the run. She was never anything less than sweet to me. Imagine."

"I remember her as a kind, affectionate woman with an easy laugh. Is she still alive?"

Lailani held up her hand, signaling she would answer that question later.

"Mama was an avid reader and she got into the books about

France I was assigned while I was taking my French classes: Molière, Balzac, Hugo, Fitzgerald, Hemingway. After she read M. F. K. Fisher's books about the South of France, she became obsessed. It was kind of fun, especially coming from a very traditional Hawaiian background. We began to share a fantasy and talk about it all the time.

"I saw no reason not to go there. The Protection Program supported our request. We were moved to a tiny *village perché*."

"A what?"

"Oh, Kaito, a perched village. It's a stunning little town, a medieval cluster of buildings hanging precariously from a rocky hilltop. It's on the Grande Corniche roadway above Monaco and the views are panoramic and spectacular. It was like a dream to us."

"I've seen splendid photography and read about the South of France," Kaito said. "Never been there. Never been anywhere out of our islands except here every September. So keep going. What happened to you after you moved there?"

"I attended classes at an excellent language school in a magical town called Villefranche-sur-Mer. There actually was bus service right into that village so I didn't have to drive the crazy roads to get there. I did eventually get used to driving around, though."

"What did the other people in the village think? Did they question you?"

"The French have a great capacity for privacy. We got to know each other slowly. More through observed behavior than information. One day we realized we'd become accepted as part of the village community when neighbors began dropping off vegetables and fruit from their *potagers*—everyone had a little garden—and eggs from their chickens. Life is simple there."

Kaito was fascinated. "Did you ever slip?"

"Our new identity said we were of Filipino heritage, but we never elaborated."

"And never let down your guard?"

"Never. Except with my husband."

Kaito looked at her with surprise.

"Yes, I married a wonderful Frenchman, Dominique Carpentier, and I have his two children, his sons—we never used the 'step' part—and an adorable grandson, Jacques." Her eyes lit up as her voice caressed the name of her grandson, and she continued with a smile. "Dom was a widower, a bit older. I finally had a family and a full life when I was forty. Mama was beside herself with happiness, and so was I."

Then a veil of sadness slipped across her face. "Dom passed away three years ago. An unexpected and sudden heart attack."

"I'm so sorry," Kaito said.

Lailani nodded. "We had a lovely life. I miss him very much. My mother passed away just a few months later. It was a difficult year."

CHAPTER 32

"*lors*, enough about me. Back to you, Kaito. Tell me more about Hana's condition. I remember the last time I saw her as clearly as yesterday. She had been raging on and off for months, after she exploded over Kiana's sixteenth-birthday plans. Nothing we tried seemed to work on the bad days. On this particular day, you asked me to come over while you waited for the doctor to make a house call. You wanted to be able to speak privately with him."

Kaito sighed. "You know, I remember that day too because it was the first time that the doctor prescribed stronger medication for her. It was a turning point, but not necessarily in a good way."

"Meaning?"

"Medication always was the treatment of choice for Hana's behavior. No one was getting to the root of the cause. So if she took her meds, things were calm for a while. If she decided not to take them, for whatever reason, all hell broke loose or she sank into deep depression."

Lailani reached over and patted Kaito's hand. "I'm so sorry to know that things did not get better."

"You know how troubled Hana was. Because no one was able to truly diagnose her condition; there was always confusion. We struggled along and she became angrier and increasingly bitter. Kiana meant everything to me and Hana resented that. You know very well how she was always mean to our daughter."

"Of course, I saw that. No wonder Kiana ran off. I recall Hana's rages and all that tension. Kiana gave as good as she got when she was a teenager."

Kaito nodded. His voice cracked as he told her, "When she left she wrote that life would be better at home for me if she went away."

His eyes welled and glistened. "She had no demons. She was good and kind and wanted the best for me, and for herself. She always sounded happy, and I learned later that she was also a very loving mother. Did I tell you her daughter was named Kailani—after me ... and you."

Lailani was completely taken aback by that information. She swallowed back tears and took his hand. "Oh Kaito. That is almost too much for me to bear."

Lailani's touch brought back an instant sense of intimacy that held the love and trust of the friendship they had shared for so long.

Kaito bowed his head. "It was an emotional bombshell when she wrote me that. Such a tribute to us both—and made me realize how much she missed us and treasured the memories."

"I'm glad you have those loving memories of her," Lailani murmured. "And I'm grateful you have given those memories to me now too."

He paused, as if considering his next words carefully. "I missed you ... we all missed you. Hana was bereft—and angry—that you had died. But she never spoke of you again. It was bottled inside. Something to add to her fury." He looked away, seeming to regret his words.

Lailani looked at the ground. "I'm sorry," she whispered.

"You were the only friend who never abandoned Hana. It was amazing how she would listen to you and you could talk her down from some of her episodes. Kiana looked to you for friendship and even, to some extent, mothering. You were a vital part of our dysfunctional family."

Tears flowed down Lailani's cheeks again. "And then I was gone. I abandoned her too."

This time her shoulders shook as she hunched forward.

Kaito turned to her. It had been more years than he cared to remember since he had put his arms in comfort around anyone but Hana. He felt it would be the right thing to do again now, but could only reach out and pat his friend's forearm, lest they both break down again.

"There, there," he said. "This is all so much in the past. I'm sorry I caused you to feel so sad."

Her speech was labored between sobs. "Seeing you here. Speaking of all this … makes the pain feel real. Today. It has been buried a long time. As much as I was grateful Mama and I were safe, I often was angry about having to leave everything and everyone."

"Lailani, Lailani. Buddha says, do not dwell in the past, do not dream of the future, concentrate the mind on the present moment. So let us do that now. We both have experienced so much pain. Yet anger solves nothing. We need to find a way to forgive all that has happened and move on."

She nodded as she wiped the tears from her face. "That truly is the only way. 'Forgiveness is not an occasional act. It is a constant attitude.' I remind myself of this often. Thank you, Martin Luther King."

"So true," Kaito said. "I have learned that forgiveness is everything."

Lailani took a deep breath. "Twenty-two years of catching up with each other. Heavy stuff! I must tell you, it seems strange to hear you call me Lailani. I have been known as Céleste ever since we moved to France." She pronounced her name with a distinctly French accent.

"Céleste ... Carpentier," Kaito repeated.

"From the beginning in Japan, I made a conscious effort to move away from every vestige of my Hawaiian life. Although Mama didn't speak of our heritage, she kept it close to her heart. There was one sentence she would always say to me. *Ma'ane'i no ke aloha.*"

Kaito smiled as he repeated the words. "*Ma'ane'i no ke aloha.* Love is here and now."

Céleste continued her explanation. "There were lonely days when those words lifted my heart. After the adjustment and then disappointment of Tokyo, Mama loved our life in France and for the most part, she was always a happy person. She had one final request that her ashes be returned to Hawaii at some point. They currently sit in a marble urn on my mantel."

"Then, Céleste it shall be from this moment on!" Kaito exclaimed. "At least I will try my best. It won't be easy, this is all so bizarre. Now tell me what you are doing here. How on earth is it possible that we were both on that path this morning?"

CHAPTER 33

*K*aito ordered more tea and Lailani switched to water. There was so much more to say, they agreed.

Lailani shook her head at his last question and gave him the most perplexed look. "How indeed?"

Kaito said, "Even Buddhism cannot explain synchronicity. We like to think we are in control of our lives, but here is the perfect example of how one random incident turns our lives upside down. Let's not look for an explanation and just accept what has happened. Our friendship has survived."

Kaito could see his friend relax as her voice filled with lightness.

"So here is my reason for being in Koyasan. Photography is a hobby I shared with Dom. If you recall, Kaito, it was you who first encouraged my interest back in high school. Remember taking all those photos when we hiked with Hana? She sketched. You and I were busy with the cameras."

Kaito smiled at the distant memories and nodded.

"I didn't keep up with the hobby when we were first relocated. But Dom was avid about it and he rekindled my interest.

We traveled Europe with our cameras, since Asia was mentally off limits to me. He was a baker and worked long hours running our *boulangerie*—sorry, our bakery—every day except for three weeks in August each year. Then our children would go to camp for two weeks and he and I would travel. The last week we saved for family time."

"So, if Asia was off limits to you, what are you doing here?"

"Koyasan was a place that intrigued Dom, but he knew I would never come. After he died, I thought about it more and more. Kind of a challenge to moving my life forward, conquering demons and all that. I decided to come on my own."

"That's brave of you. But doesn't surprise me. You never were one to duck a challenge."

Céleste stared intently into Kaito's eyes. "We are getting old. Who knows how much time we will have? Some people get old and stop taking on challenges. They miss opportunities ... and are okay with that. I know many who make that choice. I want to keep living. To keep exploring possibilities."

"You always were an inspiration. I've lived such an insular life for so long, I never think of stepping outside of the box."

"Then what are you doing here? If I may be so bold as to ask."

Kaito was silent for a long moment. "Coming here the first time was an enormous step. I will never forget the date of that trip. It was when the big hurricane hit Hawaii – 1992. Hana was barely communicating, but on the other hand her embroidery work had never been better. I felt she was in a safe place. To help myself deal with the hours of solitude, I began to study the teaching of Buddha more intently. A friend at the temple recommended this was a place where I might grow in under-standing. I was struggling with my own sanity in a way. So I came for two weeks. I knew Hana would be fine with Auntie. Those two weeks were the beginning of my salvation. The more I learned from the monks, the more peace I found within myself that strengthened the resolve I always had to stay with Hana. Since then I have returned every September for the entire month."

"What do you do while you are here?"

"At first, I was committed to simply staying at the temple and immersing myself in the monks' program of meditation, studying teachings, learning sutra copying. Then I began to take longer hikes in the area for part of the time and focus on my photography as well."

"And Hana remains at home?"

"I made a promise to myself that she would stay in our home as long as it is possible to care for her properly. I continue working as an engineer and I still own the martial arts studio, so my income can provide good care. For twenty-two years—since we lost you, as I mentioned, Auntie takes care of everything. Hana is quite passive now and spends all her days ... and many evenings ... sewing. Medications have dulled her desire for everything else unless she goes off them. Then it can be trouble. She is still able to rage! Her physical health is reasonably good although I'm told her heart is weakening."

He paused. A sorrowful expression clouded his face and his voice stilled. Then he said softly, "Our beautiful Hana is a sad shadow of the woman she was, trapped in her body."

Céleste's eyes welled with tears. "What a sorrowful portrait you paint. And you, Kaito, do you feel trapped as well?"

Startled by her directness, Kaito knew this was a thought he had ignored throughout the years. His pulse quickened. The question brought back to him how closely connected this friend had been in his early life. From anyone else it would have seemed invasive, but from her, it felt caring; something that was glaringly missing in his life.

"I don't ask myself that. I have built my own life within my soul. I meditate. I read and have my photography. I raise bonsai. I build and repair paper lanterns for the memorial lantern celebration. I study the teachings of Buddha and reflect on them as I meditate daily. I practice aikido, which focuses on unifying the soul as well as keeping fit. Buddha would have liked it." His last comment was accompanied by a wry smile.

Céleste looked at him with a sympathetic expression. "It sounds like you keep yourself occupied. And alone."

"Are you staying at a temple?" Kaito asked, clearly changing the subject as a look of pain flashed across his face. It did not go unnoticed by Céleste and hurt her heart.

"No, I'm at a small guesthouse at the end of the bus line, next to the entrance to the Shinto cemetery. I've been there for five days and I return to France the day after tomorrow. I spent a few days in Tokyo and Hiroshima before I came up here. I decided I needed to see some of the things I missed when Mama and I lived in Japan. In truth, perhaps I was banishing some bad memories as well."

"Would you like to join me for the shojin ryori at my temple this evening? They prepare it better than anywhere else. Trust me, I've sampled a few through the years."

Kaito knew the question was rhetorical. There was absolutely no way he was going to let her refuse.

"Well, I honestly don't know what that is, but whatever they're serving, I'll have it if it means spending more time with you. We have many years to catch up on, Kaito." Her eyes and voice transmitted a soulfulness that only comes from a deep connection and familiarity with someone. "Seeing you here is like discovering a long-lost treasure."

"I am still in disbelief," he agreed, feeling a long-forgotten eagerness for the honest intimacy of such a close friend. He felt overwhelmed to suddenly have this missing piece of his life restored. "I will take the bus and collect you at six p.m."

Céleste smiled, remembering his old-school manners from decades before. "It's not necessary, Kaito, but thank you for the offer. I'll walk into town and meet you where you suggest. I like to walk whenever possible."

They stood on the street outside the coffee house and Kaito bowed low as he said, his voice filled with emotion, "I am stunned ... and happy that this incredible coincidence has occurred. Truly, it is miraculous! Let's meet here again at 5:45 and I will escort you into my temple. Aloha."

Céleste spontaneously leaned in and gave him a light kiss on each cheek. A shy smile lit her face and her eyes sparkled with the zest for life Kaito remembered she possessed. "I feel the same. I'm not even going to try and make sense of how or why this happened. I will see you later. À tout à l'heure."

As Kaito walked back to his shukubo, thoughts swirled through his head and at times he felt almost nauseous. To suddenly discover alive his dearest friend that he thought—no, make that knew—was dead, was almost beyond comprehension. How could it be? And yet, there it was. He felt joy mixed with disbelief and hoped meditation would help him find some balance in his thoughts before he and Lailani ... Céleste ... met for dinner.

CHAPTER 34

𝒦aito and Céleste knelt on cushions at the low table along with eight other diners in the austerely lit room paneled in rice paper.

As soon as they were settled, Céleste reached for Kaito's hand. "I have to keep touching you to convince myself you are really here ... that we are really here together. I think I'm in shock, Kaito. I'm confused. I'm happy and sad and completely discombobulated. Honestly!"

He felt her eyes searching his and sensed her need for some sort of understanding and confirmation that he was experiencing the same.

"We are *ohana*," she said.

"*Ohana*, my *kika*, my sister," Kaito said. "I happen to know that's the new slang."

Robed monks padded about in white socks, silently moving through the room, delivering a tray of colorful dishes to every person. Each contained small amounts of different foods.

As they sampled the varied offerings, Kaito explained the food. "*Shojin* means continuous purification and *ryori* means cuisine, in particular vegetarian cuisine. Monks meditate at the temple throughout the day, even as they prepare the meals. To them, meals are not for enjoyment or for satisfying hunger, but for sustaining their health so they can continue to live in purity, devoid of sin."

"Well, I have never been into meditating but I appreciate their efforts because this food is delicious. It's bringing back memories of our years in Tokyo," Céleste commented, grinning and handling her chopsticks with expertise. "Food was the best part. I'm not anything close to a vegetarian, but everything here is scrumptious."

Kaito grinned. "I've learned the approach here is that it's not about being a vegetarian just to be one. It's really more about the state of mind you achieve."

Céleste's comments made him laugh as they tried to identify the flavors. Bitter, sour, sweet, salty, mild, and hot were amongst the red, white, black, green, and yellow colors.

"The monks suggest we think about what we're eating and where the food comes from. The food as well as its preparation is supposed to put you in tune with Buddha's teaching. Not only does the food make you *feel* better, but it also makes you think."

"In France we call that *le plaisir*. It has a different sense when you say it in French," Céleste told him. "That's one of many lessons I've learned in the country I now call home."

"I'm so curious about your life in France," Kaito said. "What a dramatic change after Honolulu."

"We couldn't have chosen better. And, in fact, I've lived there so long at this point, it really does feel like home," she said. "It's funny how things work out sometimes … like now … meeting you again." Her expression became serious and her voice was tinged with fear. Her eyes held him with a piercing stare.

"Please, Kaito, don't say a word to anyone about meeting me. I've never had to worry about it before. The one instruction I was given from the very start was never to admit my identity to anyone."

Kaito sensed her anxiety. It jolted him into realizing exactly what Lailani and her mother had given up for their safety—everything in their lives except each other. He wondered how his response could even begin to express the admiration but also sympathy he felt for what they had faced.

"Don't worry. You know you can trust me. I won't even mention it to Hana. There would be no point anyway. But I don't want to lose touch with you. It wouldn't be right."

"I would never have responded to anyone else who approached me. You can't imagine the shock of seeing you—that's not even the right word. It was something out of body. I knew it was you immediately. And for you to be here, and for us to be brought together—it was meant to be. Pure synchronicity. Serendipity. *Un heureux hasard.* I believe that, as bizarre as it seems."

Their eyes met, captured in a cloud of nostalgia.

Kaito blinked rapidly and looked away. He didn't know what he believed. It was so hard to process how she had literally returned from the dead. A family member he had loved and buried was now sitting across from him.

"You aren't in Koyasan because you are Buddhist," he said. "Am I right?"

"No. Although I like a lot of the Zen philosophy, I follow nothing in particular except to live the best life I can. I'm here for the photography and I guess to tie up some loose ends in my life. If this had not been on the list Dom and I made ... we called it our Wish List, not Bucket List ..." Her voice trailed off as her mouth twisted, battling with emotion.

Kaito waited, feeling awkward and helpless as he watched the struggle on his friend's face. He also knew emotion like this. The pain of loss. But for even more reasons. His emotions about grief were not only about the loss of happy times and loving people, but also about living without those things for so much of his life. About being denied.

"I'm sorry," Céleste apologized after collecting herself. "I still tend to lose control at times. I miss Dominique very much. We had such a happy life together …"

"Never apologize for grieving that. I envy you that kind of marriage and I'm so glad to know you experienced it. I'm sorry for your loss."

Céleste nodded her gratitude.

"In fact," he continued, "I'd like to stay in touch. Is that possible? How would we do that? Since you're here for another day, let's see each other again and try to figure it out."

"I agree. It feels as though I've been given an amazing gift finding you." She stopped speaking and stared at him in silence for a moment. "They serve a delicious curry where I'm staying. Since we both have commitments during the day tomorrow, please come and have dinner with me." Then she added, almost bashfully, "If you'd like …"

Kaito's heart jumped at her reply. How could he not want to spend more time with her? And how could they ever let go of their friendship again?

THE NEXT DAY Kaito committed himself to a full retreat of silence and meditation. He moved as though in a dream and had a multitude of thoughts to process, including shock.

Gradually, his stream of jumbled thoughts became untangled and a sense of inner peace prevailed. He felt calm and welcomed the anticipation he felt, almost like old times, at going to meet Lailani.

During dinner that evening, he began to relax and feel almost social.

In the presence of Lailani, he was reminded of his much younger self and a time when he felt optimism about life in spite of the challenges he was facing with Hana. A time when he thought he knew who he was and not the lost soul whose mind and body he had long inhabited after he lost Kiana as well as Lailani.

The two spoke of fate and how their lives had changed dramatically, in such divergent ways. Lailani's path had been determined entirely by forces outside of her control and beyond the sphere of her ordinary life.

"I mean, really, a serial killer?" she said. "The Witness Protection Program? Changing my name, my world, and living with secrets? It sounds like a detective movie."

They smiled ruefully at each other before she continued. "Thank goodness for Mama. What she never abandoned about her Hawaiian heritage were the principles of life passed through the centuries by the Kahunas. She always lived by those ancient beliefs."

Kaito nodded. "Unwrap your mind. Live in the now. It's much like Buddhism."

"Those are words Mama often repeated to me as I struggled to find purpose in my life again or worried about what would happen to us. She would tell me that when I lived in the past or the future, I was missing out on the peace of the present."

Over the course of their two evenings together, their former bond comfortably reestablished itself. Memories were revived. Kaito was not surprised how pleased he was to feel their connection as it had always been. The years of absence seemed to melt away.

After dinner, they strolled through the quiet streets, back to Céleste's lodging. Their conversation was punctuated with easy laughter.

Abruptly, Céleste stopped at one corner and offered a most unexpected suggestion. "Kaito-san, come to France to visit me and meet my family. You have plenty of time. Why not?"

Never one to do anything spontaneously, Kaito was taken aback. He had never been impulsive. He had walked along the straight and narrow path of his relatively set routine for so long, it would never have occurred to him to suddenly make such a decision.

Céleste, in her good-natured way, continued to offer a convincing argument. Kaito uttered concerns about how it might look to her family or friends to have a married man stay with her.

At first, Céleste thought he was joking. "Kaito, we are family. Such old friends! And besides that, it is 2010! Nobody even thinks about those old standards anymore!"

In many ways Kaito knew he was still stuck in old-fashioned thinking—no matter how good friends they were.

"Okay, there is a cozy two-star auberge just down the street. But I am certain my son and his family will insist that you be their guest, if you won't be mine."

"And how will you explain me to your family? I don't want this to cause any problems with the story they already know."

She smiled and raised her eyebrows in a comical gesture. "Remember, I have become adept at creating believable histories. I propose to say you are a very dear childhood friend from the Philippines who has lived in Hawaii for a long time."

Kaito nodded. "That sounds plausible."

"And," she continued, "we can describe our surprising story of discovering each other in Koyasan ... which is absolutely true ... and a fantastic coincidence I would like to share with my family. What do you think? Please come!"

Try as he might, Kaito could find no reason she would accept to decline her invitation. He was not changing his arrival date back home. And now, in the world of cell phones, Auntie could reach him wherever he was. The twinge of guilt he was feeling about going to France began to subside. "I need to start living for me in some small ways," he mused.

Surprising himself, he eventually agreed.

Céleste threw her arms around him, unable to contain her excitement. "Magnifique! You won't be sorry, I promise!"

Kaito returned her hug and grinned. "You always did drive a hard bargain, my friend!"

The next day Kaito awoke with a sense of permission to be happy about his decision—and he changed his plane ticket.

After completing his ten days of meditation he would fly from Tokyo to Paris and then down to Nice.

His old friend would be waiting at the airport.

Kaito felt a surge of unfamiliar emotion—joy.

CHAPTER 35

2010

The overnight flight from Tokyo to Paris was a long twelve hours and Kaito was glad he slept for most of it. Then he had a two-hour layover at Charles De Gaulle airport before catching the one hour and twenty minute flight to Nice.

Lailani had reminded him to book his seat for the Nice flight on the right side of the plane.

"You will have magnificent views all along the coast from Italy to Nice once the plane reaches the Mediterranean! Have your camera ready."

Kaito made a mental note to thank her for that.

The dramatic approach to Nice International Airport provided a spectacular view of the Côte d'Azur. The copilot offered a commentary on the scene out the airplane windows, pointing out towns from the Italian border, past Monaco, and along the coast, set against the backdrop of foothills that eventually climbed to the majestic Maritime Alps.

From his window seat, Kaito captured image after image as his shutter worked nonstop. There were brightly colored sails bobbing in the sparkling sea amidst yachts of all sizes. The biggest of those he would have sworn were passenger ships but knew they were not, from what Lailani had described to him. On shore, apart from the sprawl he identified as Monaco and Nice, red-tiled roofs of clusters of villages were sprinkled over the hills. The hills appeared to rise up in verdant layers to jagged mountain peaks that looked surprisingly close to the coast.

The runway itself, jutting out into the Mediterranean, brought a hint of the landing back home in Hawaii. The glistening azure and turquoise shades of the sea were as brilliant as the oceans of his Islands, he thought. But that was as close as the comparison went.

As they taxied to the terminal, Kaito took a few minutes to gather his thoughts and reconnect with the calm he had achieved at Koyasan during the previous ten days. He hoped his decision to visit Lailani at her home in France had not been too impulsive. Or improper.

He was concerned about how her French family would react to this ghost from her past or how she would explain how he fit into her life. After all, they only knew the false narrative that she had been living and not the truth about her life.

He would spend ten days in the South of France, if it was a comfortable situation for everyone involved. Deep inside he hoped it would be.

After that he would return to Honolulu and Hana, and wait patiently for the next September. His annual escape might bring even more promise into his life.

After landing, any sense of familiarity vanished the moment he walked through the arrival doors into the terminal.

There were no orchid leis draped over necks or fragrant frangipani perfuming the air. Rather, the sound of French, Russian, Italian, and English voices created a cacophony around him. For a moment it was difficult to know exactly in what country the plane had touched down.

Céleste waved to him from their arranged meeting place at a

front table in the Bonne Maison café, near the rental car office. A demure black and white French bulldog sat at her feet.

Kaito had a repeat moment of wonderment that Lailani was there. Alive.

They approached each other rather awkwardly and almost bumped heads as Kaito began to bow towards her and she instinctively leaned in to greet him with the standard French *bise*—an air-kiss to each cheek.

Laughing, they both stepped back and greeted each other with a bow.

"I'm sorry, Kaito, but you will have to get used to the French *bise*. It's such a part of our culture."

"I will try my best," he promised.

"And I would like you to meet my best friend, Bébé!" She said, picking up the dog, whose tiny bit of a tail wagged furiously.

Kaito reached out to pet her and was greeted with a gentle nuzzle of her velvety nose.

"She's my constant companion," Céleste said. "I hope you don't mind her hanging out with us."

Kaito grinned and shook his head. "I'm delighted."

KAITO WAS spellbound as Céleste drove him along the breathtakingly scenic routes of the Riviera and up into the steep switchbacks that led to her perched village. He was accustomed to stunning panoramic vistas in Hawaii, but these were in another category. Ancient villages clung to rocky hilltops and Roman ruins dotted the landscape. History came alive.

Like so many who visit that part of the world, Kaito was captivated. His camera shutter continued to click incessantly.

"I'm sorry to be so rude, Lailani—er, Céleste. Do you mind if I keep taking photos?"

Céleste laughed, explaining everyone had the same reaction when they visited for the first time. "Enjoy being a tourist!"

As they drove along, she pointed out walking paths that were visible throughout the hilly landscape. "You will discover that France has an amazing system of *sentiers*, our hiking paths. Thousands of miles of them all well marked and maintained to a high standard. It's part of our religion!"

He was impressed as she described the three categories of long paths, regional paths, and local paths.

"You can pick up trail maps at any *tabac*—newsstand—in any village. And then off you go! A broken-in pair of hiking boots can be found in any French person's closet."

She suggested to Kaito that they explore a few of these paths during his visit, if he would like. He nodded vigorously.

"*Bonne idée!*" he said.

Céleste swiveled her head with a look of surprise.

"I've been practicing," Kaito said with a chuckle. "But that's about as far as I've gotten with Duolingo."

As they rounded a corner, Kaito suddenly exclaimed out loud as a massive and majestic monument, partly in ruin, sat poised on a hilltop overlooking a large cluster of red-tiled rooftops.

"What is that?" he gasped.

Céleste had known exactly what would happen when she turned the corner and was already exiting onto a side road to stop.

"That is our pride and joy ... La Trophée des Alpes! Also called the Trophy of Augustus, as it was commissioned by the Roman Emperor Augustus in 6 BC to celebrate the victory of the Romans over a number of tribes in the area. This was an important trade route linking Rome to the South of France and continuing west to Spain and north to Gaul. It was built with limestone from nearby quarries."

"Wow! That is impressive! It's huge!"

"And it is only a small part that remains from the original massive monument. Needless to say, various rulers throughout the centuries had parts dismantled. Some of the stones were used to build houses in the village. There's an excellent museum in the village with all sorts of history, a replica of the original and schematics that I will take you to visit. And that town is La Turbie, where we live."

Then she gestured to Kaito to look down and take in the breathtaking panorama below where the principality of Monaco and the coastline to Italy in the east along the Mediterranean lay before them.

He was spellbound by the views, the history, the obvious love Lailani exuded for her adopted homeland. He felt awe and excitement and anticipation for what was to come.

"How do you get used to living in such spectacular surroundings?" Kaito asked.

"The same way you get used to the stunning settings all around you in Hawaii," she replied with a smile. "We start to take them for granted, *n'est-ce pas?*"

Kaito chuckled at the ease with which Céleste slipped in and out of her English/French personas. "You have a point."

After excusing herself and making a quick phone call, Céleste continued to relate more history of the town as she navigated narrow streets and stopped in a parking lot.

"As you might imagine, having a private garage here is practically unheard of. But we are just a short walk to the house."

As soon as she stopped the car, Bébé's head popped up from where she had been sleeping in the back seat.

"She always knows when we are home," Céleste said with a chuckle. "I could pull in somewhere else and she would not wake up."

A tall, muscular young man and a small boy appeared to be waiting for them.

Kaito was introduced to Céleste's eldest son, Martin, the town baker, and her grandson, three-year-old, Jacques, who had a mischievous look about him. When Kaito bowed out of habit, Jacques was quick to bow back with a grin. They had come down to welcome him.

Céleste explained that Martin and his wife, Danielle, would join them for dinner, but he had to return to the boulangerie soon to prepare the afternoon baguette mix for the ovens. "You will see how our days begin and end with a perfect baguette," she teased. "Bakeries are the heart and soul of French life."

As they walked under a vine-covered arch and up a narrow cobbled street, she described how this part of the village dated from medieval times. Kaito could feel the history surround him. He was also amazed that Bébé simply trotted along, unleashed, with them .

In answer to a question from Martin, Céleste explained to Kaito that they would drop his bags off at the auberge she had mentioned, just down the street from the home she had shared with Dominique. "But Martin wants you to know you would be welcome to stay with him and his family."

Kaito's face flushed with embarrassment as he nodded his gratitude but explained it would be best to stay on his own.

"I wish I could explain properly in your language," he said to them.

Martin smiled and nodded his understanding as Céleste said, "Absolutely not a problem. I had already explained to him. You will enjoy being a guest here. The owner, Jake, and his wife, Annie, are charming and go out of their way to create a comfortable experience."

"I am delighted to be here and look forward to meeting the rest of your family and exploring this beautiful area," Kaito said.

"You've had a long day of travel. Why don't you have a rest and we will collect you at six for an *apéro* and dinner."

"An apéro?" Kaito questioned.

"Oh, sorry … a cocktail before dinner. It will be a perfect evening to sit on the terrace and watch the sunset."

CHAPTER 36

*A*fter a shower and brief nap, Kaito felt refreshed and, so far, not affected by the time change. The Côte d'Azur was eight hours behind Tokyo time, so it was early in the morning for him when Céleste met him to go to her house, just up the street.

"Kaito, you must promise to say if jet lag starts to kick in during the evening. We have planned an early dinner ... well, it's all relative," she chuckled. "But earlier than our normal time."

Again, Kaito noticed that Bébé was accompanying them without any direction. "Do you never have to put Bébé on a leash?" he asked.

Céleste shook her head. "You'll notice a lot of dogs in France are extremely well behaved and trot along with their owners, or even lead the way if they know where they are going. Bébé goes out for a little stroll by herself every morning and stops in to say hello to shopkeepers and bartenders who she knows have a little treat for her. She ends up at the boulangerie. She has a bed there and usually waits for me to arrive. If I'm not there on time, she comes looking for me."

Kaito shook his head in amazement.

"But now there are stricter rules about leashing pets and when we go to Nice or other places, I must do so. Much to her annoyance. The problem really was with poop on the sidewalks —pardon the indelicacy. We French have a terrible reputation for not picking it up! But everyone is becoming more educated about it, I'm happy to say, and the streets are cleaner."

When she ushered Kaito through the massive wooden front door of her home, he was immediately enthralled. The stone walls and wooden beams of the centuries-old village house had obviously been lovingly restored and created an atmosphere unlike any he had experienced. A massive stone fireplace with a heavy, well-aged wooden mantle covered most of one wall. The front windows, set within deep limestone walls, overlooked life in the main square while the ones in the back offered magnificent views down the coast.

One wall of the room was covered with sagging bookshelves, reminding Kaito of the love of reading he, Hana, and Lailani had shared so long ago.

Framed photos of the happy life shared with Dominique and their sons filled tabletops and shelves. She made no secret of how they all missed her husband but she also embodied a zest for life. "Every day is a gift, Kaito. Dom taught me to believe that. Find the good even though it may be difficult at times."

Kaito replied. "Agreed. Buddha says every morning we are born again. What we do today is what matters most."

They exchanged knowing looks.

As they stepped through the French doors and onto the terrace, Kaito had an immediate sense of homecoming. Colorful flowerbeds overflowed with lush plantings, many he recognized from his own garden; and for a brief moment he felt the same comfort he had known there.

Martin, Danielle, and Jacques were waiting on the terrace along with another couple. Jacques and Bébé were playing a rousing game of fetch over by the garden.

Céleste introduced Kaito to her younger son, Raphael, and his wife, Yvette, and explained they lived further along the coast to the west in Antibes.

"Raphael is an artist and a curator at a gallery in Antibes and Yvette is a teacher in the village school," Céleste said proudly.

"We look forward to welcoming you to our town soon," Raphael said.

When glasses were filled with champagne, a toast was proposed.

Martin raised his glass. "Monsieur, we are delighted to meet such a longstanding friend of our mother's and welcome you to our village. We look forward to making many fine memories. *Bienvenue et santé!*"

As they wished each other good health, Jacques ran around repeating the toast with his sippy cup. Everyone laughed and relaxed in the comfortable lounge chairs on the terrace as vivid shades of pink and gold began to swirl into a stunning sunset.

Bowls of glistening olives and toasted almonds along with a plate of crostini with foie gras were the simple appetizers served.

Céleste stood and raised her glass. "This is a particular champagne that we have served for many years only on very special occasions. And this certainly is one of those.

I am still in shock at how we stumbled into each other's path … in Japan, of all places. To meet you again, dear Kaito, after all these years, is like a dream. I am thrilled to have you meet my family and only wish our dear Dominique was here with us. Somehow I feel he is watching. It is something he would have enjoyed very much."

There were low murmurs of affection as everyone toasted.

Next, it was Kaito's turn. He stood, raising his glass to all the family. "I also am still in shock at how I have come to be here with you. But it is my immense pleasure. Thank you for welcoming me in such a fine manner. Santé! Cheers! *Hipahipa!*" The latter being a Hawaiian toast, he explained.

There were many questions about Kaito and Céleste's family connections in the Philippines, but Céleste managed to easily steer the conversation back to their recent experiences in Japan and how they met up there. She and Kaito had agreed they would talk about their early friendship as it was in Hawaii but just say it had been in Manila, so they would not get caught in their deception.

Of course there were a few questions about Kaito's life in Hawaii. He explained that his wife had been a housebound invalid for many years and that the month of September was his time to travel, with her blessing. He spoke about Auntie and the excellent care Hana received, but made no mention about extended family.

Everyone was empathetic and understanding. Céleste had mentioned how the French respect privacy, and he was thankful for that.

Kaito knew this was as difficult for Céleste as it was for him. She had told him she would have loved to tell her family about how Hana was like a sister to her.

He had examined his conscience painstakingly before making the decision to come to visit Céleste, and he had no misgivings about it. He wished he could have shared with Hana his excitement and amazement about his reunion with her dearest friend, but he would deal with that when he was back home.

The stunning sunset and panoramic view offered good opportunities to change the subject. Kaito was speechless that such a view was simply part of their daily life.

Martin and Danielle served dinner, insisting Céleste sit and entertain Kaito. The entrée was a chilled vichyssoise followed by a delicious *salade Niçoise* with a small seared tuna steak on each plate.

During dinner, Kaito asked the young couples about their lives.

Martin told how he had taken over the bakery after apprenticing there in his teens with his father. He explained he and his family lived in the attached ancient residence that originally had been their family home. Céleste described how she and Dominique had always had their eye on the village house they were in.

"When we had the opportunity to purchase it, the time was right for Martin to take over our original home. And Raphael was ready to move out on his own and live the life of the starving artist for a few years. It was another of those serendipitous times."

"Ah *oui!*" Raphael said, "The starving artist indeed … and what a life it was at school in Paris. Where I also met the love of my life."

He took Yvette's hand and kissed it. She smiled radiantly and laughed.

Raphael continued, "But somehow we survived those years and have been fortunate since to do what we love—"

"And live in the most beautiful place," Yvette interrupted. "You must visit soon."

"It's an easy drive, less than an hour," Céleste said to Kaito. "We will go soon—although you may not want to leave once you see the town!"

"I can't imagine it topping this," Kaito said, reaching his hand out to the view.

Everyone spoke at once with such enthusiasm, telling him that the thing about the Côte d'Azur was that there were endless places to visit and that all inspired the same response.

Kaito shook his head. "I can't wait to experience all of it."

All through the meal, Kaito could not help but feel the affection of the family for each other and the easy humor they shared. It was a painful reminder of how that was missing in his life.

The cheese tray brought to the table caused Kaito's mouth to drop. "Never have I seen such a selection! I've heard about the French serving cheese with each meal, but could not have imagined it to be quite like this!"

A small *boule* of bread and a bottle of port also were placed on the table with this course.

"We take our cheese very seriously," Danielle murmured as she asked Kaito to choose a few pieces he would like to have.

"Looking at this selection, I would call it a passion," Kaito remarked, sweeping his gaze approvingly around the table.

Danielle delicately cut or sliced small pieces and put them on a plate with a knife and fork for him.

Cheese was served in this manner to everyone, including little Jacques, still at the table despite the hour, and Kaito could see this was an important part of the meal. The conversation centered around cheese for some time as they all discussed, for his benefit, the merits of the various offerings this evening.

Then they regaled Kaito with tales of Céleste helping in the bakeshop during the busy "baguette hours."

"I just cannot stop myself," Céleste said, looking abashed. Kaito's heart warmed to see the loving relationship she had with her family. He envied her that and could not help regretting how it contrasted with the absence of such warm exchanges in his life since Kiana left. He was not about to have a pity party for himself, but he felt more aware of an emotional void that he lived with and accepted.

To end the meal, Raphael did the honors flambéing crêpes suzette at the table for dessert.

By this time, Kaito was having a difficult time keeping his eyes open. Everyone bid him a fond *bonne nuit*. Céleste and both her sons walked with him the few doors down the street to the auberge.

CHAPTER 37

$\mathcal{W}$hen Kaito awoke the next day he was horrified to see it was almost noon. His body clock had taken charge and made certain he got the kind of sleep he needed. He sent Céleste an apologetic text saying he would come to her place after a quick shower.

She replied immediately, encouraging him to take his time.

"Bébé and I are sitting in the garden reading. I expected this might happen after your long day of travel and am happy for you. I did not plan anything special today other than poking around our village. Come for a light lunch whenever you are ready."

She finished with a smiley face emoji.

Kaito lay back in bed and took in the view out the window that overlooked foothills crisscrossed with hiking paths through the low-growing greenery. Thoughts tumbled through his mind reviewing all that had happened since he discovered Lailani in Koyasan.

He wondered if Hana would have any understanding if he shared this incredible news with her. She had loved Lailani so much and they had shared a friendship that was as close as any two sisters. Perhaps even closer. Somehow he doubted she would absorb what he told her. But it didn't matter. What was most important was that he could absolutely not share the news with anyone. Period.

That reality made him sad for a moment. But then he considered the improbable twist of fate that had brought these two old friends together. After all this time. And worlds away from where they would normally be living their lives.

He questioned how this could even happen.

Then he got up, stretched, and took a hot shower to clear his head.

He pondered the mystery of what life has in store for each of us. There were times when Kaito lapsed into self-pity, and for a moment this was one of them. He allowed himself to wallow briefly in the swampland of wondering what he had done to deserve so many heartbreaks in his life—the *duhkha* of life, the Sanskrit word for disappointment, which Buddha explained as suffering. The first of the Four Noble Truths of Buddhism is that life is duhkha. Suffering that can be transcended by mindfulness and awakening, but first suffering is not to be avoided. One must walk into it to learn the meaning of life.

How many years had he done just this?

He closed his eyes and meditated.

He was happy that Lailani had been gifted with the chance to start over in her new persona and find love and a family as well.

For whatever reason, Lailani's rising from the dead had happened. This visit to France had happened. He would accept it all and enjoy being back in his dear friend's company. He had felt the sincere embrace of her family and could see what a close, loving kinship they shared. Conversation, laughter, and all the signs of people genuinely enjoying each other never stopped. He felt happy for Lailani … Céleste …

When their lives had abruptly parted, she still had been living with the sadness of her fiancé's passing in Vietnam. At that point he knew she had not been focusing on the prospects of having her own family. She had been dedicating herself to Kaito and Hana's family.

As hot water streamed down his body, he tried to feel release. He let himself continue down the road of self-pity as he thought about Hana's illness that robbed her of any ability to love. And then his sweet keiki, Kiana, leaving her loving father for a life he couldn't imagine. And then to have her die without ever holding her close again. Then to lose the opportunity to know his granddaughter, Kailani. What a disaster his life had been! At least to his heart.

And yet he had soldiered on through it all—and made it to age sixty. He had stayed the course and was faithful and caring to Hana. That had been his life. And so it would be.

But for some inexplicable reason, he had the opportunity now to see how Lailani's life had evolved into something wonderful. This made his heart sing. He would absorb and enjoy all of it and later try to make sense of it. Or maybe never. It just was life.

As the hot water turned to cold, Kaito let that wake him up and snap him out of his thoughts.

CÉLESTE ORDERED an espresso for her and a tea for Kaito.

"Croissant? *Pain au chocolat? Pain aux raisins?* What's your pleasure? Or just baguette?" she asked.

They were sitting at a table outside a small café next to her boulangerie, after enjoying a lunch of salad and fresh fruit and baguette on the terrace at her house. Bébé sat between Céleste's and Kaito's chairs with her own little bowl of water.

"One of each," Kaito replied with a grin. "Seriously, a plain croissant would be a joy. I will gradually work my way through the array of deliciousness that I see in your bakery window."

Céleste nodded. "Good plan! Bonne idée!" and they both laughed.

"I had no idea how useful those two words would be," Kaito said. "But I think my vocabulary will need some expansion."

They had decided that this first day together would be spent relaxing and exploring the little streets of the village. "And of course, I will introduce you to La Trophée. You can hardly miss it here."

They ambled narrow cobblestone laneways, with Bébé often leading the way. Time was not of the essence and they paused often as Céleste shared the history of the village.

Within minutes he said, "Leaving my camera behind for now was a good decision. We would not have gotten far. There's so much detail I want to shoot."

"In France you quickly become a true *flâneur*," Céleste told him. "A stroller, yes—but more than that, someone who takes the time to be an acute observer of everything around him. It's a French word I quickly grew to love."

Kaito looked at her and gave her the Hawaiian *shaka* sign.

"You mean we are hanging loose."

They both laughed.

"That's something I have not seen for a long time," Céleste said. "But you are right. It's like being on Hawaiian time ... Hawaiian style ... no rush. It's all good."

There were many pauses as Kaito admired the surroundings.

"This is all a feast for the eyes," he proclaimed. "It's so interesting how stone walls, timeworn doors, shutters with peeling paint, and tile rooftops can present the most irresistible visuals."

"Even after living here all these years, I still feel the same way," Céleste agreed. "And remember that many of these homes were built using stones taken away from the ruins of La Trophée. It's what happened in the Middle Ages. There was really no appreciation for Roman ruins or other historic buildings. Finding materials to build one's home was the important factor."

Soon they came to the end of a street that opened up to a broad expanse. Before them was the astounding ruin Kaito had seen from the road and from Céleste's terrace. There was something almost spiritual to be standing beside it and know this had been there for thousands of years. Although it was only a small part of the original structure, it was still imposing. Four columns remained and a few large panels on the base with inscriptions.

Céleste pointed to some Roman words on the monument close to where they were standing. "Here's my history lesson for you. This was built in 6 BC to honor Julius Caesar's nephew Octavius, who became the Emperor Augustus. It celebrated his victories over local tribes and at the time this was the frontier between Gaul and Italy."

"What a statement it must have made. Even as a ruin it is breathtaking to see," Kaito said.

As they walked around the ruin, he expressed amazement that it was simply sitting there without any restrictions or security. When he rubbed his hands over the smooth limestone, his entire nervous system tingled as he thought of these stones being cut and put in place two thousand years before.

As they went to the museum entrance, Kaito said, "Céleste, there's no need to come in with me. You must have been here more times than you can count. Let me meet you later."

"That makes sense, although I would have been happy to accompany you. But to be honest, I think I know all the information by heart," Céleste said with a chuckle. "I will go to the boulangerie to help out and you can come over when you're through. We hope you will join us for dinner again. This time at Martin's, if that is all right. We don't want to smother you with our hospitality."

Kaito replied, "That is kind of you but absolutely unnecessary."

Seeing her exaggerated crestfallen look, Kaito laughed. "I remember that face! Some things never change! Of course I will be happy to join you. I will come to the bakery as soon as I finish here. I know the way!"

"You will be right on time for the afternoon baguette!" Céleste gave him a bise and waved as she and Bébé left him.

BY THE TIME Kaito finished asking questions of the guide in the museum, it was almost closing time. The display and information had obviously been put together with a great deal of care, and as an engineer he was intrigued by the building techniques. The museum guide had enjoyed his conversation with such an enthusiastic and well-informed visitor.

Kaito easily found his way to the boulangerie. He chuckled as he saw the lineup out the door and down the street. He took his place in line and soon was inside, watching Céleste chatting with customers, taking orders, and efficiently sending them off with their bread and pastries. He noticed how affectionately the customers greeted her and exchanged pleasantries.

Martin waved to him from the back of the bakery where he was taking the next baguettes from the oven. The mouthwatering aroma of fresh bread filled the shop.

"Here you are!" Céleste greeted him.

"Just in time for an apéro!" Kaito joked.

"Exactly! You're a fast learner! We will go to my terrace and relax for a while."

Danielle was standing by Céleste and added, "We're expecting you two for dinner at eight."

"*Avec plaisir, ma chérie,*" Céleste replied. We will see you then."

"I didn't mean to rush you," Kaito said. "If you are not finished here, I will meet you later."

"*Non, non!*" Danielle said, grinning, "The two of you run off now. I will finish up. Céleste has the customers out the door before they know it. And yet, they all feel like they had a friendly visit."

Yet again Kaito could not help noting the warmth amongst the family members. He felt another jolt of regret at how moments like that in his life had disappeared when Kiana left. That void had never been filled.

"I thought you might want to take some sunset photos this evening. Conditions are perfect for a grand display," Céleste suggested.

"Bonne idée! Let's stop at the auberge and I will get my camera and tripod."

CHAPTER 38

*a*s they set up their equipment, Kaito and Céleste compared different techniques in shooting sunsets and how they approached the composition they hoped to achieve.

"It's so easy to simply point and shoot," Kaito said. "Particularly with the excellent cameras we have on our phones now. But I still look for satisfaction in the challenge of using different lenses on my SL and shooting at different exposures."

Céleste had other thoughts to offer and the conversation about photography went on and on, never lacking enthusiasm.

Kaito began taking photos of flowers. "I have to tell you that your garden brought me an immediate sense of comfort when I stopped out here yesterday. In many ways it reminded me of ours in Honolulu and I was astonished."

Céleste nodded. "The first thing I did when I planned it was research what plants from home would grow well here. Et voilà! Of course there are some differences but I have always had a sense of my past in these flowerbeds. And I've often thought about the happy hours with Kiana planting and weeding so long ago."

Her voice broke slightly and her expression became serious.

"Sweet sweet Kiana. She brought such lightness to my heart and was the child I never had, until my life in France began. I have never stopped thinking about her."

Kaito felt a lump in his throat. He struggled to find words. "She often expressed how she wished you were her mother. In truth I often wished that for her."

They both paused for a moment, gazing into the garden. Then Céleste gently picked a rose and slipped it into the pocket of Kaito's shirt as their eyes met.

In a quiet voice, Céleste continued. "No matter how many years have passed. No matter how much I embraced a different life. Hawaii has always lived in my heart. I can't tell you how good it is to feel I can talk about it with you. It's like the key to a rusted lock has been found. But it still must remain our secret."

"I understand only too well. Please don't worry about that." Kaito assured her.

"*Pas du tout!* Not at all. Not with you." She said as the sparkle returned to her eyes. "You were always the most trustworthy and honorable person I knew. Now we have about half an hour before the action starts. Shall I pour us a pastis?" Céleste asked.

"I'm sure you can, but first tell me what that is," Kaito said.

Raising a finger, Céleste said she would be right back and went into the kitchen. Bébé raised her head from where she was lying in the last rays of the sun. Then she looked at Kaito and went back to her snooze. Kaito felt he had received the seal of approval as a welcome friend.

Céleste returned with a tray. "Ah, this is such a classic beverage in France. It has been a part of the culture since after Prohibition, and was kind of preceded by absinthe, which has its own history and bad reputation. But pastis is an anise-flavored spirit and a truly popular aperitif. You'll find people who love having one first thing in the morning and others before lunch and most, like us now, for an apéro. The French would be horrified if one ordered this after a meal! It's an aperitif and definitely not a digestif."

She set a bottle on the table along with two narrow glasses, a bowl of olives, another with peanuts, and a pitcher of iced water.

Next, she poured three fingers' worth of pastis in the glass and then slowly added the cold water, not allowing any ice to fall in. "For the most part, French people do not like to add ice. Pouring the pastis over the ice causes a slightly crystalizing effect, which we feel spoils the smooth effect of this drink. But you can add the ice later if you must."

Kaito watched as the amber liquid became cloudy and opaque when the water was added. "It's a lovely visual before I even taste it."

"Yes," Céleste said. "Perfect alchemy. The French word for the drink going cloudy like that is *louche*. We say one can become *louche* if too much is drunk quickly. You get it?"

"Aha," Kaito said. "Sip is the operative word!"

"Bonne idée!" Céleste replied with a wink.

They raised their glasses.

"*Santé!*"

"*Hipahipa!*"

Kaito murmured approvingly. "Delicious! It's a bit like ouzo, only smoother ... and a taste of black licorice."

"It's such a melange ... of aromas. Breathe it in, *n'est-ce pas?* And of flavors. I loved it from the first time I tasted it. But to some visitors it is an acquired taste."

"I agree. It's very good."

Céleste regaled him with more of the backstory about absinthe ... *la fée verte*, the green fairy ... and its origins, the social problems that evolved as the entire country seemed to be addicted to it and how it finally came to be banned in 1915.

"That's the drink that caused problems for van Gogh and Toulouse-Lautrec and other artists of the time. Am I right? And didn't Oscar Wilde have much to say about it?" Kaito commented.

"Absolutely correct. There's been much written about absinthe—some of it grossly exaggerated, of course. But nevertheless, artists were drawn to it and stories abound. You're reminding me of what a great reader you were!"

"And continue to be," Kaito murmured. "Books have been a great escape for me. Now I'm living some fantasies they provided for me!"

Céleste passed the olives and peanuts to him.

Kaito expressed his appreciation as he sipped. "I definitely could get used to this."

The sun was slipping slowly into the horizon, softly coloring the sky in golds, blues, and pinks. The view stretched a long way down the coast past Cannes, providing uneven silhouettes of foothills to one side, balancing the sea to the other.

Kaito was feeling content at the decision he had made to come to France, but there was a niggling regret at never having traveled before, apart from Japan. A sense of time wasted seeped into his mind. He repressed the negativity that accompanied those thoughts. Now was not the time to dwell on the past; he needed to enjoy every moment of the present.

CHAPTER 39

*C*éleste and Kaito toured all the must-see spots in the hills and along the coast.

He found Monaco disappointing, in spite of the beautiful setting. "What a shame there has been such overbuilding. All of these condominium towers seem so out of place," he commented, as Céleste made a point of slowing down to show him the examples of stunning Belle Époque architecture crammed in between the modern buildings.

The town of Nice, as Céleste described Kaito's reaction, was a *"coup de coeur."*

"It's love at first sight, plain and simple," she told him. "And you aren't the first to fall under the spell of Nissa la bella. Until Mama and I went up into the hills, we almost chose to live here."

Whether they were exploring the narrow alleyways of the old town or the broad expanse of the promenade, he was enchanted by the blend of French and Italian ambiance and the access to so many galleries. The pastel colors of the buildings enhanced the atmosphere, and he knew this was a town he would like to return to again and again.

Another day they relaxed in a beach restaurant with fresh

seafood for lunch and then drove to Antibes to visit Raphael and Yvette. Kaito exclaimed with pleasure the entire half-hour drive along the Bord de Mer, the main road that bordered the sea all the way to the town.

"The setting is stunning and the colors of the Med are exquisite. The entire scene is so full of life with people swimming, sunbathing, and fishing right here as we drive along. It's such a different type of beach scene than I'm used to. I have to say, as you well know, they don't hold a candle to the beaches we know and love in Hawaii. But somehow they have their own distinct charm, although I think those stones might take some getting used to."

"Ah, *les galets*," Céleste said with a chuckle. "Yes, everyone has to adjust to them. Beach shoes certainly help. Actually they are lovely to lie upon … kind of like a hot rock massage! But fear not, on the other side of Antibes the beaches are all sand."

Kaito was shown around the cobbled maze of alleys and the harbor setting of the old town of Antibes. "I'm beginning to understand why the French Riviera is such a popular destination," he said with a sigh of pleasure. "There's simply one fascinating, enchanting place to visit after another … all of them oozing history."

As THE TIME of his visit was drawing to an end, Kaito had been fully drawn into the allure of the South of France. As much as he was awestruck by the ancient towns, he also was drawn to the sentiers, the hiking trails for which France is so famous, and the vistas they offered.

Some days he and Céleste hiked together. She was fit and agile on the trails and they pushed each other with friendly rivalry. There was always a breathtaking view at some point that made the effort even more worthwhile.

On other days, Kaito would go off alone so Céleste could continue with the normal routine of her busy life. He appreciated the solitude and didn't want to be a constant drain on his old friend's hospitality.

On those days to himself, Kaito spent a lot of time battling conflicting feelings. He had moments of uncertainty and guilt as to whether he should be accepting these new experiences in his life; his place was in Honolulu with his wife. Then he would convince himself that no one was being hurt by his actions; Hana had no idea of and no ability to be affected by his absence. All of this had fallen into his life by accident—by fate, he truly believed.

He knew Buddha looked upon this as "heaven's will," predestined by a universal force and out of the individual's control. Kaito meditated on these words and found acceptance within himself.

Until the next round of guilt.

As he and Céleste explored, she took great delight in his enthusiastic response to each discovery. She said that as a person who had the privilege of traveling throughout her life, she found it sad but understandable, given his circumstances, that Kaito had missed so much. She wanted to help him make up for that time.

"Life is a collection of moments, Kaito," she reminded him in her constantly gentle and upbeat manner. "Live for the good moments, the happy ones, the ones that light your heart and mind."

This was the same attitude he remembered from all the years he had known Lailani. From the carefree schoolgirl to the woman she was when she vanished.

It wasn't that Kaito didn't know this philosophy. Much of the Buddhist beliefs were very similar. And he knew, in spite of all his meditating and work on balance in his life, this was not how he lived his life since losing Kiana. He'd always been aware of the joy he'd lost in his life, but never so acutely as these days in France.

There were moments, as he was drawn into the pleasing family life surrounding Céleste, when he squeezed his eyes closed, trying to shut out regret. He had become adept at ignoring anything that reminded him of what he'd been missing; that was his means of survival. But he had never experienced anything as special as this—with Céleste and her family. Even with his caring parents there had not been the same warmth and openness.

In his room some nights, he put himself through rigorous aikido workouts, pushing through the anger that occasionally gnawed at him about time lost. He had to admit he did not always feel as peaceful inside as he tried to portray on the outside.

Kaito was constantly on guard to protect Céleste's secret, but at the same time he felt blessed to have this friend back. Someone who knew his history. Someone who understood why he was as he was.

As they all bade him au revoir at the end of his stay, Kaito knew he would be only too happy to return again, as the entire family beseeched him to do. For the first time ever, he felt a twinge of concern about how he would feel when he was back in Honolulu. He would miss these people, this life.

He suspected his homecoming with Hana might have a few new bumps.

CHAPTER 40

2010

*K*aito's return to Honolulu was unlike any other. His attempts to sleep on the ten-hour flight from Paris to Seattle were constantly interrupted as his mind worked nonstop to process all that had transpired. After a brief stop, he could not settle down for the final six-hour leg to Honolulu. His travel had never been so restless.

Finding Lailani again ... the words spiraled through his head. How was that possible? What forces were at work in the universe that brought this about?

Visiting France and being so welcomed by Lailani's—Céleste's—family. He smiled as he thought she would always be "Lailani" in his heart.

HE ARRIVED BACK at the house in the evening after Hana had gone to bed. Their first contact was in the morning at breakfast prepared by Auntie. Hana, dressed in a colorful muumuu, looked at him without any sign of surprise he was there. She nodded her replies to comments he made about the food and the weather and ate sparingly while Auntie coaxed her on. After not more than fifteen minutes, Hana folded her napkin and bowed as she got up to return to her studio.

The change from the joyful, positive environment that he'd left behind in France was jolting. Kaito knew he had his work cut out for him in slipping back into this reality.

Shikata ga nai. It couldn't be helped.

As usual on that first day, Kaito sat down with Auntie while she shared her daily reports with him. For almost twenty years, Auntie and her husband had moved into the house for all of September to stay with Hana. As he read through the pages now, he noticed Auntie's observations that Hana's physical health seemed to be declining and she recommended a visit to their doctor.

He felt a weight of sadness and even greater heartbreak for Hana clouding his days. He wanted desperately to be able to share the news about Lailani but could see her name elicited no response from Hana when he mentioned it in a casual remark.

After the warm family atmosphere in which he had been immersed in France, the cold starkness of his home life had never been more amplified. Loneliness plagued him as it had never before. He was surprised to realize how those two weeks with Lailani and her family had affected him.

Auntie made certain each day that Hana ate something for breakfast, even if it was simply a protein drink, before Kaito left for work. On good days he would entice her to sit in the garden and feel the morning sun on her face. There had been a time when they could have a reasonable exchange of conversation and he could tell her his plans for the day at work or at the studio. Some days she would remain in the garden after he left and then go for a walk with Auntie.

But those days were becoming a thing of the past, as Hana wanted only to return to her studio as quickly as possible.

Kaito's therapy counselor had helped him understand that

her sewing studio was where Hana felt safe and he should not dissuade her from wanting to be there. He would open the windows and let in the refreshing breeze, sweet fragrances, and birdsong, even though he knew she would close them the minute he left.

Without fail, Auntie arrived at the house early each morning with a smile and a cheery story. Kaito suspected she made up some of her tales but he really didn't care, as she brought the gift of laughter into the house.

At the end of the day, she would quietly bid him aloha after reminding him to eat the meal she left. Hana, having eaten earlier, might be in her studio or in bed reading or watching television. For a while, Kaito would go to her room to sit with her.

A dull stare accompanied by an infrequent nod was Hana's standard response to his visits to her room, due to the strict regimen of medication. She had been a pretty young woman, but her mental illness had stripped her face of beauty and left it deeply etched with the scars of anger, suspicion, and confusion.

Kaito went in each evening to bow respectfully and wish her good night. For many years, she shrank from physical contact, which he gave up on after she rebuffed his attempts to hug or kiss her cheek. When he was ready to sleep, he retired to the spare bedroom that had been his for far too long.

Once jet lag was under control, Kaito slipped into his regular routine at the office. With the company's constant focus on environmentally based new projects, there was always a challenge he could set his sights on. He had progressed to become a partner and the senior project manager of the Green Buildings division that explored ways to create eco-friendly and energy-efficient living spaces.

Soon after his return, he began chatting online with Céleste. At first it was occasional. But in time they agreed that every Sunday they would have a video conversation on FaceTime. It was easy to work around the time difference. They spoke when it was nine in the evening in Honolulu and nine in the morning in La Turbie, which suited them both. Hana was asleep by then and Céleste sat on her back terrace, often just home from helping with the morning baguette at the boulangerie.

Kaito also made more effort to have a social life by reaching out to Bob and Gail, who welcomed his new enthusiasm. Occasionally, some of his co-workers would mention an evening out for dinner or a concert, and for a change he joined them.

CHAPTER 41

 arly in the new year, Kaito was stunned to receive a letter from Jake Akana.

In truth Jake was still, legally, Kiana's widower, but to Kaito he was a nonentity. The very thought of the man, when Kaito saw his name on the envelope, caused a bitter bile to rise in his throat and the fierce sensation of a word Kaito had never used in his life. *Hate.*

This was the one area of his life where Buddhist teachings had not removed these negative feelings about the man whose name he could barely speak. There was work to be done, he knew. But it felt easier to ignore it.

Apart from the contact when Jake's lawyer brought Kiana's ashes to him, Kaito had resisted anything further.

Jake had written a few letters after going to prison. Kaito marked them "return to sender," resisting the urge to spit on them and reviling himself for even harboring the thought. There were days spent overcoming the distress even the mention of the man's name caused him.

Criminal. Drug dealer. Stealer of Kiana's heart. Killer.

He had to banish the thoughts and not go there. His heart ached. His head hurt. His entire body was in torment. He knew the pain of the loss of Kiana was something from which he would never recover. The loss of a child. What parent can?

A few years after Kiana died in the plane crash and Jake was sent to prison, a lawyer had reached out to Kaito to see if he would agree to meet with Jake. The thought filled Kaito with contempt and he had steadfastly refused.

There had never been any further attempt at written communication from Jake. And Kaito had no desire to change that.

Then this letter.

Kaito's immediate reaction was to sign it "return to sender" and put it back in the mail. Instead it sat for weeks on his desk.

It was Céleste, after he told her about the letter, who suggested that he not return it just yet.

"Kaito, we had so many deep conversations about Kiana when you were here. I felt in my heart that somehow a bit of healing had occurred in those moments. Perhaps it is time to see what Jake wants to say to you."

In the years since Kiana ran away and then her fatal accident, Kaito had spent countless hours meditating on forgiveness. Mostly he sought forgiveness for himself as he blamed a lack of parenting skills for Kiana making the choices she did. Kiana said many times he had done everything right, that it was Hana she blamed. Yet he had not forgiven himself.

In his exchange of letters with Kiana, he often asked her to forgive Hana and remember it was her illness that controlled her behavior, not her wishes.

Now, as Céleste's words resonated with him, after several Sunday conversations, Kaito made the decision to open the letter.

He was not prepared for the message it contained.

"Tanaka-san, I beg your forgiveness in time.

I hope with all my heart you have opened the letter and will read my words.

I know that the constant ache in my heart at the loss of Kiana does not begin to compare to yours. And I know that I will never find the words to help heal that pain. I know too that I am to blame for the root cause of it. I took your young daughter from you when I should not have done so. I know now there was a better way.

During these thirteen years in prison, I have responded to participation in rehabilitation programs. When I was transferred to Halawa Correctional Facility, I had the opportunity to volunteer in a clinical trial for rehabilitation that was long and grueling and ultimately helped me to become the man I am today.

I have also found God and celebrate his forgiveness and acceptance of me into his embrace. I have completed an undergraduate degree in Philosophy as well as earning a Master's degree in Theology. Truly, I am a changed man.

Throughout all of the years of studying, learning, and becoming who I am, my thoughts have all centered on my wife, my daughter, and you and your wife.

I am fortunate to have enjoyed communication with my daughter, Kailani, for many years. Much of my gratitude for that situation is to your cousin, Sara, who has wisely nurtured and guided Kailani.

One unachieved goal of mine is to be able to apologize to you and Hana in person. Kailani has told me that Hana sadly has been ill for many years, and I send you my sympathy for that. But I owe you both my humble atonement.

My sentence will soon be completed. I have never applied for parole.

Please consider my request. I will understand if you choose to deny it, but I am hopeful you will find it a possibility to meet one day.

Sincerely, Jake"

"Can you believe it?" Kaito asked, after he had read the letter to Céleste. "I can't tell you how many times I have read and reread this. It seems incredible."

Céleste was quiet for a few minutes. "I'm thinking," she said. "That is a pretty profound letter, Kaito."

Kaito snorted. "How could that criminal ever be considered profound in any way? It is probably all self-serving b.s."

With a gentle tone Céleste asked, "Do you remember when we were talking about the anger I felt over having to walk away from everything that was important to me?"

Kaito nodded.

"You quoted this to me and it touched me deeply. You told me that Buddha says, 'Do not dwell in the past, do not dream of the future, concentrate the mind on the present moment.'"

Kaito nodded again. "And you reminded me that forgiveness is a constant attitude."

"Perhaps it's time to concentrate on the present moment with Jake Akana."

Kaito's words were slow and measured. "I'm not sure I am up to that. I have always thought I am a forgiving person, but this goes beyond forgiveness."

"This anger will always be a part of you. It is like grief in many ways. But I know that letting go of at least part of it is a path to peace within you. Why not give it a try? You have a granddaughter to consider in this too."

After they said goodbye, Kaito sat at his computer for a while. It felt so comforting to talk with Céleste. It was hard to believe that since her "accident" in Honolulu, he really had no one in his life with whom he could speak so frankly. No sounding board.

As Hana's illness progressed in those earlier years, he had to be careful how he spoke to her. There was never a clue or a signal as to what would set her off. So their conversations had been superficial.

But now someone was listening to him, and that made Kaito feel good—feel lighter. He recognized a difference in his first waking moments. The positivity with which he faced each dawn came more easily.

He was no longer alone.

CHAPTER 42

$\mathcal{J}$t took weeks of meditation, long hikes, and more encouragement from Céleste before Kaito reached the point where he was ready to reply to Jake. The man had been released from prison by that time and was living in a halfway house in a suburb of Honolulu.

After much deliberation as to where and how this meeting should happen, Kaito invited him to the garden for tea. He did not want him in the house. He looked to the calming ambience of this private oasis, so much of it planted and nurtured by Kiana, to providing the strength he sought.

Kaito thought having Auntie there would be a good buffer, in case he felt himself losing control of his emotions. His stomach churned the entire morning as he wrestled with doubt about his decision.

He also realized he wanted as much of the memory of Kiana as possible to be there. Although it pained him to even think the words, her spirit would hover between these two men who had shared her life.

Auntie called Kaito, who already was in the garden, when

PATRICIA SANDS

Jake's car pulled in the driveway. Hana was working in her studio.

Kaito went around the side of the house to where Jake was exiting his car. Kaito was surprised to discover a subdued man in his mid-forties and not the brash personality he recalled. He had never forgotten the handsome face of the young man with piercing blue eyes with whom Kiana had been so smitten. Now Jake's face was weathered and his closely cropped hair was peppered with gray. But he was still striking in appearance.

Kaito's first glimpse of the man brought back a torrent of negativity. He felt his hands tighten into fists and his teeth clench. He closed his eyes and exhaled deeply, bringing him into his heart chakra and with it the peaceful equilibrium he needed.

Jake bowed to Kaito. With his head still down, he offered his hand. "Before anything, I bring you my most humble apology. I cannot remove the mistakes of my past ... and there were many ... but I hope you can find it in your heart to forgive me for taking your daughter away from you."

Kaito bowed his head. Reaching out to accept Jake's hand was the most difficult act he had ever done. With a strong grip, he said, "To forgive is to find peace within oneself. I will work on this. To be here together now is the first step."

Jake nodded and bowed solemnly again. "Thank you for giving me this chance. You requested we not talk about Kiana today but I need to say this. I want you to know that she loved you with all her heart and never stopped thinking about you. I hope one day you will let me tell you more."

Kaito squeezed his eyes closed briefly, fighting back the intense emotions pushing to the surface. He led the way around to the garden, hoping the peaceful setting would calm him. Birdsong and the intense fragrance of early-blooming gardenias filled the air. He knew that day began a path to healing.

In advance, Kaito had written to Jake and set parameters for their time together. He did not want Jake to say anything about

262

his life with Kiana. He repeated the boundaries as he went through the steps of preparing tea. Auntie had everything waiting on the table.

"That conversation about your life with Kiana may occur in the future ... or may not. At this time I am not prepared to hear anything about those years. We will talk about your years in prison and why you feel I should find forgiveness because of the changes you are making in your life now."

Jake spoke in detail about the programs in which he participated and the degrees he had earned. "My regret is immense for the choices I made in my younger years. My goals and work from within prison for the last few years have focused on making amends. I have been working with young offenders and prisoners involved in the drug world. This will be my commitment for the rest of my life."

As they drank their tea, Kaito listened quietly, not judging but rather asking questions about this work from time to time. He noted how modest Jake appeared, but at the same time he could see pride on his face as he mentioned some success with his rehabilitation and the satisfaction it brought.

Jake explained that he would be on probation for many years. "Just as I never sought early release from my sentence, I will not seek a change in my probation restrictions. All of these punishments are as they should be and are what has led me into the light of my existence now."

After a short time, Kaito knew this was enough for one day. He suggested they end the discussion and meet again in a few weeks. The very act of sitting and listening to Jake had been stressful as he battled internally with unsettled feelings.

This man had brought shame to his family. He had inflicted immeasurable pain. And now he asked for forgiveness.

At times he felt elevated above the scene, as if watching it from a distance.

He needed some space.

～

"I DID IT, CÉLESTE," Kaito told her in a video chat the next day. "It wasn't easy but I felt Kiana there the entire time whispering it was the right thing to do. There were moments I wanted to get up and leave him sitting there. But I didn't."

Her face was serious as she nodded. "I cannot imagine how it was but knew you could get through it."

Yet again, Kaito's heart swelled with gratitude and the ongoing feeling he was not alone.

CHAPTER 43

*I*n the next few months, Kaito and Jake met in the garden on more occasions. During their second chat, Kaito asked him to speak about his life with Kiana. He wanted to learn about the years he had missed. He hoped he was strong enough to handle it.

He focused on his breathing as he absorbed Jake's words and the intense feelings with which he delivered them.

Jake's voice was hushed and often cracked with emotion. His eyes never left Kaito's as words tumbled out. "I can only imagine how bizarre this must all sound to you. But please believe me—it is the truth. I lived a double life. One that involved the worst kind of criminal activity, controlling the flow of illicit drugs, and the other an idyllic family life. After my early crazy years, before I met Kiana, I did a lot of drugs. When I met her, I gave that up. I want you to know what a positive influence she was. And at first she did not realize that I was in charge of the distribution of drugs in the Islands. I lied about what I did. It was a long time before she understood the depth of my involvement and that nearly ruined our relationship. But by that time we were deeply in love with each other and devoted to our daughter. I gave her my promise to never bring the ugly side of what I did home, and that was enough to make her stay. I had proven that to her. We were committed to each other and the life we built away from everything else."

Kaito listened intently. He had worked hard to prepare himself for this. His goal was to keep his emotions in check until Jake left. Then he gave himself permission to break down, as he was sure he would. There would never be enough words to describe the hole in his heart that would never heal.

Kiana's letters to him always stressed that she felt loved and respected by Jake. At the time, for his own peace of mind, he believed her. He needed to believe her. He prayed it was true.

The scenario Jake described was hard to believe but seemed to reflect what Kiana told him. And as much as Kaito found it difficult to accept, his voice rang true. His eyes reflected sincerity.

Somewhere in the midst of listening to Jake speak about the quiet, loving life they had shared on Kauai, Kaito began to feel deeply entrenched emotional hurdles soften. He understood his daughter and granddaughter had been loved and cared for. He wanted to believe it. But it was not that simple.

He could not let go of all the anger and bitterness so easily. Jake was a con man—involved in serious criminal activities. The prison authorities Kaito had spoken with had highly praised his rehabilitation. But on a personal level Jake had brought dishonor to his family and torn it apart. How dare he ask for forgiveness?

Kaito could not find the words to respond and eventually stood to indicate the conversation was over.

He nodded permission at Jake's request to bring him some photos. He knew the images would reduce him to tears and that time would be necessary to make his way through them.

Then he bowed briefly, gestured toward the walk to the driveway, and went into the house.

A few days after this conversation, Jake left a box of photo albums that Kiana had organized.

KAITO WALKED with Céleste on video through each of his conversations with Jake . She listened to him, cried with him, and together they tried to work through their separate issues of grief around Kiana's life and death.

"I have prayed for her soul's peace every day since the plane accident," Kaito told her, "and I beg each time to understand the reality of what happened. In recent years I've tried to repeat to myself the Japanese proverb 'mizu ni nagasu' … let it flow in the water. You would say forgive and forget.

"Honestly, my initial overwhelming sadness is slowly easing through this process of getting to know Jake and discovering the years I missed with Kiana. I've learned how she matured and what a fine young woman she was, and that makes me happy."

Céleste smiled. "And that makes me happy for you. Who knew things would turn out this way?"

"And all of this has inspired me to invite Kailani to come to Honolulu for a visit. I don't think Hana's behavior would be a factor now," Kaito said, his voice rising with excitement. "What do you think?"

"Here's what I think," Céleste replied. "Bonne idée!"

KAITO KNEW THAT KAILANI, now twenty-two, was aware of the bond that was growing between him and her father. Both men had written to her about it and also told her in video chats.

Kaito knew that Jake had invited Kailani to come to Honolulu for a visit and stay with him, but she had so far not accepted the invitation.

There was nothing that Kaito would have liked more than to have her stay with him and Hana; but, in spite of his exchange with Céleste about it, he continued to be nervous about extending the invitation. He waffled as to whether the risk was too great. Sara had always said she did not want Kailani exposed to Hana's "poison," and he understood. There was no way of controlling her behavior, although her personality was growing more docile as time went by.

Then, before he did anything about it, Kailani wrote to Kaito with a suggestion that made his heart soar.

Dear Ojiichan,

I hope this finds you well. Sara tells me that Obaachan's condition continues to regress and I am finally mature enough to realize I would like to come and help you. I guess my nursing studies have awakened some realities in my life that I have long stifled and now I have a strong desire to connect to my roots.

Would you consider having me come to stay with you for two months through the summer? I would like to be Obaachan's caregiver and to spend time with you. My heart is hurting for all the years we have not had together, and I would like to try to make amends.

Think about this.

Jake has asked me to come and stay with him. I would like to get to know him better but I would prefer to stay with you. What do you think?

Our family has been fractured for such a long time ... like my entire life! I want to do my part to help repair that.

I am waiting to hear from you, with love.

Kailani

This was another landmark moment for Kaito. He was stunned to have his granddaughter make this suggestion. Stunned and thrilled and nervous.

But after his visit to Céleste and all the new experiences to which he had opened himself, he felt ready and strong enough to give this a try. This newly released side of Kaito's personality, his belief in himself and taking chances, was telling him to go for it.

For a few days he thought through the possible problems that might arise. He concluded that if things were not working out with Hana, he would rent Kailani a nearby apartment.

At dinner with Bob and Gail one evening he told them about Kailani's letter. Without hesitation they offered to have her stay with them if need be.

Now that he felt there were options, Kaito asked Auntie how she felt. He respected the fact that she was Hana's primary caregiver and wanted to be certain she was happy to have this assistance.

Her response was no surprise. "I am so thrilled for you. I know how much this means. Of course, welcome Kailani to your home and we will see how things go. I might enjoy having a little time off. You know I will do all I can to help in every way."

He arranged to join Auntie when she was sitting with Hana in the garden. He explained the plans to Hana, anticipating some pushback but hoping for the best.

Hana listened impassively. When she spoke, her voice was hushed and tentative. "Kailani? Our granddaughter?"

Kaito held his breath.

Hana stood, expressionless. "Where has she been? Of course she should come. Now I have sewing to do." And with that she turned to go into the house.

Kaito and Auntie exchanged glances. That was the most Hana had said to Kaito in a long time. They wondered if she truly understood.

Before Auntie left that evening, she told Kaito that Hana had said nothing more about Kailani. "I will continue to mention she is coming and talk about what help she will be. I will let you know if there are any concerns."

Kaito felt a sense of peace when Auntie placed her hand on his arm in the most reassuring way. She patted it gently and nodded her head as her eyes glistened. "We will make this work."

CHAPTER 44

2011

*S*cattered cotton-puff clouds danced across the cerulean sky, lifting Kaito's spirits on the morning in mid-April as he waited at the airport to welcome Kailani. Still, the experience felt bittersweet, as it was impossible to stifle memories of Kiana.

But he felt this was a pivotal moment. Another forward step in his life that had been stuck for so long.

Finding Lailani the previous year had opened his heart in so many ways. He had begun to believe in life again—to be reminded that there is magic in the universe and change can happen. Karma.

He had never imagined he would become unstuck, but his world was opening up.

Now, something else he had hoped for but not expected was about to occur.

Kaito had never stopped sending his granddaughter a birthday card that included a short letter and money each year. She had always responded with polite, well-written letters giving him some windows into her life. When she turned sixteen and received a phone for her birthday, they began texting and having conversations on FaceTime. When Kailani was ready to go to university, they had reached an agreement that he would pay her tuition even though she had explained again that her trust fund more than covered the costs.

"My sweet Kailani, this is one way that I can try to forgive my absence in your life and that of your mother." She understood.

Kaito thought he already had a good understanding of his granddaughter's personality through those conversations.

Kailani had requested that he alone meet her at the airport. She explained she had talked with Jake and said she wanted to meet him after she had settled in at Kaito's.

To Kaito's surprise, Jake called him to say he understood her wish and would wait patiently for her to want to see him. It was another example of how Kaito saw Jake's commitment to living a life of peace and understanding.

Holding a delicately fragrant purple orchid lei in his hand, Kaito nervously paced as he awaited the plane's arrival. His heart palpitated wildly and he rubbed his free hand over his head every few minutes, a sure sign he was jittery.

There was a constant flow of large groups of enthusiastic lei-wearing tourists moving through the terminal, calling out loud alohas and exclaiming at the dazzling scenery they could see out the expansive windows.

The arrivals board indicated Kailani's plane had touched down. Kaito scanned the crowds anxiously. He had considered making a sign with her name on it and thought perhaps now he should have. What if they did not recognize each other? He knew he was being paranoid because they had just spoken on a video call recently. But still …

There was no mistaking the wide grin and sparkling eyes of the excited young woman who rushed up and threw her arms around him. There were no tears, just pure happiness and a strong personality thrilled to have her grandfather in her life.

After the hug, Kaito placed the lei around her neck. He swallowed back his own tears and allowed her high spirits to lift him.

"Aloha, Kailani ... granddaughter ... I am so very happy to have you standing here beside me ... and hugging me!" Then he bowed.

Kailani laughed sweetly and bowed back. "Sara told me you would bow! She has really become so American and not retained much of her Japanese culture. She said you were always such a gentleman, even in high school! I am so eager to learn our family's traditions from you."

Kaito laughed in return. "I believe we have much to learn from each other."

He looked into her deep, dark eyes and felt an instant bond ... as well as a sharp pang in his heart. They were the eyes of her mother.

He knew they both needed to take their relationship slowly. There were wounds to be healed.

Forgiveness. He sought forgiveness from Kailani. He sought it from himself.

As they drove through the city to his neighborhood, Kailani looked around and commented on how excited she was to be back in Hawaii. She sighed and clapped as they drove along Waikiki Beach.

"I can't wait to go surfing and swimming at Waikiki! The waters of the beaches in Oregon don't quite compare!" She ended with a laugh. "They are stunningly beautiful in their own rugged way, but the water temperature? Brrrrr!"

Kaito laughed with her. "I can only imagine."

"I have very strong memories of how it was to live on Kauai, even though I was nine when the accident happened."

Kaito felt himself tense at the mention of the plane crash. He reached over and touched Kailani's hand. "That must be a terrible memory for you."

"It is. Because I lost Mama—and Papa too—and my whole world fell apart. But I have to tell you, she prepared me for whatever might happen in life, even at that age."

Kaito took his eyes off the road for a moment and looked at her. His heart was jolted to hear Kiana spoken of so easily.

"That's quite a statement. It says a lot about your mother ... and you. Your voice is surprisingly calm talking about it. Tell me more, if you are comfortable doing so."

"Mama talked about you all the time. She told me how strong and kind you were and how you always made her feel loved. She talked about *Obaachan* too, Grandmother ... the good as well as the not so good. She tried to help me understand why we never saw you."

Kaito spoke softly, trying to control his emotions. "I never imagined this."

"She showed me how to do the tea ceremony like you and my great-grandparents would do. And she told me bedtime stories about the hikes you took her on, making up funny legends. We made up mythical creatures and drew them to color. She was so artistic and she said that was from Obaachan and her beautiful needlework and sketches. I learned a lot about you. And about Lailani. Mama loved her like a mother."

Gulping back his emotions, Kaito nodded and stared straight ahead knowing he had to concentrate on his driving.

"I'm sorry if I am upsetting you," Kailani murmured as she touched his arm.

It took Kaito a moment to reply with control. "You are helping me to see sides of Kiana that I missed. Please do not stop."

After they pulled into the driveway, they sat talking for a few minutes.

Kaito had so many questions he wanted to ask. But he had promised himself he would wait and let them come slowly as he got to know his granddaughter and she him.

He also realized he might be stalling. He had no idea in what mood they would find Hana.

Finally Auntie poked her head out the door to see if everything was all right.

Kaito indicated with a wave they were coming.

"Auntie is very excited about meeting you. Her name is Rosie but she prefers that we call her Auntie. She was busy preparing a special lunch when I left for the airport. You will love her and see why I feel blessed to have found her. She's thrilled that you will help with Hana and she is also looking forward to some time off this summer … an unexpected bonus you have brought."

Kailani grinned as they got out of the car.

Auntie greeted Kailani in Hawaiian and placed a kiss on each cheek. Kailani responded back perfectly. "I want to practice speaking Hawaiian while I'm here. I hope you will be happy to help me."

Auntie nodded enthusiastically. "'A 'ole palikir! No problem!" Then she made the shaka sign with her thumb and pinkie extended and her other fingers curled under.

Kailani laughed and returned the sign. "I love the shaka and have all my friends in Oregon doing it."

Auntie gestured toward the dining table she had set up in the lanai.

"Auntie!" Kaito exclaimed. "Are we having the entire neighborhood for lunch? We could feed them all easily with this spread."

Auntie laughed and explained that it looked like more than it was and leftovers would be good for a day or two. "There's your favorite lobster salad with papaya and Maui onion, steamed baby bok choy, coconut basmati rice bundles, ginger-glazed salmon fillets, of course some poi, and baby pineapples with pineapple sherbet. Kailani, I hope you will enjoy it as much as your grandfather will."

"Auntie, you promised you would join us, so I hope you have not changed your mind," Kaito said.

With a chuckle, she replied, "Why do you think I made some of my favorite dishes? I would be delighted to join you."

Kaito gave Kailani a quick tour of the house, saying the garden tour would come later. When Kailani entered Hana's studio, her eyes lit up.

"How magical! It's like walking into a painting with all of these colors arranged so beautifully! I was so looking forward to seeing this. I hope I can watch her work one day."

Kaito shook his head. "She is very controlling about what happens in here, so don't count on that. I'm just so grateful this has been the heartbeat of her life for such a long time."

Kaito had explained to Kailani, in online conversations, that Hana had never lost her ability to sew and still worked on projects, although to a lesser degree.

He peeked in on Hana, who was sleeping in her room. He felt relieved that the moment of her meeting Kailani would not happen just yet. "She's having her own post-lunch nap right now so we will see her when she wakes."

CHAPTER 45

They lingered over lunch in the lanai with the sweet fragrance wafting in from the gardenia blossoms blooming profusely throughout the garden. The conversation centered, in between expressions of how delicious everything was, around Hana and how Kailani could help.

She and Auntie agreed to sit down in a day or two and work out a schedule. Auntie would continue to be there every day until Kailani felt comfortable doing things on her own.

"After that, if you agree, I am going to drop off dinner on Monday, Wednesday, and Friday, no matter what. So you can choose any of those days—or all of them—to have time off," Auntie said. "That is what your grandfather and I agreed upon. And once a week I will clean the house. Again, with your permission."

Kailani looked at Kaito and began to object, but he interrupted. "No, I insist. Auntie is accustomed to doing everything and I am going to continue her salary. She is the boss of these matters. Trust me, you will appreciate having her help when you see how your time will be taken up caring for Hana. And you need to have time off to enjoy living on our beautiful island."

Auntie nodded her agreement. "Bathing, dressing, eating ... everything takes longer. And you will need free time to have some fun here too."

Kaito continued. "And remember. If you do not want to continue at any point, that is not a problem. It is very sweet and kind of you to want to help, but that might change and that is okay. I want you to be happy here. Just looking across the table and realizing you are here makes my heart swell with joy."

He did not mention a thought he was saving. Perhaps a visit to Kauai could happen and she could show him where they lived.

While Auntie served the dessert, she and Kailani spoke about the nursing degree and the courses Kailani was taking. Kaito was certain Auntie was assuring herself that the young woman was well prepared to look after her grandmother.

His mind was spinning as he worked to process how the day had unfolded to this point. Not only was his granddaughter sitting across the table from him, but she was a confident, exuberant young woman who had opened his heart in the most unexpected ways on a half-hour car ride.

She had brought her mother, his daughter Kiana, to life in those thirty minutes and placed healing salve on some of the deep wounds in his heart. He felt in a state of shock—but in the best way.

He wished he could tell her about Lailani. However, he knew that was something he could never share with anyone. The heartfelt thoughts about her that Kiana had shared with her daughter were a good place for her memory to rest.

AFTER THEY HAD DONE justice to the delicious lunch Auntie had prepared, she gestured to Kaito and Kailani to leave the table. They all insisted on helping clear up and Kaito felt satisfied that the summer was going to be one of collaboration and positivity.

"*Ojiichan*, do you think *Obaachan* will be awake now?" Kailani asked.

Kaito's happy feelings came to an abrupt halt as he realized this moment he had been avoiding had to be faced. He was worried how Hana would react to Kailani and if she would recognize anything of Kiana in her. The last thing he wanted was for his granddaughter to be the victim of hurt in any way.

Kailani touched his arm and Kaito was astounded at her level of intuition. "Ojiichan, I can see the worry on your face. Please don't be concerned. I can handle whatever comes next."

He put his hand over hers. "You are so perceptive. Remember her dementia is becoming more advanced and she rarely speaks, even if she flies into a rage. She often shrinks from touch, so keep that in mind."

They had discussed whether or not to tell Hana at the first meeting that this was her granddaughter. It was Kailani who had convinced Kaito it was right to do it and she could handle whatever the reaction. She would not take it personally.

It had been another moment when Kaito felt such pride in this young woman.

Kaito tapped lightly on Hana's bedroom door and opened it a crack. She was sitting in a chair looking out at the garden. She would have had a clear view of the three of them at lunch when she woke up.

He noticed Auntie had helped Hana bathe and dress with care that morning. She wore a fresh lei around the neck of her colorful muumuu and had a bright pink hibiscus blossom tucked in her hair.

With his heart in his mouth, Kaito led Kailani to her grandmother. "*Pulele*, you have a special visitor."

Hana still looked straight ahead, out the window. Kailani bowed to her and gently took her hand.

Kaito held his breath.

"Obaachan, I am so happy to finally see you. I am Kailani, your granddaughter."

Slowly Hana's gaze turned and rested on Kailani.

Kailani bent down as she softly repeated her words. "Obaachan, I am Kailani. I am your granddaughter."

Then the unexpected occurred. Hana placed the palms of her hands on Kailani's cheeks and looked into her eyes. The corners of her mouth turned up in the semblance of a smile.

Kaito felt tears pushing behind his eyes. He gulped them down as it seemed his heart might burst.

Hana said nothing but held Kailani's face for long moments.

Kailani's eyes glistened. "I have come to spend the summer with you. To help you. To love you." She gently slid her arms around Hana and held her in a light embrace. Hana did not respond but she also did not react negatively.

As Kailani began to straighten up, Hana stood too and took her granddaughter's hand as she led her back to the bed. Then Hana climbed on the bed, put her head on the pillow and closed her eyes, still holding Kailani's hand.

Kailani found enough room to sit beside Hana. Not letting go of Hana's hand, she softly stroked her grandmother's hair until the old woman fell asleep again.

KAILANI NEVER CEASED to surprise Kaito with her ability to fit into their home life and look after Hana with a perfect mix of love and professionalism. She connected that first day she held Hana's hand, and from day one Hana smiled whenever Kailani entered a room.

Kaito allowed himself to hope for miracles when he saw how competent Kailani was in dealing with Hana's challenges.

"I can see there isn't anything we can repair, Ojiichan. Auntie explained everything to me in great detail. The doctor's papers you have shared with me only clarified what you told me before I came here. What we can do is help her to be comfortable every day. I can do that."

And do that she did. Between Auntie and Kailani, there was a sense of peace in the house that had been missing. Kaito gradually realized that part of that peace came from his having a sense of purpose in having his granddaughter there to teach and guide, as well as being someone to talk to and laugh with in the evenings rather than spending so many long hours alone.

The photo wall fascinated Kailani. She regularly asked Kaito to tell her details and barraged him with questions. He took pleasure in reliving with her the memories the pictures held, and she seemed happy to learn more about her family history.

CHAPTER 46

*I*n the weeks that followed, the barrier to forgiveness began to break down between a father and grandfather who both had much to regret.

Surprisingly, after an initial awkward reunion, Jake sometimes joined them for a meal or a visit in the garden. He spoke openly about his remorse for his past life and his desire to fill the years he had left doing whatever good he could.

The three of them had conversations about his volunteer work at the local halfway house for youths fighting addiction. Kailani and Kaito went with him one day so he could show them around. His pride was obvious and there was a definite sense of healing for all of them.

Through Jake sharing his stories of life with Kiana, Kaito had gradually begun to accept him and heal his hatred. Kaito's talking about Jake with Lailani also helped.

In his daily prayers to Kiana, he asked for her permission to find forgiveness for Jake.

Now they all were making forgiveness happen together. It was part of the glimmer of hope he held in his heart—that the sense of family he had been denied so long might be returned to him.

In the days immediately after Kailani's arrival, he suggested they repair memorial lanterns as a way of having a project to share as he had with Kiana. While they worked on patching the wood and painting the rice paper shades, he answered many probing questions as they talked about the past and she discovered some of her history.

Weeks later, they attended the emotional service at Ala Moana Beach Park on Memorial Day. Gail and Bob joined them, as did Jake. It seemed as though the entire town was there remembering so many who had given so much during the war as well as their own lost family members.

Kaito, Kailani, and Jake floated lanterns for Kiana. Kaito had prepared a lantern for Brett and Lailani's memory, as he did every year. It was difficult for Kaito not to reveal the truth about Lailani, but he continued the pretense.

He was almost afraid to admit how happy he was to have his granddaughter back in his life. Deep within him was the fear that she might disappear from him, like her mother.

Gail and Bob introduced Kailani to their children who now were married and living in Honolulu, and they in turn introduced her to younger friends of theirs. Some evenings and weekends she socialized with people her age; Kaito was delighted to see her have fun.

She was excited to spend time at the K&K Studio. "Mama told me many stories of doing aikido and all the kids she played with here. They were part of her happy memories and you made those happen. I hope you cherish that."

Kailani had a knack of turning bittersweet into something that fed his soul and helped smooth some of the sharp edges of the regret that lived inside him.

He relished the time they spent together and was encouraged to see Jake's efforts to be a father figure cautiously acknowledged by Kailani.

She spoke often about her love for her Aunt Sara and the family she had grown up with in Oregon. Her memories of Kiana were strong and deep, and she often referred to her mother. This filled Kaito's heart with love.

He took such pleasure in her presence. She was the image of her mother and grandmother, with sleek black hair and dark ebony eyes.

When Kaito first held his daughter in his arms, he had lost himself in her eyes and said they were like molten pools in Hawaiian forests. Now he saw that same image in his grand-daughter's eyes. He was overjoyed to discover she also shared her mother's love of nature and was happy to accompany him on hikes.

To his surprise, Kailani had some warm memories of her childhood that involved both of her parents. When she first spoke of those times in Kaito's presence, his face paled and his body language betrayed his discomfort. But Kailani was relentless in her ability to drill down to the heart of those times and bring to life the love and laughter that she treasured. It was impossible not to be drawn in and feel happy for her. And for Jake.

She expressed to Kaito on many occasions, much to his surprise, how Jake was always a loving father and doting husband when he was around. She remembered there were often long absences. All of this helped Kaito picture a glimpse of how their life had been.

"Of course, I know now he was a kingpin in the drug world and I'm not proud of that. When I first was told, it almost destroyed me. I wanted to hate him. But I also know he shielded us from that to give Mom and me a happy life. He was simply my daddy. I never knew what he did. We lived a separate, almost normal life in a beautiful home on a quiet beach on

Kauai. I played with friends, went to school where Mom volunteered. We surfed and had fun. My mom was always kind and
loving. I guess we were our own little unit."

In ways he would never have imagined, Kaito went to sleep
many nights feeling proud of Kiana. She had somehow created a
decent, happy life for her and her daughter in spite of the one
choice he could not understand, no matter how hard he tried.
His heart would always hurt knowing he had not been able to
protect her from the hate she felt from her mother.

This stung. In the worst way. As he wrestled with tortured
and conflicting knots of guilt, frustration, and anger that were
buried deep in his soul, meditation was his primary relief. But
now he also knew he had the opportunity to talk through these
feelings with Lailani during their Sunday chats. The more he
spoke with her, the less often he felt the need to see a counselor.

He also spoke with Kiana through his prayers to her at his
little shrine at home. He would light incense and tell her all
about her daughter, wishing her happy feelings to know these
things.

He put a great deal of effort into banishing the painful negative thoughts and tried to focus on being filled with admiration
for his granddaughter. There was no denying it was truly a
blessing that she had come into his life.

Two blessings in one year was more than anyone truly could
hope for, he reminded himself often. He approached each day
with more gratitude than ever.

As much as she appeared to feel comfortable and welcome in
Hawaii, Kailani always indicated that her future lay in Oregon.
But she promised she would return to Hawaii for visits.

Kaito's hope was dashed that his granddaughter might want
to return to Honolulu permanently. But this disappointment
was tempered by the knowledge that his retreats in September
had turned into so much more.

Thinking back to Koyasan, he reflected how the days he had

spent in Vipassana meditation had been curative. But what had impacted his life more than anything was the serendipitous reunion with Lailani.

He wondered if he would ever get over the shock of that. But it turned out to be a shock in such a positive way. To have a friendship of such depth be delivered back into his life was beyond comprehension. There always would be a mystical sense to it … something that was meant to happen. For what reason, he could not possibly imagine. But happen it had.

Ironically, as Céleste, she had also pushed him more into the current use of technology. She introduced him to Skype and encouraged him to use email for personal reasons, instead of just his business mail.

"Really, Kaito! It's not too late for you to catch up with the rest of the world."

Kaito felt that he had begun to build strategies for this new chapter in his life that included Lailani. But first he would have to solve the problem of Lailani/Céleste's identity. He might have to accept that this would remain a secret forever.

CHAPTER 47

*T*he summer months passed by quickly. Kailani's infectious spirit of lightness brightened life in every way. Each day Hana was bathed and dressed in muumuus. Kailani had gone through her wardrobe, donating old items to the local women's hostel and purchasing stylish new clothes that suited her body that was again as slender as she'd been in high school.

Kailani put so much love into her care of Hana that Kaito had a sense even Hana was being touched by it. Her tantrums were fewer and there were many more days where she could be brought to sit in the garden with an expression that was more peaceful than he had witnessed for a very long time.

Her desire to converse had gradually disappeared, but she would nod and sometimes even smile when spoken to. Whether she actually understood was a question none of them could answer. The doctor had indicated that most of the time Hana was now lost inside herself.

But where Kaito had despaired that Hana was broken, he now saw signs that she may actually have pleasurable moments from time to time.

The greatest surprise had occurred not long after Kailani's arrival, when Hana had led her by the hand to her studio. She indicated to her granddaughter to sit beside her and proceeded to show her how she stitched.

After that there were times when Kailani sat with her own piece of silk and learned some basic patterns. Hana would look at her wordlessly, model a stitch, and smile warmly as Kailani copied it.

Kaito and Auntie were reduced to tears when they saw this for themselves.

"Truly a miracle," Kaito whispered.

Kailani would sing to Hana and play music on the ukulele that Auntie kept at the house. If Auntie was around, they were sometimes treated to a duet of traditional Hawaiian songs. Auntie never needed much encouragement to perform a lengthy hula and Kailani would sometimes join her. These were moments Kaito had never dared to dream about.

Not that everything was peaceful. At random instances Hana would become agitated and go off on loud streams of indecipherable babbling. Kailani had an ability to temper these outbursts and guide Hana back to her room with soothing words. She would stay with Hana and read to her or put on quiet music until she fell asleep.

THE AFTERNOON KAITO and Jake drove Kailani to the airport was filled with a mixture of emotion. So much had been accomplished—the most important thing being forgiveness. A sense of family had been reestablished. There had been joy and laughter and a feeling of normalcy that Kaito had longed for.

"Thank you for everything, Ojiichan. These months here with you and Obaachan have been more than I could have hoped for," Kailani said as she hugged him tightly and gave him a very loud kiss on the cheek.

Kaito grinned, knowing she did that in public to tease him.

Then Kailani's eyes grew serious as she continued. "You have given me something that I have missed all my life. I cannot thank you enough."

"It is I who should thank you, my sweet granddaughter," Kaito said, his voice filled with emotion. "You have given me not just your presence, but the spirit of your mother as well. Thank you for taking such loving care of Obaachan. This was a gift that could never have been imagined. You brought family back to us."

Kailani hugged him gently once more and then they bowed to each other, as she grinned. "I will be back next summer to do this all over again. Enjoy your visit to Japan again next month. I hope you will be safe after the dreadful earthquake last March. Send me some photos this year now that I know what you do there."

Kaito assured her he would be very safe and he would be happy to send photos. "Now that you have shown me how easy it is to do with my cell phone and on the computer."

"You are turning into quite the techie," she teased.

He grinned ruefully. "Apparently old dogs can learn new tricks."

Kailani turned to Jake and said, "Papa, you have become the father I remembered. What has happened in the years we missed must be buried. I know you did not mean to hurt me and I believe you have always loved me. I loved a memory. This summer you have done everything possible to be a father to me again. Thank you."

She reached out her arms to accept a hug from him. "I admire all you have done to change your life."

Jake nodded silently, his face twisted with emotion, before he finally whispered, "You are your mother's child. I see her in your every action and I am so very proud of you. I am blessed to have you accept me in your life again when you really have every reason not to do so."

There was a pause before he continued, his voice quavering, "I love you very much."

Kailani met his gaze and leaned in to lightly kiss his cheek.

The two men waved goodbye as she disappeared down the hall to the departure lounge. Then they looked at each other with expressions of mutual satisfaction.

"What an amazing daughter you have," Kaito said.

"And an equally amazing granddaughter you have," Jake replied. "How lucky we are." Then he bowed in respect to Kaito and said, "Thank you for giving me this chance of family again. It all begins with you."

Kaito felt his entire being fill with a warmth that could only be the result of loving and being loved within the embrace of family. It was something he had envied in others, certainly most recently with Céleste's family, and something he had long given up on for himself.

CHAPTER 48

2011

$\mathcal{T}$his year's trip to Koyasan was decidedly different from any of the others. It was the first trip where Kaito knew he was staying for just two weeks and then going to visit Lailani in France.

But there were other emotions involved as well.

As it happened, Bob was also going to Koyasan at the same time, as the two had done on occasion before. They had both determined to take the trip together after the shocking earthquake and tsunami at Fukushima in March. Their connection to the country and the people had become a strong one after so many visits, and the trip became of vital importance.

They had offered prayers at the temple in Honolulu, but there was another dimension to being in Japan to offer prayers and burn incense for the recovery from the disaster there. Both men shared a feeling of gratitude to the country for all they gained from years of visiting Koyasan. They wanted to see how they might give back.

Bob was surprised when Kaito explained he was only staying for two weeks but that he would not be going on the return flight to Honolulu with Bob.

Kaito had been disconcerted initially. He had never been in a position where he felt he had to be deceptive to someone he cared about. At first he hoped that Gail and Bob would be meeting up somewhere afterward, but that was not happening this year.

He gave himself a shake for feeling guilty ... about nothing really, he told himself.

"I've taken your advice about traveling somewhere else, and I'm going to visit friends ... a family in the South of France."

Bob was excited for him. "Oh man! I can't wait to hear all about that. It's somewhere we have always wanted to go!"

The weather in Koyasan could not have been worse. It poured every day. There was no opportunity to hike or enjoy nature or even meditate in the gardens. Although Kaito did venture out in all-weather gear one day to experiment with photography in the rain, it was not an enjoyable undertaking.

There was a feeling of despair throughout much of the town as the citizens were still in shock after the terrible tragedy of the earthquake and tsunami in Fukushima just six months earlier. Kaito joined in special prayers for lost souls and survivors and spoke with several people who had gone to help search for family members in the area, which was about five hundred miles away.

These were times when it was difficult to rejoice for the good things in his life. He searched the teachings of the monks for guidance and to accept that all things are transient. There was no going back. *Gaman.* From adversity we must move forward, be mindful and accept change.

He hoped that the ten-day Vipassana he had registered for would immerse him in this state of mind.

He had recognized during the past year that his time of daily meditation at home since his last visit had increased and he wondered if there was a subconscious reason. There were times he felt guilty for his reconnection with Lailani.

He always dismissed this as quickly as he could. She was a friend. A friend he thought had died. And he was filled with joy to have her in his life. If Hana had not been ill they would have been able to share that joy. But that was not the case.

He hoped that ten days of concentrated introspection with no eye contact or any other sort of connection with anyone or anything would help assuage his concerns. Since he had experienced the shortened Vipassana many times, after a day or two he was able to journey to the most important part of the process: that of maintaining focus solely on the ever-changing flow of breath as it enters and leaves the nostrils. Essentially the goal is to free the mind to do nothing and to achieve a state of calm and goodwill.

Kaito often wondered afterward whether he was just convincing himself that he was making progress. He knew he would never stop seeking the peace, balance, and absence of noise in his life. But he did know that he felt like he was progressing to higher levels, and he told Bob that was the best he could hope for.

"Well, that's kind of it, isn't it? It's so individual," Bob said. "After you've done it often enough, you can move through those difficult times that brought you to meditate in the first place."

"When I hit that 'no-mind' state, I feel my mind clear and I've trashed the bad karma at that moment. There's a feeling of inner peace and I know I am reaching a new level. But the seeking never stops. There is always more to strive for. That's why monks never stop learning and they model that for followers like me."

They shared a fist bump. "I never see the monks doing this," Kaito said, and they laughed.

"That's a whole other level we need to keep working towards," Bob quipped.

On his final day at Koyasan, Kaito remained in the presence of the monks as they chanted prayers. The peaceful drone of their voices, the ringing of cymbals and bells, and the fragrance of incense filled him with a serenity he hoped to carry with him.

CHAPTER 49

2011

$\mathcal{K}$aito's arrival in Nice for the second year felt comfortable and familiar. He had again booked his seat on the right side of the plane, and even though he knew he had taken the same photos on his previous trip, he couldn't resist taking more. The views were simply too splendid and there were so many factors, such as light and shadow, that would produce different effects.

As he waited in line at Passport Control, Kaito was aware of the elation he felt at being back in France. A thrill ran up his spine. He was eager to spend time with Céleste and her family and feel the warmth and affection he knew would be waiting.

Céleste waved excitedly, Bébé at her side, at their agreed meeting place. Kaito felt his grin take over his face. They bowed, shared *bisous*, and finally hugged.

"Bienvenue, Kaito! It's so good to see you in the flesh!" Céleste greeted him, as she stepped back from the hug and took his hand.

Kaito brought her hand to his lips. "Bonjour, Céleste, chèrie! My feelings exactly! Let me begin by acting French!"

After a year of online video chats, there was a comfortable easiness to their interactions.

They were soon in the car, winding their way up into the hills along the Haute Corniche. This time Kaito was behind the wheel.

"Even though I saw all of this last year, it fills me with the same wonder and joy," Kaito exclaimed. "This is such a spectacular route! I've been thinking of driving it for an entire year!"

Céleste grinned.

As he pulled into the parking lot at the edge of town, Kaito smiled to see Martin and Jacques on their way down the path to meet him as they had the year before. It all felt so familiar this time. When this visit was in the planning stages, Martin and his wife Danielle insisted Kaito stay with them rather than in the small auberge in their village.

Kaito had surprised himself by feeling comfortable about accepting their invitation. He noted at the time this was one more instance where he was opening himself to other social experiences. This previous year had been one of change.

After a warm welcome, they took Kaito's bags while he and Céleste went on to her home, a short walk away. Bébé led the way. They would gather for dinner at Martin's after the boulangerie closed for the day.

Relaxing on the terrace with a pitcher of ice-cold lemonade, Kaito and Céleste discussed the plan they had been working on that would organize their activities for his two-week stay. During a previous video chat Kaito had suggested that he have a few days on his own.

"You were the perfect hostess last year and spent every minute making certain I was entertained. I don't want to feel I am taking up all of your time. I know you have other things going on in your life."

"As I said before, Kaito, you can't deprive me of your

company after all these years. It simply would not be fair!" she insisted again.

But she also remembered what a private person he was and how she needed to be understanding. So they agreed that he would go on a two-day overnight hike with the local *randonée*—touring—group to which Céleste belonged, but without her.

FOR THE FIRST few days of his visits, he and Céleste had put together a list of specific places new to him, and others he hoped they would revisit. Now that he knew what was waiting for him there, he eagerly anticipated the trip.

One day was spent at the Oceanographic Museum in Monaco. The elegant example of Baroque Revival architecture looked like it hung off a cliff that dropped into the sea in the old town of Monaco.

"It was inaugurated in 1910 and used over 100,000 tons of stone from our town," Céleste proudly told him. "From 1957 to 1988, Jacques Cousteau was the director."

They each went their own way and met up for lunch on the roof terrace early in the afternoon.

After he stopped raving about yet another spectacular view to enjoy, he added, "There are so many amazing exhibits that call for a great deal of time to properly appreciate. There's so much to learn here! I could easily come back many times again."

"*Pourquoi pas?* Why not? So you shall!" Céleste agreed.

RAPHAEL AND YVETTE invited them for a sunset dinner cruise on a friend's boat. They would leave from the harbor in Antibes and slowly make their way to Cannes. The weather promised to be perfect.

Kaito and Céleste left early in the day and spent the morning touring the magnificent Villa Ephrussi with its magical gardens and musical fountains on St. Jean Cap Ferrat. Then they lingered over a late lunch of fresh seafood at the edge of the harbor in Villefranche-sur-Mer.

The stunning scenery, delicious meal, and slightly chilled rosé had lulled Kaito into a very relaxed state. His eyes rested on Céleste's face. An umbrella shaded her from the intense sun. She was gazing out over the harbor and unaware of his focus on her. In this moment, it occurred to Kaito how beautiful she was with her glowing complexion, sparkling eyes, and full lips. He felt he was seeing her as never before, as a woman of desire and not simply an old friend.

He felt his own heartbeat and was suddenly flooded with warmth. As Céleste turned her attention back to him, the waiter appeared and engaged her in conversation. Kaito picked up his glass and sipped his rosé, quickly banishing the mood of pure romance that had overtaken him and left him feeling rather shaken.

Céleste fanned herself with a silk hand fan she always carried in her purse. As they watched people enjoying the popular beach and boats of all sizes coming and going, Kaito was philosophical. "The beauty of this part of the world is like something I never really imagined. I feel as though I am just discovering so many possibilities that were never a consideration in my life."

"But surely, you had dreams of travel to places like this, did you not?" Céleste asked.

He shook his head and looked at her with a serious expression. "To be honest, I can't say that I dream much when I sleep. And if you are referring to daydreams. I don't really have them."

She reached over and put her hand on his. "I have read that we dream to give ourselves hope. I know that I have dreams all the time. Surely you must have some."

Kaito felt a moment of intimacy with her hand on his. It was such a simple gesture. Friendship. Kindness. Caring. Something he had not experienced for such a long time … probably since Lailani disappeared.

He took a moment to consider her suggestion of dreams. "It's just not what I do. For so long my life has been laid out before me and there was no hope of it being different. Perhaps I do dream but I don't realize it or remember."

"Well, dear friend, my wish is that you begin to dream again. It is always good to have hope."

Kaito looked out pensively across the water. He had been without these kinds of thoughts for so many years. "I wonder if it is too late for that."

"It's never too late."

CHAPTER 50

The hiking group gathered at 7 a.m.

Céleste went along for a few minutes to introduce Kaito to her friends, some of whom remembered him from his previous visit. They were a friendly, lively group, keen to get started and very welcoming to Kaito.

Kaito was still affected by the moments he had experienced at lunch the day before. He felt he needed to shake off his moment of being seduced by the erotic ambiance of the French Riviera. He was stunned that such feelings had come to the surface so quickly. He was not looking for this. Not looking for anything except this beautiful friendship that had been returned to him.

After an hour's train ride up into the hills, the group disembarked with trail maps in hand. It was market day in the village and they stocked up on fresh fruit before setting off on well-trod paths up through the woods.

This particular trail was part of the ancient *route du sel*, salt route, across these hills from Italy into France. It was used to transport salt and other goods by donkey and cart from the Middle Ages through to the nineteenth century. Kaito found himself caught up in the historic ambiance of the surroundings and the complete transformation from the tropical setting of the Riviera to the distinctly mountainous environment.

The hikers enjoyed sharing the history of the area with Kaito. The goal of the day was to reach the formerly fortified mountain village of St. Martin-Vésubie that dated back to the 12th century. It sat nestled high up on the edge of the Parc National du Mercantour, near the Italian border.

The hiking was strenuous at times with some steep inclines but also sublime places where pristine streams flowed by and waterfalls tumbled down cliffs. Stopping to refill empty bottles, Kaito enjoyed long drinks of the cool, refreshing water. Along the way they passed through herds of cattle, sheep, and goats grazing in vast meadowlands and sighted a few mountain goats on rocky outcroppings.

By the time they reached their auberge in St. Martin-Vésubie, Kaito was ready for a rest but also curious to explore this village that had a decidedly alpine atmosphere. Shops sold hiking and skiing gear and there was also a mountain rescue station. He noted many inviting-looking restaurants with menus describing natural local products.

In the picturesque oldest part he was fascinated to see a rushing torrent of water running in a narrow channel down the middle of the main street. It had to be stepped over when crossing from one side to the other.

"It's called a *gargouille,* and there is just one other village nearby that also has one. The water is part of a mountain stream that originates high up and carries on below the village," Kaito was told.

He also noticed plaques in the town expressing gratitude during WWII for offering safe haven and escape to many French Jews. During dinner Kaito was told the story by his companions.

"In November 1942, the town was occupied by Italian

forces. The local Italian authorities were sympathetic to the plight of Jews and offered a safe haven to around twelve hundred of them. They were able to live without fear, housed and accepted by the local populace who themselves were already impoverished by the conditions of the war. When the Germans took over in 1943, alerts were sent out secretly and the Jews helped to escape into Italy, on a long hazardous trek along the paths by shepherds and other locals. Although many perished, over 600 survived and the town has always been remembered for this. The citizens are extremely proud of it."

Kaito was deeply touched by the story and texted to Céleste that he would love to return with her to explore the area in greater detail. He was aware how natural it was for him to think of her at a time like this and to want to share the experience with her.

She replied, agreeing and adding that he would love to do the drive. "It's full of hairpin curves and was once part of the Monte Carlo car rally each year. There's also a ski area up there."

It was not lost on Kaito how well she knew him and what he liked to do. They had shared so many experiences during the impressionable years of their youth.

Kaito climbed into his simple but comfortable bed, his head spinning with the events of the day and the history. He contemplated how different an experience he was having compared to his solitary hikes in Hawaii and even in Japan. This time he was part of a large group that enjoyed socializing and, to his surprise, he was feeling very comfortable about joining in their conversations. He was touched by how thoughtful they were about speaking as much English as possible so he would feel included.

He slept soundly after the exercise and fresh mountain air of the day's exertions.

The group set off after a light breakfast. The terrain was

more challenging and there was much talk of wolves in the area. Kaito learned of the Alpha Loup Wolf Park where packs were kept in their natural habitat. Wild wolves had been hunted and their numbers decimated mostly by angry sheep farmers. In 2005 there was an undertaking to return wolves to the area but keep them in a safe, contained—but large—space.

Kaito made a note to see about visiting that park with Céleste as well.

During the lunch stop that felt pretty much like the top of the world, the guide pointed out how they could make out the mountaintops of Corsica on such a clear day.

Kaito noted the good shape of all of the hikers and the steady pace they kept on the walks. By mid-afternoon, they reached a charming semi-abandoned village hanging from the edge of a cliff. At the local bar, cold beer was the choice of some and strong espresso of others. A bus was waiting to take the group back to their original starting point.

On the bus he sat back, again as if looking at himself from a distance, and recognized how he was enjoying socializing with these people, strangers really. It was something he had cut out of his life. And now he was finding he enjoyed the camaraderie … and moved easily into it. Somewhere inside him, doors were being opened that he had kept firmly closed.

He also could not believe that all he had experienced on these two days had taken place just over one hour's drive away from the Côte d'Azur.

CHAPTER 51

*A*lthough Kaito had prepared himself for hiking with his usual stretching routines, he felt the effects of the two days in the hills for several days after.

Céleste suggested they spend a few quiet days reading on the terrace and floating about in her pool. Kaito did not have to be persuaded and was happy to have some quiet time to describe his hiking experience to Céleste.

"I know you have been up in that area and have done so many hikes with that group, but I have to tell you what a positive experience it was for me. Not just the hiking exercise, but the camaraderie and stunning scenery ... and the history. I was so moved by the stories people told about what happened during WWII."

Céleste nodded. Her voice was charged with emotion as she told him, "*Absoluement!* The Résistance was so active throughout France. You know, part of the story in St. Martin is that when the Germans first arrived, there were several children who were not taken on the escape trek because people thought they would not survive the arduous trip. So some families in town claimed them as their own. Fake identification had been prepared and they kept those kids alive right through the Occupation."

The emotional conversation continued for some time as Céleste answered Kaito's questions and told more harrowing tales.

He shared with her how surprised he was to feel comfortable with and enjoy the company of a group of strangers.

Céleste smiled knowingly. "It makes me so happy to see the old Kaito I knew. You always were sociable and liked by everyone. But I know from what you have told me that this is not how you have conducted your life for a long time. Hana's illness has kept you a prisoner."

Kaito's expression was pensive. "But it was not her fault. That was my choice. It was easier not to have to explain our home situation to anyone. I chose this way to live to protect her."

THE PACE of this visit was more relaxed than the first one. Part of the charm of this area was that they could pop out for a half hour drive and be in another stunning setting, stop for a beverage of some sort, and be back by the pool in no time.

As part of their advance planning for Kaito's visit, Céleste also agreed that he should spend a couple of days in Nice. He had been fascinated by the town the year before. Céleste made a few suggestions and he booked a room for two nights at the Hôtel Beau Rivage.

The location was perfect with the Cours Saleya old town and daily market just down the street and the Mediterranean and Promenade des Anglais across the street in the other direction. He could easily walk anywhere to places he wanted to see.

Céleste spent the first day with him, guiding him around, and left him with a list of places she recommended, along with the Rick Steves walking tour. They agreed that on his last day there she would come down to have lunch with him at the hotel restaurant right on the beach.

~

NICE CAPTIVATED KAITO. The colorful, Italian-influenced architecture gave the town a unique presence that appealed to his senses in every way. He filled his days with sightseeing, galleries, fine meals, and walking or biking the four miles of the Promenade des Anglais each morning.

Rental bikes were available all through the town and Kaito climbed on one for the first time in decades. In no time, he felt as though he had never stopped biking and vowed to look into getting a bike when he was back in Honolulu.

He strolled the daily market on Cours Saleya, absorbing the atmosphere. His shutter clicked endlessly. Colors, smells, sounds—all senses were engaged. Whether it was the displays of fresh local products, flowers, or the lively banter of the vendors, the atmosphere was electric.

The days were hot and the sea beckoned. The hotel had its own beach right across the street and by mid-afternoon each day Kaito organized a lounge and was settled in with a book and large bottle of water. The Mediterranean was refreshing, and floating on his back he looked out at the evocative architecture that spoke of another era and the unfolding hills beyond the town.

He contemplated the vast difference between the stunning beaches of Hawaii and this Mediterranean treasure. There definitely was no surf here, no underwater sea life that compared, the setting was urban, and the only palm trees were back on street level, and those stones—only a few small sections with trucked-in sand. And yet there was a distinct allure.

He thought about how he was enjoying being the consummate tourist and wondered if he was being teased by this culture that was so much the opposite of his home territory. Or was he falling in love with it?

On his first visit everything was new. But this time he knew what to expect, yet none of his initial pleasure had worn off. If anything, it had intensified.

On the third day, Céleste joined him for lunch in the more formal dining area at the beach restaurant. White linen and fine silverware settings brought an elegance to the beach setting. The menu made it difficult to choose with its varied selection.

"Somehow in France everything just works," Kaito said to Céleste as he pulled out her chair and the carafe of rosé he had ordered in advance was delivered to the table. She smiled knowingly.

"Oh, I know I'm generalizing," Kaito went on. "And there is much more than what I'm being exposed to on my trips ... the same cultural, economic, societal problems that plague us all no matter where we live. But from what I've seen here in the south there are basic components to life that are shared by everyone ... the weather, the scenery, the art that lives all around in the architecture, and ... the light. Now I understand what all those artists meant when they talked about it—Monet, Chagall, Matisse, Renoir, Picasso, Cocteau, the list goes on."

Céleste looked him straight in the eye. "I do believe you are smitten, *mon ami*. The South of France has invaded your soul."

They toasted with their glasses of chilled rosé.

THE LAST FEW days of his stay passed quickly. Saying goodbye to the family this time felt easy as everyone spoke not so much of his leaving but in positive terms about his next visit. It seemed that, as sure as September would come around again, so too would Kaito's arrival in La Turbie.

Kaito had been touched that during his stay, all of the family had inquired into Hana's health and expressed kind thoughts about the situation. He could not escape the heartache he felt whenever he thought about Hana. But it was such a part of him and after burying it from others for so long, it was almost a relief for him to speak openly.

As they parted at the "kissing spot" by the departures gate in the Nice airport, Kaito was aware of his eagerness to return. Céleste waved her hand at him graciously as he thanked her for the warm hospitality and wealth of memories he was taking with him.

"We've already got ideas for next year, mon ami," she said. "Give Hana a hug for me; I wish she could understand I still love her and think of her. And take care of life in Honolulu. If only things could be as they were so long ago and she could be here with us."

The reality of that never happening hung in the air between them.

In a moment of solemnity, their eyes met. A look of sorrow crossed Kaito's face and he nodded.

Céleste put a hand on his shoulder. There was sympathy in her eyes, understanding. "You are taking time for yourself here and I am so happy to be part of your life once again. Before we know it, Bébé and I will be collecting you here!"

Kaito nodded and felt his heart lighten. "I will never understand what brought us together in Koyasan. But I am so glad this has happened. We can't bring back the Hana we once knew but our lives go on."

They hugged. Céleste gave him a bise and Kaito bowed.

"I will see you online," were Kaito's last words. He could already feel anticipation for the next trip.

CHAPTER 52

2012

*T*his winter seemed like the longest Kaito could recall.

After years of little variation in his life, now he could look forward to not only his visits to Koyasan but also to France with Céleste and her family.

Kaito felt more alive than ever. However, he occasionally berated himself for feeling happy about it, even though he knew it would mean nothing to Hana.

Nothing changed in Kaito's dedication to Hana's care. He often looked at her tenderly and pictured her in France with him and Céleste. There had always been times through the long years of Hana's illness where he had fantasized about how life might have been had she been well. Those were moments when he had turned to meditation to ease the sorrow from his mind and keep him grounded in reality.

The months went by at what felt like a snail's pace until Kaito was once again at the Honolulu airport. Spring was in the air. This time he had two leis in hand. There was no trepidation, just eager anticipation.

Kailani greeted Kaito with even more enthusiasm than the

previous April. As before, her bright spirit lifted him immediately.

Cousin Sara also arrived with Kailani, at Kaito's invitation.

Kailani had asked her father, Jake, not to come to the airport, as Sara was not comfortable about seeing him for the first time. She had her own issues about him to resolve.

Kaito bowed solemnly as he greeted Sara. "After all this time, it is such a pleasure to see you and properly thank you for the good life you have given Kailani."

"The pleasure is mine, Kaito," she replied, returning his bow. "We have let too many years slip by."

She planned to stay with Kaito for two days and then go on to visit other relatives and old friends.

As they drove home, Kaito took a few detours to show Sara some of their old high school haunts. Sara exclaimed how the city had grown, and yet some of those familiar places had not changed much at all.

Kailani laughed and giggled at the stories about their teenage years.

Although he had mentioned his concerns during video chats with Kailani about Hana's not recognizing Sara, he raised the subject again now.

Sara's comforting words relieved his anxiety. "After listening to Kailani's experience last summer, I've been filled with a desire to see Hana. I know she probably won't know who I am, but as I get older these experiences have been weighing on my mind."

Auntie had been telling Kaito for weeks how excited she was that Kailani was returning. He smiled at the obvious pleasure and affection as they greeted each other.

Hana was in her studio, engrossed in her stitching when Kaito knocked on the door, which she had been leaving open since the previous summer. She looked up and saw Kailani smiling beside him. A bewildered expression crossed Hana's face and then she reached into a drawer and took out a rolled-up fabric. Still sitting, she extended it to Kailani, who unrolled the silk.

Kailani's smile grew into amazement as they watched a stunning pale yellow obi unfurl. A delicately embroidered garden with colorful flowers filled the length of the silk belt. Two splendid butterflies hovered above the blossoms and three white doves soared upwards. All around the border wound a graceful vine.

Hana waved her hand in a gesture that indicated this was for Kailani. She bowed her head with a faint smile.

Kailani, her eyes glistening, gently took Hana's hand and held a long bow. "*Obaachan,* do you remember me? I am ..."

Hana's voice whispered, "Kailani."

Kaito and Kailani stood dumbfounded.

"Thank you, my beloved grandmother. I will treasure this forever."

Hana returned to her stitching.

ALTHOUGH HANA WAS ENCOURAGED to join them for meals, she continued to spend most of her time in her studio, often taking Kailani by the hand to sit with her. They would stitch together.

The atmosphere in the house was lively and laughter-filled during Sara's brief stay as she revived memories of their school years. Auntie and Kailani were amused as Kaito filled in details of some of the stories, if Sara forgot them.

She mentioned their friend Lailani several times and that was a shock to Kaito. He hoped his responses did not make him seem weird, because it was most peculiar to speak of her in the past tense.

And Kailani was keen to know more about the stories that included this old friend, since she was in some ways her namesake. Kaito had shared some of those memories when they looked at the photo wall, and she was happy to hear more.

It was almost a relief to have Sara leave to carry on with her visits, just so the subject of Lailani was not raised again. He was constantly aware of the secrecy he'd promised to keep.

Kaito had worked to keep his expressions and words such that nothing was given away about the truth of Lailani's existence. But certainly all the talk had brought her to the forefront of his mind, and he told Céleste about Sara's visit during their Sunday chat.

Céleste's response to it all was not what Kaito would have expected. Her eyes were downcast as she said, "This makes me sad. How unfortunate that we can't tell the truth. Now that you and I are connected again, I keep thinking how nice it would be to return with Mama's ashes and see people I have missed. I've never struggled with this before and I guess it is no surprise that I would now. Oh Kaito, this is so bizarre."

Kaito felt her sadness. "Of course I understand that. But we both know you need to continue the life you are leading and your identity must not be revealed. We can do that. We must."

They ended their conversation with a commitment to that vow, agreeing it was a reality of the dual lives they lived. In her usual fashion, Céleste found a positive change of topic and ended the conversation with laughter.

DURING THE WINTER, the Hawaiian health care system had provided a wheelchair as Hana became less inclined to walk. Auntie had to cajole her for weeks to finally use it. Then she took Hana around the neighborhood every day and Kailani continued this. Kaito would do the same in the evening.

On weekends, Kailani and Kaito would occasionally pack the car with a picnic and load the wheelchair in the trunk.

They never knew for sure if Hana appreciated the heartstopping views along the scenic Pali Highway, but they went and hoped for the best. Hana usually fell asleep in her chair at some point. Still, they always agreed it had been worth the trip.

∼

KAILANI DISCOVERED Hana's stilled body one afternoon in late July.

She called Kaito to come home from work, explaining in a softly controlled voice that Hana had passed. As he drove home, his heart felt heavy. No matter how long he had anticipated this moment, the finality of it was painful.

There had been times he questioned if his marriage to Hana had been unfortunate, but he had never given a moment's thought to being without her. From the time he began to see how broken she was, so many decades before, he felt determination to protect her. He knew he had never stopped loving her. That love had changed and the romance of it had long ago disappeared, but he was committed to her no matter how badly she behaved.

At one point on his route home there was a particularly splendid panorama out over the bay that he, Hana, and Kiana had always loved. He pulled over.

Memories flooded back and the passage of years felt like nothing. A vision of young Hana, his sweet delicate *pulele*, floated before him ... so beautiful and vulnerable ... and he was filled with all of the emotions he had felt as they began their life as husband and wife.

A moment of immense sadness filled him and his face creased with the pain of remembrance and loss. For a moment, he wondered what had been the point of it all, of life, of the heartbreak, the struggle. Not just for him but for Hana. Her struggle, not voiced, must have been so much more than his. How does one live with such internal torment?

He closed his eyes and focused on his breathing as he strove to banish the thoughts. It was what it was. This had been their life and there was no need for a reckoning.

He had always told himself that we take what we are handed. The Four Noble Truths of Buddhism stated that life is full of suffering. We suffer because we live. To move beyond the suffering one must be kind, compassionate, and live without desire and be happy. Had he not been trying to do this? he asked himself. Most of the time these thoughts helped him through down times. Now was not the moment to focus on the suffering and let it drag him down.

He continued to feel anguish and pain but shed no tears. There would be a time for that. But not now. There had already been so many through the years.

He stared at the view they all loved and called upon deeply-rooted memories with a healthy Hana and a sweet Kiana. There had been good times. It was the bad times that haunted him and now he needed to banish them.

It was time to get home. People who loved him were waiting.

Kaito and Kailani shared a comforting embrace when he arrived home. Then he went down the hall to Hana's darkened room. Kailani had pulled the drapes so just enough light entered for him to see Hana clearly.

There was a peaceful expression on her face as if death had taken away the worry lines and anxiety. He sat beside her, held her hand and kissed her forehead.

"My sweet *pulele*, your spirit is now on its journey to nirvana. Who knows if you will return in forty-nine days in another reincarnation? I will mourn your passing and pray for your peaceful transition. And I will always love you."

There was also a sense of relief. It was good for all of them that her passing had been sudden. He had always hoped Hana would not suffer a lingering end, whenever it happened. In many ways he felt she had been suffering every day for years.

The doctor who signed the death certificate assured him her heart had stopped while she slept.

Kaito thought of Buddha's words: *life is uncertain; death is certain.* There was no avoiding death and Hana's time had come.

Kailani said they had spent an hour in the garden after lunch listening to music. Hana had smiled at the antics of the finches at the feeders.

Auntie came over immediately with an overflowing hamper of food and soothing words of solace. "Hana was a gentle soul who lived with devils inside her head. I saw her kindness and her sorrow. I know she had to live a life she had not chosen. Even though there were moments where she reacted in an aggressive manner, that was not the real Hana. I loved her. I saw every day, Kaito, how very much you loved her and were dedicated to helping her navigate the bumps and challenges of her life. Bless you."

She hugged Kailani. "Your presence here brought something special to Hana. I believe she did understand you are her granddaughter and that resonated in her heart. You managed to establish a close connection with her and rare positive responses."

Gail and Bob arrived to join them. Kailani had called them at Kaito's request and they sat around the table in the lanai, conversing quietly and savoring Auntie's cuisine.

Kaito called Céleste that evening and they spoke at length about Hana and Brett and the memories they had made together. There was comfort in shared sorrow.

The next day a stunning flower arrangement arrived from Jake with a thoughtful note. Kaito and Kailani were touched by his respectful gesture.

In the days that followed, Auntie and Kailani organized all of Hana's effects, sharing everything that could be used by others.

Kaito arranged for a niche in the same memorial park where the ashes of Kiana and the grandparents were placed.

On a soft summer evening, Kaito, Kailani, Jake, and Auntie watched as Hana's urn was laid to rest amongst those of the family. Kaito repeated a Buddhist prayer as the sun set not just on the day but on this part of life's journey that had set Hana's soul free. A monk Kaito had arranged to be present chanted to cleanse Hana's soul and for a safe journey forward.

KAILANI'S RETURN flight had been booked for the end of August, and Kaito was relieved when she was happy to stay with him until then.

"The house will feel empty without Hana's presence and I don't want to lose your energy at the same time," Kaito had said. "I hope you will always know this is your Hawaiian home. Return whenever you wish."

"Ojiichan, you have reconnected me with my life here and I will forever thank you for that. And you brought me closer to my father again. Of course, I will come to spend time with you."

On her departure day, there was a long hug with his granddaughter before Kaito bowed to Kailani and Jake. His heart was full as he watched father and daughter leave for the airport.

CHAPTER 53

aito mourned Hana's passing as his grief became part of his soul. He knew it would always be with him. How could it not? he asked himself.

He spent long hours immersed in memories from their youth and the early years of their marriage when she was healthy. They had shared happy, exciting times filled with laughter and joy discovering how to build a life together. He would never regret those.

He had many conversations with the temple priest exploring the random destruction that unexpected health conditions can wreak on a relationship.

Buddha spoke of *dukkha* or suffering in terms of life not necessarily always being satisfying. There was much to be learned from studying the three different kinds of *dukkha* and the noble truths to which they lead. In considering the angst of being human, he was reminded by the priest of the practice of the noble eightfold path.

The wise monk had said, "This is what assures us there is another way to find an end to suffering. It comes through achieving a cultivated state of mind. This will stay with you and help you understand there is always suffering in life and always a way out. And that is through rebirth."

Kaito held on to quotes like this from Buddha, "No matter how hard the past, you can always begin again." "Each morning we are born again. What we do today is what matters most." "No matter how hard the past, we can always begin again."

As difficult as he found it was to admit, Hana's death was Kaito's rebirth.

Almost sixty-three, he was beginning to live again.

Grief for Hana's passing remained a constant companion as weeks went by, as it had been in many forms through his adult life. He carried it with him inside and learned how to manage it. He had learned long ago that grief never leaves but becomes part of who you are. You learn from it, manage it, grow with it. On the surface he appeared a quiet and content man.

Although it felt strange and did not come easily, he found himself thinking more about what he had missed, ever since Lailani had *returned from the dead*, as he always thought of it. At first his enjoyment of his visits to her home in France were filtered through guilt and a sense of not deserving to have such pleasure in his life when it was all denied to Hana, through no fault of his.

This had not spoiled his ability to appreciate the pleasure of his visit, but it definitely had lingered in his thoughts when he allowed it to during quiet moments alone.

After his second visit, Kaito had relaxed enough to truly feel the pleasure of his surroundings and of the familiarity and affection of Céleste and her family.

There were moments after Hana's passing when Kaito felt conflicted about leaving at the beginning of September as usual. He worried it was too soon.

"Too soon for what?" Everyone who cared for him asked, as they encouraged him to go. "You need to do this for you."

Deep in his heart Kaito knew it was right.

As his priest reminded him from time to time, guilt is not part of Buddhism. Decisions must be made with the best of intentions, and shame should not be part of that. Kaito prayed and meditated.

Truly, Hana had been gone for years in spirit. Her physical departure in many ways freed him.

Now he needed to give himself permission to believe that this was his time.

CHAPTER 54

KOYASAN 2012

*T*he early-morning flight to Tokyo guaranteed a mid-afternoon arrival at Haneda Airport. Kaito walked quickly through the already noisy and crowded new international terminal with his Japan Rail Pass in hand. The pass guaranteed him a reserved seat for the one-hour ride to the Tokyo station.

After twenty years of visits to Koyasan, each year he was surprised upon his arrival at how quickly the landscape of tourism was changing. He stifled a smile now, tinged with cynicism, as he looked at the touristy signs advertising tickets to experience elaborate tea ceremonies.

At the enormous Tokyo station, masses of humanity swept through in all directions. Kaito was glad he knew precisely where to go. He always sensed that if you stopped for even a moment, you might be carried off by the titanic wave of people cresting through.

With relief, he boarded the Nozomi Shinkansen, the sleek, high-speed bullet train that would take him to Osaka with another reserved seat. Avoiding the crush of bodies that jammed these trains at rush hour was a lesson he learned on his first visit.

In Osaka, there would be a transfer to another two-hour train ride and then a final short transfer up Mount Koya to the peaceful Buddhist community built amidst tranquil woods. It all made for a lengthy trip, but from his first visit Kaito felt it was well worth the effort.

Off the beaten track, Kaito liked that these temples were missed by many visitors to Japan. He had already begun to feel more relaxed as he eagerly anticipated his time there. After twenty years, he felt a certain sense of homecoming.

As the train gathered speed, heading for its optimum 300 km/hour traveling pace, Kaito's young American seatmate proved chatty. He introduced himself as soon as he sat down.

"Hey, how're ya doin'? I'm James, but everyone calls me Jim." He extended his hand to Kaito.

As serious and stoic as Kaito appeared, he was accustomed to spending time with young men whose brash exteriors often masked a tender underside. Some of the young people who frequented his martial arts studio were veterans struggling with PTSD. He felt it was his duty to help them as much as he could through the therapy martial arts offered and his own respect for them.

His radar picked up the signs in Jim's eyes, voice, and body language. Kaito shook his hand firmly and bowed slightly. "I am Kaito. Nice to meet you."

"I'm going to the temples at Koyasan. Ever been there?"

Kaito explained he had been going there for a number of years.

"Cool. I hope you don't mind if I ask you questions about it. I'm fairly new to Buddhism ... but what I know so far, I like." As he spoke he gripped his hands, nervously rubbing a thumb over his fingers.

PATRICIA SANDS

Kaito nodded encouragingly. "Ask away." And so, Jim spent most of the time intensely sharing his interpretation of the ancient philosophy and the impact it was having on his life. "I'm telling you, sir, it's saving me …"

Kaito smiled knowingly, his eyes crinkled with understanding. "It saved me too, and now it sustains me in a calm, peaceful way. It's good you found your way to it."

"After two tours in Iraq, I needed something. I can tell you that. I'm from Iowa, stateside. Where're you from?"

"Honolulu."

Jim's eyes brightened. "Now there's a place I hope to visit one day. It's been a dream of mine to pay homage at the Arizona Memorial. I thought you were from here. Japanese."

Kaito shook his head. "I was born here but have lived in Hawaii since I was a teenager. I'm American."

"Did you ever serve?"

Normally, Kaito didn't speak of his army experience but there were times he knew it was right. This was one. "One partial tour in 'Nam. Early days." He didn't mention the family crisis that had kept him from returning to the war.

"Another place we should never have been," Jim muttered. "Did you bring it home with you?"

"Hard not to," Kaito replied, his lips set in a grim line.

Their eyes met briefly as a flicker of understanding passed between them. Then Jim turned his head to the window. The landscape flew by in a blur as the train sped on.

Kaito closed his eyes for the short remainder of the trip, pushing back memories the conversation had unearthed. He was well aware his short time in Vietnam had left him with his own nightmares, but nothing compared to most veterans.

Since Hana's passing, Kaito's thoughts had often returned to those early days and how Vietnam had become to him the cornerstone of the change in the trajectory of his life. With only a few highlights like his marriage to Hana, the birth of Kiana, and then Kailani coming into their life, it had mostly been downhill until his serendipitous reunion with Céleste.

Once again, after decades of absence, she had saved him.

CHAPTER 55

*I*n Osaka, they transferred to the Nankai line to go to the Gokurakubashi station.

"It's another two-hour ride," Kaito said. "I always pick up a bento here. If you're hungry, you're welcome to join me if you want to do the same. We will arrive at the temple after the kitchen is closed."

Jim's expression showed relief and gratitude. "I'm glad I hooked up with someone who knows what they're doing. There were so many people everywhere in Tokyo I thought for sure I was going to get lost in the crush. And then there's all the crazy signage. It's a different world. I'd be mighty grateful to go along with you."

They walked briskly to a large takeout stand and joined what appeared to be a long but fast-moving line of customers.

"I'm gonna sound stupid here ... what the heck is bento?"

Kaito nodded toward the box-shaped containers that departing customers were carrying. "It's like a Japanese lunch-box. You have a choice of selections, usually numbered, so easy to order. You can have fish, meat, or tofu and then always rice along with pickled or cooked vegetable. There are seaweed and noodle sides you can add. They're delicious."

"I learned a bit about sushi on our R & R breaks in Dubai, from guys coming from more sophisticated places than small-town Iowa. I really got to like it."

They carried their bento to their seats on the train and settled in. While they ate, Jim asked questions about his upcoming experience at Koyasan. He had prepared well with a lot of reading; but now that the reality was upon him, there was much he wanted to understand.

"Well, you should know this," Kaito said. "Tomorrow you will experience *shojin ryori*: the monks are renowned for their preparation of this vegetarian gourmet food. They skillfully cook without use of any meat, fish, onions, or garlic. No dairy or eggs either. And you won't believe how delicious it is. All the food here will be beyond your expectations."

"Wow! That's a relief!" Jim exclaimed. "I read about that but didn't think it would taste so appetizing. I'm a meat and pota-toes guy normally. Worried about the food here."

Smiling, Kaito talked more than usual. The teachings of Buddha's *four immeasurables* guided him on. He knew he was helping his travel companion feel more relaxed and eager about what lay before him at the temple.

"When you arrive at the shukubo, the temple lodging, the simple rules will be explained. You will be given a pair of slippers to wear during your time there and then you simply follow the routines they have arranged for you. How long are you staying?"

"I'm doing the basic seven-day introductory course. It's a special English course, which I hear is rare. I was sure glad I got in." Jim pulled a folded paper from his shirt pocket and read the program to Kaito. "We study meditation, sutra copying, sacred music—I dig the chants and those hand bells. And then some aspect of Kobo Daishi's teachings."

"That's a fine start," Kaito confirmed.

"I'm waiting to see how it goes." Jim paused and took a deep breath before his words flew out. "If I feel I'm getting somewhere, I'm gonna stay longer and focus on meditation. I can't believe how that has changed my attitude towards life already. It was my good luck the day I met a support person who put me onto this. Everyone else—not that there was much help for vets when I got home—was useless. I'm sorry to say that, but it's true."

With a look of understanding, Kaito said, "I hear you. There was no support for us returning from Vietnam, either. We were considered pariahs to a certain extent. Like you, I was fortunate to be pointed in the direction of Buddhism."

Jim blinked nervously. "I'm not religious, but I'm looking for a kind of inner peace I can't seem to find. It's been three tough years since I shipped home. My wife is gonna leave if I don't get my act together. She's gone back to her parents for the next two months and then she'll make a decision." His voice cracked and he hesitated before he asked, "Did you struggle with that? D'ya mind me asking?"

Kaito spoke softly. The conversation had quickly become deeply personal. "Oh I struggled, for sure. But I came home to a family crisis and didn't have time to think about myself. Maybe that helped me in some perverse way. But my search for that kind of inner calm has never stopped. And maybe it shouldn't stop for any of us."

"I hear ya," Jim murmured, his words almost inaudible. He looked down at his hands and was silent for several minutes before he told Kaito, slowly and softly, of his time in Iraq. Kaito was an attentive listener. His quiet compassion was palpable and he could sense Jim become more at ease as the young vet revealed the darkness he sought to shed.

"I want to have something positive come from all the bad I've been through. I'm hoping I can reach a place where I can do community work at home with troubled youths. Maybe as a police officer. First I've gotta get my act together."

"It sounds like you are on the right track, young man. Stay with it. Everything takes time," Kaito assured him.

After a while, Kaito explained they had options as to how to get to the temple from the next station. "You should make your own choice. I prefer the cable car. That's when I begin to leave this other world behind for a week of silence and meditation. It's my salvation. Then I'll point you in the direction of where you check in and you'll find everything well organized. I've been coming for so long, my routine is different."

"I think I'll tag right along with you, sir." The men smiled at each other, as Jim continued, "My notes say that Gokurakubashi means the Bridge of Heaven. I thought that sounded like an encouraging beginning to whatever is waiting for me at the mountaintop."

Kaito's transition truly began as he boarded a cable car to Mount Koya. He never failed to find the ten-minute ride peaceful and magical, climbing through the densely forested hillside. As they ascended to 3,000 feet, cedar trees lined the way like sentries, flanking the path to a secret world.

"Awesome!" Jim exclaimed repeatedly, as the funicular climbed at precarious angles.

Kaito felt himself breathe more easily as he arrived at the Koyasan stop, minutes from where Buddhist temples formed the small, secluded town. His back straightened and the discomfort of the nine-hour flight combined with the train travel began to ease.

A short bus ride brought them into town. Kaito never tired of his first view of the soaring temple rooftops and ancient pagodas. Faint light was already beginning to glow in stone lanterns and occasional low chanting could be heard in the air.

He had determined long ago that the increasing proliferation of touristy temptations would not spoil the sense of mystical intensity that filled him here. There was no denying the crowds of tourists that wandered during the day, but by evening he saw the small town as it was to him during his early years there.

The familiarity of his surroundings gave him a sense of welcome, of belonging. He smiled as Jim gasped audibly. "Even after seeing pictures, this place is cooler than I expected. It's just so ... so ... zen ..." he said. He stood still for minutes, his mouth open in amazement.

They stood and breathed in the air that seemed purer and fresher than what they had left behind. Kaito pointed Jim in the direction of the registration center for new arrivals and wished him well.

The young man gripped Kaito's forearm as they shook hands. The sincerity in his voice touched Kaito. "Thank you, sir. It has sure enough begun well."

"Be open to everything here, Jim. Be open." Kaito bowed low. "Until we meet again."

Jim returned the respectful bow. "Sounds good. Thanks for all the info. You've already offered me the light of Buddha in our time together today. Maybe I'll see ya."

In a move that was most unlike him, Kaito pulled a card from his wallet. "Here is how you can find me if you ever come to Honolulu."

Kaito smiled to himself as they went their separate ways. This was definitely part of the change he had been feeling after his visits to France and his weekly chats with Céleste. She had challenged him to be more open to change and possibilities. Conversing with a stranger like Jim was one example.

CHAPTER 56

*D*usk was quickly falling and few people were out on the streets. Kaito knew the dark was blacker than ink here. He shivered as he slipped into a warm jacket. The leaves would turn six weeks earlier than below the mountain, and he expected some blazing color in the hills for his photography. There were times he had seen snow toward the end of his month here.

Early nights were part of his routine. After stopping at his usual noodle shop for a steaming bowl of soba noodles, Kaito walked two more blocks along the chill, silent street. Most shops were already shuttered.

He passed through the wooden gates of the temple where he traditionally stayed, quickening his pace slightly to pass through the gates that closed at eight p.m.

"Welcome, Kaito-san, we are happy to see you back with us," greeted a familiar monk behind the counter who bowed as he handed him his room number and slippers.

Sliding open the rice-paper-screened door, Kaito entered his simple room. Many of the temple accommodations offered only shared bathrooms, but after all the times he had been coming,

Kaito had arranged several years earlier to have a room with a private sink and toilet.

He smiled at the room he had come to think of as "his" with its tatami mats for sitting and the low table for meals and writing. He set his backpack and small duffle bag by the open cupboard and went directly to the small altar at the far end of the room. He noted there was a different scroll decorating it this year.

As was his custom, after a deep bow Kaito hit a small copper bell with a wooden mallet, lit three incense sticks at the altar, and knelt three times as he placed the incense in front of the altar. The sweet fragrance filled his room. After addressing his ancestors, parents, wife, and daughter, he uttered his standard prayer in a soft, low voice.

"May I be free from fear.

May I be free from suffering.

May I be happy.

May I be filled with loving-kindness.

May you be free from fear.

May you be free from suffering.

May you be happy.

May you be filled with loving-kindness.

May all people everywhere be happy and filled with loving-kindness."

The main temple was closed to the public now. Happy as he was to have arrived, Kaito suddenly felt fatigued after his busy travel day. Traditionally, a young monk would come to guests' rooms to prepare the sleeping arrangements. Kaito, being a regular visitor, had arranged that he would do this himself.

He took down the thin *shikibuton* he found folded on a shelf. After rolling this sleeping mattress on top of a tatami mat on the floor, he lay on top of it. Pulling a comforter over him, he was reminded how this was luxury compared to his early visits when a tatami mat and threadbare blanket were all the bedding to be found. He folded the meager *makura* pillow in half, attempting to make the thin sack filled with buckwheat chaff somewhat satisfying. After all, he reminded himself every year, Buddha considered comfort of secondary importance.

Childhood recollections returned to Kaito on his first night here with every visit. Some memories never left.

His conversation with Jim weighed heavily on his mind. He felt such empathy for these young veterans. War killed in many ways but did not always leave you dead. The way battles were fought had changed with the war in Vietnam. The residual effects for those fighters returning home from today's battles grew even worse than from previous wars.

The monks' prayer bell would ring at six a.m. promptly. He knew a good night's sleep would be welcome.

His morning began in the monks' main hall of prayer. Leaving his shoes outside, he followed the vivid crimson carpet laid across tatami mats through the candlelit temple, as he had done for so many years now. It always took his eyes a few minutes to become accustomed to the light of the flickering candles.

Monks knelt in silent contemplation. Next came the beating of a single drum to signal the beginning of the prayer session. The occasional clash of cymbals that accompanied the drone of chanting always brought a sense of peace to Kaito, which he eagerly anticipated with each visit.

Kaito always felt as if he were held in a suspended hypnotic state, until it was his turn to make his way down the crimson carpet on his knees. At the altar, he dropped sweet-smelling incense into a burner, which caused the smoky "breath of gods" to waft over him. He offered a private prayer and hoped the supposed curative powers would help to heal what was broken within him. He knew he was still dealing with lingering grief from the death of Hana. His role of caretaker had been such a force in his life for so long, he sought guidance in moving forward without guilt.

He prayed that Hana would be in peace and find her path as she climbed higher in rank in her journey. He asked the deity to protect her since she had not sinned.

He joined the monks in meditation for the remainder of the hour and a half, surrounded by chanting, incense, and a slight warmth from the fire. The scene never failed to mesmerize Kaito. The steady flow of chants was hypnotic. Swirling trails of incense smoke curled through the space and the occasional muted tone of a gong punctuated the air.

Kaito reflected on the weeks that lay before him. This year, like the past two, only fourteen days of that time would be spent in Koyasan. The peace and calm within himself that he found through his meditation courses in Koyasan were what mattered now. He tried to keep his mind from thinking about what would follow.

CHAPTER 57

*F*or the next few days, after a vegetarian breakfast
served in his room, Kaito divided his time between
meditation and courses. These courses involved discussions
with senior monks about the teachings of Buddha and were
only available to regular visitors who had demonstrated their
commitment to the learning.

Each year, Kaito left Koyasan feeling he was closer to
achieving another level of purification of his soul. His efforts to
maintain that level through the year helped him find the peace
within that eluded him elsewhere.

For his last six days, Kaito immersed himself in a shortened
Vipassana. Through the years he had participated in longer
periods of this ancient technique and each time the demanding
schedule had posed a challenge. But that struggle was part of his
satisfaction in getting through it. Now he felt he was at a place
where the shorter course would bring him to where he wanted
to be.

The participants observed a strict daily schedule: wake up at
4 a.m., meditation from 4:30, breakfast at 6:30, more meditation, lunch at 11 a.m., meditation, dinner (two pieces of fruit

and a cup of tea) at 6 p.m., meditation, a talk by a senior monk, and lights out at 9:30 p.m.

During this time there was no eye contact with fellow meditators. No reading, writing, listening to music, or exercise. Nothing except sitting on the floor and meditating. As difficult as it was, at the end of the six days Kaito achieved an energy unlike anything else he had experienced.

He felt ever more deeply involved in his meditation. With Hana's passing, he knew he was on the precipice of a change in his life. There was no question that the universe bringing his granddaughter and his old friend Lailani back into his life had created possibilities about which he could never have dreamed.

The days here were curative. Kaito felt focused and more prepared for a new chapter that seemed to lie ahead.

CHAPTER 58

$\mathcal{O}$n his last morning in Koyasan, Kaito picked his spot along the path and set up for a photo shoot. At 10:30 a.m., a line of gold-robed monks floated by wearing their elevated shoes and carrying a wooden box that contained food prepared for Kobo Daishi. Every year, Kaito photographed this solemn display of devotion from a different perspective and it was always a challenge he enjoyed.

A crowd had gathered by the bridge, watching the procession. After the monks had passed, Kaito saw an arm waving at him from across the road. His travel mate, Jim, was hopping up and down behind the people in front of him and flapping his arms frantically at Kaito.

Kaito chuckled. Jim was of such tall stature and solid build that there was no need for him to hop, particularly in that gathering of relatively short people. He waved back. As the crowd thinned, he waited for Jim to cross over.

"Ohayo, Kaito. Aloha ... good morning! There! I think I covered all the greetings. I was hoping I would see you again." Jim's face was flushed with excitement and his words came rushing out. "I tried your cell number but then I remembered you kept it off when you were here and only responded to emergency texts. Even your voice mail was off."

"Aloha, Jim. How are you?" Kaito bowed politely, his face creased in a smile at the unabashed enthusiasm.

Jim bowed in return. A wide grin beamed back at Kaito. "I'm great! No, better than great! I have to get back to my next course soon but do you have a few minutes to talk?"

Kaito nodded and led the way to a small Zen garden behind a nearby temple. They sat on a bench and were absorbed by the simple, soothing design of raked sand, specifically placed stones, and moss. At one end, a tiny waterfall quietly filled a small pond.

Jim looked at Kaito in wonderment. "It's unbelievable here. I keep walking into these places that could be scenes in a movie."

Kaito smiled. "This garden dates back to the 16th century. Do you like it? The asceticism of these gardens appeals to some but not all."

Jim said, "The first time I stumbled into one of these gardens with just rock and sand, I scratched my head. Now that I've been here for a while and understand more about the philosophy, they make sense to me. Crazy! I never expected this. I'm staying longer, Kaito. I can feel myself wanting to know more, wanting to be calm."

"Bravo for you! You can only benefit from spending time in this environment. I found that the more you absorb from the teachings here, the better a person you become. All of the senses are touched here. These gardens work their own magic on us."

"Yup. There's that. It's sick ... I mean, wonderful. And what contrasts too! All these things that are absolutely ancient ... but there's Wi-Fi everywhere. It boggles the mind. Not to mention the mixture of solemnity in the cemetery with the totally bizarre!"

Kaito laughed out loud. "So true. I think that's the greatest surprise for people when they come here. Are you happy with your temple?"

Jim's expressive face supplied the answer. "It took me a while to adjust to the communal bath and toilet, and to sleeping on the floor with a flat, hard pillow." He looked at Kaito and they both chuckled. "I mean, I knew that's what I was in for. I read all about it before I came but it was still kind of a big adjustment. But I get it. You have to get past comfort to find comfort. I really am getting it. And I like it. I wanted you to know that."

Kaito's heart felt full as he listened. He could hear changes in Jim's voice.

"Yeah. So I feel it's karma that I ran into you. You gave me the best advice, 'to be open.' That's what I've been doing and I've decided to stay here for a while. I've signed up for a month-long residential training to study with the monks and come to a greater understanding of what this all means to me. My family's supportive and at the end of the month, I hope my wife will come for a few days and we'll travel a bit."

"That would be special, Jim. It would help her understand what you have been doing here. I'm happy for you."

"Kaito, you said this to me on the train and I have heard it many times here. 'Each morning we are born again. What we do today is what matters most.' I am learning to be born each day and to let go of the past."

Kaito made a slight bow forward. "The way is in the heart."

Jim checked his watch as he stood up. "I have to take this off again. I just put it on to come out to see the ceremony. Living without a watch has been a big deal for me. Now I like it. See you later, Kaito. I'm so glad we met and I promise I'll get in touch to let you know how this all goes."

They shook hands and bowed. "I would like that, Jim. See you later."

Kaito walked through another nearby garden filled with fiery Japanese maple trees, already fully ablaze. Narrow, rock-lined streams trickled through grassy spaces and simple wooden bridges guided him from one end to the other.

Back at his temple, he spent some time sitting quietly in the garden. The clipped verdant topiary offered a serene ambiance after the eye-popping autumn color he had just walked through.

His conversation with Jim caused him for the first time in many long years to reflect on his time in Vietnam. He thought about Brett and so many other of his peers who did not make it back. Or did make it back with injuries, both physical and intellectual, that impacted the rest of their lives. There was really no understanding then of the PTSD those vets were bringing home with them.

In his situation, that, combined with immediately facing Hana's burgeoning illness, had made for some dark days. He knew he looked to Buddhist teachings even more then to help him muddle through … and of course there had been the beautiful light that Kiana had brought into his life. Perhaps she had saved him then. Until that part of his life ended so tragically.

This was part of his fascination with Buddhist philosophy. There was no blind and inflexible acceptance of anything. Learn to see beauty in everything. Having a meaningful life is to understand that pain is inevitable but suffering is optional. In many ways it is that simple, he thought to himself. We all have to deal with pain to find our balance. That is when we can become compassionate and help others.

He felt satisfied knowing he had helped Jim.

And that was an epiphany to him. He had opened himself to a stranger.

As THE DAY drew near to leave for France, Kaito contemplated more about how he had found a new perspective concerning this next visit. He felt open to going down a different path, even as he admitted to himself that where it would lead was anyone's guess.

Being welcomed into Céleste's family and life in the South of France, Kaito was immersed into a whole new culture. He savored the seductive pleasure the French took in every aspect of life, particularly every meal, every taste of cheese, every glass of wine.

It was a true and honest friendship that drove the relationship he and Céleste—still Lailani in his heart—shared.

He had to admit there were moments during his second visit to France when he looked at her or listened to her voice and felt an unfamiliar stirring deep within. A desire to share more than friendship. But he was a married man, mired in his traditional values. He had long ago learned to live without yearning.

So he buried those feelings at the time and reveled in the unconditional affection he and Céleste offered each other.

CHAPTER 59

2012

*K*aito waved, feeling a surge of pleasure, as he spotted Céleste and Bébé at the usual meeting spot in Le Bar du Monde Café. He smiled at how comfortable he was with the familiarity of the Nice airport and the immediate transition to the French ambiance.

He had no checked luggage and set down his carry-on bag as they leaned into each other to deliver the standard air kiss on each cheek. Stepping back they held each other in their gaze.

"Bienvenue, Kaito. It's so good to see you. *Comme toujours.*"

"Aloha. I'm happy to see you too, as usual." Bowing as he stepped back, they smiled at each other.

Then, for the first time since their fateful meeting in Koyasan two years before, they instinctively embraced. It was an embrace driven by grief, sadness, empathy, affection … and perhaps even relief.

"I'm so sorry Hana is gone," Céleste whispered. "I will always regret that I was unable to be with her again."

"But we know her passing is for the best." Kaito's voice was low. "And she did not suffer."

"*Grace à Dieu,*" Céleste murmured.

Kaito's voice was stronger now as he continued. "My sadness is not so much for her passing, but for the loss of what she missed. A lifetime, really. That should not happen. That is the true loss."

They stepped apart and Céleste nodded, her eyes filled with sympathy.

Kaito continued. "I'm grateful for the conversations you and I've shared online. They've been immensely helpful."

"They helped me too, but I knew I would need to hug you," Céleste said, smiling warmly. "There will be many opportunities for quiet remembering and reflection together in the days to come. Sit down and unwind after your long flight."

She signaled to the waiter, who took their order for two café au laits and left a treat for Bébé.

Kaito chuckled. "My first reminder that I am in France is the waiter serving the dog before us!"

AFTER A RELAXING CHAT, they walked outside to the parking lot.

"I noticed you've organized perfect weather once again!" Kaito said as he settled into the driver's seat of Céleste's Renault hybrid. He had taken the wheel on his arrival the year before and thrilled to the drive up into the hills above Nice. There was no hesitation when Céleste asked if he felt like doing it again.

"Of course!" Céleste grinned. "Guaranteeing the weather is not exactly hard to do here on the Riviera."

Kaito returned her grin. "So I've noticed!"

For much of the drive, they chatted easily about the mundane—the children, the grandchildren, the boulangerie—as Kaito absorbed the spectacular scenery he had come to love.

Céleste grumbled about the increased traffic. Kaito responded with similar complaints from Honolulu and Japan.

"Even tiny Koyasan is becoming crowded with tourists. It's a modern-day scourge no matter where we go."

"Well, I hope we will not find it so bad on Corsica," Céleste murmured, flashing a bright smile at the mention of their planned hiking trip to the Isle of Beauty.

The first dinner was a family affair at Martin's home, just a few doors away from Céleste's. Kaito was staying there for the duration of his visit. He was still very conscious of not wanting to be a single man staying at Céleste's home.

Martin and Danielle expressed their condolences to Kaito on Hana's passing. Over time they had come to know about her health, and he was touched by their thoughtfulness.

He felt privileged to be included in their bustling household. The aromas of baking bread and pastries were always in the air and he was pleased in the past to occasionally help load supplies into the storeroom of the boulangerie.

Little Jacques, Céleste's grandson, now recognized him and brought toys to him so they could play together.

After dinner, the family cats rubbed gently around Kaito's calves—warm, soft, soothing. He had never had a pet, never known the gratification of this kind of physical contact, and was enjoying it immensely.

With a lighthearted chuckle, Céleste teased him about stealing their affection as they purred contentedly on his lap. He was reminded how he had isolated himself from so much of the pleasure in life. From now on he was determined to embrace it all.

CHAPTER 60

*K*aito was becoming accustomed to the inevitable jet lag after the trip from Japan to Nice. It was accepted that on his first morning he would not be concerned about the time he woke up.

Céleste had a light lunch of quiche and salad waiting and they ate in the shade on her terrace, reminiscing about early days in Hawaii. They had a toast to the memory of Hana, and Kaito described how he and Kailani had hiked to Manoa Falls and taken some ashes to spread in the forest along the way.

"It was always one of her favorite short hikes and, of course, back in the early days there were few tourists. She took so much delight in all the sketching she did there, and I believe she would be happy to know some of her spirit rests in those peaceful surroundings."

Céleste put her hand on Kaito's as she said, "I have such respect for everything you did through so many years to help Hana have the best life she could, and how you have honored her passing."

Kaito bowed his head to her. "We do what we can for those we love. My heart has always ached for what she missed in life."

Céleste smiled, "This sounds like the same mindset as the aloha spirit from the ancient Hawaiian philosophy of how to get through life by always being open and positive and considerate of others."

"Precisely," Kaito agreed.

They shared memories of hikes and camping excursions they had gone on with Brett and Hana. Kaito surprised Céleste by saying he had uploaded many of his old photos from those days. He had brought his laptop with him, and they spent some time looking at the images—after they promised no tears. Instead they laughed and exclaimed at the happy times from days long ago.

When he was uploading the photos back in Honolulu showing his little family intact, Kaito had his moments of sadness and regret. Now he was able to look at those shots and feel happy for what had been.

Kaito said, "Buddha says that what the caterpillar sees as the ending, the butterfly sees as the beginning. I try to remind myself of that. We are always beginning again."

Céleste excused herself for a moment and returned with a tray. "I have a surprise for you. This seemed like the right moment."

Kaito was touched to see a complete Japanese tea ceremony set with all of the accessories including matcha tea, bowls, scoop, bamboo whisk, and stand. "Everything we need," he said.

"I have such strong memories of your tea ceremonies. It would be lovely for you to do that here too."

"With pleasure," Kaito replied.

THE FIRST WEEK was filled with more of the usual day trips, which this time also included across the border to Italy. An easy forty-minute drive, Friday was market day in Ventimiglia. The morning was spent browsing and laughing at the outgoing personalities of the vendors, whose goal seemed more to make certain everyone was having a good time rather than bothering about sales.

The atmosphere was distinctly different from the markets in France, with a broad selection of high-end leather and cashmere goods. Lunch in a classic Italian restaurant with white tablecloths and waiters in tuxedos was an entertaining change. The menu was varied and the food magnificently local.

"It's like a mini-vacation!" Kaito commented. "I definitely feel we took a trip."

"Fasten your seatbelt," Céleste teased. "That's just the beginning!"

NEXT ON THE AGENDA, Kaito and Céleste planned to take the ferry to Corsica from Nice. They were organized to spend three days hiking and sampling the local culture.

Bébé was staying behind at Martin's.

"We will be footloose and fancy free!" Céleste declared with a spirited laugh. The humor she brought to each day was a constant reminder to Kaito of how this lightness of being was such a welcome part of his life again.

Familiar with the island, Céleste booked them into separate rooms at a small inn. She had emailed Kaito links about the island in preparation for the trip. She knew it well as she and Dominique had visited several times and she was eager to share some special trails with Kaito and to introduce him to the laid-back Corsican lifestyle.

Kaito had immersed himself in reading about the history, which went back to antiquity, and the rich Mediterranean culture of the island. For many centuries under the control of Italy, it had been part of France for over two hundred years.

Aspects of both countries influenced the architecture, cuisine, and language.

As they waited in line for their car to be loaded on the ferry, Kaito took in the colorful neighborhood of the old port area of Nice, Le Vieux Port. Restaurant terraces were already full as lunch hour approached and the enticing aromas of garlic and butter filled the air.

"Here's another part of the town to investigate when we get back," he said.

"You have no idea what we have yet to explore together! We have barely begun," Céleste said.

Kaito grinned. "Remember when you suggested that it was necessary for people to dream to make changes? Well, I want you to know that I have suddenly begun dreaming, and I have you to thank for that."

Céleste smiled knowingly. "That, mon ami, is very good news."

The departure of the bright blue, white, and yellow ferry, with the sea smooth and the day clear, made for some fine photography as they left the old port. Nestled at the foot of the rolling hills that led quickly to the rugged peaks of the Maritime Alps, it was easy to see how the sheltered setting provided the pleasant climate Nice enjoyed year round.

Kaito commented on that as he captured shot after shot from the stern of the boat.

"It's a good thing we don't use film anymore," Céleste teased him. "We haven't even begun and your shutter has been busy."

Kaito laughed. "After I visited you last year, I went home with more photos than I ever imagined I would take on a holiday. This whole area is a visual feast!"

The interior of the enormous boat was luxuriously appointed for the five-hour trip, with well-spaced rows of comfortable upholstered seats that reclined. A number of flat screens were distributed throughout showing travel videos and weather information. A snack bar served assorted hot and cold beverages along with pastries, and they each chose a baguette sandwich to eat at their seat.

With only half the boat occupied, there was a quiet, relaxed atmosphere. When they reached the open water with no views, Kaito napped while Céleste was immersed in a novel. The boat moved along smoothly.

Hours later, she nudged him awake at the announcement they were arriving soon in Ajaccio.

"Get your camera ready."

High temperatures created a haze hanging over the island, resulting in an almost surreal effect as the craggy silhouettes of granite mountaintops appeared through the mist.

It was late afternoon as the ferry pulled into the port at Ajaccio, overlooked by the massive citadel walls. When they planned this excursion, Céleste had suggested they go straight up into the hills to the small inn that would be their base.

"We should do the drive while it's still light so we can appreciate the scenery. If we want, we can spend time in Ajaccio before we take the ferry back to Nice at the end of our stay."

Kaito commented on the many references to Napoleon as they passed statue after statue of the town's most famous son. Their GPS led them through a labyrinth of cramped streets to the main highway. In his research he had read how proud the locals were that this was Bonaparte's birthplace.

Soon they turned onto a narrow winding road that climbed through green foothills covered in an aromatic dense carpet of vegetation and herbs. Kaito laughed as he inhaled a distinctively musky smell with gusto. "So that's why you told me to keep the windows down."

"The maquis is something that defines this island," Céleste said as she took in several deep breaths. "It blankets over half of the island. There's oak, juniper, heather, and other shrubs mixed with wild herbs and sweet-smelling flowers that flavor much of the local cooking."

"Ha!" Kaito said, "That's why Corsica is also called the scented isle. Makes sense."

"It's the ones we know like thyme, oregano, myrtle, but also others like immortelle and nepeta. Ever heard of those?"

Kaito shook his head.

"I had not either until my first visit here," Céleste said. "They truly are the scents of Corsica. Immortelle is deeply fragrant, almost medicinal, and nepeta is an indigenous aromatic mint. They both seem strange to me, but mixed with the other maquis here they produce the most ambrosial effects. So distinctive. You will see how the cuisine here is truly unique."

"And I know from reading up on the island that chestnuts have been a staple in the diet here since the Middle Ages," Kaito said. "See, I did my homework!"

Their route was impeded several times as they slowed to wait for goats or sheep to cross the road, or simply take their time deciding where they wanted to go next to forage at their leisure.

In the distance, a rocky ridgeline pierced the sky, but soon the road turned sharply downward, leading them to a golden sand inlet framing a brilliant blue cove.

"As you well know, I live in this type of natural landscape with mountains and coast, and yet here it is completely different," Kaito said, his eyes filled with appreciation. "Of course, I knew it would be different but this is more than that. This is unique to me."

"I had a terrible time putting the beauty of the Hawaiian Islands behind me," Céleste admitted. "I suffered from homesickness for years, really. Imagine the shock of going from living in Honolulu to Tokyo becoming our home in a day."

Kaito looked at her, filled with empathy. "I've had such admiration for how you and Ulani adjusted."

"It was the South of France that made our worlds right again," she said softly.

He looked at her and nodded. "That I can now understand."

They pulled up to a plain gray stone building with faded red shutters.

A short, stocky middle-aged man opened the massive oak front door as they approached.

"Benvinuto! Bienvenue! Welcome!" he greeted them warmly. "I am Salvadore and happy to have you stay with us."

After a few simple questions of identification, he pointed up a short but steep staircase and handed them their keys with the room numbers.

Kaito said they did not need help with their bags as he collected them and indicated Céleste to go ahead of him.

"I made certain we have ocean views," Céleste told him as she unlocked the door to her room. She gestured to the open shutters framing a stunning vista.

Kaito turned to his door across the hall. "Let's unpack our things later but put on our boots now for a quick hike before dark."

Within minutes they were on a trail.

Lizards darted about their feet as they followed a sandy path edged by spiky cacti. They climbed to a point where a view opened up over the hazy blue hills they had just driven and stretched beyond to the shimmering sea.

Céleste said, "I love these views. Balzac said Corsica is 'a French island basking in the Italian sun.' How perfect a description is that?"

Their eyes met.

Kaito reached out and grasped Céleste's hand.

"Céleste … Lailani … I have to say this. No, I *want* to say this. I've stifled it until now. I can't begin to thank you for all you have brought to my life since that day fate reunited us in Koyasan. You have taught me to feel alive again, to open myself to the world around me, to not be alone anymore. Every moment with you is worth living."

Kaito had not planned to say these words out loud at this moment. The feelings had been simmering for some time and in the bliss of this instant his heart had burst open.

Céleste held his gaze, her eyes aglow. "Having you in my life again is a gift. Something I never would have imagined. You've allowed me to reconnect with a past I've basically denied myself for almost thirty years. You have made me whole again. So I thank you as well."

They stood with the warm rays of the setting sun washing over them. After a moment, Céleste reached up and ran her fingers lightly down Kaito's cheek. He took her hand in his and brought it to his lips.

They held themselves in each other's gaze.

The moment was electric … and then a bit awkward.

"We should get back," Céleste murmured.

Kaito nodded.

They turned and began to retrace their steps.

Kaito's voice cracked slightly, as he tried to sound relaxed after his outburst. "I'm glad you suggested we not bring our cameras on this walk. It was a good idea."

Céleste walked ahead. "We can go this same way in the morning and take some shots when we head out on our hike."

She continued to keep the conversation light and told him about the 180-kilometer GR20 on the island. "The Grand Randonée is one of the most famous, and grueling, walks in Europe. Typically it takes about two weeks. It's something else on my wish list."

"Why don't we plan to do it one of these years? I would like that."

"Bonne idée!" Céleste replied, which always guaranteed a chuckle.

Back in their rooms, they had just enough time to get ready for dinner.

On his own, Kaito considered his impulsive confession. He had already decided while he was in Koyasan that he was giving himself permission to accept his emotions once again. Sixty-three years did not have to mean he was too old. He was fit for his age. He was certainly wiser than forty years earlier. There was so much of life he had missed, and now he allowed desire to fill his heart once more. Desire to taste all life had to offer.

He smiled as these words of Buddha floated into his head. *Life is a journey. Time is a river. The door is ajar.*

He knew he was ready to walk through that door.

CHAPTER 61

*J*ust after seven o'clock, Kaito and Céleste climbed into a waiting van with another couple staying at the inn. One of the reasons Céleste had chosen this place was the proprietor's approach to dinners.

He did not serve them but rather preferred to drive guests to the nearby village or down to the port. The explanation was that this way their guests could enjoy dinner to the fullest—meaning imbibing good Corsican beer and wine and not worry about driving.

"And this way we support our local chefs and economy!" Salvadore, the owner of the inn and designated driver, exclaimed.

As he drove, he gave a running commentary on dishes he recommended. "My cousin, Stefanu, makes the best *civet de sanglier* on the island. I swear on my family bible! You know, sanglier—wild boar, pig!"

He interrupted this to add snorting noises that made everyone laugh.

The road was bumpy and twisty. Kaito felt a shiver of plea-sure each time he and Céleste were pressed to each other. He slipped his arm around her on one heart-stopping curve and felt her relax into his side.

Salvadore didn't miss a beat as they jostled along. "This is the signature Corsican dish! It's a casserole with the meat, bien sûr, with onions, carrots, chestnuts, eau-de-vie, and our famous red wine. And you know, our wild pigs eat chestnuts all the time. So the flavor is divine!"

Salvadore went on to describe local cheeses, sausages, and other foods with such colorful language that Kaito whispered to Céleste he was getting full just listening to him. Leaving the main road, they entered into narrow streets with barely enough room for one car to pass through.

There was a surprising sense of dilapidation to the buildings with peeling facades everywhere and no sign of restoration or new painting and repairs. Kaito worried he might be insensitive but could not help asking Salvadore about the condition of the town.

"We are a poor country, especially here in the hills. On the coast you will see it is different. We do not have rich tourists buying property in our little villages. People come here for the simple pleasures of nature and hiking," the Corsican explained. "Long ago, we realized it was better for money to be spent on the inside of our ancient buildings to keep them safe and useable. Families have lived in the same building for centuries. The faded exteriors bring a sense of time and history to our towns. We do not worry about them. In fact, we are proud."

Depositing everyone in the town square, Salvadore pointed out his cousin's restaurant. "This is the fourth generation in our family to run this place. They are masters of charcuterie! Of course we recommend restaurants that our relatives own, so we are all benefiting," Salvadore informed them with an outburst that was so hearty and infectious they soon were all laughing uproariously.

It was a cozy bar with dim lighting on the other side of a

baroque church with a tall bell tower that dominated the space. The entire effect of the village was atmospheric.

The other couple left in the opposite direction saying they had eaten at the cousin's place the night before and the food was indeed divine. "Don't miss it!"

Kaito and Céleste walked in and were immediately greeted as if they were old friends by a handsome dark-haired young man who was deftly charring cuts of meat on a grill over an open fire. He called out to them to take a seat, saying his name was Stefanu. A smiling young woman introduced herself as Catalina and invited them to follow her.

"I think perhaps Salvadore gave them a heads-up about us," Céleste murmured to Kaito. They grinned.

They placed their order for the civet de sanglier and decided to begin with a rich, dark red wine recommended by the server. A small bowl of smoked butternut squash was brought as an appetizer.

The stew was rich and flavorful, and the server explained that the pork had been slow-cooking for hours to get that effect. The finishing touch was that of dipping warm chestnut-flour bread into the sauce, accompanied by contented murmurs.

Kaito took a moment to look at Céleste's laughing eyes and hear the contentment in her voice. He could not help thinking how this all felt so right. This trip was the first time that he was "away" with her as a single man. Coming to Corsica made the truth of it all the more evident to him. They were in a place that was home to neither of them and sharing the experience together, making memories.

Next, a platter of local sheep and goat cheese proved irresistible, even though Kaito and Céleste both moaned about not being able to eat another bite of anything.

Their host was not about to take no for an answer as he brought them a serving of the classic Corsican cheesecake, *falculella.* He insisted it was a "geeft" and they could hardly refuse it.

"It is made with our local *brocciu* cheese and baked on chestnut leaves," he explained, kissing his fingers dramatically.

Céleste and Kaito debated whether the flavor was sweet or nutty as they shared one piece with two forks.

Completing the meal with a glass of the local bittersweet aperitif, Cap Corse Mattei, Kaito said, "Salvadore is a wise man. I would not want to try navigating these narrow streets and roads after this meal!"

Céleste raised her glass. "I couldn't agree more."

Suddenly Stefanu's deep, mellifluous voice filled the small space with song and other men soon joined in. The singing was a cappella and emotional, which Céleste explained was the Corsican style. "Men only, as you can see. That is the custom, not just a coincidence here."

Catalina had come to stand by their seats and added, "These are the traditional Corsican songs that originated with shepherds centuries ago. They tell the stories of the trials of daily life as they tended their goats, sheep, or cows in the mountains. Some also sing of our country's violent history both from foreign invaders and also from some well-known personal vendettas between families. We do have stories to tell!"

She stayed next to them, clapping along from time to time. And then Kaito noticed her make the sign of the cross when one new song began.

"There are also many sacred songs which are saved mainly for festivals and saints days," she explained.

A few other patrons joined in from time to time, often with moist eyes. "Locals," Catalina whispered. "We are also very emotional."

The restaurant guests were spellbound and urged the singers on with applause and cheers. Glasses were refilled time and again.

Kaito slipped his arm around Céleste, and she pressed gently into him. "This is pure magic," he whispered. He wanted to tell her that she was, too, but instead kept the warm feeling inside himself, nervous that saying it might be too forward.

In the van on the way back to the inn, Céleste rested her head on Kaito's shoulder, yawning quietly. "This was the perfect ending to a wonderful day," she said softly.

"Thanks for planning this new adventure," Kaito said. "We've barely begun and it has already exceeded my expectations."

As they climbed the stairs to their rooms, Céleste said, "We will sleep well after that meal, no doubt about that. And we have a serious hiking day ahead of us tomorrow."

She leaned in to give Kaito a bise on each cheek.

Kaito smiled and raised her hand to his lips as he bowed. "Good night, my sweet Lailani …" They both chuckled.

"You see," Kaito said, "you will always be Lailani to me. Deep in my heart. But I've been doing well calling you Céleste, haven't I?"

"You have indeed." Céleste hesitated slightly. "See you in the morning."

Their eyes locked in a lingering gaze that said so much more than their words, before she turned and opened her door.

Kaito almost followed, but he knew she had made the correct decision—no matter what his heart was telling him. He did not want to rush whatever they were moving toward. They would both know when the time was right.

CHAPTER 62

*T*he next day was filled with one adventure after another.

Kaito and Céleste followed winding trails through groves of chestnut trees planted centuries before and mixed with forests of thousand-year-old pines. They discovered waterfalls and vineyards and a goat farm where they sampled the famous *brocciu* … a mild, creamy fresh cheese made from the whey of goats' milk. They made a note of the shop near their inn where they could purchase some to take back to the mainland. Céleste fell in love with the youngest kids who were bouncing around and bleating in the most irresistible way.

"I wish I could take a few of these back too," she joked.

The trails were often rocky and rough and the scenery breathtaking. The air was aromatic as paths wound through the wild undergrowth of maquis. Occasionally they were startled by a wild pig foraging along their trail. Kaito's efforts to take photos had Céleste nervously laughing, as there were moments when the animal's movements indicated they should make a quick exit. Which they did.

Passing through the narrow streets of a rustic village, they stopped for coffee and chose some mouth-watering charcuterie and cheese, which was grilled in a panini to make a "sandwich Corse" for lunch.

Later in the afternoon, they followed paths that were heading down toward the glistening turquoise sea. Within a few hours, they were sitting on soft golden sand, cooling their feet in the gentle lapping waves of the crystal-clear water and wishing they had brought swimsuits along.

"Never mind," Céleste said. "Tomorrow we will go to the Scandola Nature Reserve. After we leave the park there are some magical coves where we can swim in a setting you will long remember. I can't wait for you to see it."

Dinner was in a marina with a picturesque patio that hung out over the water. Kaito wondered if they were dressed appropriately, still in hiking attire, but sandals from their backpacks had replaced their boots.

"Take a look around," Céleste said. "This island is all about being casual and relaxed. Dress codes don't exist."

Once they were seated, the waiter suggested they begin with a local beer.

They both agreed that sounded like it would hit the spot.

Looking at the rich amber liquid already melting the frosting on the ice-cold glass, Kaito said, "I read about this Pietra beer, started in 1996 and the first ever made with chestnut flour and barley malt. It's a unique flavor—but I like it!"

"They are shipped all over the world now," Céleste told him.

A selection of vegetables, sausages, and a head of lettuce were placed on the table in a wicker basket.

"A make-your-own salad or just sample what you wish," Céleste explained.

Glass bottles of olive oil and balsamic sat on the table. The menu focused on local specialties: tuna carpaccio, octopus ceviche, oysters, lobster, and freshly caught red mullet and sea bream. They decided to share the special seafood platter that consisted of tastes of all the items listed. A bowl of lightly grilled vegetables accompanied this and a warm loaf of the local bread.

The sun set as they lingered over their meal, putting the final touch on an exhilarating day.

Salvadore was waiting for their phone call and arrived in just under an hour to return them to the inn. He was eager to hear about their day and how they had enjoyed their meal at this particular restaurant, which of course was owned by another cousin of his.

Kaito and Céleste both nodded off after a while and awoke only when the van began to jostle on the bumpy lane leading to the inn.

Kaito reached over and took Céleste's hand. "Thank you for another memorable day. I think I will hire you as my exclusive tour guide."

Her carefree laughter reminded him of the sound he'd been used to so many years before.

Salvadore dropped them off and bade them goodnight, explaining he was going in the other direction now to collect some other guests at a village down the road.

As they walked into the inn, Kaito's heart pounded as his emotions worked on a timeline of their own. He felt slightly out of control. Rubbing his hand over his hair, he tried to calm the moment.

At Céleste's door, she handed him her key.

He opened the door and their eyes met as she reached for his hand and drew him into her arms.

He gently pushed the door closed.

Their lips came together with lingering tenderness that ripened into deeply passionate kisses fueled by the pulsing rush of longing.

There would be no more waiting. In that particular moment,

Kaito felt his entire being open. He was free to love again. The chains were gone.

"This is right. Trust me," Céleste whispered as they moved in one motion toward the bed.

Kaito began to apologize. "This sounds crazy but I haven't—I mean, I—well, it's been years—"

Céleste put her fingers lightly on his lips, never losing eye contact. "But, mon cher, I have. Come to bed with me ... lay with me."

They undressed each other slowly, kissing and caressing.

"I've forgotten how beautiful it is to touch and be touched," Kaito whispered, breathing into her hair.

"I've been waiting for this moment." Céleste sighed as her lips brushed his neck. "I hoped it would happen."

Kaito lovingly stroked Céleste's face with his hands. His eyes flashed with emotions he once feared had been lost forever. "Nothing is stopping us. *Ma'ane'i no ke aloha.*"

"*Ma'ane'i no ke aloha.* Love is here and now," Céleste repeated, as her lips found his once more.

CHAPTER 63

The next morning, Kaito awoke with Céleste nestled in his arms. He pressed his lips into her hair, breathing in her scent and remembering their night of passion.

She stirred slightly and turned her head to look at him, raising her eyebrows. "Bonjour, mon amour. Was that really us last night? Or did we somehow transform into our younger selves?"

Kaito chuckled. "It was certainly a night to remember, my sweet Lailani."

They both stretched and then settled into each other's arms again. A light rain was falling and the soothing patter of raindrops on the tile roof filtered in through the open window.

"What a beautiful sound to greet us this morning," Céleste murmured. "We have no need to rush."

They lay wrapped in the tangle of sheets, speaking in soft undertones about the change that had occurred between them. There was no hesitation about their love for each other and how right it was to feel so completely committed to this.

As they shared their thoughts, their fingertips slowly began to explore each other's bodies with tenderness, until they folded into each other and made love again. This time it was an exquisite and gentle assertion of all they knew now to be true.

Kaito felt as though his body and soul had been liberated from years of bondage. All the desires filling him now had been locked away, forbidden. Here he was free in every way.

Kaito took Céleste's face gently in his hands as he covered it with kisses. He knew his heart was filled with a new kind of emotion. To be so in love later in life offered its own rewards. It felt deeper and stronger, built on so much life experience.

"I love you, my sweet Lailani."

"And I you, my dearest Kaito."

IN TIME, they got up, showered, and dressed in a deliciously relaxed ambiance, after Kaito retrieved a change of clothes from his room. There was an extra dimension to the ease between them that had not been apparent before.

They sat at a wrought iron table on the dampened terrace to eat breakfast and talked about the compatibility of the extremes of the Corsican culture that Céleste was introducing to him.

"Although I've only had a taste so far," Kaito said, "I can feel the strength of the people and the pride of their homeland and its history. You sense it everywhere—on the coast or in the hills. I'm loving it! "

Now that the rain had stopped, the warm air was filled with the perfume of the maquis. Cats appeared from nowhere to rub against the legs of the table and stretch languidly on the patio stones.

From time to time, Kaito and Céleste grinned at each other or shook their heads imperceptibly.

Céleste lowered her eyes and looked out through her long eyelashes. "Every once in a while I get this flash of feeling like a giddy schoolgirl ... and I'm quite enjoying it."

Kaito chuckled. "Whatever all these feelings are, let's embrace them. There are all sorts of sensations buzzing through me and every one of them feels fantastic."

He reached over and took her hand, lifting it to his lips, "I feel more intense and alive than I have in years, and I thank you for that."

Céleste's eyes glistened. "And I thank you for that, too."

SALVADORE EFFUSIVELY WISHED them well as they checked out. He expressed his hope they had fallen in love with his simple inn and would come again. Kaito and Céleste assured him their stay would always hold a special place in their hearts and they would plan to return.

The drive up to the Scandola Nature Reserve began along winding narrow roads through the forest. There were ubiquitous goats and sheep along the way, and at one point a nursing sow with eight piglets lay in the grass, just off the road.

In time the road joined an even more winding two-lane highway that hugged cliffs on one side and dropped vertiginously to the sea on the other. The absence of guardrails in many places was unnerving. Traffic moved slowly and with good reason. As they came around yet another tight curve, Kaito and Céleste both gasped aloud.

The view before them was stunning and dramatic. Towering volcanic peaks of deep red, pink, and ochre rock spread out before them. At the bottom of sheer cliffs, inlets pierced the coastline with water a shade of blue that Kaito had never seen. Intriguing coves issued invitations to be explored and they noted the number of sailboats that could be seen.

"I thought I had experienced in Hawaii every single variation of blue the sea might offer, but this is unique!" he exclaimed. "I can see why Corsica is a place to be visited by boat too."

Céleste nodded. "You are right. But these roads should not be missed either. I've driven this route several times and yet that first view of these pinnacles never ceases to take my breath away. I know a place a little further up where we can stop to take photos."

Once they had finished capturing their shots, they sat on a rocky ledge in sheer admiration. "Those inlets are called calanches," Céleste explained. "They are similar to the calanques near Marseille. Another place on our must-visit list. But these here are of a particular beauty and definitely unique."

Eventually their drive took them down to sea level to a tiny village on a small inlet, the red-toned buildings blending into the cliffs surrounding it. The first sight of it was from above as the road wound its way down a cliff.

"Here we are," Céleste said as they pulled up to a plain two-story building. The reservation for a second room had been cancelled.

"Right after lunch, we are booked on a boat to take us to the Reserve."

The hotel was new and basic. Kaito said, with a laugh, "I can see the whole point of being here is to be outside, not shut in a room. The builders were smart not to waste money on style and decor."

"Absolutely," Céleste agreed. "It doesn't get much simpler than this. Let's throw on our swimsuits and grab lunch."

At a dockside restaurant that was no more than a bar with a grill, they ordered fish sandwiches and sat with their legs dangling over the edge of a wharf. They had just finished when a small tour boat pulled up to a loading area and they hurried to get on.

"I booked us spots on this smaller boat rather than the

larger one you see over there. We got lucky and they had a cancellation. Even though it was weeks ago when I booked, they were already full. I have to get used to the crush of tourists everywhere now. It's amazing how much that has changed in just the short time that I haven't really traveled since Dom passed."

Kaito compared it to what was happening in Hawaii in the past few years. "When Kailani came to stay for the summer, there were places we simply could not get into because tickets were sold out. And when we did go to some tourist spots, the crush of people was so great that you could not enjoy it anyway."

Céleste pointed out that the beauty of where they were was the difficulty of the roads that prevented tour buses from reaching the town. "Because this is a UNESCO World Heritage Site, tourism is strictly controlled. Only a few boats are allowed into this particular area at a time, and that larger boat does not get to explore like we will."

THE RESERVE WAS everything Céleste promised and more. Bright sunshine at times and a light cloud cover at others allowed exciting challenges for different perspectives and photographic effects as they took their shots.

Kaito attempted to come up with the right words to describe the shades of blue that ranged from turquoise to the deepest sapphire blue, the latter giving a dramatic effect against the mesmerizing pink, orange, and yellow volcanic peaks rising from the depths.

The complex eroded-rock formations sculpted by sea and wind into coves, arches, holes, and other jagged formations created an astonishing other-worldly landscape.

"The combination of the deep sapphire sea against the pink

granite is my favorite," Céleste decided, when Kaito challenged her to choose. "My camera is loving the effect."

After a one-hour visit, the boat headed back out to the open sea before turning into the inlet that led to the village where their hotel was located. The guide pulled into a small cove and anchored near an almost-hidden grotto.

Kaito, Céleste, and the four other adults on the boat slipped into the water. They took snorkeling equipment and were directed to explore around the rocky mounds poking out of the water.

Céleste took Kaito's hand and said, "Follow me." She swam directly through an opening in the rocks into a cave-like grotto. The water was perfectly calm and the light was as turquoise as the sea, resulting in a breathtaking experience.

As they treaded water, Kaito looked at her and said, "You know what this reminds me of, right?"

She nodded. "The grotto we went to with Hana and Brett when we all went to Kauai with your parents for a weekend. It was a graduation gift. I knew this would remind you of that. Cool!"

"And so much fun," Kaito added. "What memories this brings back! I'm so glad we have all that history behind us that we can share."

He pulled her close and kissed her lightly.

"And now we're going to make a lot of new memories to add to that history."

They swam back to the boat and dried in the sun, thankful for the ice-cold water the guide had ready for them. When everyone was back, they headed out to open water once again just in time to catch a pod of dolphins feeding and putting on a show of leaping and diving in all their natural splendor.

CHAPTER 64

*S*trolling back to the hotel hand in hand, Kaito and Céleste admitted to being quite exhausted.

"After a full afternoon in that sun and out on the water ...," Kaito said.

"And not exactly a lot of sleep last night," Céleste added, looking at him with a mischievous grin.

Kaito slipped his arm around her. "Let's crash for an hour or so before heading out to dinner. I promise we will just sleep ... if that's what you want."

"It may not be what I want, but it is definitely what I need or my face will be in my soup before we finish our meal tonight."

Moonlight cast a golden glow over the port. Overlooking the shimmering water, Kaito and Céleste dined on the terrace of a busy waterside bistro. They were drawn into the bistro by the irresistible aromas drifting into the street.

Signs indicated the specialty of the house was lamb and the

packed tables told the rest of the story. Pumpkin beignets were served as an appetizer. Céleste was fully invested in the leg of lamb, slow-roasted with garlic, rosemary, and potatoes. Kaito was served five perfectly grilled lamb chops, accompanied by fresh-cut *frites* and an enormous salad of homegrown greens with a strong emphasis on mint.

Rather than dessert, they shared an olivewood board with a selection of five Corsican cheeses, to complement the second bottle of local red they were finishing. When they ordered from the wine list, Céleste had read the description with a twinkle in her eye. "Pure, alive, and complex … just like us."

Kaito raised his glass in agreement.

Looking across the harbor at the illuminated 16th-century Genoese tower perched on a rocky mound, they slowly sipped.

"It's ancient views like these that fire my imagination," Kaito said. "History comes to life. I'm having visions of the centuries of invasions and occupations."

Céleste nodded. "When you look at the stunning coast here and consider the bounty of sea life, it is fascinating to know that for centuries the inhabitants turned inland, into the hills to learn how to live and survive in that wild environment and be safe from marauding invaders."

"And thanks to all of that drama, there now exists this unique culture to which you have introduced me. This has been a wonderful interlude, my sweet. In so many ways," Kaito said, gazing deeply into Céleste's eyes. "More than anything I ever imagined. And I'm not just talking about this country, trust me."

Céleste grinned, almost shyly. "It's been a very long time since I blushed. You must know I share those feelings, mon amour. And as for Corsica, I was certain you would be as enchanted with it as I am."

She reached over and ran her fingers down the side of his face and across his lips with such tenderness, Kaito squeezed his eyes to hold back tears. It had been decades since he felt such a simple expression of love and it overwhelmed him.

"And now we are lovers, but ... to be honest ... it feels so right. It was just a matter of time," she said.

Kaito held her gaze in his and took a moment before he felt composed enough to speak. "What has connected us has always been based on love. For all of our lives, even when we were lost to each other, it was all about love ... love of family, of friendship, of memories. To share such affinity and then become lovers, surely is the best thing. I know two years ago we did not reunite with this in mind. We have grown into this ..."

He hesitated and Céleste suggested, "Organically?"

They laughed and leaned into each other to kiss.

THE HALLWAYS of the small hotel were darkened and silent.

"Hikers like to get to bed early," Kaito said. "It looks like everyone has hit the sack."

"But we are not hikers tomorrow," Céleste said. "We can be late risers. All we have to do is explore Ajaccio and catch the ferry back to Nice. We'll have plenty of time."

"In that case, let's slip down to the pool and have a moonlight swim," Kaito suggested.

The garden surrounding the pool was bathed in moonlight, but the pool itself was hidden from the view of others by the surrounding trees and shrubs. The strong fragrance of the maquis filled the air.

"Mmmm, the water is just right," Céleste whispered as she unwrapped her beach robe and slid naked into the water. "I feel like a misbehaving teenager."

Kaito stood in his bathing suit. "I feel like the klutz who hadn't even considered a skinny dip." Dropping it on the patio, he joined her in the water.

Céleste's quiet giggle ended with a snort, which set them both off struggling to control their laughter.

After a long embrace and a kiss, they floated on their backs, challenging each other to identify constellations.

"Kaito, there is something I can't stop thinking about and I want to say it to you."

"Of course, anything."

"I want to ... at some point ... go back to Honolulu with you. I want to take my mother's ashes home as she asked."

Kaito stopped floating and treaded water as he looked at Céleste and whispered, "But how can you? With your Protection Program I am sure you are not meant to set foot in Hawaii ever again."

"I want to find out and see what is involved. I don't want to stay long. I don't think I ever would have entertained this thought without you in my life again. But this would be for Mama."

"I don't know what to say. Now I'm shocked. I could take Ulani's ashes with me, but I know that is not what you want. You need to do it. But is it possible? That's the question."

"As soon as we get home, I'm going to look into it," Céleste said, sounding determined.

Concerned their voices might wake up others, they swam silently for a few minutes and decided they should call it a night. But as they reached the shallow end, they were in each other's arms as their mouths hungrily found each other's. Now it was their sighs and whispered words of passion that needed stifling as they made love.

"We are crazy," Céleste murmured eventually.

"Out of control," Kaito whispered back, wrapping her in a towel. They picked up their clothes and quietly stole to their room.

Sharing the same room, there was no awkwardness in spending every moment together. Kaito woke before Céleste and took pleasure in watching her sleep. It had been decades since he had not slept alone and he reveled in the feelings of love and belonging. But he had tossed and turned during the night as he worried how things would be when they were back in the real world of their lives.

CHAPTER 65

$\mathcal{I}$n the car on the way to Ajaccio the next morning, they laughed as they took turns exclaiming repeatedly about the stunning scenery. "Driving south these views offer a change from when we were heading north. Completely different perspectives! On the way up it was all about the verdant green hills and spectacular rocky outcroppings. Now those turquoise coves are calling to us!"

This time they were ready for the surprise of the Calanches de Piana when the rugged red peaks came into view.

"Oh man, it's still breathtaking!" They stopped at the one safe spot they remembered and took some more photos.

"Never enough," Céleste said.

Soon the rooftops and harbor of Ajaccio came into view. They had planned enough time for a visit to the Maison Bonaparte museum and a charcuterie lunch.

"It's not possible to visit Corsica and miss one of the best— no, let me rephrase that—THE best charcuterie ever. I challenge you to deny this," Céleste said, spreading her hands wide over the feast in front of them.

On a broad olivewood board with uneven edges, the display

looked too beautiful to consume. Photos were taken. Céleste described the classic Corsican essentials: figatellu, the essential star; a dry sausage of pork liver and meat flavored with spices, red wine, and garlic; cold cuts—lonzu, coppa, and prisuttu; the cheese—brocciu, tomme made from sheep's milk; a selection of local olives; local honey and fig jam; warm bread.

"You are going to have to roll me out to the car," Kaito moaned, as they finished everything with gusto.

At a shop along the street, they loaded up with honey, olive oil, cheese, sausage, cold cuts, and wine to take home.

Then they pulled the car into line at the harbor for the journey back to Nice.

STANDING at the railing on the upper deck of the ferry, with Kaito's arm around Céleste's shoulder, they watched the stunning island gradually slip away from view.

Then they settled into their seats to relax for a few hours. They looked at each other with a new dimension to the emotions they were sharing.

"I guess we have some explaining to do once we are back home," Céleste said, taking Kaito's hand in hers. "I would love to have us stay together from now on. At my house. Wouldn't you?"

Kaito did not answer right away and Céleste stared intently at him. "Do I detect some hesitation?"

"I lay awake half the night thinking about this," he said. "I know what I want. And I believe I know what you want. We have been honest with each other. But I worry about what is the right thing—mainly for you and your family. It's so easy for us to know how we feel, but ..."

Céleste put her fingers to his lips.

"Shhh. I hear you. But we are adults. Adults who know each

other better than most people do. I am certain my family will understand and embrace our love as we do."

Kaito was silent for several minutes. He held Céleste's hand tightly, rubbing his thumb over her fingers. Her silence matched his.

"Am I not speaking clearly?" she asked, her tone gentle. "Am I letting these wonderful released emotions I'm feeling color my thoughts? I'm kind of surprised that there is any question about this."

"I am shocked too. I love you with all my heart and I want us to be together," Kaito said. "But perhaps we are rushing things. It was so easy here in Corsica to be in our little bubble. But you have a whole family to consider. An entire life."

Céleste stared straight ahead. A flicker of concern shuddered through her. Perhaps she had been expecting too much, more than Kaito was ready for.

"You are overthinking this," she said softly. "Let's relax now and stop on the way home at our favorite spot to try and sort out what is concerning you, my love. I feel no hesitation."

She leaned over and kissed his cheek, then took out her book. Within minutes she was sound asleep.

Kaito's mind would not settle.

CHAPTER 66

*H*is feelings for Céleste were undeniable. He knew and loved her as a friend. That had not changed. And now they were lovers. He felt a fiery passion that had been denied him nearly his entire adult life. These were truths he understood.

But he felt deep concern for how Céleste's life might be impacted. Would her family understand and be happy for her? Would she have to reveal a secret she had kept from them all these years? Would she be risking everything that had been good in the second act of her life? Did he have the right to ask this?

Perhaps his place was to return to his life in Hawaii, his life that now was unalterably changed with Hana's passing.

Everything else was there for him. His home, his job, his studio.

Really? Do they really matter anymore? He began to question all of it.

If Céleste's family did approve of their love, could he leave everything he had worked for in Honolulu and move to France? His only family was Kailani. Would she understand? That was the one easy question. He had no doubt she would be happy for him.

Kaito found himself in an unknown headspace faced with questions barraging his thoughts. Once again fate had intervened in his life. But this time in a positive way. Destiny had knocked.

Do not dwell in the past, do not dream of the future, concentrate the mind on the present moment. The words hung in his mind.

He thought he was concentrating on the present. And yet he could not set aside worry. Or was he afraid? And if so, was his fear valid?

Was Céleste right? Was he overthinking?

He closed his eyes and meditated as the ferry drew closer to the port.

ON THE DRIVE UP into the hills from Nice, Kaito turned sharply down a gravel road to a cleared overlook. Céleste had taken him there on his first visit with her two years prior. They had revisited the spot many times. The view was simply overwhelming and to Kaito it signified the beauty that inspired him to fall in love with this part of the world.

Céleste had told him she'd been overcome with the same fervor—an almost crushing adoration—the first time she had been brought to this spot decades before.

They were standing on a section of terraced hillside held up by a decaying stone wall. Ancient olive trees and some abandoned vineyards could be seen all the way down the steep slope where they had been cultivated and nurtured for centuries on these layered terraces.

Before them a view of the sun-kissed coast stretched in both directions, east to Italy and west along the Côte d'Azur and beyond. Far below them, silhouettes of modern high-rises sparkled in the sun in the principality of Monaco. Boats of all sizes floated on the glistening multi-hued Mediterranean. Scattered villages dotted the foothills that unfolded up to the Maritime Alps. The two-thousand-year-old Roman ruin stood —right there, in your face—like a colossal sentry, compelling and overpowering in its historical crumbling elegance.

"Tell me what you see. How you feel," Céleste demanded of Kaito, slipping her hand in his.

"Exceptional, beautiful, profound, all-consuming ...," he answered, his voice low. His gaze had shifted to Céleste's face and he felt consumed by a burst of pure love. He knew those words were meant to express how he felt about her.

"That's how we see it, you and I," she said. "And many others, of course, through centuries. But now we are just talking about how we feel as we stand here together. And perhaps something else. Those words describe how I feel about us at this moment, too: exceptional, beautiful, profound, all-consuming. I echo yours."

Kaito's eyes stayed on her calm, serene face. She was repeating his joy and he wanted to let go of what was holding him back. He could feel such positive energy moving his emotions forward.

"How did this happen, mon amour?" Céleste's words floated in the air around them. "That we are here, feeling these extraordinary emotions about this view and each other? Call it what you will—synchronicity, serendipity, fate, destiny. It is something beyond our control and our hearts and minds are directing us. Why should this be denied?"

Kaito stood speechless. He felt a torrent of emotions building inside him.

Céleste continued, "We are not children. We have lived so much of our lives already. And we grew up together! We know each other so well. Who knows how much more lies ahead for us? Why should we not spend it together?"

She reached her hand to caress his cheek.

"But … but your family—" Kaito sputtered, as he brought her hand to his heart.

"Yes! My wonderful family that already has embraced you as one of their own in the two years they have gotten to know you. My wonderful family that loves me and wants only the best for me. My wonderful family that knows how much I loved their father and would wish me to have another love in my life—as would their father. Where is the argument, the worry, my love?"

She held his gaze in hers. He took both of her hands in his.

"We did not expect this. We did not go looking for it. It was meant to be. *Ma'ane'i no ke aloha*. Love is here and now."

Kaito knew she was right. He knew that every word she had said, he believed. He knew he had to let go of his urge to take care of everything, to be a protector. It was time to acknowledge this freedom to live and love. Most important, he knew this was what he truly wanted.

The last thread of hesitation broke loose as his heart burst into every color of joy he had ever wished for. His passion for this woman … his friend, his lover … was the smell of baguettes fresh from the oven, the taste of the smoothest brie and the most complex wine. It was harmony, tranquility, tenderness, and laughter. It was home.

He swept Céleste into his embrace and held her tightly before their lips met and did not part for the longest time.

EPILOGUE

"*In the end, only three things matter: how much you loved, how gently you lived, and how gracefully you let go of things not meant for you.*" —**Buddha**

KAITO'S HEART soared with relief when Céleste's family joyfully celebrated the news that she and Kaito were joining their lives together. There were tears as both Kaito and Céleste spoke about their past lives always remaining a part of them. The truth about Céleste's past identity in Hawaii would remain secret for now.

One step at a time, they had agreed.

The affection Céleste's family had shown to Kaito during his visits became a true acceptance of him, which elated Kaito. It began to fill the deep hole that had been a part of him for so long.

Kaito arranged to stay in France for a month and work remotely. The manager at K&K Studios had everything under control. Auntie would look after the house and garden. It was apparent to Kaito that his world in Honolulu would not fall apart. He felt a weight lift, allowing him to fully embrace his new home and family.

His old friend, Mitch, now retired from the police department, contacted the right people and assured Céleste she was under no risk traveling with her French identity. He provided the appropriate contact information for her to remove herself from the Protection program. The man she originally identified had passed away and the justice department agreed there was no longer any threat to her. The formalities and paperwork were not daunting.

After living with a feeling of security for her safety, this step required courage and confidence from Céleste. Kaito could see it was not easy to suddenly shed the cloak that had hidden her past for twenty-two years, and he provided the strength and support she needed as they prepared for her emotional return to her homeland.

Once this was completed, they planned to share the true story with all the family on their return to France. There would be no more secrets to hide.

Kaito explained the jaw-dropping story to Kailani. When she recovered from the shock of learning Céleste's true identity, she shed tears for their chance at happiness together. In a later video call, they invited her to visit with them in France and she promised to do so.

"Lanilani. Mother always called you that when she told me stories about you," Kailani said, her voice soft with emotion. "What happiness this would bring her."

Kaito and Céleste boarded the flight to Honolulu a month later, filled with mixed emotions. Their love for each other had only grown in the month of living together. For different reasons, they both felt anxiety over the memories that would face them once they landed. There was so much to reconcile ... love, loss, grief. But they knew together they could handle anything.

Before he opened the door to the house, Kaito took Céleste in his arms. "We are stepping into a lifetime of memories ... many of which we shared. And we are bringing love back into this house. Let us celebrate all of that love and begin making new memories. You are my love, my heart, my hope."

Céleste held him tightly. "The spirits of the past will always be with us, my love, and I know we will honor them as we live each day forward together. We can do this. You are my everything."

Auntie had filled the house with flowers and food accompanied by a heartfelt welcoming note. She recognized Kaito and Lailani might want the space to themselves at first and would wait for Kaito to call her back.

The days passed quickly as Kaito reorganized his life there. He and Céleste had talked over all the details and felt everything would fall into place. She had decided not to contact relatives on this visit but rather simply absorb the impact of returning to the land of her birth and allow her history to come alive within her again.

Kaito arranged to rent his house to Jake, who was grateful and emotional. Kaito had wrestled with his decision but knew it was another major step in accepting the past, finding forgiveness, and moving forward. Grandfather and father were both pleased that Kailani would have a place to stay whenever she visited.

For future visits to Hawaii, Kaito and Céleste were excited at the thought of renting different places on the island until they found exactly what called to them. It would be a home with new beginnings and no bittersweet memories.

He would keep K&K Studios and offered his manager a partnership in the business.

Bob and Gail could not contain their happiness for Kaito, and the couples spent a great deal of time together. For Kaito, it was a solemn reminder of the life he had once missed and now embraced wholeheartedly.

As Céleste's mother had wished, Ulani's ashes were scattered in her beloved homeland. Céleste felt great happiness to let go of the longing, which had lived inside her heart, to honor her mother. She could leave Hawaii with no regrets, particularly since she and Kaito would return from time to time.

They paid an emotional visit to the memorial garden where Hana's and Kiana's ashes rested with the rest of their family's. Tears of love and sorrow blended with feelings of loss, but also gratitude for the years they had shared and memories that would live on.

Kaito made a poignant visit to the temple that had been his refuge on difficult days for so many years. He lit a candle from which he burned incense, and gave thanks for his full heart, for all of the loves in his life—his parents, Hana and her family, Kiana, Kailani, and now Céleste and her family. He felt blessed for all of that, the happy and the sad from which he had grown, and for the understanding it was not too late to begin again.

After days and nights of living with this new love, he had been given a second chance at life. One that would have no secrets.

The words of Buddha resonated. *Each morning we are born again. What we do today is what matters most.*

THE END

NOTE FROM THE AUTHOR

Thank you to everyone who has written to me through the years or messaged me on social media. I love hearing from readers! I value your thoughts and opinions, so please continue to share them with me at patriciasandsauthor@gmail.com.

Have you signed up for my newsletter? It goes out once a month with all sorts of giveaways from my author friends and information about what's coming next. Just click on "subscribe" at my website http://patriciasandsauthor.com/

If you enjoy the photos from France I share online, please follow me on Instagram. I'll be happy to follow you back.

If you would like to find yourself in some of the beautiful settings in my photos, you might want to consider coming on a tour I co-lead each summer with my BFF, Deborah Bine (aka Barefoot Blogger). We take 16 women on a 12-day magical journey through the parts of the south of France we love the most. Many women come on their own while others come with a friend or friends (your book club?) or a sister, mother, daughter. It's all good. What we love the most are the wonderful friendships that develop on this journey every single time. Simply email me at patriciasandsauthor@gmail.com or go to this website – Absolutely Southern France Travel - to see the details of our tour.

There are photos of past tours on my website. The 2022 details are online now.

I love to visit with book clubs! Don't hesitate to ask! We usually do this through FaceTime or Zoom and it works perfectly. I would love to meet your group to chat about books, life and whatever you like!

Any time you take a moment to write a review, please know your efforts are appreciated. Comments from readers are helpful and inspiring to me. You are the reason I write and your words encourage others to read my books. *Merci mille fois!* Thanks a million!

And now . . . on to the next book. See you there!

ACKNOWLEDGMENTS

In order to reach that exciting point where a manuscript is finally ready to publish, a tremendous amount of support and assistance is essential. I'm grateful to everyone who contributed in his or her own personal way to bringing *THE SECRETS WE HIDE* to readers.

Friends and family are my rocks. My husband's patient support, encouragement, and critical first look at my words always begin the process.

Having a male protagonist in this story was a change for me and I have author Toby Neal to thank for that. Some years ago she introduced me to a character in her original crime series, set in Hawaii, and from that Kaito Tanaka has now come to life. Toby has a large body of work set in that tropical paradise.

As always, many long months of research went into preparing to write this novel.

In addition, to be certain I understood the nuances of Kaito's character, my dear friend Junko Mills (PhD, RN) was an essential guide who offered tremendous information and understanding of the Japanese psyche, culture and history. She grew up in a similar traditional Japanese family in much the same time frame as Kaito. She also has a deep understanding of the Shinto and Buddhist beliefs that are so much a part of this story. By coincidence, Junko has also spent many years living part-time in Hawaii and offered important small details that made a difference to the story. Her vast medical knowledge, as well as personal experience in supporting her husband's last years with dementia, gave added credence to Hana's mental health struggles. My gratitude to her is endless.

It was vital to me that Hana's mental health issues be written with respect and accuracy. Author Barbara Claypole White is known for her powerful novels that include characters dealing with various mental health conditions. The wisdom and experience she shared with me was invaluable.

I feel fortunate to have advance readers who offer honest, helpful comments and read my rewrites without losing their sense of humor. Thank you for giving so willingly of your time and opinions. In particular, Gail Napier Johnston, you are a star! Annie McDonnell, Tonni Callan, Denise Birt, Carla Suto and Susan Baldwin Mayfield, I know your schedules are packed and I appreciate the time you gave me.

Authors are always busy with their own writing and yet somehow manage to find time to read the new work of others. For this novel, I was fortunate to have the eyes of Barbara Claypole White, Bette Lee Crosby, Kay Bratt, Marilyn Simon Rothstein, and Kerry Schafer. I can't thank you enough.

This book could not have happened without the talents of Kerry Schafer in formatting and saving me from the technical challenges that accompany publishing. She truly is an Author Genie!

Many thanks to editor extraordinaire Tiffany Yates Martin for her time, patience and in-depth edits. I learned so much from her expertise.

My gratitude to Copy Editor, Elizabeth Brown for the essential final polish.

Thank you, Sharon Clare, of Clarity Book Cover Designs for putting all the right feels into this cover. Your patience is only outdone by your talent!

The Secrets We Hide will be launched with the expertise of Suzanne Leopold's Suzy Approved Book Tours.

And to all the members of the Blue Sky Book Chat group , especially my talented co-hosts, my Lake Union Authors family, and to my friends in Patricia's Readers' Rendezvous, mille mercis … a thousand thanks!

I'm so grateful to the writing community of which I'm proud to be a part. The collegiality, friendship and support found there is truly remarkable. Thank you to the many reviewers and bloggers who take the time to read our novels, review and write about them. I include in my thanks talented designers who create meaningful and beautiful graphics. You all are the lifeline to sharing news about our writing and helping expand our readership. The tremendous effort you put into your work is most appreciated. I began to write out a list and it became so long, I had to stop. The number of excellent online reader groups, bloggers, reviewers, and bookstagrammers could fill its own chapter and I did not want to inadvertently omit anyone. Some of these sites have thousands of followers and others are small and personal. All of them provide invaluable assistance to authors. I send a sincere thank you and hope I share my gratitude often with you personally. You all are an integral part of the village it takes to reach readers.

Which leads to more gratitude to all the readers who buy our books. I love hearing from you and appreciate the time you take to share your thoughts with me and with others. If you write reviews and spread the word, even better. And if you do none of that, that's okay too. As long as you find pleasure in the books we write, that is our greatest reward.

Read for the love of it!

ABOUT THE AUTHOR

Patricia Sands lives two hours north of Toronto, but her heart's other home is the South of France. An avid traveler, she spends part of each year on the Cote d'Azur and once a year co-leads a 16-women, 12-day tour of the Riviera and Provence. Her award-winning 2010 debut novel, *The Bridge Club*, is a book club favorite and in 2020 the *Tenth Anniversary edition* was published .

The Promise of Provence, which launched her three-part Love in Provence series was a finalist for a 2013 USA Best Book Award and a 2014 National Indie Excellence Award, an Amazon Hot New Release in April 2013, and a 2015 nominee for a #RBRT Golden Rose award in the category of romance. This was followed *by Book Two, Promises to Keep* and *Book Three, I Promise You This*. The trilogy is published by Lake Union Publishing.

Drawing Lessons, Sands' fifth novel, also set in the south of France, was released by Lake Union Publishing in 2017 and was a Finalist in the Somerset Literary Book Award 2019.

The Villa des Violettes miniseries, a follow-up to the Love in Provence trilogy, released in 2019/20 and Book 4 is anticipated in 2023.

Patricia is also busy writing a novella, *Lost At Sea*, to be included in the nine-book, multi-author *Sail Away* series that will publish in January 2023.

A lifelong photographer, follow her to France on Instagram @patricialsands.

Find out more at Patricia's Facebook Author Page, Amazon Author Page or her website where there are links to her books, social media, and monthly newsletter that has special giveaways and sneak peeks. She would love to hear from you!

facebook.com/AuthorPatriciaSands
instagram.com/patricialsands

CPSIA information can be obtained
at www.ICGtesting.com
Printed in the USA
LVHW112355120822
725822LV00002B/50

9 780986 120251